ROGUE WARRIOR®

OPTION DELTA

ROGUE WARRIOR®

OPTION DELTA

Richard Marcinko
and
John Weisman

POCKET BOOKS

New York   London   Toronto   Sydney   Tokyo   Singapore

This book is a work of fiction. Names, characters, places and incidents are products of the authors' imaginations, or are used fictitiously. Operational details have been altered so as not to betray current SpecWar techniques.

Many of the Rogue Warrior's weapons courtesy of Heckler & Koch, Inc., International Training Division, Sterling, Virginia

 POCKET BOOKS, a division of Simon & Schuster Inc.
1230 Avenue of the Americas, New York, NY 10020

ISBN: 0-671-00068-3

First Pocket Books hardcover printing January 1999

10   9   8   7   6   5   4   3   2   1

POCKET and colophon are registered trademarks of
Simon & Schuster Inc.

ROGUE WARRIOR is a registered trademark of Richard Marcinko

Printed in the U.S.A.

In memory of Col. Arthur "Bull" Simons, USA (Ret.),
Warrior and Patriot

History has shown that the Germans can be dangerous opponents. If it weren't for the fact that they have such a madman as a leader, we'd be in even more desperate straits than we are. But madmen, you see, will always self-destruct in the end. That is why we will not fail. That is why we will win the day.

—Winston Churchill, 1941

THE ROGUE WARRIOR'S
TEN COMMANDMENTS OF SPECWAR

- I am the War Lord and the wrathful God of Combat and I will always lead you from the front, not the rear.

- I will treat you all alike—just like shit.

- Thou shalt do nothing I will not do first, and thus will you be created Warriors in My deadly image.

- I shall punish thy bodies because the more thou sweatest in training, the less thou bleedest in combat.

- Indeed, if thou hurteth in thy efforts and thou suffer painful dings, then thou art Doing It Right.

- Thou hast not to like it—thou hast just to do it.

- Thou shalt Keep It Simple, Stupid.

- Thou shalt never assume.

- Verily, thou art not paid for thy methods, but for thy results, by which meaneth thou shalt kill thine enemy by any means available before he killeth you.

- Thou shalt, in thy Warrior's Mind and Soul, always remember My ultimate and final Commandment. There Are No Rules—Thou Shalt Win at All Cost.

Inhaltsverzeichnis (Contents)

ABSCHNITT EINS

Chapter

1

GOD, HOW I DO LOVE BEING COLD AND WET. AND IT IS LUCKY THAT I do, because cold, and wet (not to mention tired, hungry, and suffering from terminal lack o' pussy), is precisely how I have spent a large portion of my professional life. Take my present situation. (Oh, yes indeed. Please, *take* my present situation. All of it. Each and every molecule. Every single fucking bit.)

And exactly what *was* my current situation, you ask? Well, to be precise, I was one of four SEALs crammed inside a spherical steel tank built for two—we're talking roughly eight feet high by five feet in diameter—in total blackness, squashed atop and against the three similarly chilly and claustrophobic occupants, and clinging to a ladder attached to the side of the cylinder so I wasn't stepping on the head of the man below me. Just to make things interesting, cold seawater from several vents was being pumped into the tank. Currently the water was at crotch level, and it was frigid enough to shrink my Rogue-sized balls to hazelnuts, even through a thick, black neoprene foam wet suit, which covered me head to toe.

I waited quietly, patiently, until the tank was completely filled. As the water came in, I could hear the air as it escaped through the collar of the air bubble hood manifold above me. Under what might be called normal circumstances, I could have monitored our progress on the chamber's interior pressure and air gauges courtesy of the two waterproof battle lanterns that are mounted six feet above the bottom hatch cover. But Mister Murphy (of Murphy's Law fame), or one of his Murphyesque minions, had already decided that light was an unacceptable component of the night's activity, and thus he had caused the lanterns to malfunction as soon as the bottom hatch had been sealed, the pressure equalized, and the water begun to flow.

Even so, I might have followed the action by using my waterproof flashlight. But my waterproof flashlight was safely stowed in my equipment bag. And my equipment bag was being transported on the fucking deck of the fucking nuclear attack submarine on which I was currently a passenger, lashed to a cleat behind the sail, where I would retrieve it after I'd completed lockout.

Under normal circumstances, we wouldn't even have been in this particular fucking sewer pipe, which is how SEALs refer to subs. We'd have been aboard one of the retrofitted SpecOps craft, attack subs that have been specially outfitted for us shoot-and-looters. We'd have had the advantage of Mark-V SDVs, or swimmer delivery vehicles, which are carried on the decks of SpecWar subs in bulbous clamshell devices called DSS, or dry-dock shelters. But there are only three such boats available, given the current drawdown to our 296-ship, twenty-first-century Navy. And so, we'd had to make do with what was on hand. Which was, to be precise, the USS *Nacogdoches* (SSN 767), a third-generation Los Angeles-class U-boat, equipped to kill other subs, launch Tomahawk missiles, lay mines, wage electronic warfare, and do many other, sundry top secret tasks. But the list did not include the capacity to accommodate and launch eight SEALs and all their equipment on a clandestine mission.

The result, as you can probably guess, meant that we'd had to

4

jury-rig everything from our sleeping quarters (we'd hot-bunked in the forward torpedo room with the Tomahawk missiles, Mark 48 ADCAP—ADvanced CAPability—torpedoes, and Mark 67 SLMMs—Submarine Launched Mobile Mines), to having to store our weapons and other gear outside the sub, as the escape hatches were too narrow to allow us to exit with anything more than our Draeger LAR-V rebreathers. Even our method of egress was nonreg. SSNs have two escape trunks. This one (known formally as the stores hatch, because it was where the ship's stores are commonly on-loaded) was the most forward trunk. It was located just aft of the control room and abutted the triple-thick insulated, lead-shielded wall surrounding the nuclear reactor compartment.

SSNs modified for SpecWar have enlarged escape trunks so that SEAL platoons, which number sixteen, can lock out quickly. Unmodified SSN escape trunks are, as I have just pointed out, built for two men at a time. But given the parameters of my current mission, which included the necessity of a quick exit, I'd changed the rules. And so, we were locking out four at a time. Which currently gave the escape tank the crowded ambience of a frat-house telephone booth during a cram-the-pledges contest.

Thus, I stood immobile in the darkness, teeth chomped tight on my Draeger mouthpiece, trying not to stick my size ten triple-Rogue foot in Gator Shepard's size normal face, while trying my best to stay out of range of Boomerang's bony elbow (he has a nasty habit of flailing his arm like a chicken's wing when he's under stress), running and rerunning the night's schedule in my head. Oh, yes, it was much easier problem solving than thinking about my iced-down nuts and my other chill-packed nether parts. And so I stood there in the cold and the wet, anticipating everything that can, could, will, would, shall, should, may, might, or must go wrong, so I'd be able to outwit Command Master Chief Murphy who, experience has shown, likes to tag along on these kinds of ops.

Finally, I sensed the water flow had stopped. When I was

positive no air remained in the escape chamber, I flexed my shoulders, worked the cramp out of my neck, and then started to pull myself toward the steel ladder bolted to the escape trunk bulkhead. I knew that I had to climb three rungs, then reach above my head in the total blackness to the spot my mind's eye had muscle-memoried as being the first of the six dogs that secured the trunk's outer hatch cover.

Wham! My action was interrupted by a rude elbow (or other sundry Boomerang body part—it was dark after all, and who could really tell), which smashed into the right side of my temple. I went face first into the ladder rail and saw goddamn stars. Belay that. I saw the whole Milky fucking Way. Oh shit. Oh fuck. Oh, doom on Dickie. Which, as you probably know, means I was being fuckee-fuckeed in Vietnamese.

My mask came off—the back strap separating from the clasp and disappearing into the void between my legs. And then the sonofabitch hit me again—this time *smack* upside my wide Rogue snout, which knocked my mouthpiece clean out of my mouth. I gagged and snorted, which just about fucking drowned me, because as you will remember I was completely underwater, and gagging and snorting when underwater means inhaling what in SEAL technical language is known as the old double-sierra: a shitload of seawater.

It occurred to me that perhaps I should yell "CUT!" and start this process all over again. But that, of course, was impossible. This wasn't fucking Hollywood, where you get as many takes as you need to Get It Right. Or a goddamn training exercise, where you can take a time-out to regroup, rethink, and reapply yourself to the task at hand. This was for real. And there was a mother-blanking, bleepity-bleeping schedule to keep.

You what? You want to know what that schedule *was*? And you want me to explain it all *now*? When I'm in serious fucking pain?

Geezus, have you no sense of timing? Okay, okay—you paid good money for this book, so I'll be fucking accommodating. To be brief about it, the mission tonight was for me and my seven

SEALs to lock out of the *Nacogdoches*, swim undetected roughly eighteen hundred yards to the northeast, and make our way under half a dozen picket boats manned by armed and dangerous nasties. Then we'd locate *die Nadel im Heuhaufen*[1]—in this case it was a certain seventy-five-meter boat—board it, obliterate any opposition, and then capture a Saudi royal yclept Prince Khaled Bin Abdullah. We would do all of this *sans* any hullabaloo whatsoever.

The reason for our stealth was that Khaled baby was the forty-seven-year-old scion of the Abdullah family, third cousins of da king, and Saudi Arabia's sixteenth most wealthy clan. Khaled's annual income was somewhere in the $400 million range, which works out to something like thirty-three million U.S. smackers a month. Educated in Germany, England, and France two decades ago, he'd eschewed the lavish single-malt scotch, Cristal champagne, beluga caviar, and hooker-rich lifestyle most of his fellow princes took up. Instead, he'd somehow gotten involved with the campus radicals, e.g., assholes from the Baader-Meinhof gang, the Red Brigades, and others like them. So Khaled wasn't into conspicuous consumption like most of your Saudi blue bloods. Instead, he'd invested his profits from Microsoft, Dell Computer, Cisco, and Intel, his circa 1980 12.5 percent zero coupon bonds, and his ARAMCO oil royalties in transnational terrorism.

Khaled funded Hamas suicide squads, Algerian GIA (Armed Islamic Group) death squads, and Kurdish car bombers. You could say that his money endowed "chairs" in murder and assassination at two of the five "universities" the mullahs have set up outside the Iranian cities of Tehran and Qum to train transnational terrorists. He'd provided financial support and logistics to the Harakat-ul-Ansar's program to assassinate westerners in Kashmir and Pakistan. He'd even given money to American neo-Nazis, German radicals, and Puerto Rican ultra-nationalists. This scumbag was a real equal-opportunity tango.

[1]That's Kraut for needle in the haystack.

RICHARD MARCINKO and JOHN WEISMAN

And until now, between the reluctant but constant protection of the Saudi royal family (he was, after all, an illegitimate third cousin to the current Saudi ambassador to the United States, which made him a directly indirect relative of da king), and his residence in rural Afghanistan, where he was protected by a brigade of Come-Mister-Taliban-Tally-Me-Banana-clip-on-your-AK-47 gunmen, it hadn't been politically prudent, tactically practical, or diplomatically realistic to lay our hands on him without creating what the State Department tends to describe as "a deplorable, regrettable, and unfortunate violation of sovereign territory involving United States military personnel."[2]

But tonight, his illegitimate ass was going to be mine. Because my guys and I would nail him in international waters, where the State Department has no jurisdiction. Once he'd been properly TTS'd—which as you know means tagged, tied, and stashed—we'd turn him over to the proper authorities, i.e., a team of special agents of the Federal Bureau of Investigation, who were already waiting on a close-but-not-too-close VSV.[3] They'd ferry him to an aircraft carrier cruising off Malta, where he'd be put on a plane that would, through the marvel of in-flight refueling, not touch down until it reached the good old U.S. of A. Bottom line: he'd stand trial for financing the bombing of the Khobar Towers complex in Saudi Arabia a few years back and killing nineteen American military personnel.

Yes, friends, when it comes to terrorists, the United States has

---

[2]Have you ever noticed that the fucking State Department has the habit of almost always taking the other guy's side whenever there's an international dispute? It has occurred to me to ask who the fuck these pin-striped fudge-cutting cookie-pushing bureaucrats work for. The answer, of course, is that they work for you and me—the citizens of the United States. But don't tell *them* that—most of our professional diplomats get upset if you require them to stand up for America.

[3]Very Slender Vessel, which is a fancy way of talking about the kind of high-speed cigarette boats favored by drug smugglers and other stealthy types.

8

a long, long memory. And sometimes, despite the current State Department's best efforts to the contrary, we even act on it.

Ninety-six hours ago, Khaled, the TIQ[4], had been lured out of his safe haven in Afghanistan to these here international waters, which happen to be eighty miles due southwest of Akrotiri, Cyprus, by the promise of securing something he'd been trying to buy for the past decade: a ready-to-go, .025-megaton Soviet special demolition munition device, popularly described as a suitcase atom bomb, (even though the goddam thing does not come in a suitcase). The bomb was real—and the man selling it to him, a former Stasi[5] officer-turned-black marketeer, smuggler, and arms merchant named Heinz Hochheizer, was a bona fide no-goodnik. Neither Heinz nor Khaled realized they'd both been set up in a protracted, complex, and very intricate sting by the CIA, which thought that getting its hands on one of the old Soviet devices at the same time Khaled was being scooped up made an excellent idea.

It had taken more than nine months to get this far, but Khaled had finally nibbled at the bait, and the folks at Langley had allowed the hook to be set—hard. Still, Khaled was a smart sumbitch. He knew that Fawaz Yunis, one of the tangos involved in the hijacking of TWA 847 back in 1985, had been seduced into international waters by the lure of pussy. But as we all know now, the PIQ (look it up in the Glossary) had been a female FBI agent, an integral part of the FBI's aptly named Operation Goldenrod (sometimes the Bureau actually *does* have a sense of humor). And Khaled remembered all too well that Mir Aimal Kasi, the wealthy Pakistani who'd killed two CIA employees and then fled to his homeland, had been sold out by his fellow countrymen—his bodyguards, actually—and scooped up in the summer of 1997 by a joint task force of CIA officers, FBI Special Agents, and Delta Force shooters.

---

[4] As you can probably guess, it stands for Tango-In-Question.
[5] East German secret police.

And so, Khaled was real careful about leaving his Afghan sanctuary, even with the wonderful prospect of securing an atom bomb staring him in the puss. It had taken three months of negotiation before he'd agreed to meet Heinz in a non-Islamic venue. Only the threat that others were interested in securing the weapon had finally brought him out of hiding. And Khaled had insisted on making all the arrangements for the exchange— arrangements that changed daily, sometimes even hourly, all posted in encrypted messages on the Internet.[6]

But he was being watched by a joint CIA/FBI team. And so, Khaled's progress was noted as he flew in his private jet from a small airstrip southwest of Meymaneh, to Tehran. He was shadowed as he'd driven through Damascus, to Beirut, where his chopper awaited him for the final leg of the journey. It was in Beirut that Mister Murphy showed up and our intrepid American gumshoes lost him. Khaled climbed into his limo and drove to the airfield where his chopper was waiting to take him on the final leg of this nasty odyssey, a 230-mile flight onto the deck of the transatlantic-capable, seventy-five-meter boat I'll call the *Kuz Emeq*, which had sailed from Cannes to the anonymous rendez-vous point Khaled had chosen in the middle of the Med. But when the big Mercedes limo pulled onto the tarmac, Khaled was nowhere to be seen. He'd pulled a fucking vanishing act that would have done David Copperfield proud.

The team panicked—and with good reason. This op had cost us a bundle—not to mention more than a dozen assets. The alarm bells went off, and our people combed the whole goddam Mediterranean from Libya to fucking Marseille. But Khaled had disappeared. And then, after thirty-six hours of nothing, they

---

[6]Though a great boon, the Internet is making the tracking of tangos much more difficult, as it is almost impossible to intercept encrypted E-mail and other postings. Note, however, that I said *almost impossible*. Our alphabet-soup agencies have developed certain proficiencies in recent years that keep 'em half a step ahead of the bad guys. Half a step may not be a lot—but it's enough.

spotted another of his private choppers, a CH-3C with a range of more than six hundred miles that we'd originally sold to the Saudi Air Force. It was flying south, threading the needle between France and Italy. When it refueled at Cagliari, Sardinia, one of our people got a peek inside. And guess what? Khaled was there, sipping on his Evian water and reading the Koran. Two hours later, he was sitting in the main salon of the *Kuz Emeq* as it steamed eastward toward the rendezvous point, with us, and the USS *Nacogdoches,* in hot pursuit.

Khaled had arranged for the bomb vendor, Heinz the East German (he had Russian Mafiya ties, worked out of a mail drop in Frankfurt's red-light district, and, as I've just mentioned, was an unwitting accomplice in this little charade), to be brought in by another of his choppers, so even the Man with the Bomb would be ignorant of precisely where the meet was going to be, and therefore unable to bring any of his own hired guns along. For his part, Khaled made sure that his security people, six fast boats of well-paid Corsican Mafiosi, as well as a dozen fanatical Taliban shooters aboard the *Kuz Emeq*, were handy, and well armed. For a quick getaway, he had his chopper sitting on the *Kuz Emeq*'s chopper deck, its engine warmed up and its pilots ready to go *am geringsten Anla2J*, which is how the scumbag had learned to say "at the drop of a hat" at the Free University of Berlin back in the late 1970s.

But every once in a while the folks at Christians In Action (which is, you recall, how we SEALs refer to the Central Intelligence Agency), get things right. This was one of 'em. The Agency's sneak-and-peekers had managed to plant a beacon aboard the *Kuz Emeq* so subtly that even Khaled's head of security, a former KGB one-star technical guru, failed to spot it during his twice-daily ELINT/TECHINT/SIGINT[7] sweeps. And by modifying the sub's ESM—it stands for electronic support measures—equipment and then glomming onto the beacon's

---

[7]ELectronic INTelligence/TECHnical INTelligence/SIGnals INTelligence.

signal, the *Nacogdoches*'s skipper, a bright young Annapolis ring-knocker named Joseph Tuzzolino, aka Joey Tuzz, aka Captain Tuzzie, had stealthily slipped his boat to within just over a mile of Khaled's yacht.

Now all that was left was for us to lock out of the sub, swim in, while keeping the beacon signal dead ahead of our position, slither onto the yacht, and perform the actual takedown. There were even a couple of bonuses for us if everything went right: that suitcase full of cash was one—I like being able to help pay down the national deficit—not to mention that compact, man-portable Soviet atomic munition device.

And, hey, this was gonna be a piece of cake, right? An easy swim followed by an effortless shoot & loot. Oh, *sure* it was—and if you believe that, I have this nice bridge in Brooklyn to sell you. Anyway, so much for background. Now let's get on with the fucking action sequence, shall we?

I bent forward to try and retrieve my mask strap, and was knocked into the ladder again by yet another elbow to my head. What the fuck was Boomerang trying to do, kill me? I reached around and grabbed the offending arm and shook it hard, as if to say WTF.

In answer, I received two taps on my right bicep, and a squeeze back. Which meant he was being properly apologetic—and would S^2, which as you probably know stands for sit the fuck down and shut the fuck up, until I signaled otherwise.

I found my air hose, clamped it back in my mouth, swallowed more seawater to clear the line, and then took a very welcome gulp of oxygen. I bent forward again—not an easy task, given the thick respirator on my chest—and fumbled between my legs. Gator reached up, his fingers finding mine in the darkness, and handed me the missing mask strap. I reattached it, pulled it snug, then vented air through my sore-as-a-gangbanger's-dick nose until I'd cleared the fucking mask.

Murphy-time over, perhaps it was time to do real work.

I climbed the ladder, reached up, found the first dog, and twisted until it released. Once I'd cleared the first one, I went on, working my way counterclockwise. The fourth one stuck, but I muscled it free and wrenched until it opened.

Then, the sixth dog undogged, I braced my feet as best I could against the ladder rung and pushed upward with all my strength. The hatch opened outward, and I pulled myself through, and struggled up and along the deck until I found the half-inch nylon line we'd run from one of the midships cleats to the sub's mast so we could find our way in the darkness.

I pulled myself along the line toward the sail. I could sense the current moving against my body as the sub continued on. Nuclear subs are like sharks—they hardly ever stop moving. And so, locking out is an intricate exercise in which the sub's captain has to keep his boat on a perfectly flat plane while moving at the slowest possible speed—that's between one and two knots—so that the swimmers can exit without being swept off into the current, unable to catch up with the sub as it continues onward and out of sight.

In fact, that was one of the potential goatfuck factors of tonight's escapade. Los Angeles–class submarines are built for speed. They do not like to be driven slowly. And so, Joey Tuzz, the CO of this particular sewer pipe, currently had his hands full. Launching me and my guys was going to give him a Rogue-sized headache.

I felt a hand on the knife sheath strapped to my left calf. Good news. That meant my guys were following. I kept moving, pulling myself foot by foot until I felt the rough surface of the mast. I worked my way around until I came upon the elastic netting that held our equipment bags. Reached through to find the outer compartment, where I'd stored my dive light. Found it. Attached it securely to my wrist, then turned it on, so I could see what I was doing. If it had been daytime, we could have seen one another clearly, as the deck was only sixty-five feet below the surface. But it was just after 2100, three hours after sunset, and the only way to describe things was *d–a–r–k*. None of the phosphorescence you normally see in the water; no hint of light from above. Or anywhere else. Which added to the goatfuck factor. You can easily become disoriented in these sorts of conditions. Down becomes up. Up becomes sideways. Distance, time, and direction get obscured. You can die.

Boomerang's narrow face came close to my own. I put the light on him. Then, using hand signals, I asked him if he was okay. In answer, he gave me an upturned thumb. Behind him, I could make out Gator Shepard and Duck Foot Dewey as they pulled their way along the line.

I took the light and slid past my guys, working my way back toward the escape trunk hatch. I secured it, then twisted the wheel atop the domed steel until it was tight. I paused, counting the seconds off. Finally, I heard the sounds I was waiting for: water was being pumped out. The clearing process would take four and a half minutes. Then, after the pressure had been neutralized, the bottom hatch would be undogged, my final four shooters would load, the chamber would be flooded once again, and the whole process repeated.

Meanwhile, there was work to be done. I crabbed my way back to the mast and checked the big watch on my left wrist. The shine-in-the-dark display read 2113. Fuck me. We were already three minutes behind schedule, and we hadn't even begun.

2119. The rest of my crew arrived. Half Pint Harris, Nod DiCarlo, and the Rodent led the way. They were followed by a big, burly, eager puppy of an FNG (look it up in the Glossary) named Terry Devine, aka Baby Huey.

No, I do not like operating with cherrys—in other words new personnel—especially on jobs as important as this one. But on tonight's particular mission, there'd been no alternative. The shooters I call the Pick and Nasty Nicky Grundle were in sick bay with badly broken bones. It was doubtful they'd ever be able to operate with the same balls-to-the-wall efficiency they'd once been able to. Doc Tremblay'd retired—he'd had enough of the new, zero-defect Navy. And Stevie Wonder had finally passed his chief's exam. That was good news and bad news. Good news because the Navy needs more chiefs like Wonder. Bad news because the Bureau of Personnel—BUPERS in Navyspeak—had, in its infinite wisdom, transferred Chief Wonder from his sinecure at the Navy Yard down to Norfolk, and I was going to have a hell of a time getting him back under my Roguish wing. Shit, I was going to have a hell of a time bringing him back long enough to give him the sort of proper, old-fashioned, rocks-and-shoals chief's initiation that he deserved.

All those developments had left me one man short. I'd checked the personnel files and, mindful that one officer's scum is another officer's jewel, selected Baby Huey, who was just about to be tossed out of the Teams for disciplinary infractions. He was my kind of kid. First of all, he'd graduated dead last in his BUD/S class. The training officers had given him a black mark for his low standing. To me, it said that the kid had determination and grit—he'd stuck things through until the bitter end.

Second, he'd been a SEAL for less than a year—still a pup—when he'd been scheduled to receive a captain's mast for off-duty brawling. In today's zero-defect Navy, one bar brawl or DUI is enough to get a chief with fifteen years as a SEAL shit-canned from the Teams. As for Boatswain's Mate Third Class Terry Devine, another black mark was placed next to his name, which meant he was unofficially classified as LTWS[8] by the pucker-sphinctered, holier-than-thou, bean-counting, teetotaling bureaucrats who run NAVSPECWARGRUTWO these days. Oh, and run it they do: right into the fucking ground, so far as I'm concerned.

To the SpecWar panjandrums at NAVSPECWARGRUTWO, Baby Huey's brawling suggested that he might be overly aggressive. Which meant he might actually kill something someday. And that possibility put his future as a SEAL in jeopardy.

---

[8]Lower Than Whale Shit

That's what they saw. But as we all know, Rorschachs mean different things to different people. What the LTWS blot told *me*, was that Terry Devine was yes, aggressive, and that he liked to play the kind of up-close-and-personal, body-bruising games that relieve the pressure of being a SEAL. But I saw that as a positive, not negative, attribute. Frankly, I don't think you can ask a man to risk his life every day, train at the very edge of the envelope, and then tell him to go out and relieve the stress by playing tiddledywinks, or sipping cocoa and perusing the *New Yorker*, although there's nothing wrong with either. Sometimes SEALs need an evening (or a weekend), of full-contact boogie rock 'n' roll, smack 'em upside-the-head, rabble-rousing brawling. Like clearing a fucking barful of Jarheads, *par example.*

But no matter what my positive instincts about the kid may have been, the reality was that I was about to go shooting and looting with an untested, untried, unblooded, twenty-year-old tyke. A big, contentious, muscular tyke, but a tyke nonetheless. Until this very moment of his life, it had all been training and simulation. He'd never had to Do It for Real. Gone into battle. Been wounded. Killed a man face-to-face.

Well, this was the big leagues. Baby Huey would learn quick— or he'd be dead.

You think that sounds cold? Well, it may indeed sound cold. But it's the fucking truth. The men who work for me are always selected because they can look into their enemies' eyes and kill them dead. Not wound. Kill. Roy Boehm, the godfather of all SEALs, taught me by example that breaking things and killing people is what being a SEAL is all about. I see no reason to modify his operational philosophy even in these politically correct days of nonlethal weapons and touchy-feely military doctrine.

2121. First things first. We lashed ourselves together, and I lashed the line that tied Boomerang and me together to one of the mast cleats, thus assuring that all eight of us were attached to the sub. Under normal OPCONs, SEALs travel in pairs. Tonight, our four pairs of swim buddies would move as one until we reached the *Kuz Emeq*. Night swims are tough. Clandestine night underwater approaches are even tougher. I wanted to know where each and every one of us was, at all times—and that meant moving together. We began to unpack the gear and affix it to our bodies. We were traveling light tonight, because it is no fun swimming when loaded down with equipment. Eighteen hundred yards is an easy swim—if you are on the surface, and you can drag your gear in a flotation bag. It is an easy swim at a depth of thirty-five feet as well, despite being hampered by your rebreather, which has all the hydrodynamics of a small refrigerator. But tonight it would not be an easy swim, because tonight in addition to the Draegers, we'd be encumbered by weapons, ammo, and other takedown equipment. There would be hostiles patrolling on the surface, and crosscurrents to face. No, this was going to be work.

2127. I finally strapped all my gear on—the last step was attaching my suppressed MP5-PDW—when I received a hand signal from Boomerang that everybody was packed up and ready to launch. Good news. I undid the half-hitch that secured us all to the mast cleat. Just as I turned us loose I sensed the current intensify. The fucking *Nacogdoches* was picking up speed—three, maybe even four knots right now. Not good. Like I said, speed is not a plus when you are trying to launch swimmers.

I grabbed for the long line I'd used to pull myself from the escape trunk to the mast. But now the fucking sub began to roll counterclockwise, and the line was nowhere to be found. What the fuck was Tuzzy trying to do—drown us?

I kicked as hard as I could. But it is impossible to keep up with something moving at four knots, especially when you are tied to seven other bodies by five-yard lengths of nylon rope.

Relentlessly, inexorably, the big boat slid away from me, a receding shadow in the blackness. And then, as if snapped up by a huge grappling hook, I was whipped around, turned topsy-turvy, and—*wham*—slammed against the sub's hull.

I reached out to grab something, but there was nothing to take hold of—just smooth hull beneath my fingertips. Now the fucking sub rolled another four, five, six degrees away from me, and the current slammed me up against the hull. Oh, terrific. If Joey Tuzz kept this up, he'd roll us right into the path of his goddam screw, and we'd end up as SEALburgers. What the hell was he doing? There was no way to ask—and no way to find out. Once we'd left the escape trunk, we had no comms. Oh, this was not the way I'd fucking conceived this mission.

My instinct told me the sub's speed had just increased again. Maybe up to six, six and a half knots. Yes, I know that six knots is just about the speed at which most joggers jog. But underwater, when you're being bounced against a fucking submarine hull, six knots is enough to get you fucking killed.

Well, I wasn't about to get myself—or any of my men—killed tonight. This mission was too important. There was too much at stake. I clawed at the hull, my fingers seeking any goddam purchase they could find. They found nothing. And now, the combined weight of my seven men started to pull me aft along the hull. I was slipping farther and farther astern—toward that goddam lethal screw.

Fuck. I would the lifeline around my left arm, stretched my right arm as far out as I could reach, summoned every particle of energy left in my body (and more importantly my soul), and kicked, trying to propel myself in the direction of the sub's roll.

Nothing.

I kicked again, and again, and again, and again, until the muscles in my calves, my thighs, my back, and my chest all caught fire.

I hurt like hell. But I made progress. My hand brushed against the rough surface of the narrow, nonskid safety track that runs almost the entire length of the sub's hull. I knew that two feet from the track, a parallel line of fixed cleats runs along the spine of the hull. I kicked, kicked, kicked. Every atom of my body fought against the water, the current, and the sub's movement. Every particle of my mind *willed* forward progress. I bit through my mouthpiece, but I didn't give a fuck—I was going to get us out of this. I WOULD NOT FAIL.

And then, the fingers of my outstretched left hand found a fucking cleat. I muscled my big paw around it, joint by joint, holding tight, my arm clenched as tight as it was when I did the last fucking pull-up in the last fucking rotation during Hell Week at BUD/S, when you are so completely fucking exhausted that you know that you can't even draw one more fucking breath—and then the fucking instructor tells you to give him another twenty pull-ups or you are gone from the program.

Yes, I gave him twenty fucking more back then—and another, just to show I could fucking do it. And the lesson I'd learned has stayed with me my entire career: when you believe it is over, it ain't over. When you think your body cannot do any more, it CAN do more, and it WILL do more. And you WILL NOT FAIL in your mission.

And so, yes, I held on to the cleat, clawing, clenching, grasping, clutching, until I could wrap the safety line around the cleat and secure us to the boat once more. With the line secure, I hung there suspended, hyperventilating, expended and sweating into my wet suit, as the sub moved steadfastly on through the dark water.

I was totally spent. I was emotionally drained and physically exhausted—completely burnt out. And we hadn't even begun the night's work yet.

2129. Just as inexplicably as it had accelerated, the *Nacogdoches* now dropped its speed and eased back to vertical, barely moving placidly through the water at the proper one-knot velocity. What had the problem been? Had Captain Tuzz been evading something one of his multiple warning systems had picked up? Had the sub started to take in water—foundering because of its slow pace? Had the boat simply begun to stall out and he'd had to act to save it—even if it meant losing us? There was no way of knowing. We were out here on our own.

And frankly, it didn't matter. We'd survived. We were locked, loaded, and ready to go—and it was way beyond the time to go to work. I released the hitch tethering us to the sub and peeled away, checking the lighted dial of the underwater compass strapped to my right forearm to get our heading. I looked at my depth indicator. We were at fifty-five feet right now. Yes, I realize that according to the current NAVSEA operational manuals, our Draegers should not, and here let me quote, "be used at depths greater than six fathoms under any circumstances without the express authority of NAVSEA."

Now, it doesn't matter than no one at NAVSEA has ever used a fucking Draeger LAR-V anywhere but in one of the fucking swimming pools in which they certify the goddamn things. That's right, gentle reader: the nitnoy, pus-nutted paper pushers who are charged with buying these items for the Teams are not the selfsame salty-balled SEALs who have to use 'em. The result is that those desk-bound bean counters don't give much of a rusty F-word whether equipment works or not, or whether it's suited to the SEAL mission profile or not, or much of anything else.

This sort of shit-for-brains U.S. Navy institutional mind-set is nothing new. When Roy Boehm created the first SEALs back in 1962, he was duly and properly authorized by the powers that be to carry M-14 rifles and .38-caliber pistols, because those are what the desk-bound bureaucrats at BUWEPS—the Bureau of Weapons—decided that he needed. Roy, to his credit, went out and bought .357 Magnum pistols, and AR-15 assault rifles for his shooters. The M-14 is a terrific rifle at a thousand yards. And the .38 Special is a good target round. But even as far back as 1962, Roy realized one of the places his new team of merry marauders would be sent was Vietnam. And Roy had studied enough war to know that the SEALs would have to be capable of disabling the Viet Cong's motorized sampans and junks with their pistols— which is something the .357 round can do. He also knew from his experience of working with the Philippine guerrillas in World War II that most of the rifle work his men would do they'd do from ambush positions—a hundred yards or closer.

Knowing all of this—and unable to convince the apparatchiks at BUWEPS that he was correct—Roy simply went out and bought his men Smith and Wesson .357s and AR-15s *without* going through the system. And the Navy tried to court-martial him for doing so. In fact, if it hadn't been for President John F. Kennedy, the Navy would have succeeded in keelhauling Roy's horsehide-tough ass, and we SEALs would have been much worse off today.

Anyway, the rebreathers we were currently using weren't Navy-certified beyond forty-one feet of depth—in fact, the Navy doesn't want 'em used any deeper than about thirty-five feet. It didn't matter that I have been using them at depths up to sixty feet for more years than I care to remember. I've just never bothered to tell the folks at NAVSEA what I've done.

2145. We moved ahead in the darkness. I felt a crosscurrent, coming from starboard to port. Now it took 50 percent more effort, as I kept my eyes focused on the underwater compass's dial, to keep us on course. Behind me, Boomerang was counting kicks (two to the yard), so he could guestimate how far we'd come, and how far we had to go. I checked my depth gauge: twenty-three feet. Maybe there'd be less current a bit deeper. I angled my body down slightly, and kicked forward into the blackness, gently bringing us down to a depth of thirty-two feet. After eighty or ninety seconds, the crosscurrent subsided and I began to make decent progress once again. I began to sense a dull ache in the forward portion of my brain—I'd probably been so intent on swimming, I hadn't been breathing deeply enough. I sucked a big gulp of O_2 to clear my head and swam on.

I checked my depth gauge as my legs kicked rhythmically. Steady as she goes at thirty feet. I liked that depth: it gave us a big safety margin. Highly unlikely we'd be spotted. Shit, with the night this dark, we could come in at six feet and they'd never see us. But as my old platoon chief, Everett Emerson Barrett, used to tell us tadpoles, "Never assume, you worthless, pencil-dicked geeks: *assume* makes an ASS of U and ME." And so, I wasn't about to assume anything. A whole bunch of agencies had actually come together and worked their butts off putting this op together, and I wasn't going to screw things up for any of us.

2203. *There was something above my head.* I couldn't see it. But I could feel it, as if, despite swimming in the darkness, a shadow had loomed over me. The sensation was completely and absolutely palpable. Instinctively, I angled myself downward, slowing my pace. From the angle of the safety line attached to my waist, I noted that the SEALs behind me did the same. I fought the urge to turn the light on and go take a look. Instead, I kicked on single-mindedly, moving in the heading my compass was pointing. And I prayed to the God of War that whatever was up there didn't have a sonar system deployed, or any other detection device for that matter. I didn't need any more fucking problems than I'd already had.

I swam on another 150 kick strokes, then paused long enough to let Boomerang and the rest of the team catch up. My head still ached—in fact, it now felt as if a vise was tightening down between my ears. Well, fuck it—I had work to do. We all hung suspended in the water, nose to nose, and conversed with our hands.

"There was something up there, right, Skipper?" Duck Foot gestured.

I shrugged, giving him the universal sign for, "Your guess is as good as mine." But I think we both knew we'd passed under one of Khaled's picket boats. Well, whatever it was, Duck Foot had sensed it, too. It was the hunter in him.

I asked Boomerang how far we'd come. His hands told me we were almost halfway there. Hmm, I realized my thigh muscles had lied to me. From the way they were burning, I'd have guessed we'd have made a lot more progress than that.

2257. On the target, my ears were was now ringing like Big fucking Ben, and my head was pounding like I'd just been kicked by a steel-toed boondocker. WTF was causing it? There was no time to ask or answer that question. Too much else to think about. Like the *Kuz Emeq*. We were, to be precise, twenty-nine feet below Khaled's vessel. Not that we could see anything. But there was ample evidence that we'd hit the spot.

Boats, you see, make a shitload of noise—much more than you might expect. And this one was no exception. We could hear the ship's generators and pumps working; I could discern the ebb and the flow of the crew as they moved around the ship. Even make out the reverb from some rock and roll someone was playing up above. We knew it was the right vessel because the homing device told me that I was dead on. And, to make our lives easier, Khaled's crew had obligingly deployed a pair of sea anchors to keep the yacht's movement at a minimum. Indeed, I was currently hanging on to one of the anchor hawsers.

Time to make ready. For those of you who have been through the process with me before, think of this as a refresher in Roguish SpecWar philosophy. For those of you who haven't, pay fucking attention, because you will see all of this material again.

Okay. Here's a fundamental SpecWarrior truth: whether you are taking down an aircraft, a train, a bus, a car—or a luxury yacht, the three elements most crucial to the success of your operation are, one: surprise, two: speed, and, three: violence of action.

And here is another vital but essential rudiment of SpecWar. At its core, each special operation pits a small but highly trained and motivated force against a larger but less well-motivated unit. The spec-operators achieve their victory through achieving something called relative superiority, or RS.

Simply put, relative superiority is when that small, elite force achieves a swift tactical advantage over the larger body of defenders. The obvious truth of the matter is that if you do not overwhelm the bad guys quickly, ruthlessly, and efficiently, they will overwhelm your shooters before you can kill enough of them to achieve RS.

That's where the speed and the violence of action comes in. There can be no hesitation, no doubt, no restraint. You must balls-to-the-wall ATTACK. And when you do ATTACK, you go in, as my old shipmate, Colonel Charlie Beckwith,[9] the godfather of Delta Force, used to say, to "kill 'em all and let God sort it out."

Now, the most critical period in a special operation has come to be known as the Area of Vulnerability, or AV. The AV in an aircraft hostage takedown, for example, starts when the assault group begins its approach to the plane. Because if the shooters are spotted before they Get There, the hostages will be killed before a single rescuer makes it into the cabin. When you go over the rail of a ship under way, you are most vulnerable as you are making your climb up the caving ladders. There's a thin line of shooters, spread out as they muscle their way up and over the rail.

Oh, sure, you may have a security team in the boat below, but the fact of the matter is that the defenders hold the high ground—i.e., the deck and superstructure of the ship—and if a tango decides to take a cigarette break, spots you, and calls for reinforcements before you can neutralize him with a head shot from a suppressed weapon, you're dog meat. Even so, tonight's assault was marginally easier for us than if we'd been tasked with boarding a ship under way.

Obviously, it is much simpler to clamber onto a craft that's not moving than it is to have to factor in all the myriad components of current, velocity, wind, waves, and other Murphy-prone elements of underway assaults. Second, the size of the *Kuz Emeq* made our job getting aboard less problematic. Oh, the boat may have been over a hundred feet in length, but it had the sort of shallow draft common to pleasure craft, with the happy result that its custom teak side deck and ebony-inlaid gunwale wasn't ten feet above the water's surface.

---

[9]Now, as I've said in the past, Charlie wasn't literally my shipmate, meaning that he and I had served in the same ship together. But Charlie and I worked together; we were friends and colleagues; we stood back to back and fought the powers that be to make things better for our men—and kill as many of our nation's enemies as we could. So far as I am concerned, that makes him my shipmate.

Moreover, there was a diving platform suspended from the transom, and since the crew had obligingly set out sea anchors, we now had lines to climb.

2301. We jettisoned our fins, lashed all our extraneous equipment to the sea anchor lines, and made ready to hit the *Kuz Emeq*. Each man knew exactly where he had to be, and just how he'd go over the rail.

Our final assault plans had been assisted by satellite surveillance photographs of Khaled's yacht courtesy of a specially diverted National Reconnaissance Office *Lacrosse/Crystal/Flagpole* satellite, which provided us with thermal simulations as well as 0.039-meter imagery, which comes out to be a resolution of about 1.5 inches from a constant trajectory of 287 miles above Earth.[10] And when the intel squirrel wonks and photointerpretation dweebs at NRO and DIA's labs had finished playing with—read computer enhancing—those satellite snapshots into the two-thousand-pixel-per-inch range, we'd been given a bunch of real Kodak Moment–quality pictures from which to work. Ain't science grand, folks?

---

[10]Oops. I think that the *Lacrosse/Crystal/Flagpole* designator is still compartmented information. In civilian-speak, that means it's Top Fucking Secret. Do me a favor: please cut this entire page out of the book, shred it, then send the shreds back to the publisher as evidence you've complied. Otherwise, the fucking Feds are probably going to come after my Roguish ass for giving away the nation's secrets.

Chapter
2

2303. *SHOW TIME.* I SHOOK MY HEAD TO CLEAR IT—I WAS REALLY getting fuzzy now—double-checked my Knight-suppressed MP5-PDW to make sure the lightweight mag was locked firmly in place and the safety was on, slapped the bolt forward to chamber a round, then slung the nylon strap over my shoulder. With this new model suppressor, the HK would fire coming right out of the water. Shit—it would even fire *one* shot underwater. Strapped to my right thigh was the bulky ballistic nylon holster package containing my backup weapon (a suppressed HK USP nine millimeter, fifteen in the mag, one in the pipe), and three spare fifteen-round mags all filled with subsonic hollowpoint rounds. My big, nasty saw-back dive knife was strapped to my left calf. High above it, a nylon thigh pouch held two waterproof flashbang distraction devices, one waterproof concussion grenade, and three spare thirty-round MP5 magazines.

A pouch secured to the nylon web belt at the small of my back held a roll of duct tape—like your American Express card, we SpecWarriors don't ever leave home without one—a dozen nylon handcuff restraints, a small bolt cutter, and a five-yard coil of eighth-inch nylon line. And if you think that swimming a mile or so underwater with all this shit strapped to your body is easy, guess again, bub. I fucking *hurt* right now. But then, as you know if you know me at all, if I'm not hurting, I'm not living. So you can guess I was very much alive tonight.

Since I believe in Roy Boehm's two-word definition of leadership ("Follow me!"), I'd assigned myself and my senior enlisted man—Boomerang—the hardest and most exposed responsibility: the stern. We'd surface alongside the dive platform (and just above the yacht's nasty twin screws, which were idling), hoist ourselves across the dive platform and over the transom, neutralize Khaled's aft security force—the largest cluster of armed & dangerous fuckers aboard—then move across the fantail, which was totally exposed to fire from the quarterdeck and chopper pad, and make our way through the big double sliding glass doors into the yacht's main saloon. There, we'd take down Khaled and the Kraut bomb salesman before they had time to deep-six any of the evidence—or the money.

Gator and Duck Foot would come over the starboard rail just aft of the bow. They'd clean-sweep any security off the deck, then drop through the *Kuz Emeq*'s forward hatch and clear the forward cabins. Half Pint and Rodent were responsible for the port side, where there was an amidships ladder leading to the bridge. They'd neutralize it, close down the adjacent communications shack, then head for the engine room and temporarily disable the yacht. I say temporarily, because if something went wrong and the cavalry—read FBI—didn't show up on time, my orders were to sail the *Kuz Emeq* to the closest U.S. warship and make the transfer there.

Nod and Baby Huey would insert starboard amidships, up the accommodation ladder that sat alongside the main cabin. They'd take another ladder to the chopper deck, charge up, disable the chopper on its landing pad and neutralize the crew and any security personnel. Then they'd double-time it to an adjacent passageway, which led below decks to the crew's quarters, where they'd handcuff and lock down the *Kuz Emeq*'s staff. If

27

they met any resistance they were authorized to have the kind of lethal fun that SEALs seldom get to have these days when the ROEs[11] put out by the White House for counterterrorism missions stipulate more first aid for wounded tangos than wounded SEALs.[12]

The plan was KISS-simple, which is the way I like to do things. Yes, we were outnumbered. There were a dozen Taliban gunmen, and a crew of sixteen. But we would retain the tactical advantage, and therefore we would win through surprise, speed, and violence of action. Timing the assault was not a problem. We'd synchronized our watches aboard the *Nacogdoches*; besides, we carried waterproof radios. Once we'd broken the surface, we'd be able to communicate through our lip mikes and earpieces—if, that is, Mister Murphy hadn't screwed with the equipment.

I hand-signaled and we separated, each pair of swim buddies moving to locate their assigned insertion points. Boomerang and I moved away from the sea anchor line and had started to ascend gently—no telltale signs from us accomplished sneak-and-peekers—when I fucking passed out. I mean: one moment I was swimming, and then I don't remember fuck-all. Nada. Zero. Zilch. Somebody turned my fucking lights out.

Now, the fucking Draeger LAR-V is fed by a 1.5-liter oxygen bottle. Under what passes for normal operating conditions, it is expected that an experienced swimmer can operate for up to five

---

[11]Rules Of Engagement

[12]That's to be expected. This administration, after all, is the one in which a highly paid Pentagon consultant told the secretary of the Army that the military is too "manly" and demanded that in the future, training should not accentuate such "manly" attitudes as aggressiveness and combat skills, but instead pattern Army training after such organizations as religious orders and Alcoholics Anonymous. That way, the consultant wrote, "the Army will achieve the desirable goal of becoming non-violent, less sexist, and ungendered." What is most unbelievable about all this unmitigated horseshit, is that the fucking secretary of the Army actually accepted the criticism without comment.

hours underwater. Unless something goes wrong. And obviously, something had gone wrong.

Anyway, next thing I knew, I was being rudely shaken. I opened my eyes and saw Boomerang's face up against my own. One of his hands was holding my face steady. With his other, he pulled the mouthpiece out from between my teeth. Then he drew his hand across his neck to tell me, "Don't breathe." Then he passed me his own mouthpiece.

Someday, I am actually going to meet Mister Murphy. When I do, I am going to kill him. Slowly. Painfully. With extreme prejudice. That would be then. For now, all I wanted was a little fucking oxygen—just enough to get me to the surface. I didn't know what had gone wrong with my rebreather. Maybe there was water in the Barrel Lime, maybe it was cursed by dry rot, maybe . . . well, who cared. All I knew is that I'd blacked out, and if it hadn't been for Boomerang, Mister Murphy would have won this little contest.

I held on to my swim buddy as he passed the mouthpiece to me and we shared air for the final four fathoms as we eased ourselves toward the surface.

At about two fathoms we began to pick up the *Kuz Emeq*'s lights. Bright halogens, directed toward the water. That would make popping the surface more difficult. But it wouldn't necessarily help the folks aboard pick us up. The surface of the ocean is not mirrorlike. There's the chop—which tonight was about a foot—as well as surface winds, currents, and other elements. Bottom line is that unless you are looking—and I mean really looking—it will be hard to make out a swathed-in-black combat swimmer when he pops the surface adjacent to your ship. Especially if said combat swimmer knows enough to come up as close to the hull as possible, so that to see him, you have to lean way over the rail and look straight down.

I swallowed water, took a last gulp of O_2 from Boomerang's mouthpiece, and pushed off, giving him the air hose back. I exhaled gently—didn't want a bunch of bubbles giving my position away after I'd come so far undetected—and turtled the surface at snout depth at the port side corner of the transom, protected by the shadow of the dive platform.

Taking air through my nose and mouth quietly but rhythmically so I wouldn't start to hyperventilate and tunnel-vision, I eased the MP5's thick muzzle suppressor up, brought it out of the water next to my head, reached down and illuminated the waterproof electro-optical sight, and took a firm, one-handed grip on the weapon. Switched the radio on. Carefully inserted the earpiece and brought the lip mike into play.

I *tsk–tsk*ed. No response. I waited another fifteen seconds and *tsk–tsk*ed again. Nothing. WTF? Played with the radio and tried once more. Result: silence. Eased my right arm up far enough to check the dial of the big-watch-little-cock dive watch on my big hairy wrist. Despite all the goatfucks we'd endured, and the various dings that still made my teeth ache (not to mention running out of O_2), I was still ninety seconds ahead of schedule. I gave it fifty-five seconds (and believe me when you are fucking sitting in hostile territory, fifty-five seconds is a long, long fucking time), then *tsk–tsk*ed once again.

This time, seven *tsk–tsk* echoes came back at me. All the signals were five by five. That meant everybody's radios were on—and working. Will wonders never cease?

Now that I knew we were all set, it was time to prowl and growl. My body told me it was ready for combat: my breathing had become shallow; there was a slightly hollow feeling in the pit of my loins. My heart was pumping at about 150, my adrenaline level was off the charts—and I'm willing to bet you couldn't work a single fucking strand of *capelli d'angelo* up my sphincter right now no matter how much *olio* you doused it in.

I scanned (so as not to tunnel), breathed evenly, and pushed myself slightly aft to gain a better position and a better purchase on the dive platform.

Scan . . . and . . . breathe. Moved my left arm oh so *s-l-o-w-l-y*

30

onto the sea-bleached teak, my fingers grasping through the wood.

Scan and breathe. Peered across the wide transom to see Boomerang's narrow face mirroring my own movements, so that he'd cover my blind-spot areas and I'd cover his.

Scan, breathe. Except I held my breath as a shadow fell across the dive platform.

Scan breathe, goddamn it. I fought the impulse to move my arm, which lay up against the transom. Eased the suppressor of the PDW up so it angled into the shadow. Waited. Watched as the shadow lengthened and intensified.

Now, I perceived a hint of something physical—edge of head; hair; a whiff of . . . *garlic.* The motherfucker was starting to bend over the transom.

Scanbreathe. Scanbreathe. A dark, bearded face came into view, bisecting the V between transom and dive platform. *Scanbreathe.* I saw his eyes widen as he discovered my arm and leaned farther out to see what it was attached to.

I reached up, put the muzzle of the gun under the thick beard on his chinee-chin-chin. Squeezed the PDW's trigger before the sonofabitch could react. Put a three-round burst up and into his head.

This all took place under the physiological condition that piled higher-and-deepers[13] at graduate schools of psychology call "tachypsychia," which is a fifty-dollar word for the kind of time-stands-still slow motion under which so much combat seemingly happens. There was almost no noise—the surpressed sound of the hammer *pu-pu*-popping was lost in the ocean's chop and the ambient sounds coming from the yacht. Then the top of his Talibany turban exploded, and I was showered with blood, brain, and bone fragments.

He dropped like a sack of shit, collapsing over the transom, his weapon clattering to the deck out of sight. Then—this is in real

---

[13]That's how SEALs refer to a Ph.D.

time—he fell forward, onto the dive platform. Precisely where I had to be.

I heard the babble of Babel from SOD—somewhere on deck—followed by the long, deadly r-r-rip of automatic weapons fire. They were shouting to one another. Was it Arabic? Urdu Pak? Pashto Afghani? Who knew. More to the point, who cared.

The transom just above my head splintered as a barrage of rounds cut through it. Instinctively, I ducked behind the Taliban's corpse. Fuck me—sitting here in the water wasn't going to do anybody any good—especially if any of the motherfuckers on deck were carrying grenades.

I let go of the PDW, reached up, and pulled on his corpse, dragging it into the water, shouting "Go-go-go!" into the mike. No need for stealth anymore—what we needed was fucking violence of fucking action. Lots of both.

"Boomerang—let's go!" I grabbed one of the distraction devices out of its pouch, pulled the pin, heaved it over the transom, and pulled myself onto the dive platform.

As the two-hundred-decibel concussion and 1.8-million candlepower flash rocked the yacht I rolled over the transom, and came up on one knee, my MP5 up and ready to rock and roll, my Roguish eyes scanning for threats.

And because the God of WAR is a great and beneficent God, and because the God of WAR loves me as I was created in His image, He provided me with manifold threats to neutralize.

Threat One was that Taliban over there with the AK pointed vaguely in my direction. I smote him from his crotch to the bridge of his nose with three three-round bursts, and yea he went down and verily he died most nastily.

Threats Two and Three were still blinded from the flashbang. I shot them as they fought to see WTF was happening, holding the HK's front sight center-mass on their bodies and filling them with one-two-three-four-five three-shot groups until they fell and didn't move.

I heard Boomerang roll over the transom behind me, and the welcome sound of his surpressed PDW in triple-burst. A body fell off the aft starboard side of the upper deck, landing off to my right with a hollow thud. "Gotcha covered, Boss Dude—"

"Roger." I moved forward, listening to the sounds of my assault team as they commandeered the *Kuz Emeq*. Gator'd cleared the forward cabins and was already on his way aft. Rodent was inside the radio shack. Seconds later I heard him shout, "Commo hut clear."

I heard Baby Huey's hyperexcited voice report he'd taken care of the chopper and its crew. "Chopper clear chopper clear chopper clear," he screamed *sans* punctuation. *Yes*—this motherfucking operation was going like fucking clockwork. In fact, I was the only motherfucker behind schedule.

"Boss Dude—" That was Boomerang's urgent voice, coming from somewhere behind me. "Red four o'clock."

I concentrated on the sounds coming through my earpiece and kept moving toward the wide glass doors to the main saloon, where I could make out two, three, four people inside. My focus was diverted as Boomerang's voice exploded inside my ear. "Chopper pad! Red four o'clock," he screamed. Then he yelled, "Can't get a shot, going right, going right, going right."

Okay, enough already. Boomerang was telling me in SAS shorthand that he was moving to our right. I would have said something military like "Roger," except that the fucking expensive wood that Khaled had bought for *Kuz Emeq*'s fantail splintered right in front of me, and a long, nasty splinter of that selfsame very costly teak—it was about the size of a chopstick but much, much sharper—drove itself all the way through the meaty portion of my left calf.

It occurred to me right then that perhaps Boomerang hadn't been telling me where he was going, so much as trying to warn me that there was another fucking threat on my right-hand side—and that he didn't have a clear shot. It occurred to me right then that perhaps the God of War was angry with his child— that's *moi*—for exhibiting what the ancient Greeks called hubris, and Izzy Cohen, who ran Izzy's Kosher Deli & Numbers Running Establishment back in the old New Brunswick, New

Jersey, days of my ute, used to refer to as chutzpah. Hubris, chutzpah—either way, I was fuckee-fuckeed.

I swung the PDW's muzzle toward the threat. But I couldn't perceive any fucking threat. I swept left. I didn't see a fucking thing. I swept right. I didn't see bupkis there, either. That was when I realized that I was neither breathing nor scanning. Not good. I was tunneling: focused on the narrow, pie-shaped field of vision directly to my left and to my right. But that's like going into combat wearing blinders. Tunneling cuts off about 80 percent of your vision. Most crucially, it cuts off your peripheral vision—and peripheral is where most of the fucking action is going to take place.

Like the area above me—the edge of the chopper pad, from which, now that I'd bothered to raise my eyes, I saw a nasty, turbaned sonofabitch drawing down on me.

Just as he fired I rolled left and shot without aiming, stitching the rim of the cantilevered pad vaguely in his direction. Well, to be honest, that is an overstatement. I fired. But unlike all those fucking Hollywood movies where the good guy somehow manages to eke 218 shots out of his single-stack hard chrome frame and aubergine purple finish slide Bill Fabus custom-made hybrid Caspian .45 *sans* reloading, this was the fucking real world, and the thirty-round magazine in my PDW had just gone dry.

Now, a big part of being a SpecWarrior is training for situations such as this one. Saturation training. Hours and hours on the range, working out the most fluid way of dealing with stoppages, stovepipes, malfunctions, empty chambers, and just plain fuckups.

And so I didn't panic. I didn't even have to think. My mind went onto autodrive. I shouted, "Cover—Cover!" rolled under the sheltering lip of the quarterdeck and dropped to one knee.

"Gotcha, Boss—" That was Boomerang's voice as he lay down a comforting blanket of suppressive fire. It was even more comforting when a body dropped off the chopper pad onto the fantail.

The muzzle of Boomerang's HK followed its trajectory, and as it hit he pumped two shots into the Afghan's head. Yeah—I hate to waste ammo, too. But this way Boomerang was certain that this motherfucker wasn't gonna come back to haunt us.

I racked the bolt back. Dropped the mag. Took a new one from my thigh pouch, jammed it *sans* any foreplay into the receiver and shook it to make sure it was secure, then slapped the bolt forward. Total time was less than six seconds—an eternity when you're under fire, but better than anything I'd ever managed on the range.

I was ready to rock and roll, and I shouted, "Clear!" so Boomerang would know it.

Sometimes, friends, I am given to understatement. This was one of them. I was not *clear*, in any sense of the word. In fact, I was in what the former Leader of the Free World, George Herbert Walker Bush, has referred to so genteelly (and presidentially) as, "deep doo-doo."

Tonight's deep doo-doo was located inside the saloon, where an enterprising Taliban or two realized that he/they could fire the heavy rounds from their AKs right through the heavy, reinforced safety glass of the doors without shattering the glass itself. This was not especially good news to me. See? I told you that I am sometimes given to understatement.

I received this not especially good news in the form of half a dozen bullets directed at me. Luckily, these Taliban, while resourceful, were religious shooters. By that, I mean they were of the "spray and pray" school. I scampered on hands and knees out of the line of fire and retreated to shelter alongside a steel bulkhead adjoining the saloon.

"I can't keep their heads down, Boss Dude—" Boomerang's voice called urgently from across the fantail. "My HK ain't gettin' through the friggin' glass."

This was a problem we hadn't anticipated. The AK fires a heavy 7.62-×-39 round that punched clean through the double panes of half-inch thick tinted safety glass. Our suppressed,

9-mm hollowpoint rounds basically shattered on impact. They'd been designed that way for CQC (Close Quarters Combat, don'tcha know) in steel passageways, aircraft fuselages, and narrow hallways, where you don't want ricochets slamming into your own men or killing innocent hostages.

Fuck me. Belay that. Fuck us. I was dangerously behind schedule. By now the goddamn Corsicans had to have heard the shooting, and I'd wanted to be in total control of the fucking yacht by the time they'd had time to react.

Wild-eyed, I looked around. Saw a boat hook hanging on the bulkhead. Six feet of stout hickory, tipped by a steel shank with a solid spur. Grabbed it. Rooted around in my thigh pouch until I retrieved a distraction device. Fumbled until I came up with my duct tape and the coil of nylon line. Taped the distraction device to the steel shank of the boat hook, setting it so that the spoon was horizontal, and the ring head of the grenade pin pointing toward the deck. Half-hitched six feet of nylon line to the ring. Then, *c-a-r-e-f-u-l-l-y*, straightened the grenade pin.

I crouched to give myself a better swing and edged forward to the corner of the saloon. Then I took the fucking boat hook like a baseball bat, wound up, and swung the motherfucker hook first into the glass. Just before I made contact I pulled the nylon line, releasing the grenade pin, which kicked the spoon out and lit the device's second-and-a-half fuse.

I knew enough to look away as the fucking thing went off and shattered the saloon's safety glass doors into dust. Even so, I was virtually blinded by the blast. I charged through the opening where the doors had been, seeing stars and spots instead of targets or threats. Finally picked out two targets three maybe four yards away. Fired from the hip. They both went down. Closed the distance and discovered one *Mausetot*[14] Taliban.

Great, I was now seeing double. I heard Boomerang behind me. Turned to make sure (never assume). There were two of him,

---

[14]Kraut for dead as a doornail.

too—kind of a parallax view. Fuck me. I am getting to damn old for this kind of fun and games.

Swung back. Vaulted over the twin pianos, which were looking a lot worse for wear since I'd loosed half a mag into it (them?). Picked the wrong piano to vault—the one that obviously didn't exist—and landed flat on my Slovak snout. Since I was down, I took the time to reload the PDW—one fuckup like that a night is all I allow myself—then I gathered myself up and kept moving.

There was a passageway at the rear of the saloon, ending in a set of antique wood-and-multipaned French doors that led to the master suite. I knew that's where Khaled would be. Of course I bounced off the door frame—I really don't like this double-vision shit at all—and caromed crazily along the bulkheads, skimming across the oriental carpet.

Whoa—there were two single-compartment doors on opposite sides of the passageway about halfway to the master cabin. Here is a CQC rule that will keep you alive: never go past an unsecured space. I stopped just shy of the first, rubbed at my eyes, which were almost back to normal vision by now, and turned the handle. The door opened. I let it swing back up against the interior bulkhead. It opened all the way. I eased around, and peered inside. Reached in and flicked the light switch.

It was a guest compartment—a rectangular cabin with a double-sized bed, a big closet with two louvered doors, a sofa, coffee table, and two armchairs. The bathroom—I could make out the door—was off to the right. Subgun at the low ready, I worked my way around the perimeter of the room. Checked behind the sofa and under the bed. Worked my way past the credenza. Opened the closet doors. Inspected the bathroom. The cabin was empty.

I wedged the door open and went back out into the passageway to see Boomerang working his way up to the doorway opposite the one I'd just cleared. We stacked and made entry, working quickly and efficiently. It took less than thirty seconds to clear the second compartment, a mirror image of the one I'd done solo. That left the master suite.

Now, let's just stop the action for a minute or so here, so I can give all of youse some Roguish pointers about what we in the counterterrorism trade call dynamic entry operations. As I've pointed out recently, the key to success in these kinds of ops lies in surprise and in violence of action. But (there's always a *but*, ain't there?) there is one condition in which a dynamic entry is both foolhardy and dangerous. That is when someone knows you are coming, all surprise has been lost, and you still decide to go through the door into unknown hostile territory. Yes, sometimes it's absolutely necessary to do so. But in 99 percent of all cases, it is ill-advised, misguided, and downright foolhardy.

I have seen it happen. Some young, energetic SWAT cop on a dynamic entry sees a malefactor run down a hallway. The perp disappears around a corner, or into a room. The cop's adrenaline is pumping. So he gives chase and busts into the room, or turns the corner of the hallway. The perp is waiting with three friends and five guns, and the cop becomes dog meat.

Remember this piece of advice and take it to fucking heart: when some asshole scarpers down a hall or into a room on you and you lose sight of said AS—which stands for aforementioned sphincter—you have lost surprise. The dynamic entry portion of Show Time is over. Finished. Complete. Elvis has Left the Building. Now what you have is a barricade situation, and it should be treated as such.

So, instead of charging into the room or down the hall, you must RRXING—in other words, stop, look & listen. You must wait for backup, so that your firepower will absolutely positively completely suppress and overwhelm anything that may be inside that room or down that hall.

And then, instead of doing a Light Brigade and charging half a league, half a league, half a league onward into the valley of death, you must try to call the mutt out to you.

"Yo, scumbag inside the room, come on out or I'll use a year's supply CS gas on your worthless pus-nuts ass and then interrogate you with the help of a fuckin' plunger," is one way to open the dialogue. Sending Caesar the Squeezer K9 killer is another viable option. Or, if the scumbag has hostages, you just bottle him (or her, or it, because in these politically correct days we can and we do have female scumbags, and indeterminately gendered scumbags, too, y'know) up, cut the water and the power, commandeer the phone lines, and wait for the hostage negotiator.

But to be honest, most of the time, you'll get a response. It may be a hostile response, but it will be a response. And, from that first exchange, if you are agile, and sharp, and you play the situation right, you will be able to talk the perp out. And if he decides not to cooperate, and you have to escalate things, then the grand jury in front of which you will appear will find that you used prudent and reasonable force when confronting an armed and dangerous suspect, and your ass won't be hung out to dry.

Okay, so you realize right now that I wasn't about to kick in the French doors, just in case Khaled had trained an RPG or a machine gun on 'em. Boomerang and I held in the guest cabin. I peered around the door and yelled, "Khaled!"

No answer. I shouted his name again. This time I got what the social scientist dweebs sometimes call a nonverbal negative response: a long burst of automatic weapons fire shattered the glass panes of the French doors and ripped past us, down the passageway.

Now, we knew from our surveillance imagery that there was no way out of the master cabin except down this passageway. The suite had two rooms—a bedroom and a sitting room—plus a huge bath. But no back door. No escape hatch. Just six portholes on the starboard side, and six on the port side. And Khaled was a chubby little motherfucker with a forty-four-, maybe forty-five-inch waist, and those portholes, which opened out onto the deck, weren't more than eleven-and-a-half to twelve inches in diameter. I did the math in my head: no way he'd squeeze his royal bulkness through *them.*

I tried one more time to get him to do the right thing. "Hey, Khaled—you're bottled up. Just come the fuck out and stop this shit, and nobody gets fuckin' hurt."

Khaled's only response was another long burst.

. Well, fuck him. You can't say I hadn't tried to work things out like Mister Nice Guy. But it didn't look as if Khaled wanted to play my game. And there wasn't a whole lot of time to waste— remember all those nasty Corsicans just over the horizon. I hand-signaled Boomerang to tell him what we were about to do. Then I plucked the last of the distraction devices out of its pouch, straightened the pin, yanked it, reached around, and softball-pitched the fucking thing through the shattered French doors right into the center of the cabin. At first I thought I'd tossed a dud—because the goddamn flashbang didn't explode for three, four, five seconds, and the Mark 2 Mod 3 distraction devices I was carrying all had 1.5-second fuses. When the damn thing finally blew, the explosion made the whole fucking yacht shudder.

That's when I realized that what I'd tossed wasn't a fucking distraction device, but a goddamn Mark 3A2 concussion grenade. We are talking about half a pound of TNT here, folks. And it is spelled *l-e-t-h-a-l.*

I charged the French doors, my PDW working straight ahead. Boomerang was at my heels, his MP5 over my starboard shoulder. I kicked through the shattered double doors into the cabin. The fucking place was totally destroyed—broken glass and wood fragments everywhere. The draperies and furniture were on fire. The marble tabletops and counters had disintegrated— the explosion had turned the stone into lethal flechettes.

Khaled lay on his back, faceup—well, what was left of his face, anyway—behind the smoldering sofa, the Styr-Aug assault weapon he'd fired at me was still clutched in his right hand. From the look of things, he'd caught the brunt of the grenade blast directly. He wasn't a pretty sight. But I wasn't about to waste time admiring my handiwork. After all, I had the bomb salesman—and the Russkie device—to worry about.

The Kraut obviously wasn't in the sitting room. That left the bedroom, the closet, or the head.

Bedroom first. I silent-signaled Boomerang. We stacked outside the port side of the doorway. When he was ready to go, he squeezed my shoulder. I "cut the pie," working my muzzle around the doorway, exposing as little of myself as possible while scanning the ever-widening wedge of bedroom that I was able to see.

What I saw made the hair on the back of my neck stand straight up. Oh, the little Kraut was there, all right—all four feet eleven of him. He was standing in front of the bed. His left hand was in the air, minuscule palm facing toward me, waving in surrender. He was braying, *"Kapitulieren, kapitulieren,"* which even my *kleine* Deutsch managed to translate as "I surrender, I surrender!"

I nodded. And then—*holy shit*—I focused on what the Kraut was resting his right hand on. *"Machen mit* der hands up, *schnell, schnell, schnell!"* As I gestured with my weapon, the expression in my eyes left no doubt about what I'd do if I wasn't obeyed *right now*. The tiny Kraut's paws shot above his head.

Now I could concentrate. And like I just said, holy shit. What had me worried was a capped metal cylinder about two feet long and four inches in diameter. The top of the cylinder had a small rod protruding from its center. Below the cap was a thick collar, in the middle of which sat a large keylock device, surrounded by a series of buttons and switches.

The cylinder itself was fixed in what looked like a trio of ten-kilo weights—the same sort of iron plates that sit on the outdoor weight pile behind Rogue Manor. But I knew all too well that I wasn't looking at iron here. No—these plates were made of U235. What was even more disturbing was the fact that my contacts at Christians In Action had been inaccurate. The Kraut hadn't been about to sell Khaled a *Soviet* atom bomb. What sat in front of me was a USGI[15] SADM, which is the U.S. military acronym for a Small Atomic Demolition Munition, more popularly known as a tactical, man-portable nuke. This guy'd been about to sell Khaled one of *our* fucking atom bombs.

The question was, where the fuck had he got hold of it. The answer to that mystery was something I was going to make a point of finding out—and soon.

2313. We secured the ship. Gator kicked the *Kuz Emeq* into "ahead, one third," and we headed west-northwest through the gentle current, toward our rendezvous point. One additional piece of good news was that the Corsicans never showed up. I considered that good tactical judgment on their part; after all, it hadn't been their fight. Like many mercenaries, they'd simply taken the money—and then they'd run.

While my guys put out the remaining fires and searched all the bodies for papers and other assorted intel, I got on the radio to the Feds with the bad news about Khaled's untimely demise. The SAC—for Special Agent in Charge—had some choice words for me, few of them suitable even for *this* book. Well, fuck him—he hadn't been on site and I had. Besides, I had the Kraut, and I had the weapon, and two out of three (as the old country song goes), ain't bad.

Moreover, one might well argue (*I* most certainly would argue) that Prince Khaled Bin Abdullah dead actually made a lot more sense than Prince Khaled Bin Abdullah alive. First of all, it paid him back in kind for the nasty things he'd been doing over the past ten or so years—illustrating in no uncertain terms those old biblical and Koranic maxims about living by the sword results in dying by the sword. Second, Khaled's demise got him out of the Saudis' hair permanently, and *sans* any further embarrassment to them. The royal family would be spared seeing one of its own on

---

[15]United States Government Issue

trial in the United States—so the king wouldn't have to posture about tossing all the Americans out of his kingdom (big fucking chance of that, as it is the United States military that protects his fat-assed royal butt), or threatening an oil embargo, or whatever. Perhaps most important so far as I was concerned, killing Khaled prevented what I call the NRE, or Negative Ripple Effect, of counterterrorism. Whenever you capture one of these assholes and hold him for trial, there's always the risk that the asshole's pals will cause ripples: take hostages, blow up an embassy, send a series of suicide bombers into your capital city, or do some other heinous, nefarious, nasty shit, just to force you to let the guy go.

Finally, since it's the good old U.S. of A. we were talking about bringing Khaled back to for his trial, there was always the possibility that one of the prince's $500-an-hour pussy-ass liberal lawyers would be able to find a fucking Let 'Em Loose, Bruce judge, and get the scumbag off on some outrageous technicality. Well, given the chain of events, all of the above were problems we wouldn't have to face anymore so far as His Royal Corpseness, Khaled Bin Abdullah, was concerned.

But that wasn't the way the FBI saw it. Indeed, the very same instinct that has saved my life in the past caused me to forget to tell the FBI we'd taken the Kraut bomb merchant alive. We had ample opportunity to hide him before they came aboard, which is exactly what we did.

And my innate sensitivity to such situations turned out to be absolutely on the money. In fact, by the time the six-man crew of Special Agents showed up in their state-of-the-art VSV, the self-important SAC of shit who considered himself top gun in this little operation had already called Washington to complain about *moi*. He strode onboard the *Kuz Emeq* and, *sans* any of the usual formalities, began to dress me down like some wet-behind-the-balls recruit at Quantico. Now, this sort of behavior offends me. And so, provoked, I replied in kind.

I could replay the scene for you here. But why? Frankly, the sight of a pair of grown men screaming obscenities at each other doesn't do much for me, and it certainly doesn't move the plot of this book forward.

Moreover, there was no way I was about to submit to the Bureau's demands. Said SAC of shit wanted the SADM, and he wanted no part of Khaled's corpse. For my part, I was unwilling to part with the SADM, although I was willing to let the corpse go.

And so we called each other a lot of compound, complex names that included the *F*-word in most of its forms. But I was not about to give in. You see, so far as I can recall, it is the United States military, not the Federal fucking Bureau of Investigation, that has responsibility for the nation's arsenal of nuclear weapons—especially our tactical nukes.

Let me put it to you this way. I've been on the fucking FBI tour half a dozen times, and while I have seen John Dillinger's Colt .45, Machine Gun Kelly's Thompson submachine gun, and Lee Harvey Oswald's sniper rifle, I've never seen a SADM (or any other atomic device) among the collection of weapons stored and displayed there.

And what about the Kraut? Well, so far as I was concerned, he was my very own material witness to the theft of U.S. government military property. I wanted to interrogate him about where, when, and how he'd obtained the device. There was no way I was about to let the FBI know I had him.

So, suffice it to say that the SAC and I agreed to disagree, and when he threatened to call the attorney general's office and have me ordered off the case, I called the private line of General Thomas Edward Crocker, the Chairman of the Joint Chiefs of Staff and the officer for whom I work, reported to the Chairman the nasty details of my discovery, and received formal instructions from him to protect the device.

I even turned the phone over to the FBI's aforesaid SAC of shit so he could hear General Crocker for himself. It did no good, of course. Said sad SAC kept insisting that he didn't come under the fucking command of any fucking general except the one whose title began with "Attorney." Well, it was getting late, and I was wet, cold, worn out, and—with no pussy in sight—I was feeling decidedly antisocial. And so I ended the discussion abruptly by unceremoniously tossing the SAC's self-important butt, and his cellular phone, overboard, and ordering his six-man detachment off my fucking ship at gunpoint.

No, it might not have been the smartest thing to do. But watching him sputter and kick in his $1,500 suit and fancy Italian loafers gave me a certain amount of transitory, visceral satisfaction. After all, it had been a hard night, and we gotta take our small pleasures where we can, right?

Yeah, well the priests used to tell us kids at St. Ladislaus Hungarian School that for each act of pleasure, there will be compensatory pain. Or, as the famous Italian street philosopher, Detective Anthony Beretta, once said on TV, "If ya do da crime, ya do da time."

In my case, the pain came at dockside at Mazara del Vallo, Sicily, where my men and I did not pass "Go," did not collect even a single fucking lira, but were ordered forthwith, at once, immediately, and *tout de suite* to promptly surrender everything we'd removed from the *Kuz Emeq* to the proper authorities, and then promptly remove ourselves onto a Frankfurt-bound aircraft.

Surrender—WTF? Remove—WTF? Frankfurt—WTF?

WTF indeed. We'd been received at this out-of-the way port on the very southwest coast of Sicily by an unlikely welcoming committee that included more than a score of representatives from four of the five armed services (only the Air Farce was missing). A Coast Guard cutter escorted us the final fifty nautical miles into Sicilian waters. There were sailors and marines galore on the dock awaiting our arrival.

And there was a tall, lanky BDU'd colonel, complete with loaded side arm, spit-shined boondockers, and the white-walled buzz cut that's fashionable amongst gonna-be generals at the John F. Kennedy Special Warfare Center at Fort Bragg, North Carolina, pacing up and down on the quay as we nudged the *Kuz Emeq* alongside. Tucked under his left arm was a big, well-worn, brown leather document folder. Off to the side, a platoon of green-bereted Special Forces shooters in full battle gear ringed a big, black Pave Low chopper that sat, Ready to Go, at the end of the dock.

Once we'd made secure and shut the engines down I had Nod and BH lower the accommodation ladder. I lifted the rail, secured it, then clambered down onto the low concrete pier. The colonel headed in my direction.

"Captain Marcinko."

It wasn't asked as a question, so I guess he recognized me from the salt spray in my French braid and my Roguish good looks. "Datsa me. *Bon giorno, colonnello* . . ." I stopped cold, because I'd been staring at the breast pocket of his neat but well-used BDUs looking for a name tag. Hmm. There was none. I guess he was one of those generic-type officers.

"Suter, Captain. John Suter." He extended his hand. "Pleased to meet ya."

I took his big hand. The grip was firm, his skin was cool and dry to the touch, and his fingers were as rough as sixty-grit sandpaper. This guy was no desk jockey. "What can I do for you, Colonel Suter?"

"Hey, let's dispense with the formality, okay? Just call me John, and I'll call you whatever you want," he drawled in a soft southern accent that was somewhere between North Carolina and West Virginia.

"Dick sounds good to me." I paused and waved my arm toward the uniformed assemblage on the quay. "So, John, what the fuck—over?"

When he laughed his eyes crinkled. That was another good sign. "Well, since you asked so nice, I'll tell ya. First thing is, according to the message that ripped me and my guys a bunch of new assholes, ya got your hands on a device that once belonged to us."

"You have a copy of that message, John? And maybe some kind of ID, too?" I didn't want to be unfriendly, but since ADMs are valuable commodities these days, I wasn't about to take any chances. Frankly, it's reasonably easy to get hold of starched, well-worn BDUs and colonel's eagles. In fact, it's not wholly inconceivable to purloin a Pave Low, either. I know—I've done it.

"Gotcha." He retrieved a current ID card from his breast pocket. I checked the holographic device carefully. It was real. Then he cracked the brown leather folder, so I could see what was inside. There was a red-tabbed fax message lying there, secured by leather straps top and bottom. It was printed on TS/SCI paper, so I knew that it was authentic, too.

The message was on JCS letterhead, and signed by Thomas E. Crocker, General, USA, and Chairman of the Joint Chiefs of Staff. It was also, as is General Crocker's habit, PFS—which stands for Pretty Fucking Straightforward. Since it's brief, let me show it to you in its entirety.

TOP SECRET

From: Chairman of the Joint Chiefs of Staff
To: Colonel John C. Suter, Fifth Special Forces
          Security Group, USA
          231077-042/1250
SUBJ: Recovery of ADM Serial Number 79-20113

1. It has come to my attention that ADM 79-20113, originally supplied 03 September 1982 to components of Fifth Special Forces, Patch Barracks, West Germany, has been seized by United States Naval Special Warfare personnel during a TS counterterrorism operation.

2. As part of your current project (see Tab A) you are ordered to retrieve the device from Captain Richard (NMN) Marcinko, USN, at Mazara del Vallo, Sicily, immediately upon Captain Marcinko's arrival.

3. You are ordered to use all appropriate means to secure the device and transport it to Patch Barracks under Threatcon Charlie conditions.

4. You will report using encrypted means to this office and only to this office at the earliest opportunity, giving precise details of how and when ADM 79-20113 was removed from under the military control of the United States.

5. You will treat this matter in strictest confidence.

6.   (signed):   Thomas E. Crocker
                            General, U.S. Army
                            Chairman, Joint Chiefs of
                                            Staff

REF: 10 USC 167
Att: Tab A (TS/C)
       Tab B (Unclassified)

TOP SECRET

48

John Suter looked at me, his face Huckleberry Hound long. "Maybe I'm being paranoid, but from the way I read this, my whole group's been fucked." He pursed his lips and focused on imperfections on the concrete of the quay between his boots. "Y'know, I don't mind taking a fall. That's my job as an officer. But my men had nothing to do with this. Most of 'em weren't even in grade school when the fucking ADM was first deployed here."

It was good to meet this guy. He was the kind of officer Roy Boehm would have liked. I shook my head. "That's not the way the Chairman works. Sure—he wants results. And he's reamed me so many new assholes that my hind end looks like fucking Swiss cheese. But he's not looking for scapegoats. So far as I can tell, the memo's written to satisfy the politicians—and keep your ass out of it. So I don't think you have much to worry about unless you lose the fucking nuke between here and Stuttgart, in which case I hope you like life in the brig. Hey, the Chairman's tough, but he's fair, and he's a fucking War-rior."

Suter nodded. "That's good to know, given the pussy-ass can't cunts I have to deal with most of the time." He patted the Beretta on his pistol belt. "It took me six hours of wheedling to get the one-star weenie in charge of base ops to sign the req form for us to draw ammo this morning. And this is with me holding this fucking note from the fucking Chairman of the Joint fucking Chiefs telling me I'm supposed to provide Threat-con fucking Charlie security for a fucking stolen nuclear fuck-ing device."

While I appreciated John Suter's familiarity with ironic use of the *F*-word, the sorry truth, my friends, is that antimilitary behavior from flag officers is all too common these days. Or, as the godfather of all SEALs, Roy Boehm, puts it so well, "There are too fucking many dickless fucking admirals and pussy-ass fucking generals who choose to fucking sit down whenever they have to go fucking wee-wee."

Y'know, in the old Navy, the Navy of wooden ships and iron men, they say (and *they* is right) that leadership comes from the top. And y'know what? It does. But in today's Navy (which had been morphed into a Navy of iron ships and wooden men), the Navy of which the fucking commander in chief is a draft-dodging, pussy-whipped, hate-the-military coward, you can just imagine how all those one-stars who'd like to become two-stars will act when a decision that may appear to be warlike has to be taken. It's doom on warriors time, hence we are all fuckee-fuckeed these days.

Endeth the soliloquy. "Amen, bro." I extended my hand in John Suter's direction.

"Yeah," he grinned. "Those pus-nuts would probably shit a brick if they knew I'd cumshawed a two-pound block of C-4 when I drew the ammo."

That brought a smile to my face. "You grabbed a block of C-4?"

"Hey, you never know when you're gonna have to redecorate, right?"

I liked this asshole. He thought like I do. I slammed him on the shoulder. "Well, good luck, John. I hope you kick some ass, and do some redecorating." I paused. "By the way, can you give me a hint about what's in the attached tabs?"

He looked at me strangely. "Say what?"

"Chairman's message has a tab attached—tab A. Top secret. Compartmented."

Suter's face reddened. "I'd love to, Dick—but y'know how it is with TS/SCI."

I did—although I'd have loved to have known what the Chairman had asked him to do. I shook my head. "Message received. What about the other tab—the unclassified one?"

A crafty smile crept across his face. "I think I can bring you up to speed on that one, Dick." He reached behind the TS fax and pulled out a folded sheet of paper. "Tab B," he said, as if he was remembering a piece of trivia, "it's a love note from the Chairman for you."

I unfolded and perused. There was no classification on this one and it was just as KISS as the message to John Suter. No need to repeat it, but the gist was that I was to hand all the intel I'd gathered on the *Kuz Emeq* over to representatives of the judge advocate general's office. I would then transport myself, my men, and all our equipment up to Rhine Main Air Base, just outside Frankfurt, within twenty-four hours of transmission of this message. At Rhine Main I was to check in with an 0-5 (that's a lieutenant colonel) named Smith, who worked in the Intelligence section, and comply with his instructions. That was all. Over and out.

I looked at the time stamp on the fax. Then I stared at the little-dick-big-watch watch on my hairy left wrist. Sixteen hours had passed since the Chairman's transmission. I was standing on a fucking dock on the fucking southwest coast of Sicily in a wet suit I'd been wearing for three days. I had no papers, no travel orders, not even a fucking ID card. When one goes to war, one don't usually bring the fucking AMEX or driver's license along. On most of *my* missions, which tend to be clandestine, covert, or UNODIR,[16] I tend not to carry any identification at all. That way, should my Roguish ass get waxed and wasted, I won't be an embarrassment to my country.

I scanned the single sheet of fax paper again. Transport myself, my men, and my equipment, the message ordered. Forthwith, the message ordered. WTF was I supposed to use, a fucking oxcart?

It was about to be doom-on-Dickie time, and I said so in the sort of SEAL technical language that made Colonel Suter roar with laughter. He clapped me across the shoulder. "Hey, Dick, we can probably come up with eight sets of coveralls, if you don't mind wearing Army OD. I took the liberty of bringing a

---

[16]The acronym stands for UNless Otherwise DIRected, and it's how I prefer to operate when I'm surrounded by can't cunts.

pair of Conex lockboxes with me so you can stow your weapons and ammo and whatever other goodies you may have."

I was grateful, and told him so. You don't find many officers these days who'll take that kind of initiative.

"Hey," John Suter said, "You'd do the same for me, right?"

I offered him my hand. "Anytime, John."

"Cool," he said. "And look—I can give you a lift as far as Sigonella. It's less than an hour if we put pedal to metal. They're always running shuttles between there and Frankfurt. You'll make it, no sweat."

That was easy for him to say. After all, he had his own fucking aircraft. My men and I were about to become hitchhikers. Mendicants. Untouchables in the hierarchy of the fucking military air transport system. But since the Chairman is my boss these days, and he and I are on a first-name basis (He calls me "Dick," and I call him "General"), and I like my work, I groaned, said a silent "Yes, sir," took the Chairman's message, and set about complying.

Well, sorta. I didn't hand over the suitcase of cash I'd removed from Khaled's stateroom. Nor did I surrender the interrogation notes I'd taken during the fifty-three hours it had taken us to sail the *Kuz Emeq* to Sicily. Interrogation notes? Yup. Lots of 'em. And believe me, the ex-Stasi agent, *der winzig* Heinz Hochheizer, had been extremely talkative during the cruise.

That was to be expected. Y'see, I have this certain, shall we say, *persuasive* quality about me. Especially when *you* are naked and duct-taped to an uncomfortable chair, and *I* am waving a hot soldering iron in my big, Roguish paw. Now, Heinz hadn't actually survived the trip to Sicily. He'd died on me—a heart attack, probably, but without a medic aboard, who could tell. Hey, it wasn't my doing. He just fuckin' croaked. Anyway, we gave the former Stasi agent a decent burial at sea, which was probably more than he deserved. And since neither John Suter (nor anyone else) mentioned Heinz, I didn't bother to bring the subject up either.

Anyway, back to what I'd discovered. I'd learned that Heinz had paid $800,000 for the damn thing—bought it from a Georgian Mafiyosi named Gabliani, for cash. It was his understanding, Heinz told me, that the *vor*[17] had traded the weapon from a Russkie colonel working for the Ministry of the Interior in Moscow. The Russkie'd paid off the man who'd sold it to him— some German—with three vintage-1985 Soviet suitcase nukes. Gabliani took the Americanski ADM off the Ivan by paying him with a ten-kilo chunk of Afghan flake heroin and fifty keys of Bolivian cocaine.

I didn't give a shit about the drugs. What I wanted to know was how the Ivan had scored a USGI[18] ADM in the first place.

"I think the German was from Düsseldorf," Heinz had wheezed.

That's not what I'd meant. What I meant, was how had the Kraut gotten his hands on the bomb in the first place.

"But then, you *do* mean Düsseldorf," Heinz had insisted.

"Okay, *Ja*, Düsseldorf," I'd said, humoring him.

He shrugged his shoulders as best he could, being taped up to the chair. Before Düsseldorf, the little Kraut insisted he had no idea where the ADM came from. I was convinced that he was telling me the truth, too, because he, and I (and the soldering iron), went over that ground a number of times, and no matter how well he might have been trained (and the Stasi trained its operatives pretty damn well), I can sense when I'm being lied to. And Heinz wasn't giving off any bad vibes, except, that is, for his BO, and all the shit in his skivvies.

But Heinz did share one piece of disturbing information with me in the course of our lengthy interlocution. He was absofuckinglutely certain that the ADM he'd bought wasn't the only American device for sale. In fact, he mentioned that before he'd

---

[17]That's Russkie for a crime lord.

[18]United States Government-Inspected. Yes, I know last time I used this acronym it stood for U.S. Government Issue, but that's the way things go.

been able to contact Gabliani the Georgian, he'd gone to Düsseldorf himself to check the market out, because word on the street was that Düsseldorf was the happening place, so far as pocket nukes were concerned.

I made a mental note of that factoid, then wondered aloud if the little Kraut had found anything out.

Heinz was quite proud of himself. After all, he was a former intelligence operative. He bragged that it hadn't taken him even half a day. He'd called one of his old agents in Berlin, a West German government official code-named Rottweiler, whom he'd run during the Cold War. Rottweiler wasn't especially happy to hear from Heinz, but the Stasi man knew the West German wouldn't give him away. If he did, Heinz would see to it that Rottweiler learned a whole bunch of new tricks—in prison.

Anyway, it didn't take long for Rottweiler to put him in touch with someone from one of the neo-Nazi fringe groups, who put him in touch with some fucking ultranationalist scum, who tried to peddle Heinz two hundred kilos of Semtex plastic explosive.

The story was getting a little long. I licked my finger and touched the end of the soldering iron, and after Heinz had heard the hiss, I told him to pick up the pace.

The little Kraut began talking so fast he sounded like a 33-RPM LP playing at 78. The Semtex dealer knew a cocaine dealer, who sold to someone named Franz. Franz had an expensive habit. Franz needed money to support that habit. The cocaine dealer allegedly told the Semtex dealer that one night, at one of Düsseldorf's pricey discos, Franz had told him that he'd be willing to exchange a Russkie pocket nuke for a hundred pounds of grade-A, uncut, highest quality Colombian blow. For a hundred *keys* of coke, Franz said he could perhaps get his hands on an American pocket nuke. Much better quality than the Soviet nukes he already had in stock.

Now Heinz was beginning to make sense. "And who is

Rottweiler," I asked, the soldering iron in my hand closing in on Heinz's withered weenie.

Unlike his old boss, Markus Wolff, who went to jail rather than name names, Heinz saw the Roguish look in my eyes and decided to spill his guts. "His name is Grüner. Peter Grüner," the little Kraut wailed.

"Did Peter Grüner put you in touch with the coke dealer," I asked.

"Nein," Heinz said. He'd started the ball rolling, but before things fell into place, Heinz had received the call that finally put him in touch with Gabliani, the Georgian mobster he'd been trying to contact for a month, and who, Heinz had already confirmed, had an American ADM for sale. That was it: Heinz checked out of his hotel, took a cab to the airport, and climbed on a flight to Sofia. He'd never checked out Düsseldorf Franz, or the disco.

And what was the name of the disco, I asked rhetorically (I'm *real* good at rhetorical when I have a hot soldering iron in my hand).

"Die Silbermieze," Heinz caterwauled. "The Silver Pussycat."

I asked Heinz why he hadn't taken the easy route and scored one of the Russkie suitcase nukes on the market. I mean, the eight hundred thou Heinz paid for the SADM he'd planned to sell Khaled was at least twice the going price of the stolen Russkie devices I knew were being sold to Iraq, Iran, and Libya these days.

The little German told me he'd actually tried to save the Saudi some cash by obtaining an Ivan bomb. But Khaled had insisted on nothing but American goods. He'd gone on and on, Heinz bitched, about the Koranic justice of using the captured sword of the oppressor to put him to death. And since money was to be no object, and since Khaled was such a first-class putz, Heinz had decided to buy high and sell even higher. So he'd gone straight to Sofia, been picked up at the airport by a squad of goons, blindfolded, tossed in the back of a big black Zil, and driven who knows where. Finally, he was taken to a godforsaken house where he sat, guarded by a couple of real thugs, for two days. "I guess they were checking my bona fides," Heinz whined. Then he was blindfolded again, and driven to meet the Mafiyosi.

He first set eyes on the *vor v zakonye*[19] named Gabliani in the back room of a Georgian restaurant in the back streets of Sofia. They haggled for three days over plates of mayonnaise-enhanced salads, greasy herring, and black Georgian bread, all washed down by countless glasses of Napoleon cognac, Chivas Regal, and vodka. Well into his cups (his tumblers, actually), Gabliani the Godfather had bragged to Heinz that, given the price of flake heroin in Afghanistan, and his high-level contacts with the old mujahideen leadership, his mullah friends in Iran who helped him transship the drugs, and despite the higher cost of payoffs for authorities in Turkey, Albania, and France, the fucking weapon hadn't cost him even two hundred thousand dollars.

And so, Gabliani had said, since he'd cut himself such a good deal, he'd pass some of the savings on to Heinz—more profit for them both. A price had been agreed on, half the money had been transferred, and three weeks later, a messenger with the ADM had appeared one night at Heinz's apartment in Frankfurt.

And indeed, money *had* been no object. Not for Khaled, anyway: there were two and a half million dollars, all in used hundreds—that's twenty-five thousand $100 bills—in the suitcase. It weighed more than the fucking SADM.

Now, my long conversation with Heinz had left me perplexed, aggravated, and apprehensive. First of all, there was the Chairman. One missing ADM had already given Chairman Crocker a fierce case of WHUTA (which, of course, stands for Wild Hair Up The Ass). Once I told him that I suspected more were gone—something I hadn't been able to do thus far because I lacked the secure communications to do so—he'd probably develop the worst fucking case of hemorrhoids ever known to man.

---

[19]Mafiya godfather

And then there was me. I don't like the prospect of going up against nuclear weapons in the hands of no-goodniks, scumbags, and other assorted assholes. And these sorts of tactical weapons can be employed quickly, effectively, and with deadly consequences. Just imagine, friends, what would have happened if the bomb that went off in the garage of New York's World Trade Center had been a SADM. Or if Timothy McVeigh had been able to find the financial resources to obtain a Russkie suitcase nuke to use on the Murrah Federal Building in Oklahoma City.

The nasty possibilities are endless. And so, while I'd get my Roguish butt to Rhine Main and deal with Lieutenant Colonel Smith, just as the Chairman ordered, what I really planned to do was to slip away from Smith and get my behind up to Düsseldorf, find Heinz's ex-agent, Peter Grüner (aka Rottweiler). Maybe we'd go together to that disco called the Silver Pussycat. But I wasn't interested is shaking my booty—or anybody else's. No, I planned to spend some time sneaking and peeking to see who the fuck this Franz was. It was he, after all, who claimed he could sell the kinds of lethal nuclear devices that would put my country in jeopardy.

I don't like that. Yes, I am a Rogue-type Warrior (in fact, I am THE fucking trademarked Rogue Warrior®). But I am also an unabashed patriot. Full stop. I love this country, no matter how much I bitch about the military system in which I exist, the C_2C0 assholes with whom I am too often forced to work, and the current lame-dick administration, which is ruining our armed forces.

Now, when the nation's in jeopardy, I am not a happy Rogue. In fact, when the nation's in jeopardy, I become a very extremely dangerous Rogue. And therefore, when I discover who the guilty party is—and believe me, friends, I will find out—I will put my Roguish hands around his, her, or its cocksucking throat (I am an equal-opportunity executioner after all) and s-q-u-e-e-z-e until there is no more life within.

Chapter

3

John Suter and I gossiped all the way to Sigonella. His life had been miserable lately: a series of probes—skinheads, or neo-Nazis, or both—had compromised security at half a dozen Army installations between Stuttgart and Frankfurt, and he'd been tasked with finding out who/what/where/how/why.

Over at Patch Barracks, for example, the goddamn sensor system kept crapping out, and the fucking general in charge—the same asshole who'd almost denied John his ammo—was in denial. He insisted that the fucking foxes and rabbits and other varmints had gone crazy of late, when John Suter and the rest of the shooters knew damn well they were being probed by varmints of the human kind. Worse, some local crackers[20] had hacked into the computer system used by Army Intelligence at Nuremberg and made off with several hundred crown jewels, and the idiots down there didn't have the sense to repair their fucking firewalls, so the system was just as vulnerable as it ever was.

---

[20]Criminal hackers

And now there was this fucking ADM thing. "I tell ya, Dick," he said, "I don't mind a full plate, but this one's overfucking flowing—and it all smells suspiciously like shit on a shingle to me."

I had to laugh—because misery really does like company. But I did more than laugh. John and I struck a deal—we'd cooperate. Because what we'd discussed was troubling.

See, Germany is going through a transition period right now. The absorption of what used to be East Germany has caused the Krauts some hardship—high unemployment, for example. But unification also has its pluses. Germany wields more power in Europe than it has in more than half a century. Berlin is a key player in European economics and politics. Meanwhile, America, which used to be the big kid on the block during the Cold War, has got other strategic fish to fry these days. We're more concerned with the Far East, for example, than we are in Europe's internal affairs. Which means, Germany and America are drifting apart—not necessarily a Good Thing, in my estimation. Why is that, you ask?

Because it allows ample opportunity for a few no-goodniks—Germany's growing ultraright factions for example—to start making trouble. And from what John Suter said, that was exactly the case in his AO.

So John and I would stay in touch. And if the circumstances warranted, we'd share information.

I'm a big believer in that sort of thing. There are folks who close-hold info and intel because they treat it as their property. So far as I'm concerned, any intelligence, or tactical info that can save a shooter's life, should be shared. John Suter had been handed a tough assignment. If I could be of help to him, I would be. And I'd expect the same in return.

We set down on the tarmac at Sigonella fifty-three minutes after we'd lifted off the quay. And John Suter had been right: about half an hour later, we cadged eight spots on a grungy C-130 making its thrice-weekly garbage-and-beer run to Rhine Main. John waved as his Pave Low lifted off. He shared more than gossip, and the promise of sharing info. Inside one of the Conex boxes he'd given us sat his two-pound block of C-4 plastic explosive, six pencil detonators, two yards of det cord, and three electronic timers. Someday, I hoped to be able to pay the debt back.

I spent much of the time on the just-over-three-and-a-half-hour flight up to Frankfurt stretched out on a greasy canvas tarp, my head resting on the big bag of cash, thinking about the ADM we'd taken off little Heinz. I'd never worked with portable nukes. Three of the grizzled chiefs from UDT 21 and UDT 22— my old platoon chief, Everett Emerson Barrett was one of 'em; the tough old goats known as Grose and Mugs Sullivan were the others—had trained with early versions of SADMs (Small ADMs) and MADMs (Medium Atomic Demolition Munitions) in the 1950s and 1960s. They jumped out of planes and locked out of subs with them, no mean feat, because the earliest of the MADM devices weighed in at about 135 pounds.

They were also as cumbersome as hell. Grose said it was like jumping out of a plane tied to a fucking washing machine on full spin cycle. He said that it was almost impossible to throw a hump and get stable, which meant you had a real good chance of your chute collapsing on you if you weren't real careful. And cutting away a collapsed chute and riding in on the reserve was almost impossible, given the weight and bulk of the MADM.

According to Mugs Sullivan, more than a dozen Frogs burned in and croaked during MADM jumps. But worst of all, the earliest ADMs—both the *M* and *S* versions—were capacitor-driven. And let me tell you, capacitors can be devilishly unstable, especially if they come in contact with moisture or cold.

But—at least Ev, Grose, and Mugs hinted so—the tactical possibilities were endless. I once asked Mugs Sullivan once why the fuck he'd volunteer to jump out of a plane with something that could vaporize him in a millisecond.

"You worthless pencil-dicked shit-for-brains pussy ass wet-behind-the-scrote dumbshit," Grose growled affectionately by way of response. "Let's just for argument say that we're working with a nuclear device that has a power of point one zero megaton. Think about it. That's the friggin' equivalent of two hundred thousand pounds of TNT. Two hundred fuckin' tons of explosive, in a package that I can carry on my friggin' back if I have to. Okay, let's say we have a dam we want to blow up. Take your choice, asshole—two hundred tons of TNT, or a hundred pounds of ADM. You'd have to put *two fucking thousand* five-hundred-pound bombs on the fucking target at once to do the same job I can do with less than a platoon of Frogs. How many sorties do you think it would take to drop two thousand five-hundred-pound bombs?"

When he put it in terms like that, it made perfect sense—even to me. Still does, in fact. Then, in the early 1970s, so the story goes, half a dozen SEALs from SEAL Team Two had been S³d, which as you can probably guess stands for selected, shang-haied, and sheep-dipped. They went to work for some superse-cret alphabet soup entity created, it was whispered, by direct order of the president, our late and much-lamented Richard Milhous Nixon, his own roguish self.

One day, they'd been drinking beer on Team Two's quarter-deck with their shipmates. The next, their names had been expunged from the Team roster, their families had been moved who-knew-where, and we never saw any of 'em again at Little Creek—or anywhere else, for that matter. The RUMINT was that they'd volunteered to work on some program that involved covert stay-behind tactics in the event of a Soviet invasion of Western Europe. The whispered scuttlebutt was that they'd volunteered to hit Warsaw, Prague, Sofia, Moscow, Leningrad, and other assorted Soviet and Warsaw Pact targets with man-portable atomic weapons, knowing that the projected mission mortality rate was 100 percent.

But in the 1970s, dying for your country was something men volunteered for. Back then, patriotism wasn't a dirty word, or an idle concept. Back then, the military wasn't touchy or feely, or built around the idiotic concept of giving recruits better self-esteem.

Back then, recruits were expected to ACHIEVE. Full stop. End of story. And if they didn't have the drive to do it on their own, there were a lot of size eleven, double-E boondockers that drill sergeants, gunnies, and chiefs would employ in that old-fashioned, highly effective motivational technique known as "a swift boot in the ass."

But I'm getting away from the point here. The point is that back then, the folks running the military realized that the only reason to have an army is to kill our enemies, not to make people feel good about themselves. And since our biggest enemy was the Soviet Union, it made perfect sense to me that these six SEALs had volunteered to kill as many Sovs as possible, even if it meant their own deaths.

During the Cold War, the Major Land-War Scenario, as it was known back then, ran like this: Soviet and Warsaw Pact troops, buttressed by air support and medium-range missiles, would sweep from the Baltics, Poland, and Czechoslovakia, directly through Germany. Like the ripples in a pond, the Soviets would move across Western Europe to the Atlantic in the west, and the Mediterranean in the south.

One of the major elements of NATO's defensive strategy was that in the case of that massive Soviet invasion, Special Operations forces—Green Berets, SEALs, and others—would infiltrate the Russkie lines to attack the Sovs from behind, destroying their supply lines, their command-and-control centers, and their communications. To aid this plan, the United States clandestinely cached tons and tons of military equipment all across Europe. Most of these stay-behind stockpiles, which included weapons and ammunition, vehicles, food, spare parts, ordnance, civilian clothes, and huge numbers of bogus IDs, were hidden in Germany and Austria. But there were also caches in France, Norway, Italy, Greece, and Turkey. These clandestine nest eggs were known as POMCUS—for Positioned Outside the Military

Authority of the United States—caches. Coordination for POM-CUS was run from Patch Barracks, the Army's red brick SpecWar headquarters, located just outside Stuttgart, Germany.

Obviously, the precise sites of the POMCUS repositories was a close-hold, need-to-know kind of thing. I am privy to a dozen or so locations—most of 'em in close proximity to a maritime environment, in Norway, Italy, France, and Greece. But there are hundreds of POMCUS sites. Did any of them contain ADMs? It is probably that they did. But I cannot say for sure, because I just don't know. None of the caches I'd ever been to held any. That was on the one hand. On the other hand, I knew from the Chairman's rocket to John Suter that the SADM *der winzig*[21] Heinz sold to Khaled had been delivered to Patch Barracks in the early 1980s. Then at some point it disappeared from everyone's radar screens. Ultimately, it had been snatched. Not a good situation.

We arrived at Rhine Main just after 1200 hours. I left the guys and all our gear in the cafeteria, and headed toward the low red brick building on the far side of the field, which housed the Intelligence staff. Inside, I checked the building directory for a lieutenant colonel named Smith. No one by that name was listed. I found the admin office, stuck my head inside, and discovered a perky, young E-5 who peered at me over the screen of her desktop computer. The sign atop her desk told me I was talking to First Sergeant M. Walsh.

"Hi, First Sergeant Walsh, I'm Dick Marcinko—looking for a Lieutenant Colonel Smith. He doesn't seem to be listed on the directory."

"*You* are looking for Lieutenant Colonel Smith," she repeated. She gave me a TVE—a Thorough Visual Exam—and I could see that I came up heavily in the debit column. "And your name, again, is . . ."

---

[21]It's Kraut for *tiny*.

"Marcinko—Richard. Captain. Navy."

I received another TVE. She didn't say a word, but her body language was FLFC—Fucking Loud and Fucking Clear. It said, Oh, sure you are a U.S. Navy captain—and I am the fucking queen of Bavaria.

I unfolded the Chairman's faxed message, smoothed it out on the corner of her desk, and proffered it in her direction.

She accepted the sheet, slid it under her button nose, and examined it, her lips moving as she read. She checked a large Post-it note attached to her computer screen, and as I leaned forward to try to read it, she removed the sheet of yellow paper, folded it once, and put it in her skirt pocket. To further keep me from prying, she hit a series of keys, which blanked her CRT (if you don't know, go to the Glossary and look it up). Then she rose, walked across the office to a four-drawer document safe that sat under a bad photograph of a one-star Air Farce general, and standing with her back to me to block the view, she spun the dial, opened the combination lock, flipped the red-letters-on-white-background magnetic sign that read CLOSED over, so its white letters on red background read OPEN, opened the top file drawer, and retrieved a sealed red-tabbed folder. She removed a letter opener from atop the document safe and slit the seal, opened the file, peered inside, then looked closely at me, as if she was comparing my face with a photograph.

Obviously satisfied, she pulled a thick brown manila envelope from the file, slit it open, replaced the letter opener on the safe, then handed me my very own wallet, complete with my Don't Leave Home Without It[22]. That was a neat fucking trick, and I told her so. She smiled wryly in return and continued extracting goodies from the big envelope. First came a proper military ID card with my hair-rich face and my real name on it, noting that I was a NILO[23] attached to the Rhine Main Intel unit. There were

---

[22]American Express card
[23]Naval Intelligence Liaison Officer

similar cards for each of my men, and a thick wad of German marks wrapped in a rubber band. She laid a sheet of paper attesting to the inventory atop her desk.

"Sign in the highlighted area alongside the little red tab, please, Captain Marcinko."

I retrieved a big Spyderco folder from my waistband and flicked it open. "Do you have a pen—or should I just stick myself and sign in blood?"

Sergeant Walsh actually thought about it for ten seconds or so, then looked at me and with a perfectly straight face said, "A pen will do, I guess." She gave me one from her desk drawer.

She retrieved the signed form from me and held an upraised palm out until I laid the pen atop it. The pen was Put In Its Proper Place. Then the signed form was replaced in the red-tabbed folder, the folder was snapped shut and slipped back into the file drawer. First Sergeant Walsh closed the drawer with a satisfying *thwup*, twirled the combination lock, and reversed the magnetic sign all in one fluid motion. It was all so well choreographed that it was more satisfying than watching the Rockettes do their Christmas routine—and let me tell you, First Sergeant M. Walsh had better legs than most Rockettes.

She caught me staring, betrayed the merest hint of a smile in my direction, and said: "Lieutenant Colonel Smith has left the base, Captain Marcinko. He requests that you and your men meet him in Mainz."

"Mainz."

She nodded. "Do you know where Mainz is, Captain?"

Of course I know—and I told her so in a playfully Roguish way that brought a flush of embarrassed color to her cheeks. For those of you not familiar with der layout of Deutschland, Mainz is about twenty-five miles west of Rhine Main Air Base, at the confluence of the Rhine and Main Rivers. It's a small city located in the middle of one of the Rhine Valley's best wine-making districts. But make no mistake: it may be small when compared to, say, Frankfurt, or Düsseldorf, or Berlin. But it's good-sized—

not some one-street Rhine River, Main River, or Mosel Valley town, and the fact that Lieutenant Colonel Smith, whoever-the-fuck-he-was, said he'd meet us in Mainz didn't help much at all in re a *treff*.[24] It's like saying, "I'll meet you in Santa Fe."

I scratched at my beard. "He didn't happen to say just where he'd like to link up, did he?"

She reached into her pocket, retrieved the Post-it note and scanned it again. "Go to Mainz and check in to the Mainz Hilton—the one on the riverbank," Sergeant Walsh said. "There are rooms reserved for you and your men." She waved the yellow rectangle in my direction. "According to this, Lieutenant Colonel Smith will find you."

Now that we had IDs, we hit the Rhine Main commissary and picked up a few basics—like jeans, T-shirts, sweats and jackets, boondockers, socks, toothbrushes, razors. Then, freshly outfitted, we searched for transportation. Much to Duck Foot's annoyance, we did not boost any of the Mercedes sedans in the BOQ parking lot. Nor did we borrow—read steal—an Official U.S. Air Farce vehicle. Instead, we caught one of the base minibuses that run the circuit, dropping pilots off in the commuter suburbs that surround Rhine Main. And thus we meandered through Florsheim (now I know where all those frigging shoes come from), Weilbach, Biebach, Erbenheim, and Wiesbaden, then crossed the Rhine at Schierstein and turned east, paralleling the river, driving through an industrial zone that slowly metamorphosed into the city proper, until the big Hilton loomed in front of the windshield. We unloaded and watched as the little diesel bus chugged off in the direction of Bodenheim, with two very tired pilots still aboard. It took two luggage carts to hold all our equipment. Then I gave the desk clerk my name, and he gave me the key to a suite on the fourth floor.

There were four big bedrooms, each with two double beds.

---

[24]That's a *rendezvous* in Deutsch.

The suite had two bathrooms, and a huge sitting room that looked out over the city. And there was a note addressed to me sitting on the minibar.

I slit the envelope. *"Willkommen, mein Kapitän,"* it read in block letters. "Then let's meet and talk. See you at the Alt Deutsche Weinstube—it's a wine bar behind the *Dom*—1900."

I checked my watch. It was 1525. If the meet was set for 1900, I wanted to recce the neighborhood and the wine bar for at least two hours beforehand. No, I am not being paranoid. I am simply following my own fucking SpecWar Commandment—the one that says Thou shalt never assume. So, we grabbed quick showers and then, as we were beer-deprived in the hotel room, secured our gear in the steel lockboxes John Suter had provided, and set out to explore.

1605. We strolled the narrow modern streets. It had been some time since I'd been in Mainz, and I was amazed at the Americanization of the place. The city dates back more than two thousand years. It sustained heavy bomb damage during the World War II, and so most of the construction is less than fifty years old. But that's not what I'm talking about. What I mean is that these days, Krauts buy their sneakers at Foot Locker stores, eat at McDonald's, Burger King, and KFC, and snack on Pizza Hut pizzas instead of all those wonderful wursts.

And if you want to go native and look just like the locals, forget about der lederhosen und der high-ge-zocksen, or der loden coats und hats mit der feathers in der brim. Just slip into an oversized UCLA sweatshirt, a pair of Levi's or Gap jeans, a pair of Air Jordans, and one of those fucking Oakley "No Fear" baseball caps—worn backward, of course, and you'll look just like 80 percent of all Krauts these days. We wandered through Mainz's crowded shopping district and believe me, it was like we'd never left Georgetown, except everyone was *sprechen sie Deutsch*ing.

Well, my own personal feeling is that ven you iss in Chermany, you vill eat der Cherman food—und you vill LIKE IT. Und zo, we as headed toward the *Altstadt*—the old part of the city where we were scheduled to meet Lieutenant Colonel Smith—I was drawn like der moth to der fire, toward the thick glass counter of a stall that sold the kind of old-fashioned *Fleischwurst mit Saft* (that's sausage with mustard), on *Brot*—that's bread—which is so absolutely, completely, perfectly, intensively, utterly *German* that it brings tears to your eyes (not to mention kilos of saturated fat to your arteries). I *schniffed*. I *schnorted*. I succumbed. I told the guys, who were looking longingly at the Mickey D's not a hundred yards farther down the street, that we were going nowhere until we'd sampled every fucking variation sitting in the big glass case.

They bitched und moaned—until, that is, I'd made 'em taste the goods behind the counter. One bite is all it took—I knew they were hooked. And so, we *schtood* und *gemunchened*, the fat dribbling down our chins, the mustard clotting in my mustache. Oh, gentle reader, I was in fucking *schwein* heaven.

And then, satiated, with the guys pulling on my sleeve like kids always do when they'd been given only half a treat, we reconned the narrow streets between the cathedral and the river until we found ourselves a beer *Stube*.[25] The task was harder than you might think, given the fact that Germany is supposed to be to beer what Switzerland is to chocolate. But Mainz, you have to understand, is a wine-making town. Hence there are scores, perhaps even hundreds, of *WeinStuben*. But old-fashioned German beer halls, the kind that line the streets of Munich and Stuttgart, or even the sorts of bars you can find in Düsseldorf, Berlin, Hamburg, Köln, and Bonn, are fewer and farther between.

We finally found a likely candidate a few blocks south and east of the cathedral. It was on a narrow, graffiti-rich side street, halfway between a housing project and a small industrial block

---

[25]Literally, a beer room. What a wonderful concept.

of what looked to be metal shops and garages. As we walked past the housing project, a four-story block of prefab concrete with louvered windows, many with small satellite TV dishes attached, the rich smells of Turkish cooking wafted down on us.

The sign outside the bar read BINDING EXPORT, Mainz's local brewski. The place was one of those medieval reproductions. There was lots of dark wood trim, and thick machine-made-to-look-hand-hewn-timber beams framing the doorway. The smoked glass windows were small, opaque, and mullion-intensive. You could smell the beer and cigarette smoke from twenty yards away. I held the heavy door open for my guys, and we trooped inside.

As the door closed behind us, we froze. Have you ever been someplace that, the moment you walk in, you realize that you have made a humongous mistake? You have? Good—because that's the way I felt right then.

The vibes herein were all wrong. This was not a happy environment for Dickie and his guys. Oh, it was authentic, all right—the long, wooden bar; the hand-wrought bar stools; the tables, some of them made from antique beer barrel tops; the ancient brass taps from which *der Barkellner*[26] could draw the local pils or lager from huge barrels in the basement. But the ambience was fucked.

And what was that fucked ambience, you ask? Well, there were one-two-three-four-five-six-seven-eight-nine-ten drinkers at the bar. Another trio stood at the beer keg–table to my starboard. Two more lay to port. And each and every one was clad in some version or other that included black leather over greasy jeans cinched by chromed chain links and/or garrison belts, and sporting the kind of thick-soled Dr. Martens steel-toe boots that hurt like hell whenever they make contact with your rib cage— or any other portion of your anatomy, for that matter. Even in the

---

[26]Bartender

dim light, I could see lots of body-piercing, too. Hairwise, they wore the kind of close-cropped buzz cuts inflicted upon first-week boot camp Marines. Yup: we'd walked into a skinhead bar.

You want to know about skinheads? Well, I guess there's time for a short sit-rep. We're talking right-wing, punko, pseudofascist dilettante bullshit, for the most part, mingled with neo-Nazi racist philosophy, cowardly attacks on foreign laborers, and an ultranationalist, anti-American outlook on life. Heard enough? Good.

I 20-20'd the sorry bunch of scrotes arrayed in front of us, and took note. Why is it that assholes like these have such bad skin and seldom remember to bathe? Let me put it another way. My friends, where the fuck's *gemütlich* when you need it?

Let me say here and now that despite the fucked vibes, we weren't about to back out the door and go somewhere else. SEALs do not—repeat, NOT—ever back away from a situation, or a fight, just because it may be prudent to do so. Not my SEALs, at least.

I select my people for their aggressiveness and their love of kicking the proverbial ass and taking the proverbial names. I want each and every one of my men to have a playful manner—and if "play" includes tossing you and twenty more like you through a plate glass window, well, so be it.

Besides, we'd had a hard couple of days. We'd swum and we'd climbed and we'd been shot at and we'd had to kill a bunch of nasty, dangerous, and well-armed tangos. We'd been cold and wet and we'd shit on ourselves and we'd suffered dings aplenty. And frankly when you have done all of that, it's actually quite a relief (and an emotional as well as physical release as well) to get the kind of deep satisfaction that whupping the shit out of some sphincter-minded skinhead in a bar gives you.

Hold on, hold on—there's someone out there yelling a question. Repeat it once more, will you?

You what? Oh—you want to know if kicking ass in a bar is as effective in releasing the pressure as a long session of pussy.

Hey—*nothing* is as good as pussy when it comes to releasing the pressure. But you know as well as I do that there was no pussy in sight. Not a fucking female in the bar. And thus, these leather-clad, body-pierced schmucks were going to have to do. And so, we sailed ahead full, bellied up to the bar, and asked for *acht Bieren, bitter.*

Der Barkellner, who sported three small silver rings on the outside corner of his left eyebrow, five similar rings through the cartilage of his right ear, and a large, ornately crafted silver monkey's paw stud embedded just below the center of his lower lip, looked at us with undisguised hatred. He stood with his arms folded across his old black leather apron, a cigarette dangling from the middle fingers of his left hand, and said, "Ve don't here zerve *Amerikaners.*"

"Hey, fuck you, you fucking asshole." Baby Huey put his petulant puss right in the bartender's face. "We want some fuckin' beer and we want it—now."

I know, I know—he's only a wet-behind-the-balls kid, and therefore he's impetuous by nature. But behavior like this is unacceptable. Like Don Vito Corleone once said, *"Nevah let anybudy know what you ah thinkin'. Nevah reveal yawself to yaw enemies."* Well, so far as I'm concerned, da Godfather could have been a SpecWarrior from the way he thought.

I was beginning to have my doubts about BH. My hand settled around the back of the kid's neck. I physically removed him from his face-to-face with the bartender, and brought him nose to nose with *moi.*

"Nobody elected you the fucking spokesman for this fucking delegation," I said. "So you get the fuck over there"—I pointed to a bar stool one table away from the pair of port-side skinheads—"and stay there until I say so."

His eyes went wide. "I didn't mean anything, Skip—"

There he went again. I cut him off with a look, and he stopped in midsyllable.

"Terry—"

The kid's big lower lip stuck out about an inch and a half. He let out an audible sigh, his big shoulders hunched, and he shambled over to where I'd directed. The closest skinheads watched him, nudged one another, and schnickered. Oh, that was gonna be their problem.

I turned back toward the bar, hoping I'd kept things on an even keel and knowing I'd accomplished my goal when I heard derisory laughter from the rest of the skinheads. Oh, I knew we were going to have to clean this place out. But I wanted to do it on my terms, not when the resident assholes chose to act.

"I apologize for this young man's behavior," I said. "How he said it was wrong. But we would like some beer."

The bartender's arms were still crossed. He glared at me.

"That'll be eight beers, please." I checked my watch. It was currently 1656. You will remember that I wanted at least an hour and a half in the *Altstadt* to reconnoiter the meet with Lieutenant Colonel Smith. I looked over toward the very rear corner of the bar and saw that Mister Murphy had snuck in behind us and was sitting there with a big fat *schmirk* on his ugly puss. Oh, doom on Dickie. From the shit-eating look on Mister Murphy's face, I knew that we were going to end up way, way behind schedule.

Off to my right, Boomerang giggled. I shifted my stance slightly—just enough to perceive that each of my men had selected a target and a secondary. The great thing about traveling with Warriors is that you don't have to talk a lot about situations like this one. They simply know WTF to do, and they Just Do It.

Boomerang giggled again. Most people read it as a sign of nervousness. It's not. Boomerang giggles before he kills things. In fact, that's one of the reasons I like the boy so much. He has a truly perverted sense of humor, which exhibits itself at times like these. Maybe it's because he's the only California surfer in my band of merry marauders. At six foot one, two hundred pounds, he's a former linebacker from the UCLA who tells people he enlisted in the Navy because he wanted to get paid to surf. He's called Boomerang because during BUD/S he just kept coming back for punishment, no matter how dinged up he got. During Desert Storm, he chased SCUD missiles in the Iraqi desert, blowing up three launchers and killing nineteen Republican Guards in the kinds of one-on-one encounters he likes best— late at night when Boomerang's out and about all alone, with his K-Bar and his piano-wire garrote.

Next to him, Nod cracked his knuckles, then his neck. Eddie DiCarlo is a former blankethead—a Green Beret for whom Special Forces got *b-o-r-i-n-g*. And so, at the age of twenty-nine and a half, he enlisted in the Navy. At thirty, he went through BUD/S. Now, the average age at BUD/S is twenty-two. And Nod's knees were kinda beat up, due to the fact that he had six hundred jumps to his credit, and more than his fair share of rough landings, before he became a Frog. But he persevered. In fact, he excelled. He's a moody, quiet kind of guy who didn't have much success in the Teams because he had no respect for the can't-cunt officers who lead from behind these days—and he showed that disrespect at each and every opportunity.

But, you see, Nod had been to war, whereas most of the SEAL lieutenants, lieutenant commanders, commanders and captains with whom he dealt had not. As an E-6 Green Beret, Nod chased drug dealers in Colombia and Bolivia and tangled with Manny Noriega's Israeli mercenaries in Panama. As a SEAL, he worked as a countersniper in Somalia, and he has nineteen varmints to his credit. That's three more than the normal bag limit there. But after Mogadishu, things went sour. The administration changed, the Clintonistas came into power, and all of a sudden Warriors like Nod weren't appreciated. In fact, back in the mid-1990s officers discovered that they didn't get promoted if their units were filled with the kinds of men who liked to pull the trigger.

Under the Clintonistas, aggressiveness was a no-no. You want a star? Teach your troops to recycle. Send your men to Save the Rain Forest School. The sorry result was that Nod's post-Somalia fitreps read like shit. Some of the better descriptions included insubordinate, recalcitrant, uncontrollable, stubborn, and over-aggressive.

In fact, most of my men were considered scum by the current

RICHARD MARCINKO and JOHN WEISMAN

Powers That Be. That's why they were assigned to me. I got "stuck" with the brawlers, the incorrigibles, the aggressive, pushy, cunning, tricky sonsofbitches that nobody else wanted.

Well, friends, lemme tell ya. I'm an old-fashioned kind of leader. I like all those above-listed qualities in a man. Roy Boehm, the godfather of all SEALs, used to say that given the choice, he'd rather get his men from the brig than from the Naval Academy, because guys from the brig were more likely to delight in breaking things and killing people, than the tea-sipping, memo-writing, ring-knocking ossifers and gentlemens they breed these days at Annapolis. (Oh, yeah—it's a sorry situation when the school that gave us Arleigh Burke, Chester Nimitz, and Bull Halsey now produces dope-dealing, test-cheating manager-officers who quake at the thought of making WAR.) How right Roy was (and is). Moreover, Roy taught me how to channel those destructive energies; how to harness all that drive and determination. And so, I lucked out when Nod as well as the rest of my recalcitrants were assigned to Red Cell as a way of quashing their careers (and mine, too).

But talk about tossing a squad of Br'er Rabbits into the fucking briar patch! And—whoa, hold on a sec. I'd rhapsodize a bit longer on this theme, but *der Barkellner* just spat some Kraut in my direction, and he's looking at me very strangely. So, I'll tell you more about my guys later. Right now, things are about to get very interesting.

"Excuse me?" I leaned across the bar.

"Nicht serviert Amerikaners hier—ve don't zerve here *Amerikaners,"* the bartender said once again, jabbing the air in front of my face with his cigarette for emphasis. Off to my port side, one of der skinheads added an exclamation point to the *Barkellner's* statement by slapping his chrome steel chain across the bar and laughing.

Things were getting far Teutonic for me. And so, I wide-arm shrugged (as if I wasn't really in the mood to argue), and began to turn, as if we were actually going to leave, and said "Well-l-l-l . . ." in a passable imitation of Ronald Reagan, or Jack Benny.

Now, as all of that is taking place, allow me to give you the Rogue Warrior's First Law of Physics.

It goes like this. "Grab an asshole by the monkey's paw stud in his lip and pull hard enough, and the rest of the body will always follow the lip."

Und now, I vill illustrate.

I whirled, reached across the bar, grabbed *der Barkellner* by the stud in the center of his lower lip, yanked him clear over the beer-stained wood, grabbed him by the scruff of the neck and the rear of his belt, and slammed him into the floor face first.

There was this incredible momentary lull—the skinheads were too fucking shocked to react. That was when Boomerang, that big smile on his face and a giggle in his throat, sucker-punched the skinhead closest to him. Oh, it was an astonishing, amazing, pile-driving hit. I mean, Boomerang used every bit of power in his legs, torso, back, shoulders, and arms to bury his left fist wrist-deep in the poor asshole's solar plexus. The punch lifted the Kraut eight inches off the ground. He puked about a gallon of lumpy, beer yellow puke on the way down, and collapsed in a heap on the floor. I sidestepped just in time to miss getting puked on—hey, I was wearing clean clothes for a change.

My friends, let me give you a tactical suggestion about bar brawling: do not get absorbed in the action, because you will not pay attention, and you will get surprised. That's what happened to me. I was admiring Boomerang's handiwork when someone wearing four silver skull-shaped death's head rings on his right hand grabbed my French braid and tried to use it like a slingshot to throw me through the window. I stepped back, slamming my bulk up against him to jam him and keep him from leveraging me.

A real-world, European aside: God, he stank. What's with the counterculture vultures here on the Continent? Don't these scumbuckets ever fucking believe in taking a fucking shower? Okay: back to real time. This asshole was a handful—six inches taller than me, and probably forty pounds heavier.

We bumped around against the bar like a couple of pinballs, all elbows, knees, chins, teeth, and feet, fighting for position. I thought I'd managed to slow him down a little: a gentle love tap to the nose here, an affectionate poke to the balls there—until he push-me-pull-you-do-si-do swung me around, looped my braid around my throat, and tried to garrote me with my own fucking hair.

That sort of chutzpah wasn't appreciated. I stomped his instep—ineffective, dammit, because he was wearing these big high-top Dr. Martens steel-reinforced boondockers. He caught me with his free hand—a solid blow to my big, wide, Slovak snout that brought tears to my eyes.

Oh, that hurt. But there was no time to deal with the pain. I slammed him in the balls, which bent him forward, and followed up with a quick backhand to the face with the trailing edge of my fist. But the *Schei*Ⓐ*kerl*[27] had my hair wrapped around his hand and wasn't letting go.

I shifted gears, wound up, and elbowed him in the gut as hard as I fucking could. Progress: I dropped Herr *Vier Ringen* to his knees. But he took me with him (I told you, he vas a *Schei*Ⓐ*kerl),* slamming my chin against the edge of the bar hard enough to loosen several molars as he dragged me floorward. Yeah: right into the huge, fucking puddle of fucking lumpy fucking puke (you remember the aforementioned puke; it's courtesy of Boomerang's fucking sucker punch). Since Mister Murphy saw fit to make an appearance at this point in the festivities, I (of course) careened into said fucking puke face first, catching a good snoutful of the stuff.

Believe it or not, that was GNBN. BN is that puke stinks. GN is that puke be as slippery as a horny seventeen-year-old prom queen's pussy. And more BN (for Herr *Vier Ringen)* was that I am a former pea-snorting, spaghetti-inhaling geek enlisted man. In fact, as a young tadpole, I used to trade snot with my teammates.

---

[27]Sonofabitch

So, practiced in the green arts, I simply snorted puke and kept on going. Herr *Vier Ringen,* on der other hand, tried his best to keep his face out of the stuff. That was BN for him and GN for me. While he was scrambling ass over teakettle, I broke away, swung my right arm, and caught him nicely with my elbow, nailing him in the cheek with a solid *thwack,* sending him pukeward on his back.

Herr *Vier Ringen* struggled, cockroachlike, to regain his hands and knees. He crawled doorward through the puke. I grabbed him by his ankles and dragged him back, facedown, to me. Desperate, he caught hold of a bar stool and pulled it between us.

Lemme tell you something, folks: when you are spending all your energy trying to hold on to a bar stool, you are not trying to kill the ol' Rogue. That gave me the opening I needed. I pulled myself up the length of his body as if I were going up a caving ladder. Using my forearm, I smashed the back of his head into the floor, wrestled the stool away from him, and used it to leverage myself onto my feet, then I reversed it, brought it around by the legs, and swung it—*fore!*—like a fucking golf club, catching him square in the Adam's apple as he struggled to regain his own footing. He collapsed mit much *gürgeln* und *schpittin'* der teeth.

I'd just started to admire my handiwork (don't I ever learn?), when another FSK[28] armed with a yard-long length of chrome tire chain launched himself across the floor in my direction, traveling chain-first, a nasty expression on his round, double-chinned FSK face. Oh—he was another big, fat one, with a shaved head and a blond mustache that gave him the look of the guy on the Mister Clean liquid detergent labels.

Feeling my oats like a fucking thoroughbred, I whirled away just as the fucking steel came down toward my head. The chain slashed past my ear, heading for my shoulder, and would have broken my clavicle, except that I got the fucking bar stool up in

---

[28]Foul-smelling Kraut

time. The wood took the brunt of the hit, shattering, but absorbing the energy of the blow. I reached out, grabbed the end of the chain, and—since I'm a damn Yankee, I yankeed hard and reeled the lard-laden asshole toward me.

But FSK realized what I was up to—and so he charged, closing the distance between us faster than I would have liked. But it didn't matter—you see, I had taken control of his fucking chain. And since I bench-press 450 pounds, 155 times a day, rain or shine, hung out or hung over, on the outdoor weight pile at Rogue Manor, I am very much stronger than your average, everyday skinhead. I am, in point of fact, very much stronger than your above-average, extraordinary skinhead. I am also more Roguish, which means I'm nastier, too.

So, as I reeled the sonofabitch in, I was wrapping his chain around my hand and arm. And since he'd obliged me by getting up close and personal, I decided to do the same with him. I stepped up and caught him with a downward, sledgehammer blow from my chain-augmented fist—*wham!*—right above the heart. His eyes crossed, an incredulous, porkish expression came over his face, and he collapsed into the puke puddle beneath his feet.

Quickly I scanned, searching for other threats, but there were none.

"All clear, Skipper," BH called out.

Boomerang shook his head. "Negatory. Not fucking clear, yet, Baby Huey."

He turned the tadpole to starboard to observe as Rodent upended the last standing FSK, ran him headfirst into the bar, and stood back as the Kraut krumpled kaput.

"*Now* we're all clear," he said. He put his arm around the young man's shoulder. "That's the third fuckup, kid—it's time for you to start paying some fuckin' attention to what you do. You almost got Boss Dude and me whacked on the *Kuz Emeq* when you said the chopper deck was clear, but it wasn't, and we had to take out somebody you should have dealt with. Just now, you almost blew our fuckin' cover. And here you go again, shoutin' 'Clear' when it ain't clear yet." He paused. "Baby Huey, my man, you better start payin' better attention to detail if you're gonna make it in this little unit of ours."

Gator Shepard, who wasn't even breathing hard, nodded in agreement. "Amen to that, bro."

Baby Huey's round baby face fell. He clenched his fists. "Hey, look, I was just trying—"

"Look, BH," Gator said, "We don't *try*. We *do*. There's a difference."

Duck Foot put his hands up. "Yo, kiddo, lemme tell you what a chief once told me when I was an FNG at Team Four. He said the most important thing I could do was S^2—which meant I should sit the fuck down and shut the fuck up, and learn from the more experienced guys."

"You wouldn't be here if Boss Dude didn't think you had potential, my man," Boomerang said. "But be cool. Lay back. Like Duck Foot says, S^2. Learn how we work as a team. Then you become part of it."

"Because if you don't," Nod said, "your ass is gonna go out the door. We don't have room for loners."

Baby Huey stood there, his big eyes moving from one SEAL to another. Finally, he nodded, and swallowed hard. "Got it," he said, his big jaw moving up and down.

Gator clapped him on the back. "Cool."

I watched as they all piled on BH as if he'd just scored an eighty-yard touchdown, tackling him, roughing him up, rolling him around in the puke. Now, this is why I truly love my men. I didn't have to ream Baby Huey a new asshole. My men did the job for me. And did it in the Old Navy style, by which I mean the kind of tough talk that inspires, stimulates, and motivates. Moreover, from the way they were acting, I knew they'd accepted the kid, flaws and all. And they'd told him in no uncertain terms that from here on in he'd have to pull his own weight or he'd be gone. But their actions had said, "You're one of us."

"Screw all this touchy-feely shit. I need a fucking beer," Rodent chirped, separating himself from the pile of puke-coated bodies. The tiny SEAL vaulted the bar and began searching for unbroken glassware. "Any of you assholes want to join me?"

"We all will," Half Pint said. "But we'd better drink quick, then get back to the hotel and clean up. I mean, I don't wanna walk around stinking of some fucking skinhead asshole's puke. We're supposed to be low profile, ain't we, Skipper?"

It was 1948 before we arrived, double-time, in front of the Alt Deutsche Weinstube. Like most of the wine cellars in the *Altstadt* the restaurant was built into a three-story timber-framed, seventeenth-century house, with wonderful vaulted roof, dormer windows, and intricate gables. We cut around the wide market square in front of the *Dom*[29] and turned into the *Altstadt*, jogging along narrow cobblestone streets, slaloming past knots of locals walking their dogs, tourists gawking at the sights, and university students threading their way home on the sorts of ubiquitous, old-fashioned single-gear bicycles one can still see in Europe.

Outside the wine cellar, a dozen or so tables were filled with groups of Krauts in animated conversation. We slowed down, split up, ambled closer, and recced the folks sitting al fresco from a distance. Baby Huey and Boomerang window-shopped the souvenir stand ten yards downstream from the tables to make sure there was no one nasty lurking in the shadows. Half Pint, Nod, and I perused the display window of a wine store while we took the street's pulse from the upstream side. And Duck Foot, Gator, and Rodent—all animals of the party kind, after all— checked for beaver and pussy at Murphy's Farm, one of the Irish pub franchises that are so popular in Germany these days, which sat diagonally across from the wine cellar.

It didn't take long for me to sense that everything was kosher.

---

[29]You'll remember that's what they call cathedrals in Germany.

Now, if circumstances had been different, I'd have broken us into three groups, run three separate SDRs—that's Surveillance Detection Routes—and been in position by 1700, watching, looking, and listening to see if any bad guys were in the neighborhood. Frankly, urban countersurveillance is much more difficult than it is in the field. In the boonies, you dig in, camouflage your position, and wait for the flora and the fauna to go back to their natural patterns—birds singing, crickets chirping, and insects buzzing. If those patterns are disturbed you know that there's someone else in your neighborhood. Same thing goes for a small town. In the Kraut Kuntryside (or just about any other rural location anywhere in the world), a stranger *fallt entsetzlich auf*—schticks out like der sore thumb.

But in the city, things are much harder. Instead of listening to the sounds of nature, you have to search for untoward patterns— teams of watchers passing through on a regular, or irregular basis. Customers at the street cafés who don't blend in with the regulars. But how do you know? Cities like Mainz (and Rome, and Paris, and London) are populated with transients, and tourists, and one-day-trippers, as well as the huge pool of residents. Oh, sure, you can handle things if you have a week or two to detect those normal patterns. But to do it in a day, or worse, in a couple of hours, is virtually impossible. And so, I've discovered that urban countersurveillance requires a sixth sense kind of gestalt, which you must develop over time. I treat it the same way I deal with taking point: I follow my instincts.

Tonight, my instincts told me things were okay. No hair was standing up on the back of my neck; no klaxon horn was sounding; the bullshit meter that sits below and behind my pussy detector read "zero." This was no ambush. No setup. And so, after twenty-five minutes of watching for watchers and spying none, I signaled the guys, we assembled, and made our way past the crowded outdoor tables, through the narrow open door, and inside the candle-lit restaurant.

It was one of those old-fashioned places made up of half a

dozen or so small rooms filled with tables. The ceilings were low and accented by real, antique hand-hewn beams. The tables were heavy and ornately carved, as were all the chairs.

I squeezed past a knot of English tourists working their way toward the front door and squinted into the dimly lit room directly in front of us but didn't see anyone I recognized. I began to move toward a small alcove to my left, when a maître d' in a well-worn, shiny double-breasted tux approached, a fistful of menus in his hand.

"Willkommen," he said, a big smile on his perspiring face. "Gut naben, mein herren."

I answered him in kind.

He ignored my German and continued in flawless English. "And how many will you be tonight?" he asked, shifting so he could peer past my shoulder.

"We're eight—but we're meeting someone," I said. "A Mister Smith. Has he arrived yet?"

"Ach, sooo—Herr Schmidt," he said. "So, you are his party." He gave me a fidgety but not angry little frown. "Herr Schmidt has been waiting for you—very, very patiently." From his tone, Herr Schmidt was a big tipper. The maître d' did a passable Veronica as a tray-bearing waiter sidled past him into the alcove. "Please, follow me. Herr Schmidt has reserved one of our private rooms in the wine cellar."

He turned on his heel and strode back through the narrow, smoky room, turned to his right, took a second sharp turn to the right, and descended a long, creaky, bannisterless staircase. At the bottom were three doors. Through the first, which was open, I could see the restaurant's bustling kitchen and the dumbwaiters on which the food was sent upstairs. The second door had a big padlock on a hasp. That left door number three. The maître d' swung it outward, and stood aside to allow us entry.

The cool, dank air of the wine cellar washed over me. It was twenty degrees cooler down here than it had been up in the restaurant. That was because the room was all stone—floor, walls, ceiling—all of 'em had been hewn from the solid-rock foundation of what was obviously a very old building. Suspended from the ceiling were three large, wrought iron chandeliers that hung, evenly spaced, over the sort of long, wide, majestical table that you see in old King Arthur movies. Huge wine racks lined the walls; each of the six-foot-high structures was filled with bottles whose brown and green glass reflected the dim light.

A single figure sat at the far end of the long table, an open bottle of wine and a small-bowled, half-filled *Rhinewein* glass in front of him. Four place settings were arrayed on each side.

"Herr Schmidt . . . ," the maître d' said by way of introduction. He closed the door behind us.

From the head of the table, Thomas Edward Crocker, Chairman of the Joint Chiefs of Staff, and no less of his general's bearing in the thick tweed jacket, cashmere turtleneck, and hunting cap than if he were in his Class A uniform, pointed his trademark thumb and forefinger like a locked and loaded Colt .45 at my chest. "You're one goddam hour and six goddam minutes late, Dick," he growled.

Then he stood up, extended his hand in my direction, and a big wide smile washed over his face as he took in my bruised puss and smashed nose. "What's the problem, Dick—had a little trouble on the way over?"

Chapter

4

WE SAT DOWN TO A MEAL OF PORK SCHNITZEL COOKED IN WINE AND shallots, red cabbage, *rost*—which means grilled—potatoes, and the wonderful, buttery German form of pasta they call spaetzle, all topped off with more than a case of the best Rhinegau *Kabinett* I've ever had. The Chairman was in an expansive mood, which was fortified even more by the great wine. He brought us up-to-date on the latest Washington gossip, joked about the pukes on the Joint Staff, reported that his former aide (and my old compadre) Joanne Montgomery was rehabilitating nicely from the shotgun pellet wounds that had put her in physical therapy for eight months.[30]

He even told us a bizarre story about a senior White House staffer who'd been caught in flagrante delicto by one of the Marines who work the security detail at the State Department the previous week. Said senior White House official's main squeeze was a speechwriter for the secretary of state, and the

---

[30]If you want to read more about Joanne, you can go out and buy *Rogue Warrior: SEAL Force Alpha.*

Marine had caught them in full flagrant fudge-packing, or however two guys do it, on SECSTATE's very own antique desk.

Once everyone was at ease, he looked around the table and asked each of my shooters about themselves. From the way he asked the questions, I knew he'd spent time reading each man's file. He queried Duck Foot Dewey, whose real name is Allen, about growing up on Maryland's Eastern Shore, and hunting quail, dove, geese, and deer with his father and uncle.

"Maybe you'll take me up there one day," the Chairman said. "Nothing I like better than the first day of deer season."

Duck Foot's eyes brightened. "Any time, sir. Just ask."

General Crocker teased Nod about trading the Army for the Navy. He reminisced about college football with Boomerang, and talked law enforcement with Gator Shepard, who'd worked as a SWAT deputy before joining the Navy. And believe me, Gator's good. Gator can hit a frigging dime at fifty yards with an MP5.

He even asked Rodent how he'd come by his nickname.

"My big brother's called Fat Rat," Rodent chirped. "He enlisted in the Navy six years before I did—went through BUD/S and made it to Team Two. By the time I enlisted he was an E-5—and he had a lot of friends. So when I went through BUD/S, he made sure the chiefs knew I was coming so they could give me an especially hard time. There was this one bad-ass instructor—I'll never forget, his name was Denny Chalker, and he was the biggest, meanest sonofabitch I'd ever seen—and the first fucking day (pardon my French, General, but you know what I'm talkin' about), he took one long, nasty look at me as I clambered out of the pool all cold and wet, and he said, 'You are not only lower than whale shit. You are also so much fucking smaller, so much fucking weaker, and so much fucking more insignificant than your fucking fat rat brother that you are nothing but a fucking rodent.'"

He laughed. "And I guess it stuck, 'cause I've been Rodent ever since."

The Chairman turned his gaze toward Half Pint. "You're Mike—the one they call Half Pint." As Half Pint nodded, General Crocker looked at me. "Isn't he the one who likes to eat ears?"

Half Pint's eyes went wide. Some years back, during one of the regularly scheduled SEAL-versus-pilot brawls at a rough-and-tumble bar called the Ready Room (for those of you who are into naval trivia, the Ready Room sits just behind the main gate of Oceana Naval Air Station), Half Pint bit off most of an Airedale lieutenant's right ear. The Ready Room's owner, who has a very weird sense of humor, wanted to pin the fucking thing behind the bar for a month while it dried out. But the Airedale insisted on snatching it back and taking it posthaste to the Naval Hospital in Portsmouth, where he had it reattached.

Said Airedale got a new radio handle out of the fracas—he's still known as Frankenstein. And Half Pint is greeted by cries of "Yo, Jaws!" every time he walks his five-foot-five frame into the Ready Room.

Finally, General Crocker's gaze settled on Terry. "You're the newbie," he said. "How's it going, Terry?"

"There's so much to freakin' learn, General," Baby Huey burbled in SEALspeak. "But I'm gonna freakin' do it. All I freakin' know is that I wanna be the best freakin' SEAL who ever freakin' lived, and I'm gonna keep freakin' trying until I freakin' get there."

"Hoo-ya, BH," Boomerang said, lifting his glass. "And fuck you very much—that's the kind of attitude we like in this here unit."

Me, too. When I recruit, I don't look for gazelles, the sorts of sailors who do everything effortlessly. I want the grunts. The guy who came in dead last in his BUD/S class but kept on going no matter how bad it got. I look for the little engines that can, the tadpoles who thwam and thwam right over the dam. My goal is to mold Warriors in my own image—with a Warrior's fucking heart and a Warrior's fucking soul. I believe that General Crocker thinks the same way I do, which is why he keeps me around— and is why I stay.

A silence came over the table. General Crocker rose, lifted his glass, and toasted fallen comrades. We stood and did the same. Then he continued in the serious vein. He reminisced about his days as a company commander during Vietnam, and how three tours in the field had taught him something he'd never learned at West Point. "I discovered the value of loyalty *down* the chain of command," General Crocker said. "Because it was something I never received when I was young. The generals I served under didn't give a shit about me—all they wanted was numbers; to be able to check things off their lists and report them as 'done' to Washington."

He drained his wine and poured himself another full glass. "My men and I got no backup, no support," he said bitterly. "I remember one time when I sent an after-action report up the chain of command. One of my recon platoons had spotted two dozen North Vietnamese tanks, and I thought that was pretty damn significant. Well, the day after I sent it up the line, I got a rocket back from division. I was ordered to change my report— delete all references to tanks." The Chairman set his glass back on the table. "I did a little recon of my own, and discovered the reason behind the order was that the damn one-star J-2 staff intel idiot in charge in Saigon had already guaranteed to General Westmoreland that the NVA had no tanks within fifty miles of my AO, and Westmoreland had already passed that info on to President Johnson as solid. Officially, therefore, no tanks existed, and my report had to reflect the official position."

The general rapped the table with his knuckles. "But y'know what the problem with that situation was? The problem was that, since there weren't any tanks, I couldn't receive antitank weap- ons." He grimaced. "The damn bureaucrats. They wouldn't even let me draw LAWs or bazookas," he said. "The only thing I could do was scavenge what I could—RPGs off NVA corpses—and try to cumshaw as many LAWs and other weapons as I could lay my hands on." His face grew grim. "I lost soldiers, Dick—lost good men, because the officers above me were too busy trying to save their own careers to give us grunts in the field any support, even though those sons of bitches demanded my total loyalty to them."

He looked us over in a paternal way. "You and your men have been loyal to me," he said. "You've come through. Delivered the goods. And so, it's the least I can do for you."

Indeed, the Chairman was imbued with the sort of old-fashioned command loyalty we used to have in the Teams. Which is precisely why he'd come over in mufti to waylay us. The Cabinet, he said, was in disarray. The president was up to his ears (well, the precise anatomical point was somewhat lower) with a scandal involving a female political appointee who the tabloid press had labeled "SAP/BJ," which as you can probably guess stands for Special Assistant to the President for Blow Jobs.

The vice president was busy trying to raise enough money to blow all his potential political adversaries out of the water while fending off a special prosecutor. And so, things were pretty much being run by the White House chief of staff these days. Which meant that nothing was getting done—except for a lot of political infighting among the Cabinet members.

The FBI director, it seemed, wanted my head on a fucking pike. So he'd gone to the attorney general, who'd gone to her old law-school classmate, the chief of staff, to demand it. The national security adviser, who doesn't particularly like me at all (and *that* is a goddamn understatement), had jumped into the pot, too. He'd been more than willing to put my head—not to mention the rest of my svelte Slovak body—on the old chopping block. The current chief of naval operations is a fucking bureaucrat who does what he's told. No support for Dickie there. And his assistant, a three-star named G. Edward Emu, is probably the only man to have made it through BUD/S and wear a trident who faints at the sight of blood.

So, only SECDEF and the Chairman had been around to speak

on my behalf. And they realized that the best thing they could do was keep me away from Washington until things blew over.

Well, I've always believed in turning adversity to my own favor. If eight bogeys are coming at me, my only question is, which one of 'em do I kill first. And so, I told the Chairman that staying here in Germany fit into my plans just fine. In fact, I said, I wanted to head straight for Düsseldorf. That's where my little Kraut had started nosing after the ADM for Khaled—and it was where I wanted to start schniffing around, too. There were traitors afoot—somebody was selling ADMs—and I told the Chairman we'd be ready to go and start kicking some ass at zero dark hundred.

General Crocker had other ideas. "Every time you go off and start one of these—what is it you call 'em, snooping-and-pooping exercises?—we seem to have an international incident," he said. "The Saudis threatened to kick all American military forces out of the Kingdom because of what happened on the *Kuz Emeq*. You know the Saudis—they don't mind what we do if we keep everything quiet. But they walk a fragile line in the Arab world—and they can't allow themselves to be seen as dependent on us, even though *they* know, and *we* know, that without American military power backing 'em up, that Kingdom would collapse like a house of cards. But the politics of the situation is touchy. And I have to tell you straight: killing Khaled didn't do us a lot of good in the political arena." He laughed bitterly. "Hell, Dick, the State Department doesn't like you any more than the FBI does right now."

Well, I don't give a shit what the frigging State Department does or doesn't like, which is precisely what I told Chairman Crocker, in what can be called RUT—Roguishly Unvarnished Terms.

My RUT response brought a bemused grin to his face. But he was adamant nevertheless. "I want you invisible, Dick. Totally stealth. And running up to Düsseldorf and scamming to buy pocket nukes doesn't come under the stealth category."

Instead, the Chairman said, my men and I were to do a little hunting right here in the Rhine Valley. There was a small logistical problem that needed some work, and we were the perfect ones to help him—and SECDEF—solve it.

Uh-oh. When officers start talking about small logistical problems, I am transported back to my days as an enlisted man. Because back then, when someone who wore gold braid on his sleeve started talking about my helping him with a small logistical problem, it meant I was about to draw a nasty dose of KP, swab out the latrines, or pump the bilges.

Actually, once the Chairman explained things, this particular logistical problem turned out to be slightly more interesting than latrine swabbing. It even related to my current ADM problem.

To put the best spin on things, it seemed that the precise locations of several of the POMCUS caches containing ADMs had been, in the Chairman's words, unfortunately misplaced. A total of six ADMs were unaccounted for, and he wanted me and my unit to find two of them.

Now I see you out there, the dweeb editor at the front of the pack, all jumping up and down like FMs (look it up in the Glossary) and telling me that what I've just written is impossible; that the frigging government just don't go and misplace half a dozen tactical suitcase nukes.

Well, friends, here is a lesson from real life. The world we actually live in is a lot more strange and much more bizarre, illogical, absurd, and just plain loony than any fiction—even fiction with my name on it—could ever be.

And here is the unhappy truth of the matter. We already know that, with the exception of SECDEF, the current administration doesn't give a shit about the military. Well, one of the peripheral developments resulting from this attitude of nonbenign neglect, animosity, and just plain vindictiveness, has been a series of personnel cutbacks at the Department of Defense. As a part of those drawdowns, most of the folks who'd been assigned to keep track of our POMCUS caches had been early-retired and/or

RIFed. That move made sense to the bean-counting Schedule C[31] deputy assistant secretaries in charge of fucking our men in uniform. After all, why keep a GS-14, step 8, around at eighty grand a year plus benefits, when you can hire a part-timer from a consulting firm to do the same job for fifty grand—and no benefits.

The problem is that by firing your professional staff and replacing them with part-timers, you lose what's known in the bureaucratic trade as institutional memory. Now, as you know, I'm not big on bureaucrats. But they do serve a purpose—and so long as they don't get in my way, I tolerate 'em. Chairman Crocker explained that over the past decade the Pentagon had managed to lose track of half a dozen POMCUS locations. The paperwork had disappeared. Maybe it had been lost when hard copy had been input on DOD's computer network. Maybe they'd sold off the safes containing the relevant files and hadn't bothered to check beforehand.

Oh, shit. There's the fucking dweeb editor again, waving his blue pencil in circles, saying things like that don't happen and even fiction has its limits and I'm stretching the suspension-of-disbelief thing too fucking far. Hey, Ed, first, don't interrupt me when I'm on a roll. And second, yes they *do* happen. I've actually seen that precise situation with my very own eyes. Back when I was serving my one-year sentence at the Petersburg, Virginia, federal penal colony and mayoral blow-job facility, we'd had a bunch of Executive Grade One file cabinets from the State Department dropped off at the prison's UNICOR facility for refurbishing. Inside one of 'em, one of our more enterprising cons—read burglar—found a bunch of MEMCONS[32] dealing

---

[31]A Schedule C employee means that no experience in the field is necessary, as said employee has been given his/her/its job because of work in the presidential campaign, or influence from whatever party won the White House.
[32]MEMorandums of CONversation

with our START nuclear treaty negotiations with the Soviet Union. All top secret stuff. So the fact we'd misplaced six POMCUS caches was not something I found improbable.

Now, my little task force wasn't the only one assigned to this ADM retrieval mission. The Chairman said he'd given the bulk of the job to John Suter's Special Forces security group out of Stuttgart—and when (I found it significant that he didn't say, "if") I retrieved my ADMs, I was to get hold of John chop-chop and hand the goods over to him.

That made sense. No reason for me to travel around schlepping any pocket nukes. Besides, I liked John Suter and knew I'd be able to work with him. What the Chairman said next, however, I liked a lot less.

What he told me was that if I came upon anything of political significance during this exercise, I was to go through the normal chain of command, which meant reporting what I'd discovered through CINCUSNAVEUR, the acronymed title for the Commander-IN-Chief, US NAVal forces, EURope.

I objected. I have a hard time dealing with the Navy, and the Chairman knew it. More to the point, I have a hard time dealing with the current CINC in London. His name is—well, since he's an Irish sonofabitch, let's just call him Eamon the Demon. He's one of those apparatchik Annapolis ring-knockers whose BA degree was in engineering and whose MA was in systems management. Assholes like Eamon detest war and abhor warriors. In fact, Eamon has been a staff puke for his entire career, with one or two minor sea-tour exceptions.[33]

---

[33] I don't have time to get into this right now, but it's important for you to know that most of our admirals and generals do not get promoted because they are good at making war, or will be able to lead men. They get their stars because they have spent most of their time as staff assistants or aides to senior generals or admirals. The most recent Navy board, for example, selected thirty-four captains to be promoted to one-star rank. Of those thirty-four, twenty-three held the positions of executive assistant, or chief of staff to a four-star admiral. Seven were senior military aides or executive assistants detailed to the White House or the Pentagon. Only four came from an operations slot.

But the general was adamant. "Goddammit, Dick, I have no choice in the matter. I'm not the God damn emperor. I'm a part of a damn chain of command—and so are you, whether you like it or not. I have to keep peace among the services, and let me tell you that the chief of naval operations and his deputy are steamed over the fact that you and your men work for my office." He paused, finished his wine, and rapped his knuckles on the table. "You don't have to like it, Dick—you just have to do it. Case closed."

I wanted to mention a few of the things I know about Eamon the Demon, but I bit my tongue and kept silent. The Chairman has taken a number of shots directed at me—and if he wanted things to move this way, well, then so be it, although I knew his decision was going to complicate my life.

The politics dispensed with, General Crocker continued talking about our new assignment. It boiled down to this: since he didn't want my big Slovak snout poking where it shouldn't be right now, and I couldn't return to CONUS, he'd assigned us a piece of the ADM action. We would search the area that lies between Mainz and Koblenz, bordered by the Rhine River on the east, and the Mosel River valley on the north—an L-shaped area roughly a hundred miles on each side.

Hey, piece of strudel, right?

You bet. So far as I was concerned, this was an urgent "go" for a number of reasons. Most obvious was that the recently demised Heinz had bought the USG ADM he'd tried to sell to Prince Khaled—and it had probably come from one of the missing caches. That meant there were bad guys out there prowling and growling, not to mention pawing through our POMCUS caches. Not good news.

I told the Chairman we'd brought some of our own supplies— weapons, ammo, and other tactical goodies—with us from Italy. But we'd need other equipment.

Done, said the Chairman—give me a list, and you can pick it up at Rhine Main within twenty-four hours. Then there was the matter of funding. That was no problem at all. Remember, I had buried-at-sea Heinz Hochheizer's suitcase filled with all those hundred-dollar bills. General Crocker's eyes actually went wide when I told him how much cash I had on hand. The good news was that Heinz's money would fund our operation—and then some. That left only one piece of equipment: a state-of-the-art radiation detector.

To which General Crocker, who obviously thinks of everything, replied, "I brought you two of them, Dick. They're stowed in my hotel room, along with a bunch of maps and charts and other papers you'll be needing—so let's have a nightcap there."

Chapter

5

BY 1300 THE NEXT DAY WE'D CAMOUFLAGED OURSELVES IN THE style befitting clandestine ADM hunters. While Boomerang, Half Pint, and I bought supplies in Mainz, I dispatched Nod and BH to Rhine Main Air Base, where they purchased enough camping equipment to qualify for the Outward Bound discount. Meanwhile, Rodent, Duck Foot, and Gator hit the used car lots on the southern outskirts of the city. Three hours and six greasy hands later, they chugged up the Mainz Hilton's driveway in a well-used RV, a Mercedes sedan that was older than Baby Huey, and a pair of sleek, well-worn BMW five-hundred-cc bikes.

I gave the RV an approving once-over. It wasn't going to attract any fucking attention at all. What they'd bought was a beat-up Fiat Gran Tourisimo, which bunks five—although we'd all somehow manage to find ourselves some space if we had to. It was precisely the same kind of vehicle that tens of thousands of Germans own so that they can go touring with their families and friends, complete with a huge red-and-white sticker on the rear bumper that told the world we loved Oktoberfest in Munich. Like I said, cosmetically, the RV wasn't much to look at. But under the hood, where it counts, it was perfect. They'd even installed davits, so we could hang the motorcycles off the back of the camper.

The Mercedes was a fifteen-year-old diesel, and it may not have been the fastest car on the autobahn, but it, too, was in terrific mechanical shape. Our radiation detectors could be concealed in the vehicles. Hell, they were almost small enough to be carried in our pockets. I really like miniaturization. It makes my life as a sneak-and-peeker a lot easier—and our presence a lot less obvious.

Now, let me say a few words here about what searching techniques would and would not work in our current situation. We SEALs do most of our search work underwater. There are three basic techniques for underwater searches. The first is called the running jackstay search. The running jackstay search requires four buoys placed in a rectangle 250 meters long and 50 meters wide, with grid lines attached on the long sides. The divers—up to five of them—then run a 50-meter running jackstay between the grid lines, and then work their way down the grid, searching the bottom below meter by meter. This technique is generally done in clear, shallow water, with currents under one knot. Well, the running jackstay wasn't going to be worth a running jack shit, because the Rhine current flows at an average of six knots between Mainz and Koblenz.

Then there is what's known as the checkerboard jackstay search. Guess what—same problem because of the current. Which brings us to technique number three, the circle line search. Circle line is a keep-it-simple-stupid search. You take a buoy, drop a weighted line from it, then attach a search line to the weighted line. You simply swim in ever-shorter circles, checking the bottom as you go, until you recover what you are looking for. If you come up holding nothing but your dick, the technique is known as a circle jerk search.

All of these techniques are commonly used for recovering lost objects, such as missiles, or other ordnance, that you don't want falling into your enemy's hands. Our situation was somewhat different. We had to locate the ADM in a cache that might (or might not!) be underwater. Caching material underwater is an old SEAL procedure. But I wasn't so sure that the folks who'd built the POMCUS caches knew about it. Indeed, all of the POMCUS caches I've ever seen have been dry sites.

And so, I made an executive decision. Just as General Crocker ordered, we'd work the riverbank—but we'd concentrate on the shoreline, not the river itself. Why? Because it made sense. When these devices were hidden they were supposed to be retrieved by blanketheads, not SEALs. And they were then to be used to decimate the Russkie supply lines.

And so, I had BH go out and buy us the best map of the Rhine Valley that he could lay his flippers on. And then we overlaid all the major highways and rail lines.

The *letzte Zeile*, as they call the bottom line over here, is that I was able to reduce our search area by about two-thirds. The biggest rail yards on the west bank of the Rhine within a hundred kilometers are just to the northwest of Mainz, in Budenheim. After that, there was nothing worth blowing up until you get to the outskirts of Köln—almost two-hundred kliks to the north. We'd run a check in the Budenheim area, but I didn't expect to find anything there. You can blow a rail yard with conventional explosives very efficiently. And there was no control center near Mainz—that, too, was farther downriver, between Köln and Bonn.

No, I decided that the target environment was much richer highway-wise. German megaroutes, which as you probably know are called autobahns, run more or less parallel to the Rhine. Autobahn number 3 parallels the river's east bank, and Autobahn 61 parallels the west bank. If one were going to disrupt things (and blanketheads, like SEALs, just *l-o-v-e* to disrupt things), then you'd cache your explosives near one of the hu-fucking-mongous bridges spanning the gorges that run through the countryside. I'm talking about two-klik-long, reinforced concrete, arched bridges, eight lanes wide, that would take a fucking year to rebuild.

The biggest of those spans was right outside the AO General Crocker had given me, just to the west and north of a good-sized city called Koblenz, which sits at the confluence of the Rhine and Mosel Rivers. I checked the maps. There are no fewer than six bridge crossings within twenty-five kliks of Koblenz. Now, if I were a war-planner back in the good old days of the Cold War, and I were trying to cache an atomic weapon or two where they'd do my Special Forces some good, I'd put 'em close to where they could blow a whole bunch of bridges at one time— thus bringing the Ivan resupply line to a screeching halt. There was a second factor in looking in the Koblenz area. Koblenz is just about an hour and a half south of Düsseldorf. And despite what the Chairman had said, I wanted to nose around Düsseldorf—check out the places Heinz had pointed me toward.

Which brings me to executive decision number two. We'd take a quick pass through the Mainz area—and then go straight to Koblenz. Yes, I knew it was a risk. But if you will look at the same maps I do, you'd see that the Rhine Valley itself is of little strategic value these days. This is not World War II, when the Allies' main objective was to move waves of personnel and materiel across the Rhine bridges to press the Nazis farther and farther into Germany. The Soviet war plan called for massive air and chopper assaults, followed by a huge army of occupation. The Soviets, therefore, were preoccupied with keeping their supply routes open. And we were just as intent on destroying those major arteries and letting the invasion bleed to death.

So I wasn't all that concerned about examining every kilometer of the north-south rail line that ran along the riverbank. But I wanted to check the areas around the huge east/west autobahn bridges. And I also wanted to look in the areas close to those gorges northwest of Koblenz.

It didn't take us long to verify my hunch. We took a day and a half, cruising the side roads between Mombach and Bingen, working the land-locked equivalent of a checkerboard jackstay search. The RV and Mercedes provided the grid borders, and the two BMWs, ridden by Boomerang and Half Pint, who concealed the devices in shopping bags tied to their handlebars, did the searching. We drove up and we drove down, and we drove all the fuck around. But our jackstay search didn't turn up jack shit. Not even a hint of anything—except a persistent and nagging sensation in my Slovak skull that ve veren't alone.

I made sure that we played all the countersurveillance tricks we knew: doubled back on our tracks; abruptly changed course; everything. Our senses were primed. But we found nothing. Saw nothing untoward. Maybe I was getting paranoid. No. I'm never paranoid; I'm only careful. But, since we saw nothing, I circled the wagons, and we headed north.

We hit our first paydirt near a small town called Bassenheim, which sits eight kliks from a pair of huge, multilevel autobahn junctions. When you're looking to fuck with your enemy's supply lines, there's nothing as good as being able to destroy not one, not two, but three or four highways at one time—and major junctions are where you do that. The first interchange, at the junction of Highway 411 and Autobahn 61, crossed the Mosel River gorge and Highway 416, near the tiny town of Dieblich. It had the additional attraction of two sets of railway tracks—one on the Mosel's northern bank, the other on its southern. A pair of MADMs placed just right would cause months' worth of devastation, as well as send radioactive debris down the Mosel. It's the kind of target I'd eat a yard of shit to be able to blow.

The second interchange, five kilometers away, was an even more intricate fabrication. It merged three autobahns and two smaller highways. Now, you gotta hand it to the Krauts. They do a wonderful job building highways. The road surfaces are built for speed—in wet weather or dry. The exits and on ramps are clearly marked, and even though some folks tend to drive more than a hundred miles an hour, there are few accidents. That's because they PFA—Pay Fucking Attention—to what they're doing; they don't drive drunk, and they drive according to the rules.

The second interchange—its proper name is the Koblenz-

Metternich interchange—is a six-level affair near Bassenheim that forms a triple cloverleaf arrangement so fucking intricate it looks like a department store Christmas bow. The whole thing is built of preformed concrete sections. The highways sit atop pillars five yards in diameter. The interchange itself reaches a 180 feet in height at its highest point (that's more than eighteen stories for you city dwellers), which occurs as the highways span a mile-long gorge. The effect is mesmerizing—all that concrete and stone looking like some great modernistic minimalist sculpture, contrapuntally poised against acre upon acre of lush, green countryside dotted with cows and sheep and other bucolic shit.

I tell you, folks—just looking at it made me want to get my hands on a couple of hundred pounds of C-4. Oh, it was beautiful. Oh, it was a structural work of art. But what can I tell you? I'm a fucking Visigoth. All I want to do when I see something as beautiful as this, is to blow it up.

But enough about my wet dreams. Let's get back to reality. Just west of the interchange sits the village of Bassenheim, looking like something out of a fucking fairy tale. It's one of those archetypal German towns you see on the postcards: a cluster of whitewashed, half-timbered houses with dark shingled roofs, looking as if they've just posed for a Disney version of Grimm's Fairy Tales, all sitting cheek-by-jowl along five streets that all meet on a tiny cobblestone town square. On one side of the square sits a medieval stone tower; on the other, a single-spired church whose clock tower rings the quarter hours with Teutonic regularity.

We eschewed the town's single pension in favor of the *touristenpark* on the outskirts. There, I let the manager run my AmEx card, we plugged the RV into the power supply and set up our own form of BOQ housekeeping—i.e., we picked up three cases of the local brew, Königsbacher, at the huge *Brauerei* that sits alongside the Rhine about three miles from the center of Koblenz. Then we piled into the Mercedes and onto the bikes, and set off in search for our new, clear Grail. It was my guesstimation that these interchanges were Class A obligatory targets, and that there'd be a cache somewhere in the neighborhood. The question was where.

I knew there'd be nothing in any of the small towns that dotted the landscape. You don't cache things in a small town because it's impossible to keep secrets in a small town—and even more impossible for a stranger or a bunch of 'em to come in and get something done without the locals knowing all about it. And so, you either find a place in the countryside that is isolated but relatively easy to access, or you cache in a city, in which you can remain relatively anonymous.

I drew a thirty-klik diameter around the interchanges, shaded off the area around the two German Army camps obligingly redlined on the map (*Ich liebe der* Krauts—they're so fucking precise. If we'd had maps this good in Grenada a lot of Americans wouldn't have been wounded or killed), and off we went.

It took us eight hours of driving to locate two POMCUS caches. The first was secreted in the middle of a small wooded tract between two farms, on a long and winding road leading to a village named Niederbach that was so small it wasn't on anybody's map—even ours. The second was in the middle of a huge fucking cattle pasture occupied by a mean-looking bull and eight big-titted heifers. The pasture was bordered by an electric fence and sat adjacent to a neat one-lane road that meandered through the gently rolling countryside, about halfway between the one-street, *ein Gasthaus* towns of Pillig and Naunheim. No, I'm not making these places up. Check your fucking maps.

Now, you ask, how did I find these cleverly hidden sites when no one else could manage? The answer is because I'm a devious sonofabitch—who knows what to look for. We dealt with the Niederbach site first—the weather was moving *immer schlimmer*, which is how they say going from bad to worse over here. The cache was concealed below what appeared to be an abandoned barn, although this "barn" had state-of-the-art door locks and security devices. The place caught my attention because abandoned barns don't usually have any locks on their doors—but as I scanned this one through my binoculars, I counted five separate devices.

We slogged through a hundred feet of brambles, along a track that appeared to have been used recently. First things first. I switched the radiation detector on. Nothing. It registered zero. Well, maybe whatever was inside had been shielded. I let Boomerang play with the locks. It took him seventeen minutes to defeat 'em. Once we got inside, we had to break through the floor of the structure to get to the cache area.

There, we were greeted by a pile of empty crates, cartons, and boxes. Fuck—this site had been looted. We ran our nuclear-detecting devices carefully—but came up dry. If any ADMs had been stored here, they'd been removed long enough ago so that there was no residual radiation.

It was raining the well-known *Katzen und Hunden* by the time we drove past what turned out to be site two—the cow pasture. We were moving slowly down a one-lane blacktop road (the kind of German byway that has yellow disk signs posted every couple of kliks, explaining in universal pictographs that the speed limit for trucks is fifty kilometers an hour and for tanks it's forty kliks an hour. That's the kind of speed signs you put up if you live in a country where tanks and army convoys used to be as prevalent as tractors and plows). Anyway, all of a sudden I saw a four-foot-high chain-link fence, *sans* any gate, surrounding what appeared to be a small, brick pump house, about five hundred feet off the road. I raised my binoculars. Small signs on the fence told me that the pump house belonged to the Cochem district water management bureau, and to Keep the Fuck Out.

Now, this fence attracted my attention because it sat splat in the middle of the sort of countryside in which chain-link fence is a rarity. In this 'hood, most farmers use electric fence—single wire—or wire mesh, or some form of board und batten to border their land or contain their animals. And the municipalities? All the municipal fences I'd seen had been made of wood post and wire. So this twenty-by-twenty square of chain link, which looked as if it had come straight from Sears or Home Depot, was enough to pique my interest.

I signaled for our little convoy to stop. We pulled the RV off onto the wide shoulder adjacent to the pasture, and parked the Mercedes and the bikes under a convenient tree about fifty yards farther up the road on the opposite side. Boomerang and Gator, who'd been riding 'em, went into the RV to towel off and grab a cup of steaming coffee from the thermos.

I climbed out into the rain and eyeballed the site. About a quarter mile off to the east, most of it hidden by a slight crease in the countryside, I could make out a one-story farmhouse. Its red roof was silhouetted against the gently rolling hills across the gently rolling hills. On the far side of the house, I could pick out two sheds, and a barn. Off in the distance, a horny Rogue rooster was crowing. Rogue, you ask? You fucking bet: I listened very carefully as he crowed, "Suck my doodle-doo!" three, four, five insistent times. All of a sudden I felt Roguishly lonely. Like, I mean, I haven't had *my* doodle-doo sucked since I don't remember when.

Ah, gentle reader, this is but one of the prices I pay to defend your freedom. But I put all thoughts of pussy out of my mind (okay, I put *most* thoughts of pussy out of my mind. You know as well as I do that putting all thoughts of pussy out of my mind is impossible), and I turned my attention to the work at hand: i.e., the pasture.

While Duck Foot and Nod distracted the bull and the cows, and BH and Half Pint provided touristlike camouflage, I grabbed the nuke detector, churlishly threw my crew the bird, vaulted the electric wire fence (it was only four feet high), and landed—squish—in a nice, moist, fresh, and very fragrant cow pie that immediately soaked clear though my nylon running shoes. That will teach me to churl. I wiped what manure I could off my feet against the rough pasture grass and made my way across the greensward[34] to the chain-link fence, as careful as a point man in

---

[34]Lovely word, isn't it? It derives from Middle English, where *sward* means turf, and *green* means green.

enemy territory watching for bovine mines. Hey, one squishy cow pie a day between the toes is enough.

I examined the fence. Its condition told me it had been maintained until maybe eight or nine years ago. That put it within the right time frame for POMCUS caches. I went over the fence and looked at the pump house. It was unremarkable—but it was no pump house. There was not a single water connection inside. No valves. No pump. This place was a shell—as in shell game.

There was a single door, facing away from the road. The door was secured by a big padlock. I turned my nuke-spotting device on and got an immediate positive response. *Ja*—this must be der *platz.*

Now, I checked the single door more carefully. What appeared to be hinges were in fact a second series of locking devices. There was probably a third device, too. Perhaps it was even booby-trapped. I'd just begun to figure out how to break in without blowing us all up when I heard an urgent, two-fingered whistle.

I looked up. Duck Foot was waving frantically and the message was loud and clear: Get your ass back here, Skipper—on the double.

I hauled butt back toward the road. "What's the prob?"

"We got visitors coming—"

That's the nice thing about country roads in gently rolling countryside—you can see for miles and miles and miles—even in the rain. And there, in the distance, making good time given the condition of the road, I could make out a pair of black cars coming directly at us. Their brights were on. And they were traveling at flank speed.

The hair on the back of my neck stood up. You know what *that* means—it means that the sensor in my brain that sits below and behind the pussy detector has just gone off. Now, this could all be very innocent. But I wasn't about to take chances—and my instincts have never let me down in cases like this one. "Gator, Boomerang, Nod—get in the fucking RV and keep your heads down." No way was I going to let anyone see how many we were.

The rest of us played at being silly tourists in the rain. It didn't take much playing, either. Duck Foot tried to entice the bull with a carrot from the RV's fridge. Baby Huey sucked his Königsbacher. I played with the camera, fiddling with the zoom lens as the cars bore down on us.

They were big mothers, too—500- or 600-series Mercedes (I can seldom tell the difference), with extraweight suspensions, oversized tires, and enough radio antennas to remind me of the armored Town Car limo that the director of the CIA travels in. The lead vehicle slowed precipitously as it came abreast of our RV, which was fifty, perhaps sixty yards down the road from the Mercedes and the bikes. The big car's single windshield wiper slapped furiously across the wide expanse of tinted glass. There was a coat of arms on the rear door. Instinctively, I squeezed off three frames, then lowered the camera and peered at the windshield. Like I said, it was tinted, but I could see enough. The driver was wearing Oakley ballistic wraparound glasses—the kind you see on shooters. Riding shotgun, I could make out a man dressed in a black turtleneck, with close-cropped steel gray hair, cruel eyes, and a scar running down his cheek. He turned as the Mercedes cruised past at SLOW, those cold eyes boring into my own. Then his expression changed. He double-taked, a look of shock and surprise washing over his face.

Hey—I'd seen that puss before. I knew him, too. He was a big ugly Kraut—police or SpecWar. But I was fucked if I could put a name to him. It had been TMY/TMB (too many years and too many beers) in between sightings.

And then, the big Mercedes sped up, and then it was gone. I peered at the chase car as it passed. Two men in the front seat— and dark smoked glass that kept me from seeing anything else. I turned to watch as the brace of big sedans accelerated out of sight. Fuck—I raised the camera, pressed the zoom button to get full benefit of the hundred and whatever millimeter lens, and pressed the shutter so I could get the license plate numbers. Thank God for autofocus.

We'd have the film developed—and then I'd check out the license plates and the coat of arms. I still have a few friends in low places here, and I wasn't going to be reticent about calling on 'em for some help. But that was for sometime in the future. Right now, we had some work to do here in this cow pasture. Like retrieving the ADM that I knew was somewhere behind all those locks and security devices.

Chapter

6

I CHECKED MY WATCH. 1540. THE RAIN WAS REALLY COMING DOWN now. But I wasn't about to be deterred—or interrupted. I posted Duck Foot two and a half kliks up the road, and BH the same distance on my opposite flank. Each man had a radio. If we were about to be interrupted, at least we'd have adequate notice.

1550. We moved the RV closer to the site, parking it on the opposite side of the road. Then Boomerang and I started work on the first of the locking devices. It was a Mark-1 Mod-2 version of something I'd seen a dozen times on nuclear weapons depots back in the States. Nothing much. The second device, however, was going to give us trouble. It was one of those keyless locks, where you punch a series of numbers and the lock drops open. You can sometimes bypass keyless locks with electronic gear, listening to the way the tumblers work. Or you can dust 'em with graphite powder and see which digits are the most used, then play with all those combinations. But I didn't have either graphite powder, or a lot of time. And I didn't have any electronic gear either. Boomerang and I went over the devices and decided that they hadn't been booby-trapped. So, we'd simply blow the sucker with some of the C-4 I'd cadged from John Suter, grab the ADM, and scoot.

1555. I'd just finished disabling the first locking device and Boomerang was in the RV preparing the charge when Duck Foot called in.

"Visitors, Skipper."

I squished across the pasture (taking the long route, because you don't want to wear a trough into the soft grass so folks will know you've come a-calling), peered up the road into the rain, and saw 'em. Two green and white Opels, blue and white flashing lights going full-tilt boogie.

Ach, du Lieber—die Polizei had arrived.

I jumped the fence and made my way to the RV just as the first of the cars pulled up and switched its flashers off. Behind the windshield sat a pair of road-weary cops, rain gear covering their gray-green uniforms. But they didn't do anything for the moment. No—they waited until Car Number Two had arrived. Only then did the first pair haul themselves out of the little car and Took Notice of the surroundings. And once I got a good look, I realized that they may have appeared to be bored, but these guys were pros.

The first team had waited for backup. And now that it had arrived, they went into action.

The first cop, a long, thin piece of work with blond hair and a thin mustache the color of corn silk, sauntered over to where I stood, next to the RV. His partner came up behind him and stood three feet back and to his left.

The tall officer touched the dripping brim of his hat. *"Guten Tag."*

I wiped my dripping face off with the edge of my hand. "Hi— good afternoon." I looked at the brass name tag that was pinned above his left breast pocket. It read: BRENDEL, K.

He nodded, as if he understood. *"Gut* afternoon," he said. "And what is it that you are doing out here in this nice German weather? Perhaps you are trying to have a picnic, *ja?"*

I laughed, raised my face skyward, and let the rain hit my

beard. "Oh, it's a great day for a picnic, officer." I paused. "We stopped to have some lunch. Cook up a little wurst. Dry out."

The cop's eyes smiled. But his body language, indeed his whole attitude, told me he wasn't necessarily buying the story. Which frankly puzzled the hell out of me, my friends, simply because he had no reason to doubt it.

He stepped back, putting an arm's length between us. "Do you have any identification?" he asked.

"But of course." I reached into the back pocket of my jeans, brought out my wallet, extracted my military ID, and handed the laminated card over to him.

He thumbed the plastic and played with the card in the light to make sure the Great Seal of the U.S. holograph was authentic. He examined the picture on it, looked at me closely, then passed the ID on to his friend, a short, dark officer with a bristly mustache whose name tag read RACKEL, V.

Rackel took the card, repeated the whole process, then walked back to the police car, climbed in, and as I watched, punched a series of characters—probably my name and my ID number—into the computer terminal that sat affixed to the dashboard.

Brendel looked over at Boomerang, who stood slightly behind me and to my right, and at Duck Foot, who'd just come up from his sentry position. "And you two—you have identification?"

"Hey dude, course I do." Boomerang ran a hand through his long, wet, silver hair and smiled.

Duck Foot's head nodded up and down. "Sure."

Brendel gave them a suspicious once-over. "May I see them, please?"

There was something awfully wrong here. German cops do not roust tourists. Not tourists who have enough money to have an RV, two BMWs, and a Mercedes. Not American military tourists. And this was a roust, friends.

Before either of my men had the chance to do anything, I stepped forward. "Excuse me, officer—"

Brendel stepped back, his hand up as if he were stopping traffic. "Please," he said, a warning tone creeping into his voice.

He stepped away from me, creating defensive space. "Stay where your are." His right hand dropped toward the Sig autoloader that sat in a flapped holster on his belt.

"Whoa—" I stayed where I was, and my eyes told the rest of my men to do the same. We had no fight with these guys. All I wanted to know was WTF. I mean, this was a little crazy.

I raised my hands. "Look, Officer Brendel—"

"*Ja.* You just wait, okay?" The tall cop backed away toward his patrol car. We stood in the rain and watched as he and his partner conferred.

Then, my ID card in his hand, he returned. This time his body language told me that everything was okay. He handed the card to me with a smile. "I am sorry for the confusion, Captain Marcinko." He said. "But it was just reported to us that a bunch of cattle thieves were in the neighborhood—what you Americans call rustlers. They"—his hand made a pistol—"shoot . . . *ja?* A cow, then they butcher it, on the spot, and they store it"— he pointed at our RV—"in something like that." He smiled, pleased with his command of English. "And zo, you realize that we had to check out here your story." He stood straight and extended his hand in my direction "I am sorry for the inconvenience to you and your friends, Captain Marcinko."

I smiled at Officer Brendel and gave him my hand. "Understood," I said. "It was nothing."

But it wasn't nothing at all. I mean, dear readers, think of the game that's just been played. First, the cops had been put on the scent by that convoy of big Mercedes sedans. And if the folks in that convoy had any juice with the locals—and I had no reason to believe that they didn't, given the quick response of the *Polizei*—then they'd also learned who I was.

But all of the above was conjecture. I needed affirmation. I decided to play dumb. "Can you do me a favor and explain how you got the report about us, because we haven't seen anyone here."

"Oh, yes, Captain. We have here, near this place, the"—he

struggled for the right word—"estate? Yesss . . . estate, of a man named Lothar Beck. He is"—Officer Brendel struggled for the right word—"a big, a very important businessman, *ja?*"

"*Ja?*"

"*Ja.* And he saw you and he called from his car to his friend the assistant minister of *Polizei* in Berlin, and the minister, he has his assistant called the local commandant, and then . . . *zooo*"—he paused and shrugged—"we are sent here, because Herr Beck he is afraid that you are schtealing cattle."

Now, this is starting to make some sense to me. Is it beginning to make sense to you? No? Let me explain.

First of all I suddenly realized, as it so often happens after the fact, precisely whose ugly, scarred Kraut puss I'd seen in the front seat of that big car with the coat of arms on its rear door. His name is Franz Ulrich, and he used to work for my friend Ricky Wegener, when Ricky commanded GSG-9,[35] Germany's top counterterrorist unit.

Franz is a big boy, who cut his teeth at Mogadishu back in October of 1977, when a bunch of Ricky's shooters took on the hijackers of a Lufthansa 737 aircraft and rescued ninety-one passengers and crew. In those days, he was the unit's point man—the first shooter up the assault ladder. He put down the first terrorist he encountered—it was a female, but you don't say "*Après moi*" when you're hitting an aircraft. Anyway, Ricky liked what he saw, and Franz went on to become Ricky's number one hood.

And then, some years ago, Franz retired. Abruptly. Oh, there was gossip at the time. Whispers about a drug problem. Nasty buzz about kickbacks on some contracts for GSG-9's weapons. Vague rumors about other, more nefarious activities. To be honest, I don't recall the specifics. But Franz Ulrich dropped out of sight like a rock in a quarry. And Ricky? To Ricky, it was as if

---

[35]Grenzchutzgruppe 9 was formed as a unit of the West German federal border police.

Franz had died. Ricky never mentioned his name again. Once I brought the subject up, but the look he gave me was more than sufficient to tell me to S^2 and not mention it again.

And now, *hier* turns up Franz Ulrich, riding shotgun in the lead car owned by a big industrialist named Lothar Beck. Franz of the rumored drug problem. Franz of the alleged kickbacks.

And now I knew instinctively where Beck's HQ was located. I decided to check anyway. "By any chance, Officer Brendel, do you know where Lothar Beck's headquarters is located?" I asked.

"BeckIndustrie?" the policeman asked rhetorically. "It is in Düsseldorf, Captain—a huge tower of glass and steel right on the river. There are even postcards of it. It is on all the tours. You can see the revolving clock on the roof from ten kilometers away."

Game, set, and match.

You are still confused. Okay. Here it is plain and simple:

• Item: Düsseldorf is where Heinz Hochheizer the RIP weapons dealer told me he'd originally gone to score an ADM.

Coincidence? Happenstance? You tell me.

• Item: The name of the man *der winzig* Heinz told me about in Düsseldorf, the very selfsame one with the cocaine problem bragging about being able to lay his hands on USGI ADMs, was . . . Franz.

Coincidence? Happenstance? You tell me.

And now I discover that Franz Ulrich, former GSG-9 shooter whose name Ricky Wegener won't even mention, works for a big-time industrialist named Lothar Beck.

And what does Beck do, I wondered? I asked officer Brendel, who consulted with Officer Rackel. "Herr Beck? Well, BeckIndustrie has *große* contracts with the defense ministry, und the ministry of interior, and many other government"—he paused and shrugged and conferred with his colleague in schmeisser-rapid German—"agencies."

Officer Rackel pointed toward the police car. "BeckIndustrie. They make the radios we use. And the"—he, too, struggled for the right word—"*zoft*ware on our computer terminals."

Golly gee, gentle readers. Let me tell you something about the folks who make radios and communications software programs for military or police use. It is: they'd better be honest, because if you make radios or software, you can install bugs in it so that you can eavesdrop on what your customers are saying. And eavesdropping, if your customers are in the shooting-and-looting business like I am, can be dangerous to life and limb.

Now, here was a sophisticated man of business, Lothar Beck, who makes many of the things that shooters like me, or officers Brendel and Rackel, use. That in itself is not ominous. But let's add a couple of elements.

Element One: Colonel John Suter tells me there have been a number of recent probes at U.S. stowage facilities and other installations. Some have used ELINT—ELectronic INTelligence to try to break in. Evidence of COMINT, or COMmunications INTelligence, has also been tracked of late. And finally, John Suter tells me he has evidence of several human penetration efforts.

What does that tell me? Well, I did the same thing when I ran Red Cell. I probed. I sent out my best sneak-and-peekers and tested the opposition. I tapped phone lines and ran lasers against their communications systems. And what did that-all tell me? It told me what my opposition's capabilities were—how fast they'd react; how easily I could defeat their security systems. It told me who was serious about counterterrorism, and who wasn't. And that is how I gauged this series of ops. Somebody was trying to get us to show our capabilities, so they could be measured.

Element Two: Chairman Crocker has Colonel John and his boys, and me and mine, working overtime to retrieve ADMs and other weapons stashed in POMCUS caches here in Deutschland. That's the political side. We had to retrieve all this stuff without letting the Germans know we'd put 'em in place. So we were walking on eggs here.

But here's Element Three: somebody is selling our ADMs—the same ones I'm supposed to be retrieving.

Which brings me to Element Four: I now discover that one of the biggest contractors in Germany's defense industry has hired what is known in the trade as a BA, or Bad Apple, named Franz Ulrich, and that selfsame big contractor sees me, and all of a sudden he calls the cops because he thinks I am . . . a *cattle rustler.*

Well, friends, whoopee ky-yi-yay motherfucker, as Bruce what's-his-name says in those *Die Hard* action adventure movies. If you believe that's why Franz and Lothar made the call, I have a real nice bridge in Brooklyn to sell you—very cheap.

Here's what really happened. Franz recognized me—we both saw his eyes go wide. He gets to my name faster than I got to his, tells Lothar who I am, and Lothar punches up the old cellular to his pals at some ministry in Berlin to find out WTF some Roguish, hairy-assed SEAL named Marcinko is doing prowling and growling nowhere near any fucking body of fucking water.

Lothar's request takes about half an hour to carom down the chain of command from Berlin, to wherever. And then, all of der zudden, officers Brendel and Rackel appear, complete with backup. They look over my ID card, count who's here, and report everything in a sit-rep to their boss.

Who sends it back up der chain of command. Und now, Lothar and Franz know for sure that I'm me, and that I'm on the scene with a squad-sized group of SEALs, and we're all parked next to a big fucking pasture. And in the middle of that big fucking pasture, there is a pump house where no pump house should be.

So far as I am concerned, it's time to stop explaining things and get to fucking work before Franz and some of his friends come back to see what they can find.

Und zooo, we made nicey-nicey with the *Polizei,* and made all the appearance of getting under way. We climbed into and onto our assorted vehicles, pulled out, turned around, and headed back in the vague direction of Bassenheim, with Officer Brendel and his pal Officer Rackel watching us closely until we were out of sight.

But we didn't go to Bassenheim. We found a nice little *Bierstube* in a village called Küttig, piled inside, and treated ourselves to double-sized portions of smoked pork chops—*Kasseler*, in *Deutsch*—piles of tangy sauerkraut, *rost* potatoes, and a couple of gallons of the local *Altbier*. Then, soon as it got dark, we paid the bill and made our way back to the pasture, where we'd be able to go to work undisturbed.

Chapter

7

2035. I DESIGNED THIS LITTLE EXERCISE THE SAME WAY MY SEAL forbears back in Vietnam ran their nighttime snatch ops. Except tonight we'd be bringing out an atomic device instead of a Viet Cong tax collector, and we'd be using a car not a chopper or a PBR. But just like Vietnam, it would be a clandestine infiltration, followed by a totally stealth retrieval, followed by a quiet exit. If things went as I'd planned 'em, no one would ever know we'd come and gone—and the Chairman would be one happy general.

We stashed the RV eight easy kliks from the target—no sense getting lost if we had to make a fast return—and piled into the Mercedes and onto the bikes to make our infiltration. It had stopped raining, but the roads were slick, and there was a thick ground-level mist that hovered, apparitionlike, two to three yards above the road surface.

Since I've always believed that war is an acronym for We Are Ready, we came ready for WAR. We dressed in our basic black *sans* benefit of pearls. We carried suppressed weapons just in case we came across any malefactors needing suppression. And I'd remembered to bring an ounce of Colonel John Suter's C-4 plastic explosive just in case the door to the inner sanctum of the POMCUS cache's stowage area needed any extra persuasion. I'd bought fresh batteries for the radios, so Mister Murphy wouldn't be able to take over our comms tonight. And Half Pint had even managed to find us some red gel to put over the lenses of our miniflashlights.

2036. Rodent, who was tonight's point man, secured the LZ on his BMW.

There was a loud squawk in my left ear as Rodent hit the transmit button on his radio. I cursed under my breath, turned my squelch switch down, and then listened to his voice in my ear: "Front door's open. C'mon up, Skipper."

I pressed my transmit button. "Roger-roger."

"Rear door's locked." That was Half Pint, who was playing rear security on the other bike, two kliks behind us. By now he'd have concealed himself in the underbrush alongside the road.

2038. There was no sign of Rodent as Baby Huey slowed the blacked-out Mercedes to about ten miles an hour, steering carefully through the mist. Good. That meant he was on his way to his position, two kliks up the road. I reached over and double-checked that the interior light switch was in the off position. It's the sort of basic operational detail you learn as a tadpole, but you'd be amazed at how many CIA gumshoes, FBI countersurveillance teams, and cops just plain forget to do it—and make themselves obvious targets as they get into and out of their vehicles.

From my position riding shotgun, I gave Boomerang, Duck Foot, Nod, and Gator an upturned thumb, smacked BH on the shoulder and told him to stay on the radio in case we needed him to show up on the double, then cracked the door open, and stage-whispered, "Go!"

We tuck-and-rolled out of the big diesel sedan into the blackness just like my SEAL predecessors in Nam rolled over the sterns of their PBRs. Well, not quite. I tucked—but since Mister Murphy was riding in the front seat with me, I caught the heel of my trailing foot on the doorjamb of the car. Now, since I didn't want to be dragged down the asphalt, I flailed my stuck foot—and it separated from the vehicle. Of course, with my progress slowed, I was about to be smacked by the car's open doors. I reached up, caught the front door, and used it to throw myself toward the shoulder of the road. The move cleared my body away from the car—but it didn't remove Mister Murphy's viselike grip on my lapel.[36]

With Murphy attached like the leech he is, I began to roll uncontrollably. I bounced off a body—couldn't see whom I'd struck, but whoever it was gave up a loud grunt—then I coasted eight or nine yards across the blacktop on my right hip (oh, *that* was going to burn like hell tomorrow), caromed down the rock-encrusted shoulder onto the slicker-than-shit wet grass, and came to an abrupt stop when I skidded—splat!—face first, into one of the fifteen-centimeter-square creosote-coated wire fence supports that sat at ten-meter intervals at the edge of the cow pasture.

I lay there in the mud for an instant or two, trying to catch some of the wind that had been rudely knocked clean out of me. I reached up and around my face—I was currently as twisted as a pretzel—and picked a trio of nasty splinters out of my much-maligned snout. Then I rolled over onto my back, caught my breath, breathed deeply, and ran my hands over myself bow to stern to make sure nothing had gotten broken.

God, how I love pain. And it is a good thing that I do, because pain and I have (as you know) a unique, even existential relationship. Oh, I was going to be one sore sphincter in the morning. But that would be then, and this was now, and dings or no, it was Show Time. So, I pulled myself to my feet, patted myself down to make sure none of my equipment had come loose. Guess what? I discovered that it was generally in better condition than I.

---

[36]Okay—I know I'm not wearing anything that has lapels right now, but this is a novel, after all, and I'm therefore allowed to occasionally use what the old editor describes as "literary license."

2040. Gator, Nod, and Duck Foot set up perimeter security. Boomerang and I vaulted the electric wire and made our way across 150 meters of squishy, cow pie–filled pasture to the four-foot-high chain-link fence surrounding the pump house.

Except that, just as I trained my minilight on the door and its locking mechanisms, I was interrupted by Rodent, squeaking urgently in my ear. "Belay, belay, belay. We got company Skipper—three cars coming up on my position—now. They're moving goddam fast."

"Roger—" Two kliks is just over a mile—less than a minute the way most Krauts drive. No time to waste. I hit the transmit button again. "Baby Huey, get off the road into cover—now! And stay with the fucking car."

The "*tsk–tsk*" in my earpiece told me either that he'd heard, or he'd made visual contact. Either way, he was complying.

I hit the transmit button again. "Snatch group—move across the road and regroup. We got company coming."

I looked at Boomerang. It was five hundred long feet back to the electric fence—and if we ran, we'd leave the kinds of deep footprints that even city dwellers can make out in soft, muddy pasture at night.

The editor has just interrupted my train of thought. He says I'm anticipating a problem when I may not need to.

Good point. Did I know that the cars coming were unfriend-lies? No, I did not. Did I believe that the occupants would stop and examine the pasture for tracks? No, I did not. But given the situation, I wasn't about to assume that they *wouldn't*. Contingency planning is a big part of SpecWar—but visitors were a contingency I hadn't planned on.

Gator, Duck Foot, and Nod were already hidden. They'd gone across the road and disappeared into the thick tree line that began roughly ten yards off the shoulder of the road. And I knew what they would be doing: they would be setting themselves up in an ambush position.

I looked up the road. Fuck: I could make the headlights out already. It was time to move.

But not toward the road. I hooked my thumb in the opposite direction. "Let's get going."

Boomerang nodded. "Gotcha, Boss Dude—" He slung his bag of break-and-enter goodies over his shoulder, I did the same, and we started off, keeping the pump house between us and the road. We made our way as carefully as any Mohican in a James Fenimore Cooper novel, walking stealthily so as not to leave telltale tracks. I could make out a slight rise in the pasture, ahead and to my right. We zigged and zagged across the open field until we reached it. I stopped long enough to get some sense of where we were. Off to my left, my night vision could make out the squared-off shapes of cattle, standing quietly perhaps a hundred yards from where we hunkered.

And then, the rude glare of halogen headlights cut through the blackness. Boomerang and I both dropped flat. I waited for a couple of seconds, then stretched out and peered over the crest of the rise that sheltered us.

The fucking cars were slowing down. The fucking cars were stopping. They pulled onto the shoulder of the road directly opposite the pump house. In the ambient glare of headlights and taillights, I could tell they were a pair of big Mercedes sedans.

I pulled my monocular from my breast pocket, raised it, and twisted the focusing reticle. I knew who these assholes were— you probably can guess, too. But I couldn't resist checking anyway. I focused the monocular on the rear door of the first car, where you and I both knew I'd see an ornate, hand-painted coat of arms.

Except I didn't. The door was unadorned. And then, all the vehicles' lights went out, and I lost the image.

Boomerang and I lay there for some seconds until we got our night vision back. You use a different part of your eye to see at night than you do during daylight. In daylight, light is picked up by sections of the retina in the center of the eye. These are called cones. At night, the retina uses rods, which are grouped around the cones, to pick up light sources. And so, at night, you use a lot more of your peripheral vision than you do in the daytime. In

120

fact, if you stare directly at something at night, you may not see it. But if you look off to the side, you'll usually pick out what you're looking for.

That's what I did here—I let my vision play with the darkness, find its own areas on which to concentrate. And within a few seconds, I was able to make out the shadows buried in the shadows, and see what these assholes were up to.

I counted ten figures. Some had spread out in a defensive perimeter around the cars. The others were unloading equipment from the Mercedes' trunks. They'd obligingly left the trunk lights on. They were removing the normal assortment of break-in tools: suppressed, automatic weapons, pry bars, and a number of what I call burglar's bags, no doubt filled with the various sorts of miscellaneous goods you need to get inside your target. Then the trunks were slammed shut, and everything plunged back into darkness.

It was time to get some more eyes on the problem. I flicked the transmit button. "Nod—"

Immediately, my ear buzzed with an affirmative response. *"Tsk–tsk."*

"How many?"

There was a pause. Then a whispered, "Ten."

We were five, unless Half Pint and Rodent were coming back on foot. Well, if didn't matter—we'd take down however many we had to. We'd—Nod's voice interrupted my thoughts. *"Ivans, Ivans, Ivans.* They're talking *Russkie,* Skipper."

Now *that* was unexpected. I mean, here was Franz, a former GSG-9 shooter, who'd retired under a cloud, who now worked in Düsseldorf for BeckIndustrie, and whose name I'd heard secondhand from *der winzig* Heinz Hochheizer, the deceased Stasi agent and bomb salesman. So, I'd have expected that Franz would see me nosing around, and then come back himself to see what I'd been snooping for.

But now, here were a bunch of Ivans doing the snooping instead.

I lifted the monocle and peered through it. I couldn't make

much out at all. But they were working. Then, I saw four of 'em vault the electric fence. Three moved straight toward the pump house across the dark pasture. The other lifted his leg up and tried to shake his foot off. I knew what he'd stepped into.

Time to check on the troops. I whispered "count off" into my lip mike. There was a half-second delay. Then a series of one-two-three-four-five-six-seven *tsk–tsks* came through my earpiece. At least we all could hear one another.

I told my guys what I wanted them to do, and received affirmatives from everybody. There's not a lot of time to explain it right now, but the bottom line was that Gator, Nod, and Duck Foot would deal with the six Ivans on the road. Half Pint and Rodent would provide perimeter security, Boomerang and I would take on the quartet of ADM-snatchers headed for the pump house—and Baby Huey would stay with the Mercedes, so we'd be able to extract at a moment's notice if it became necessary.

Yes, I realized that we were outnumbered here this evening. But it was we, not they, who maintained all the advantage. You see, we knew we had company. The Ivans obviously didn't. They were smoking, and they were talking, and they were violating so many basic OPSEC[37] procedures that I knew they weren't military types.

So, who were they? Believe me—I planned to find out.

2043. The quartet of Russkie raiders pressed on through the pasture. They'd gone over the chain-link fence with all the demure grace of heffalumps in heat, clambered across the muddy pasture, and finally come around to the side facing away from the road, where the door was located.

I watched as they began work. They weren't more than sixty yards from us now. But making out what they were doing was hard because they were working in total blackness. Well, maybe I couldn't see, but I could still hear them. Sure I could. They

---

[37]OPerational SECurity

thought they were alone, and so they nattered at one another in Ivan as they began work on the door lock. Then all of a sudden the bright beam of a halogen flashlight almost fucking blinded me though the monocle. One of the Ivans stood back and shone the light on the door, so they could begin work.

That was my cue. I slid the monocle into my pocket and nudged Boomerang. He watched as I crept over the crest and moved away from it so as not to silhouette myself against the sky, crawling slowly but deliberately toward the pump house.

This was harder to do than it is to describe, believe me. First, there was the terrain—it was squishy, acres of wet pasture accented by cow pies and piss-puddles. Then there was the absolute lack of cover. In the woods, you can use foliage to camouflage your movements. In the city, there are shadowy alleys, vehicles, and buildings that can be used to help conceal your movement. Here, I was forced to proceed in the open, which left me vulnerable to all sorts of nasty possibilities. Still, I remembered the three basic tenets of concealment—shape, shine, and silhouette—and used them all to my advantage as I crawled forward. I kept my silhouette low by moving snakelike and evenly. I allowed no telltale shape to stick out and give me away. And I provided no reflective surface: I was blacked out from my face to my toes, and nothing that I carried reflected any light.

I also followed a trio of simple rules I have developed for nighttime operations, rules that have kept me alive all over the globe. Rules that would, I hoped, work again tonight here in Deutschland.

Rule One: always keep low, because your profile offers the enemy a great target.

Rule Two: avoid open spaces if possible. If avoiding open spaces is not possible, then follow rule one and keep as low as you can.

Rule Three: always move slowly and deliberately. Creep like Kramer and you'll become dog meat. The less attention you attract, the less attention you'll attract.

And so, I slithered, and slid, and slinked, moving mere inches at a time across the expanse of pasture. The sixty yards became fifty, then forty. I began to pick up the pace a little bit. The Ivans were intent on their work now—drilling at the locking devices, their flashlight centered on the door hinges. The light was bothersome, but I knew that by keeping one eye closed, I'd retain most of my night vision.

I slowed down momentarily and looked back under my outstretched left arm. I could make out the prow of Boomerang's balaclava as he pulled himself, inch by painful inch, across the pasture. Yes—painful. Your muscles burn at times like this. Breathing is hard, because you don't want to make any noise. Every movement is deliberate. Put your hand in the wrong position, and you will cause some twig to snap, or leaf to crackle, or stone to click, or something else equally nasty to happen, and then the bad guy turns around and shines his light on you, and it becomes Doom-on-Dickie time, which is never a pleasant occurrence to yours truly.

2053. I lay prone, the front of my black BDUs smeared with fragrant cow pies, stained by mud and grass and cattle piss, not eight yards from where the Ivans had broken through the first and second locking devices, and were about to defeat the third in the series. Slowly, slowly, I slid my right hand down my side, and as I did, I brought my right knee up, so as to allow my hand to grasp the pommel of the black-oxy'd K-Bar in the sheath strapped to the outside of my right calf. The pommel was strapped, and I flicked the big snap, which cracked like a knuckle.

That's when one of the Ivans turned—abruptly—as if he'd heard something. Which, of course, he had. He took a big, healthy drag on his cigarette, exhaled with a sigh, and looked straight at me.

Now, a few graphs ago I explained about how your eyes work at night. So you already know all the shit you need to know about rods and cones. Now, let me add something to that: it is a scientific fact that if you look directly at something at night, you will not see it. At night, you see (!), it is one's peripheral vision, not one's direct vision, that is dominant.

Why? You're still asking me why? Where the hell did you learn reading retention?

Because, asshole, it's the rods of your retina that work at night, not the cones. And the rods are not at the center of the retina, but at the periphery—remember?

And so, when I caught the Ivan looking at me, I simply froze. No breathing, no nothing.

I remained where I was for what seemed like a fucking eternity but didn't last more than fifteen seconds. But I swore that the sonofabitch could hear my heart, arteries, and veins all pounding *pa-doom, pa-doom, pa-doom on Dickie.* The cigarette smell was overpowering. And then, and then, and then . . . he flicked the butt into the darkness, straight at me, watched as it hit the wet ground and went out with a hiss not six inches from my nose. And then he turned on his heel and went back to work.

2102. The Ivans defeated the last of the locking devices, opened the cache door, and went inside. No—they didn't leave anybody standing guard. Why should they? Their rear security was in place—on the road. And they simply assumed that no one would come through the back door—i.e., the pasture—and hit 'em from the back side.

Now it was MY turn. All knees and elbows I crawled to the doorway, rolled onto my side, pulled myself up and hunkered, my shoulder touching the rear wall of the pump house, waiting for Boomerang. It didn't take more than thirty seconds for him to show up. We could make out hints of light from inside as the team of Ivans opened the trap door that I knew lead to the weapons cache. I sheathed my K-Bar and exchanged it for the suppressed USP that sat in its thigh holster, and checked the weapon to make sure there was a round chambered. Boomerang unholstered his suppressed USP, and made ready, too.

2103. I *tsk-tsk*'d into the lip mike to let the rest of my guys know that we were going to work. I looked over at Boomerang, who had what can only be described as a glad-to-be-alive shit-eating grin on his long, narrow face. What can I say? Nothing, except that I love a man who loves to kill the way Boomerang loves to kill.

Boomerang gave me an upturned thumb. I returned the gesture, dropped low, and went through the doorway.

The floor was concrete. I moved cautiously, so as not to make any noise. The ambient light from below was enough so that I could make out the interior of the pump house shell. The room was square. In the front port-side quadrant, a steel trap door was propped open. From below, I could hear the Russkies talking.

We split up and crawled to opposite sides of the trap door. I rolled up alongside it and peered over. A steel ladder about sixteen feet in length and bolted to a concrete wall descended to the chamber below. I had no idea how big that chamber was, or what it held. What I *did* know—I could tell from the way the lights were moving down there—was that the Russkies had all moved way over to the far side, and that the only way to get down was to drop with our backs facing the Ivans.

Now, since you—along with Mister Murphy—are along for the ride tonight, let me present you with a slight tactical problem. They are down there. We are up here. Remember back at the start of the book I told you about the concept of Relative Superiority, and the AV, or Area of Vulnerability? Well, going up or down a ladder or a rope is an AV almost as big as my dick. The descent becomes an AV just as big as my dick if you have to go down with your back exposed toward the enemy. So, friends, my query to you is this: how do we solve the problem of getting down into the chamber, waxing the Russkies, and removing the ADM, without becoming vulnerable, and thereafter dead?

Right you are. The correct answer, of course, is that we do NOT go down into the chamber. We wait until the Russkies climb up. Because we already know that ladder is a hufucking-mongous AV. And the narrow trap door? Well, because it cuts the vision potential down to almost zero, it is what's known in the SpecWar trade as a fatal funnel. What's that? In Roguishly simple terms, it means it's gonna be fatal for the Ivans to try to funnel their way up the fuckin' ladder.

2110. I heard enough scraping and scrambling from below to know that they were on their way. I looked over at Boomerang, my eyes explaining what I wanted to do. He nodded that he understood, and we reholstered our weapons. We weren't going to need them . . . yet.

Now here is a little insight into human behavior. Most people, when they climb ladders and ride elevators, tend to look straight ahead. And INO—Ivan Number One—was no exception. He came up at a good pace. His head and then his shoulders cleared the trap door. As they did, I came up around the starboard side of his neck with my size extra-Rogue hand, clamped down on his Adam's apple, and choked off his air supply.

Before he could struggle any more, Boomerang had him under the arms, and had pulled him through the opening.

Ivan's eyes were big as saucers—he really hadn't been expecting any company.

Well, April fool, motherfucker. His surprise was my tactical advantage. I slid around behind the sonofabitch, my right elbow now a vise in which his throat was caught. It's an old LAPD[38] choke-hold, and it works. He went down much easier than you might expect. I squeezed, exerting pressure until I felt the pressure of his body slumping up against mine. Then I took his head, snapped his neck forward and wrenched until I heard the bones break. I took his jaw in one hand and put the other on his skull, then twisted his head until I knew the spinal cord and nerves were all severed. Then I rolled him off my body. Boomerang took the corpse by the shoulders and pulled it out of the way to give us an unobstructed playing field.

Not a second too soon, either. Because INT—Ivan Number Two—was already on his way up. He was struggling because he was hampered by the ADM package—eighty bulky pounds of

---

[38]Los Angeles Police Department

nuke. He'd balanced it above him and was pushing it up toward the trap door, waiting for INO to take the package from him.

Hey, I like to be helpful, and so I reached down and yanked the dark molded case out of his hands.

He started to say *"Spasíba—"* Thanks. But then he saw who he was thanking, and the word froze in his throat.

I gave him a big Rogue smile. *"Pozháluysta—"* Don't mention it.

It was about then that I realized that things had been going all too smoothly for Dickie. As if in Slo-Motion, the Ivan's right hand dropped toward his waist. It came back up—and there was a big fucking pistol in it.

Basic rule of thumb: do not use an atomic weapon as a ballistic shield. But it was all I had, so I put the package between the Ivan and me. And then, just like Ford, I had a better idea. I tossed the ADM at him. "Hey, *baklan*[39]—you take the fucking thing back!"

Now, here's how things stood: the Ivan's feet were on the ladder rung. One hand held his pistol. The other supported him. He dropped the handgun and brought his support hand up to catch the package. But of course he couldn't balance it right. And so he stretched toward the ADM like a wide receiver going for a pass thrown too high. He managed to grab it, too, a real nice shag. But his feet must have come off the rungs as he'd stretched to catch the device, because he dropped like the proverbial stone down the hatch, clutching at the ADM all the way to the bottom. He hit with a loud cry, followed by the solid thunk of nuke crate on the cement.

No time to think—I just reacted. I rolled toward the hatchway, grabbed the ladder rails with both hands, kept my feet on the outside, and dropped into the void, the steel of the ladder rails burning through the lightweight leather of my Nomex assault gloves.

I hit the floor below badly. My right foot caught the ADM

---

[39]*Punk,* in Russkie.

crate, I heard my ankle bones pop and then the fucking ankle caved. But it didn't matter, there was too much else to worry about.

I rolled away from the ladder so Boomerang could follow me. As I rolled, I pulled my pistol out of its holster, got into low ready, and—scan/breathe—searched for threats. The chamber was much bigger than I'd expected it to be. And, geezus—I'd fallen into a goddam armory. The walls were lined with ordnance, weapons, and other supplies. Stacks of ammo cases. Crates of firearms. Jerry cans of water and other liquids. Uniforms—U.S., German, and Soviet—hung on racks. But I didn't have a lot of time to take inventory. The INT may have been flat on his back—the ADM had cold-cocked him, or worse, hopefully. But off to my port, another Ivan was either playing with himself or trying to extract a pistol from his trouser pocket.

When will they ever learn how to carry weapons? I sight-acquire-fired and winged him with a shot to the right arm (oops), which sent him spinning. I did better second time around: I caught him as he turned, with a perfect hammer—tap-tap—to his chest. Hey, great sight picture and nice center mass shooting, if I don't say so myself. The bullets knocked him back against the far wall, where he collapsed against the steel-rack shelving units, a look of shock, pain, and surprise on his ugly Russkie face.

I was just admiring my handiwork when Ivan Number Four tackled me. This one was quick—he'd closed the distance between us in no time at all, and he'd come prepared to Do Nasty Business. He was carrying a short length of steel—it looked more like a crowbar than a tire iron—and he hit me hard enough with it to drive me back into the ladder, knocking me into Boomerang as he dropped.

We all went arms and legs akimbo into a heap. The Russkie slashed at the back of Boomerang's head and caught him with a glancing blow, knocking my surfer-SEAL face first into the ladder. Boomerang went down, wrapping up my feet and legs as he did so. I whirled, which just made things worse, because

Boomerang's hand slammed my wrist up against a rung, and my
USP bounced, then went skittering off across the concrete floor
of the cache room. It was now officially Doom-on-Dickie Time.

Christ, this was turning to shit. I grabbed hold of the Ivan's
weapon and tried to wrest it away. Nada. Bupkis. The guy had
hands of steel. I slipped my own hand free and grabbed him by
the throat. Ivan's eyes went buggy and he growled sweet
nothings in my ear while trying to gnash and nibble at it.
Abruptly, he wrenched away, swiveled, and slapped the short
piece of steel at my face. Instinctively, I brought my arm up. It
blocked the blow—but the goddamn shaft caught me on the
outside of my elbow and I could feel the fucking shock waves all
the way into my toenails. They may call it the funny bone. There
is nothing fucking funny about it at all, my friends.

But here is a truth of Warriordom. Pain makes the Warrior
stronger, not weaker. It is the anvil on which all true Warriors are
forged, whether it is the muscle burn, sleep deprivation, and cold
of Hell Week, the Marine Corps crucible, Ranger training, Delta
Force selection—or the kind of life-and-death struggle in which I
was now engaged. The ordinary person gets hurt—and he
retreats to deal with his pain. The Warrior takes in all that pain,
all that hurt, all that agony, and metamorphoses it, transmogri-
fies it, channels it, into pure, unadulterated, kinetic strength,
electric energy, and pure will to win.

I took hold of the bar with both my hands and twisted,
working it out of the Russkie's grasp. He would have none of it.
Instead, he brought the damn thing up, its chisel-edge under my
chin, and tried to impale me by lifting me off the floor.

This, friends, is when those 150 reps of 450 pounds on the
outdoor weight pile at Rogue Manor, hung out or hung over,
rain, or snow, or sleet, pay off. My War Face looked his Russkie
pusskie straight in the eyes—and he was the one who blinkski'd.

Oh, yes. Now he was *mine*. The growl in my throat told him it
was time to die. I put my hands outside his, so we both had hold
of the bar. And then I brought it absolutely horizontal. Then
inexorably, unstoppably, I forced it down and away, moving the

two-foot length of steel farther from my chin—and closer to his midsection.

I kept his eyes locked with mine while I pushed the steel lower, then turned it once more, so that the sharp, chisel-edged pry-blade was pointed in *his* direction. And then I drew the fucking thing back, back, back, and, with all my strength, drove it **HOO-YAH** into his thorax.

It struck with this amazing, reverberating, *thwock.* The blow staggered him back—but it staggered me, too, as if I'd hit a fucking brick wall with my fist. I've heard of abs like steel, but this was ridiculous. And then, of course—my old shipmate Doc Tremblay is quick to say *entiymah feeshmok,* which is Cairo slang for "you've got fartbeans for brains"—I realized that the sonofabitch was wearing a bulletproof vest, which had a fucking ceramic strike plate positioned over his chest and thoracic regions, and all I'd done was knock the fucking wind out of him.

Time to exchange bars. I dropped his pry bar and went for my K-Bar. While I used my body to hold him in place, I reached down, grasped the pommel, and extracted the big knife from the sheath on my leg. I took it in what's known in the killing trade as the modified saber grip—blade horizontal to the ground, thumb atop the hilt. Held the blade tip up and, my left arm and shoulder pinning Ivan to the wall, thrust the big, nasty, blade up, up, up, working it behind his vest, then twisting the blade edge to vertical so I'd cut through his diaphragm, and reach beyond, toward his heart and lung area. He struggled against me, but I was using my whole body mass, my arm, and my shoulder—not to mention all of that accumulated PAIN—to hold him down while my right arm did its work and the knife eviscerated him.

He gave me a horrible look as the blade severed his portal vein, cut through his abdominal aorta, nicked his pulmonary artery, and then finally slit his heart and lungs open. He tried to gurgle what was probably a curse in Russian, spat blood at me—it simply drooled down his chin—and then the life went out of him.

I wrenched the blade out, wiped it on his corpse, and as I

sheathed it I sank to my knees—wasted. My fucking ankle throbbed. My elbow felt like shit. I may be a grizzled old War Wolf, but right then this *Canis lupus* wasn't huffing and puffing hard enough to wheeze down a single piggy's house—even if the fucking thing had been folded out of origami. Here is some Roguish sooth: war is for the young.

But I didn't have any time to ponder the philosophical truths of battle right then.

Why not? Because the goddam Ivan I'd shot was alive and well, and on his feet, and he'd retrieved his pistol from his pocket, and he was advancing on me, shooting as he came, the gun clutched in his left hand, his useless right arm dangling absurdly at a nasty angle.

It was a little gun—a Marakov—but the sound of those 9-by-18, or .380 ACP, or whatever-the-fuck-they-may-have-been rounds in the enclosed space was deafening, even more so because the sound was augmented by the nasty sprays of concrete about a foot to my left and getting closer.

A shard of something sharp nicked my face half an inch below my right eye and I felt blood on my cheek. Oh, fuck me. I backpedaled away from the gunfire like a fucking hermit crab, grabbed the corpse of the bulletproof Ivan, and hefted it around my body and held it in front of me. The Russkie kept coming— he squeezed off two, three, four more shots. But he was panic-shooting with his weak hand and the rounds went wide again. I tripped over something. It was my own fucking USP. I bent, grabbed it while trying not to lose hold of my Russkie-corpse shield. *Got it!* I struggled to my feet, holding the dead Russkie in front of me just as the Ivan finally found the range.

I heard the *thwock–thwock–thwock* as the bullets hit the corpse's ceramic vest plate. All I could think was, *Geezus, keep shooting at the fucking vest—don't fucking try to hit me in the fucking legs, because you'd fucking be fucking successful, and I'd be fuckee-fuckeed.* And then, I'd come up on him. And guess what? Since he'd panic-fired, which means he had no fire discipline, he'd run out of fucking ammo. I tossed the Russkie corpse in his direction,

132

and when he ducked away, I was on him. Twisted the pistol out of his hand—broke a couple of his fingers, but so the fuck what, he'd been fucking shooting at me. I was in a blood frenzy now, sharklike and very dangerous. I slapped the Ivan across the mouth head with his own weapon, knocking teeth onto the concrete. He struggled, tried to get away, but I had him in a death roll and I wasn't about to let him get away again. I brought the pistol up, reversed it, and hit him as hard as I could in the face with the butt. The blow broke his nose. I smashed him again and again and again with the flat of the pistol grip, driving bone fragments up into his brain.

His eyes rolled back in his head. Maybe he was dead. But maybe not. I don't like to make the same mistake twice, so I reached down, pulled the USP, and put two bullets in his forehead just to make sure he wouldn't come at me a third time. I don't like to repeat mistakes, I prefer to learn from 'em.

Exhausted, I pulled myself up onto my feet, and staggered over to the ladder to check on Boomerang, who was unconscious and caught up in the rungs. I lowered him to the deck and rolled him onto his back. He had some dings on his arms and legs, a cut on his cheek, and one hellaciously nasty mouse over his left eye, as well as a humongous shiner that would cause him immediate pain, temporary suffering, and lots of ribbing from his shipmates. But his breathing was even and he didn't have any broken bones. Since I wasn't carrying any ammonia ampoules, I slapped him gently until he came to.

I watched his eyes focus, fog over, cross, uncross, then struggle until they focused again. He checked himself over, stem to stern, then felt at the blossoming, tender lump over his eye with his fingertips, grimaced, and said, "Oh, shit." Then he looked around, and saw the bodies. "*Geezus*, Boss Dude—WTF?"

His look of concern brought a smile to my face. "Just like always, asshole—you fucking slept through the whole floor show and missed all the tits and ass." I grinned as I helped him to his feet. "C'mon—we have work to do."

133

Chapter

8

2214. YEAH, WE'D OVERCOME THE BAD GUYS, BUT THERE WAS STILL an old SEAL technical term that covered our situation. It was: FUBAR—Fucked Up Beyond All Repair. We now had ten corpses on our hands, as well as what might be called a huge cache-flow problem. Oh, we'd be able to pack out the two ADMs I'd discovered down in the cellar. But what about all those uniforms, and weapons, and other ordnance? Not to mention the two Mercedes sedans in which the Russkies had been traveling.

Dump the corpses in the pump house and leave 'em? No way. They'd been sent by somebody—and whoever it was would come looking for 'em. Destroy the evidence? It would be possible to dump all the corpses in the cache, and then use John Suter's C-4 to blow the place—and everything in it—up. But that wouldn't help our situation vis-à-vis the Kraut cops, e.g., Brendel and Rackel, who'd return to the scene of the questioning, do the anal-retentive forensic number, remember precisely who had been seen in the area *(moi)*, and *mir erlegen*—hunt me down like the *Schurke*[40] I am. Nor would the unsuspecting farmer whose

---

[40]Rogue

134

cow pies currently decorated my BDUs and clotted my beard appreciate my blowing up several acres of his prime pasture land. Besides, I wanted to find out who these Ivan assholes were, who they were working for, and what they'd planned to do with the pair of pocket nukes.

Moreover, as you will remember, Chairman Crocker had asked me not to make as much as a ripple during the current exercise. Okay, okay, so he hadn't asked—he'd ordered. But you get the idea.

And so, I dutifully got on the horn—the cellular, to be precise—and called the number Colonel John had given me.

The phone rang three times. "Suter."

"It's your traveling companion from Italy."

"Gotcha." Oh, was he quick on the uptake. "What's up, my hairy friend?"

"You know what you've been tasked to do—I'm in possession of a couple and I'd like to hand 'em over ASAP."

"Roger that." There was a momentary pause, as if he knew another boondocker would be dropping. "Anything else?"

"Funny you should ask. I've got some extra material on hand as well. About two six-by's full, maybe more."

"Okay. Can do." Nothing seemed to faze this guy. "Location?"

I put my red-lensed flashlight on the map General Crocker had given me and read off two sets of coordinates. There was a pause while Suter checked my position.

"I've got a three-hour ETA. Does that work for you?"

"If it has to."

John Suter's voice was clear and cool. "It has to. We're talkin' complicated logistics here, friend, and since I won't be landing any Pave Lows where you are, I gotta come in to Rhine Main, proceed by land—and I gotta move mucho quietly."

I couldn't argue any of that, and told him so.

"Anything else?" he asked.

What was he, prescient? "Well, if you happen to have about a dozen body bags, it might be helpful."

The "Oh, fuck me very much" indicated that I'd finally fazed him. He cupped his hand over the mouthpiece of the phone, and I could hear muffled orders being given. Then his voice came back strong. "See you at Zero Dark Hundred, O Hairy One. Keep your head down and try not to eliminate anybody else. We have a shortage of body bags down here ever since the end of the Cold War."

"Roger-roger, Suter-san."

I slapped the cellular shut. We'd already moved the Ivans' two Mercedes off the road and under cover. The ADMs were under Gator's watchful eye. And BH, Nod, Half Pint, and Boomerang were checking over the Ivans and their effects to gather what intel nuggets they could.

Without a whole lot of results, I might add. The four in the cache carried no IDs at all—although each had about a thousand dollars' worth of German marks and another thou in American dollars, all of it in brand-new Gucci wallets. The Ivans also wore expensive clothing—good quality Hugo Boss suits. They'd taken their jackets off, but they sported dress shirts and ties. The labels told me everything came from the same department store in Düsseldorf, even the dressy, low-cut, urban cowboy shoes with tassels you don't see in cow pastures very often.

Their cigarettes were Americanski; two of the Ivans carried solid gold Duponts, which go for five grand each in Paris. Four of them were wearing gold Rolex watches. Two others had Piagets, and three others were wearing brand-new steel Tag-Heuer chronometers. We're talking huge amounts of disposable income here, friends—but little else. Oh, they'd shown up with burglar's kits—pry bars, saws, drills, lock picks, graphite dust, and other tools of the break-and-enter trade. But they weren't carrying anything that identified 'em. No hotel room keys; no receipts; no papers; no nothing.

As for weapons, we had two Marakov semiauto pistols, one Walther PPK in .380 ACP, and one Sig-Sauer in nine mil. The rear guard had been carrying suppressed MP5s. The only thing that seemed out of place was that everybody'd been wearing

German-made tactical body armor over their shirts and ties, but under the Boss double-breasteds. It was the latest German military equipment, too: Class III-A stuff with ceramic plates front and rear, as well as high-cut armholes and lots of Velcro. Weird, huh? I certainly thought so.

The two Ivans who'd been driving had German driver's licenses—recently issued, from the look of 'em—and more of the brand-new Gucci wallets that contained both dollars and deutsche marks, but very little else.

Now, my friends, this obvious conspicuous consumption, coupled with the lack of personal ephemera, made me suspicious. I mean, ask yourself, how clean is your wallet? How much junk is buried therein—even in a relatively new wallet? Not to mention the sort of wallet grunge that comes with constant use. Indeed, one of the most important things you can do when operating under deep cover is to make your wallet appear to fit your character. These dudes' wallets didn't fit shit. It was as if they'd simply bought 'em by the dozen, filled 'em with cash, and that was that.

My educated guess was that I was looking at a bunch of Russkie Mafiyosi corpses. As you may know, I've dealt with the Russian Mafiya before on their home turf,[41] so I know what to look for. And these assholes showed all the signs of being what the Moscow cops call *bandity*.

Which raised all sorts of questions in my soggy Slovak brain. The little arms dealer I'd shanghaied off the *Kuz Emeq*, Heinz Hochheizer, had bought his ADM from a Georgian Mafiyosi. Segue to the present: I discover a cache containing ADMs. I'm spotted by Franz Ulrich, who tells his boss Lothar Beck, about me—and lo and behold, all of a sudden I'm set upon by the local cops.

---

[41] I was sent to Moscow after my old shipmate Paul Mahon was murdered by an Ivan *vor v zakonye* named Andrei Yudin. You can read about it in *Rogue Warrior: Designation Gold*.

When I prove to be kosher (and, incidentally, my identity is confirmed, not to mention the fact that I'm a prowling-and-growling SEAL), a bunch of Ivans mysteriously appears at precisely the same spot I'd been visiting. The Ivans break into the POMCUS cache and attempt to make off with the ADMs.

It's like, *duh.* I mean, how obvious can it get?

The problem is, there was nothing to tie these dead Ivans to Franz Ulrich or Lothar Beck. The evidence was purely circumstantial. I had no notes in their pockets written on BeckIndustrie notepaper. There were no maps of Düsseldorf with a circle around the headquarters of BeckIndustrie in the glove compartment of either Mercedes. No receipts for gasoline from Düsseldorf-area gas stations, either.

Now, I can tell you that I found this lack of evidence hard to take. I mean, I've been doing this kind of work for years, and I can tell you, so far as I am concerned, there is *always* evidence at the scene of the crime. You just have to know what to look for—and be patient.

And since there was no place to go until John Suter and his team showed up, we started at ground zero once again, and went back over everything one more time. We checked the linings of their suit coats. We turned the corpses' pockets inside out. We checked for false shoe soles and hollow heels. We ripped out the carpets in the cars, checked the seat-back linings, examined the trunk space in minute detail. And we came up empty one more time.

Until Baby Huey, God bless him, blundered into something.

Since he was the junior-most kid, I'd assigned him the choice task of stripping the corpses and going over them, top to bottom. Yes, that included the always-fun-to-do body cavity search. Nothing like a little blood and gore, not to mention shit and piss, to get a SEAL pup accustomed to life in the real world.

Baby Huey'd tossed his cookies twice in the first half hour. But then he'd either run out of things to puke, or he got used to the smell, and the feel. An aside here. I don't have to tell you about human excrement. But human blood, in the quantities we're talking about here, is not a pleasant substance to be around, either. It has this oily, metallic, sweetish odor that makes most folks gag. It certainly worked that way on BH. But I had to hand it to the kid—he kept at it, pulling the Ivans' clothes off, handing 'em off to Nod to search, and then examining their bodies with the thoroughness of a good pathologist.

He'd just rolled one of the drivers over for the third time. The Russkie was a fat little guy, completely bald and hairless. It was like trying to work on a butchered hog—even more so because Nod had cut the asshole's throat, and he was a fucking slippery, bloody mess, and you have to remember that BH was working without the niceties here, e.g., no rubber gloves, sphincter forceps, or other operating room goodies.

Anyhow, BH'd worked his way north from the Ivan's toes. He was wiping the blood off the guy's arms, looking for tattoos, or any other identifying marks, when he called me over, his voice an octave higher in excitement.

"Skipper, look! There's writing on his fuckin' hand," he shouted.

I quieted the kid down, then checked. Indeed, there was writing on the Russkie's fuckin' palm. It had been partially obliterated by mud, blood, and combat, but I could make out a series of numbers. They'd been written in marking pen.

Oh, it's a trick I've used before. Write a memo on your hand. If you're about to be captured, you wipe it off and no one's the wiser.

But we'd waxed this Ivan before he'd had the chance to destroy any evidence. I wrote the number down. I certainly had no idea whose number it was—but the area code was 02-11.

You probably know as well as I do that 02-11 is the area code for Düsseldorf. And as for the number—well, I wasn't about to go bush league and call it. But I did want to check it out.

I even had a way to do just that. But not now. Because right now, I saw headlights approaching down the long, straight single-lane blacktop from the north. A fucking convoy from the look of things. Either we were about to be in even deeper shit than we already were, or the cavalry had arrived, or both.

You had to hand it to John Suter. He showed up with five real extralarge German Army trucks. Perfect camouflage, given the venue—and the mission.

"𝕯𝖊𝖗 𝕬𝖉𝖑𝖊𝖗 𝖎𝖘𝖙 𝖌𝖊𝖑𝖆𝖓𝖉𝖊𝖙," he said as he jumped out of the convoy's lead vehicle. He was wearing a green Nomex flight suit without any markings, and matching Nomex gloves, so he wouldn't leave any fingerprints. At a distance—or a speed of forty kilometers an hour—it could be mistaken for German Army issue. Two dozen men dressed similarly, all armed with locked and loaded CAR-15s, descended from the truck beds.

I jogged over and took his gloved hand in my gloved hand. "Good to see you, John. Thanks for coming."

"I wish I could say the same about you."

"What's the prob?"

"Problem?" he said. "You mean the rocket of a message I got not six hours ago? The one I won't go into right now, but the gist is that you are shit-hot?" He cracked his knuckles. "Whatever gave you the idea I had a problem?"

I checked my watch because it was obviously Doom-on-Dickie time. "How bad is it?"

"Bad enough. Some admiral wants your ass in London. Right Now. Forthwith. Pronto. Chop-chop. In manacles if necessary."

Eamon the Demon. "And what did you answer?"

He gave me an even look. "I E-mailed the sonofabitch I had no idea where the blankety-blank you were, but that if I ever found out, I'd let 'em know right away."

"I owe you one."

He surveyed the devastation I'd just wrought with a bemused smile. "Y'know, you have a hell of a way of showing your gratitude," he said. He looked me over once more, then wrinkled his nose critically. "And did you know you have cow shit in your beard?"

"What's your point?"

He shook his head. "I guess I didn't have one." He paused. "Okay, how do you want to proceed?"

I flicked my French braid in the direction of the farmhouse. "I guess we have to pack it all up and get it the fuck outta here before it gets almost light and one of farmer Schmidt's roosters wakes up the whole fuckin' neighborhood."

"Sounds about right to me." He called one of his people over and gave a series of commands. Eight men split off to set up a defensive perimeter. Another two ran a bypass to the electric fence, snipped it in two places, then dropped a rubber mat over the wires. The rest of Suter's shooters set off toward the pump house. John looked over at me. "Well?"

I grabbed an armful of body bags and gave the "up and at 'em" sign to my men. "Hey, guys—let's get to it." And, get to it was right. The sooner we had this site loaded out, packed in, and cleaned up, the sooner I could begin working on developing the information I needed to deal with my growing list of Roguish problems—to wit: stolen ADMs, Russian *bandity*, and a nasty double portion of soured Krauts, e.g., Franz Ulrich and Lothar Beck.

Chapter

9

WE HAD THE SITE CLEARED BY 0350, AND JOHN SUTER AND HIS convoy were on their way back to Rhine Main by 0355, the ADMs safely stowed in a triple-locked safe, and the Russkies' two Mercedes added to John's convoy. He said he'd lose the Russkie corpses somewhere between here and Patch Barracks, after he'd pulled fingerprints, and he'd dump the cars, too—after he'd checked the registrations and VIN numbers for me. No way he could show up with either in Stuttgart: too many questions from the C²s, and too few answers from Colonel Suter and his shooters.

Well, all the above was his problem now. And since John seemed to be a resourceful asshole, I knew he'd come up with a fitting solution.

After he pulled out, my guys and I stayed around long enough to do a quick site policing. We couldn't hide all the signs of what had gone on, but we did enough to make things hard for anyone but the most determined professionals.

Before he left, John reminded me it had been General Crocker's wish that I accompany any goods I'd found back to Rhine Main. And he also reminded me that Eamon the Demon had demanded my immediate presence in London, at CINCUS-NAVEUR.

I gave him a double-negatory response. You already know what I think of Eamon: he's a fucking C²CO. So, you know there was no way I was going to give him a window on what I was doing and let him begin meddling in my affairs, or worse.

No—I had to get to Düsseldorf. I had things to do, not to mention beer to drink and people to kill. So, just as the dark void of night metamorphosed into that wonderful, pastoral, predawn black-purple you can see only if you're nowhere near a city and all its ambient sodium-slash-halogen-slash-fluorescent light, it was back on the road for me.

And just as Baby Huey turned the ignition key and our Mercedes diesel ge-chugged into life, I heard that pussy-crazed neighborhood rooster *suck-my-doodle-dooing* for all he was worth, and saw a single light switch on in the farmhouse across the pasture and down the road so quickly in response it was fucking Pavlovian. Sometimes, dear friends, Mister Murphy stays away long enough for you and yours—or me and mine—to get the job done.

By 0930 we were showered and cleaned up (God but it was good to get the cow shit out of my beard). By 1000 we'd had breakfast, checked out of our pension, and were back on the road again. We took some evasive maneuvers, just because I had that nagging sensation once again that somewhere, somehow, we were being spied upon. And then, finding nothing amiss, our little convoy headed north.

Not to belabor the point, but yes, I realize that the Chairman had told me to keep things stealth—and I hadn't. And yes, he'd been adamant that he didn't want my big Slovak snout poking around Düsseldorf—and here I was heading Düsseldorfward. And yes, I knew that he'd forbidden me to go UNODIR—and that's what I was doing.

But I also knew that was then, and this was now. And since Eamon the Demon had decided to stick his pug Irish nose into my business, I'd been given no choice. Besides, the only way I was going to get to the bottom of this thorny problem of stolen ADMs was to confront it head-on: i.e., up in Düsseldorf.

Now, you should understand that Düsseldorf's nickname is "The longest bar in the world." That's because the city is known worldwide for its dozens of *Altbier* breweries and their delicious output. (It is also famous for its unique, spicy *saft*, or mustard, but thank God it's not known as the longest hot dog in the world.) Drink and food, however, weren't why we were headed there. We were going to the village on the Düssel because that's where the Ivans had bought all those expensive clothes at a certain department store in the Schadow Arcade. We were going because there was a certain telephone number from the Mafiyosi's palm I wanted to check out. We were going there because Düsseldorf was where the headquarters of BeckIndustrie was located. And we were going there because there was a disco called die Silbermieze where *der winzig*[42] former Stasi agent, Heinz Hochheizer, had told me I'd find a coke freak named Franz, who claimed he could sell pocket nukes. But before I did any of that, I had a telephone call to make, and somebody to see.

I had BH pull over at the Weilerswist interchange rest stop, halfway between Bonn and Köln, so I could make the call from an anonymous pay phone. The guys topped off the vehicles, then went to drain lizards and scarf up sausage and cheese sandwiches (are they ever not hungry?). While they did, I slipped away, found a pay phone, played with myself until I came up with a palmful of pocket change, and extracted a shard of cocktail napkin from my wallet. I memorized the number scrawled thereon, dropped the requisite coins into the slot, and waited as the phone *bring-bringged*.

It did so *ein, zwei, drei, vier* times. And then a basso profundo Teutonic voice growled, "*Hallo—Ja?*"

---

[42]Remember, it stands for "the tiny" in Kraut-speak.

"Achtung! Du Schei<del>2</del>kerl! Yo—Fuck you, cockbreath! *Bist du* der hotsy-totsy ersatz Nazi motherfucking cocksucking pus-nuts Kraut mit whom Ich bin *spreching?"*

A volcanic explosion of laughter erupted in my ear. "Screw you and all that horse piss you call beer in that godforsaken homeland of yours, you big asshole of an *Amerikaner."* I heard him clap a hand over the receiver and bark something in machine gun German. Then: "Long time no hear from you, Rotten Richard. What the hell's the matter? Is it that you're so famous now you don't bother staying in touch with your old friends anymore, eh?"

He was right, of course, about my not calling. We haven't spoken in years, and it was my fault. But I've known Frederic Kohler since I was a tadpole ensign at SEAL Team Two, and he was a junior *Leutnant* in the Bundeswehr, who'd signed on for a two-year exchange stint with the *Kampfschwimmers,* the Kraut Navy's combat-swimmer unit. We rose through the ranks at approximately the same rate, which was fast, I might add. And since Fred always had a keen interest in killing his enemies before they killed him, promoting unit integrity in an age of *"moi,* myself, and I come first" officers, consuming beer, downing schnapps, and chasing pussy (and not always in that order, either), we cross-trained the men in our units to make WAR and eat snakes, even though he was Army and I was Navy, and despite what the powers-that-be might have liked.

Once—I was a mere lieutenant commander in those days— we even managed to ship thirty of his paratroop shooters from their base of ops in central Germany to my base of ops on St. Thomas in the Virgin Islands for a month of joint exercises. We probably expended more ammo and C-4 in those four weeks than the Army does in a year. We blew up enough coral reef to give the local tree-huggers terminal strokes. We practiced covert attacks on the sub base. And we also spear fished grouper and snared langouste and grilled them all on the beach, accompanied by copious amounts of Red Stripe beer, and shots of the local white lightning, a 150-proof raw-as-80-grit-sandpaper rum known as screech.

By the end of the month, we'd learned how to work as a joint unit, something that would come in handy if ever we had to go up against the Soviet bear together. Of course, we also managed to carve out a lot of downtime for the usual unlimited rounds of rough-and-tumble male bonding and marathon sessions of pussy chasing in the local clubs and discos.

And just to make sure things were kept interesting, there were fights with the can't cunts in the bureaucracy. Indeed, when somebody at the Pentagon discovered what I'd done (I'd engineered things so that the U.S. Navy paid the freight for Fred and his men), some pencil-dicked bean counter in Washington tried to get me court-martialed. When the Ministry of Defense in Bonn found out that Fred shifted thirty shooters to der tropics without asking *"Bitter"* they tried the same thing with him. But being slippery sonsofbitches, we slithered away and emerged unscathed. Yeah, he was a maverick. Just like me.

But Fred, unlike *moi*, had managed to live and to thrive within the system. After his stint with the *Kampfschwimmers* he'd gone back to his real home: the Bundeswehr's paratroop command, where as a colonel, he'd led a brigade. Currently, Frederic Kohler was a one-star general, in charge of what was billed as Germany's newest counterterrorism unit, the Kommando Spezialkräfte, or KSK. I'd first heard about KSK shortly after it had been commissioned last year. It was lean: only 120 shooters. And it was mean: KSK's mission was proactive, not reactive. They trained incessantly. They were hunter-killers who were tasked with neutralizing the opposition, not taking prisoners.

According to the supergrade Christian In Action who filled me in on some of KSK's secrets (I'll pseudonym him Jim Wink, so make sure they used an asterisk next to that name in the Index, because whatever his real name is, it ain't Jim Wink), Fred's unit had been patterned after 14 Intelligence Company, the top secret British unit devoted to counterterrorist activities in Ireland. How so, I asked. Well, Wink said, first of all, KSK was made up of both covert operators and SAS-type commandos, just like 14 Intel Co. Second, they had been given carte blanche to use all the German government's facilities "in support."

I hate apparatchik-speak. "Put that in English, will you, Jimbo?"

"They can skim almost anything they want from any of the ministries. Intel, comms, you name it. And they've been allowed to use buildings in Berlin and Bonn to hone their mission profiles." Wink paused long enough to take a long pull on a bottle of Corona. "You know what that tells me? It tells me they've been breaking into government offices to take what they need. I mean, that's what I'd do."

He was right, of course. He's an operator, and he knows about these kinds of things because he's done 'em all himself. I'd done the same thing when I ran Red Cell, too. I took a shitload of files from the Naval Criminal Investigative Service one night when I'd been tasked to test the Washington Navy Yard's security. I'd taken a lot more goodies from other installations—everything from weapons and ordnance to equipment, intelligence files, and other operational materials. Don't think of it as theft. Think of it as creative augmentation of your operational capabilities.

When I'd first learned about KSK's creation, I'd heard rumors that the unit had a counterterrorism mission and was based near Bonn, in some sort of big, isolated complex. I was wrong on the first count and right on the second, according to Wink.

Wink, who I've dealt with ever since he ran a black program out of the White House a few years back, had just returned from a six-week TDY with Fred and his people. He'd shared the latest on COMINT and ELINT tactics with them. For their part, KSK's CO, Fred, had given Wink a peek at the unit's operational capabilities. And during the evenings, Fred had also provided a few pointers about beer consumption (not that Wink needed any).

Anyway, Wink and I had overloaded on gossip and Corona

just about three weeks before I'd wheels-upped for the *Kuz Emeq*. He'd provided Fred's phone number from memory, along with a rambling monologue (there'd been a LOT of beer) about the unit's overt, clandestine, and covert capabilities.

Let me digress long enough here to explain a few basics about intelligence gathering. It has been argued in Congress that we should cut back on military and intelligence training activities. What Congress doesn't, perhaps, understand is that such activities give us the chance to gather intel vital to our national security, as well as pass on some good instruction to our allies.

When SEALs from SEAL Team Four instruct Venezuelans or Colombians in counterinsurgency, or SEALs from Team Eight work with elite military units from Africa as part of the Pentagon's JCET program,[43] they teach them how to patrol; how to ambush; and how to interrogate. But they don't quite teach 'em the exact same way we do it. Moreover, they make careful notes about the foreign units, their officers, and their capabilities, notes that are passed on to DIA on the unit's return. We recorded their strengths and weaknesses; do personality assessments; make diagrams of their headquarters and installations. And so, if the need should ever arise—a coup d'état that installed a hostile government, for example—SEAL Team Four, or Eight, could operate against the folks they've trained, and decimate 'em. Or, they could go back and work with the officers and men they knew, helping them set up guerrilla operations against the bad guys.

For its part, the Agency sends experts who help develop counterterrorism programs all over the free world. But as they do their teaching and consulting, they also gather intel, so that we get a clearer picture of what our allies are doing, what their capabilities are, and how they plan to act if a crisis arises.

And so Wink, an observant type with a photographic memory

---

[43]JCET stands for Joint Combined Exchange Training. JCET is not subject to State Department strictures, so the units are often made up of soldiers whose human rights history is not quite all that the ACLU might like.

and a couple of decades of field experience, came home with a lot more information about KSK than Fred might have liked him to have. For example, Wink said (it seemed strange to him at first, until he realized what was going on) that KSK was kept in virtual quarantine. Its communications links were all monitored. There were no public phones in the barracks. The men were even forbidden to have cellular units. And contact with the outside world was limited as well.

"It all looked like one of these goddam South American antidrug units we used to fund at the Agency," Wink explained. "The ones where they're so worried about OPSEC, they keep the whole frigging unit in isolation, allow no comms whatsoever, and only one or two of the most senior people know what the target is until the troops are in the air and on their way."

Moreover, despite the fact that they'd tried to hide many of KSK's personnel from him, he'd managed to slip away from his minders long enough to discover that some of Fred's operators looked like skinheads, others had the kinds of tattoos favored by bikers, and still others could have passed for the everyday kinds of Germans we'd seen on the streets.

So, KSK wasn't a military unit in the conventional sense, Wink said. KSK was something different. Just like 14 Intelligence Company was different.

"These guys are going to operate inside German society," he told me. "Oh, they're pushing the military stuff: hostage rescue and counterterrorism is the overt raison d'être for KSK, and that's what you'll see at their base. And that's precisely what Fred wants you to see—the choppers, and the kill house, and the rest of it. But I tell you, Dickie, I've run six big, complicated black programs in the last twelve years, and Fred has structured KSK almost the same as the one I called Skyhorse."

I hadn't been cleared to know about Skyhorse, but there had been a lot of RUMINT[44] at the time, and I could make an educated guess. "Wasn't that the op you ran in Jordan under

---

[44]RUMor INTelligence.

Royal Jordanian Police cover? Built a clandestine unit based on 14 Intelligence Company to infiltrate Palestinian terror cells?"

Wink's eyes went wide over his Corona. "I didn't think you knew. Anyway, the way KSK is set up—it's like seeing a bigger, more sophisticated, and complex version of the indigenous undercover reconnaissance unit I trained in an unnamed Arab country"—he drained his Corona and grinned mischievously—"located somewhere between Syria, Iraq, Saudi Arabia, and Israel."

I'd written Fred's number down at the time, shoved the information in my wallet, and forgotten about it—until the previous night. I hoped Wink's beer-soaked recall had been unimpaired, and was delighted to discover that it was.

I shook myself out of the past and dealt with the present. "You're right, Fred—I'm sorry. Life's been a goatfuck—and just as always, I'm the fuckee."

He roared with laughter. "Still the shy one with words, I see, Richard." He pronounced my name in the German fashion, *Ree-kard*.

"*Jawohl, mein Brigadegeneral.*"

He laughed again. "*Und zooo*, now that you are on the phone, and since the connection sounds as if this is a local call, what is it that you want of me?"

Fred is a perceptive Kraut, and like I said, we've known each other since Christ was a mess cook. "Do you think I'd call only because I need your help? Maybe I'm in town and I want to go out and sample the local brewskis."

There was a pause on the line. Then his voice came back, and when it did, it had a serious edge to it. "Honest answer, Richard?"

"Of course."

"I think it is the former, not the latter," he said. "I believe you and I both know that you are engaged in activities that I, for one, do not want to talk about on this phone."

Sumbitch.

"Und," he continued, "I believe that you do indeed need some help in your current tasks, and that I can afford you assistance."

Son Of A Bitch. I answered in the affirmative. There was no reason not to—because it was all too fucking true.

"Fursermore," he went on, "it has been brought to my attention of late that there is a high degree of activity in—" He broke off, and I heard him cup his hand over the phone again and bark a series of orders. "Areas of shall we say common interest."

"You're right on that one, too, Fred." He certainly was up to speed on my problems—at least it seemed so in the abstract.

"Ja, I know I am correct." He chuckled amiably. "That's why I'm a *Brigadegeneral."*

That's the Germans for you. Always wishy washy. I glanced at my watch. "So, Fred, I'm on my way to Düsseldorf," I said. "And I thought maybe I'd stop by and see you for a couple of hours. Talk a few things over."

"I'd like that, *Ree-Kard."*

"Only thing I need is directions. Word has it that you're pretty much kept in quarantine these days—out of the mainstream."

"Oh, *Ja?* And who says so?" Another pause, another clap of hand over the receiver. Then: "I tell you what, Richard. You follow the BMW *Limousine* that has just pulled next to your"—he paused as someone spoke to him—"old, black Mercedes, and it will bring you to where I am."

I spun around and looked over the bustle of the rest stop. A huge black BMW 7000 series four-door sedan with half a dozen antennas sprouting from its trunk had pulled adjacent to my vehicles. I took a closer look and saw that its front door quarter panels were equipped with gun ports. From behind the opaque, dark gray smoked glass windows, the Beemer's driver flashed the brights thrice.

"Damn, you fucking Krauts are efficient," I told Fred.

"Ja," he answered matter-of-factly. "That is *because* we are Krauts—not to mention the fact that we have recently been equipped with an *Amerikaner* GPS technology, integrated into a new, computerized system of tracking phone calls, courtesy of

your *Zentraal* Intelligence Agency." He roared with laughter. "Now hang up, Richard, and follow the BMW, and I'll see you in about eighteen minutes, if you can keep up."

We couldn't keep up, of course, and so it took my two-vehicle convoy twenty-five minutes to drive the thirty-six kilometers from the interchange south, then west, until we reached a small village named Gemünde. From there, the BMW turned onto a single lane of blacktop that meandered through a long ravine bordered on either side by a thick pine forest. After three kliks, we reached a four-meter-high fence, topped with razor wire. Just inside, two five-meter-wide cordons sanitaires of freshly raked earth paralleling a ten-meter band of lumpy soil was evidence of multiple sensor systems and land mines. We wove our way through a series of blockades designed to bring vehicles to a crawl and pulled up to a single electric gate manned by a squad of locked and loaded sentries. There was an audible hum as the gate was slid open. Then, before we were cleared inside, our IDs were checked by an efficient-looking pair of security guards. As the engines idled, I did a quick target assessment and discovered two more squad-sized security teams, well camouflaged, and with heavy automatic weapons, in ambush positions. These people were serious about their security.

We drove another two, three kliks, and emerged from the forest onto a wide, grassy plain. Ahead I could see a series of chopper pads bordered by landing lights. Three dark brown, unmarked CH-53 Pave Lows sat like ominous hulks, juxtaposed against the emerald green grass. Behind them, six MH-6 Little Birds, also unmarked, were arrayed in a loose diamond formation. Behind the choppers, well-camouflaged but nonetheless obvious to my practiced eye, were the above-ground valves to the fuel farm, which was obviously buried somewhere beyond the birds. Just like Wink had said: the conspicuous accent was on SpecWar.

Off to my starboard, there were barracks, warehouses, and other stowage and training facilities. To the port side were two soccer fields, a well-maintained cinder track, and a big, square open rustic shed under whose brown cedar roof sat a half dozen press benches and a huge pile of weights, all arrayed neatly on skeletal racks. Beyond the choppers, I could see a huge berm rising in the distance, and even through the windshield of the car and Baby Huey's choice of Generation X music, I could make out the snap-crackle-pop of small-arms fire. I couldn't see everything, of course, but from the quick peek I was being afforded, the place looked like it was, indeed, self-sufficient. Just as Wink had described.

We drove around the perimeter of the chopper landing area, cruised past the high berm, and came to a fork in the road. BH followed the BMW as it steered to port. We crossed a small bridge under which a ripply stream flowed, progressed through a series of tight curves that took the road around half a dozen gnarled, thick trees that must have been a couple of hundred years old from the look of them.

About half a klik later, we emerged from the greenery into a clearing. Three hundred yards away, the single lane of blacktop abutted the outer rim of a wide, light-colored gravel courtyard, which fanned out in front of an exquisite, fully restored eighteenth-century stone country house. House, hell—this was a fucking ESTATE. It had been built in the French style— evidence of France's influence on so much of eighteenth-century Germany. It was the French philosopher Voltaire, after all, who'd been the most influential teacher that the great Warrior and king, Frederick the Great, ever had. Voltaire had even inculcated the young Prussian prince in the concept of benevolent despotism— a concept, incidentally, by which I command my own troops today. Oh, I'm a real benevolent fucking despot, believe me.

The Beemer veered off toward a wrought iron fence, with gold pikes atop its ten-foot-high pickets and intricate, scrolled torsades at ground level that ran along the right side of the courtyard. The car pulled up to a double gate. The driver must have hit an electronic release, because the heavy gates swung open and the BMW disappeared behind the big house.

As I watched the gates swing shut, BH steered us right up to the front portico, where he pulled over and switched the engine off. The RV followed suit. We tumbled out and stood around, admiring.

And there was a lot to admire. The stonework was all hand done. The long, multipaned windows that faced the courtyard all had cremorne locks of bright polished brass. The roof was slate, in what appeared to be a handmade, ornate clamshell pattern. The front door itself was exquisitely detailed with hand-carved bas-relief falcons surrounding a coat of arms that featured a crossed sword atop a medieval mace, all entwined with ivy. I took a second look. Geezus—the fucking door was one solid piece of wood. Probably weighed in at two hundred pounds. I ran my hand along the cool, grayish stone of the house, looked at how the windows were set, and checked the doorway. Damn, the stone on the house must have been two feet thick all the way from the ground to the roofline. I stepped back and did some mental arithmetic. It would take a shitload of C-4 to bring this place down. Yeah, they built things solid back then.

Then the big door swung open, and Fred came through, wrapped me up in his big arms, and swung me around. *"Will'kommen, lieb Richard!"*

"Fuck you, you Kraut cockbreath—" I hugged him back, then broke his grip, stepped clear and took a good look.

He'd hardly changed—just under six feet of kinetic, coiled-spring energy. Maybe a bit thicker around the middle, and grayer around the edges. But then aren't we all—except for *moi*, of course. Fred was still muscular as hell. He wore his flecken camouflage with its distinctive raindrop pattern of black, brown, sienna, gray, and OD shirt with sleeves rolled high to accentuate the definition of his biceps. His chest was massive and his neck and shoulders all showed evidence of a lot of reps on the weight pile. A brigadier's insignia wrapped around the epaulettes on his shoulders, and what I took to be the KSK's distinctive patch adorned his black beret.

I looked into his cool, gray eyes and held my hand up at

shoulder level. He grasped it like the fellow gladiator he is, a grin spreading across his rectangular face. "It's been too long, Rotten Richard," he said, shaking free of my hand and snatching me up in the bear hug once again. "Too fucking long."

He ushered us inside, gave us the pfennig tour, and then called on his senior NCO to take my guys off for lunch, followed by a quick tour of the facilities. He and I caught up in the house's huge, formal dining room, which Fred had made over into an office-slash-op center-slash great room. We sat across from each other at a small, round, ornately carved medieval table and consumed multiple liters of a local *Altbier* called Heimbacher. An adjacent serving table held a silver salver on which were piled a mound of handmade sausages, and huge round slices of hot roast pork, a big crock of red cabbage, and a covered basket holding piles of crusty, warm rolls.

I toasted him with the excellent *Altbier*. "Nice spread," I said.

His eyes crinkled. "*Ja*—rank has its privileges, Richard."

I shook my head in the affirmative. "I can see that."

"All in all," he said, "life is pretty damn good. Just about as good as it was when we spent time searching for virgins in the Virgin Islands."

"With few if any real fucking virgins to be found, eh? Even though we spent enough damn time looking for 'em."

"*Ja*—" He shook with laughter. "That was most certainly the truth." Fred pressed a hidden button somewhere on the floor. A green-uniformed steward materialized through a hidden-panel doorway and cleared the plates as we waited in silence.

Once the steward had withdrawn as silently as he'd come, Fred drained his beer, pushed his chair back from the table and rose, drew himself another from the ten-liter keg that sat atop the serving table, then turned toward me. His expression was serious. He hemmed and he hawed for some seconds, rocking back and forth on his heels as generals are sometimes prone to do. Then, finally, he spoke. "We have common problems, you and I, Richard."

"Common problems," I repeated. Now, Fred is an old friend. But my business is MY business, and so I was going to let him do the talking first, to see what he knew, and what he wanted.

"*Ja*—problems," he said again. He crossed the big room, moving toward the document safe that stood behind his desk. "As you know, KSK has"—he paused, searching for the right word—"*die Haftbarkeit*; the responsi*bility*"—he gave a bitter half-laugh—"the liability, I'm beginning to think, for counterterrorism in the area of what we call, ah, *double-vey-emm-day*—WMD; weapons of mass destruction."

"Affirmative."

"You've heard that, have you?"

"That's the RUMINT at the Pentagon."

"The Pentagon." Fred gave me a look that told me he didn't believe me. "And, *zooo?*" He waited for me to speak. I chose not to, and there was what you might call a pregnant pause.

"Richard," he said, "let's not play games. We go too far back."

He was right about that. "Okay, Fred. You say we have common problems, you and I. Suppose you tell me what they are."

"This is perhaps a good idea, Richard. We should . . ." He struggled for the translation, then gave up. "*Karten aufdekken*; show ze cards to one another." Fred turned his broad back to me. With the electronic dial of the safe shielded, he punched the combination in. The lock opened with a click. He turned the big handle that released the locking bolts, swung the thick, insulated steel door open, and retrieved a hefty file from inside. Then he reversed the procedure and locked the safe door, checking to ensure that he'd secured the locking bolts again.

He brought the file over to the table where I sat and laid it in front of me.

I reached down and flipped it open. On the left side, a thick sheaf of documents were attached. I riffled through them. There were transcripts of what must have been phone taps. There were copies of bills of lading. There were bank receipts. There were memos, spreadsheets, and letters. Then I looked at the right side of the file. Under a cover sheet, two dozen photocopied surveil-lance photographs were attached.

I flipped through the pages. I didn't recognize any of the surveilees at first. But at the bottom of the file, a few were familiar—even surprising. You want an example of surprising? Okay: the late and unlamented Prince Khaled's face stared out at me. That brought me up short.

I tapped the grainy surveillance photograph. "This is Khaled bin Abdullah."

"Ja," Fred said. "Khaled." He shook his head. "Nasty piece of work."

That was an understatement. "When was this taken?"

"Early last week, in Düsseldorf," said Fred.

So *that's* where Khaled had disappeared to. And he'd managed to get from Düsseldorf all the way to Sardinia before we'd managed to climb back on his trail.

But why the hell had Khaled put himself in jeopardy to come Düsseldorf? He already had a commitment for his American-made ADM from Heinz Hochheizer. He wasn't looking to buy any more—we knew that much from our intelligence. Then, I answered my own question when I looked at the next picture. There was Khaled again. But now he'd been joined by two men.

I recognized one of them: Franz Ulrich's scarred puss stared out into space, eyes alert, antennas up, as if he'd scented something amiss. Khaled, oblivious, was in deep conversation with another man, whose face was unfamiliar to me.

I pointed at the high-contrast black-and-white photograph. "Who's he?"

"Him? That is a man named Lothar Beck," Fred said matter-of-factly. He stared intently at me, gauging my reaction.

I kept *ein pokergesicht*—a poker face. But inside, I was shouting Bingo! Jackpot! HOO-YAH!! "Was this taken at the Silbermieze?"

"Affirmative," said Fred. Now it was his turn to *pokergesicht.* "And how might you have come to know that, Richard?"

"I'm prescient," I said.

"Richard, *die Karten aufdekken,* remember?"

157

I changed the subject. "What do you know about Franz Ulrich these days?"

Fred's expression told me that he didn't like Franz Ulrich any more than I did. "Don't try to change the subject, Richard. I want to know about the Silbermieze."

Since I was sitting with a six-inch-thick pile of Fred's top secret documents, I decided to give him a peek at my hand. I gave him a quick sit-rep about Khaled, and Heinz Hochheizer. I told him about the two ADMs we'd recovered, including all the details about the Ivans we'd waxed.

His face grew serious. "Did you say you have their finger-prints?"

"No, but I can get 'em."

"*Gut.*" Fred's fingers drummed on the table. "*Zooo,*" he said, "you were asking about Franz Ulrich."

"*Ja,*" I said. "What's the word?"

"He has friends in high places," said Fred. "Like Lothar Beck, for whom he works. And I'm told that he has some bad habits, too." A wry smile crept across Fred's face. "But then, you've seen him recently, what do you think?"

Now you know that the only time I'd seen Franz in eight years was when he drove past us at the pasture. And Fred knew about that. Now it was my turn to maintain *der pokergesicht.* But there was only one thing to ask, and I asked it straight out: "What the fuck, Fred."

"I told you, we're Germans," he said, "We work in our own mysterious ways."

I realized a couple of things at that point. One was that everything that Wink had surmised about KSK was correct. This was a shell game, and Fred was running a small, effective covert unit inside the big, gaudily patched counterterror shell.

"You've been tracking me," I said. You know I'd sensed it, right from the start of this little odyssey. But it hadn't been clear until now; until Fred had let it slip, and no doubt slip on purpose.

"To be honest, Richard, I don't mean to be critical, but you tend to leave a big fat wake behind you. You are easy to track."

I disagreed with him, something I explained to him in RUT.[45]

Fred held his hand up like a traffic cop. "Richard, Richard, it's simply a matter of looking closely. You have an American Express card, *ja?*"

"*Ja.*"

"Und *ven* you use it," he said, fumbling in one of his desk drawers, and coming up with a series of faxes that he handed to me, "I can track your movements."

Sure enough: there they were. My receipt from the Mainz Hilton. The *touristenpark* receipt. Gasoline chits. Even the meal we'd had in Bassenheim. I was . . . impressed with Fred, and pissed off at myself. It was such an obvious fucking mistake.

"Zooo . . . now we both know that you are here to deal with the problem that was caused by the Saudi terrorist I have here pictured with Franz Ulrich, and Ulrich's boss, Lothar Beck. Zooo, you are on a counterterrorism mission—just like my mission at Kommando Spezialkräfte. But it also occurs to me as I track your movements, that perhaps you are dealing with a thorny, potentially embarrassing political problem for your government, as well as trying to neutralize Khaled, which"—he gave me a wry smile—"is *alzo* not so different from my work here at Kommando Spezialkräfte."

He retrieved another sheet from his desk and handed it to me. It was a copy of the police report signed by Officer Brendel. My German isn't as good as it should be, but I know enough to pick up on the important stuff. And the important stuff was that I'd been identified as a Navy SEAL, and Brendel'd had enough doubts about what my men and I were doing in his neighborhood to put 'em down on paper.

"I also know from our time together what SEALs do, and how," Fred said. "And I know that your government has a problem with missing ADMs—" he pronounced the acronym *ah–day–emm*—"these days."

---

[45]Roguishly Unvarnished Terms

I started to protest, but Fred held up his hand like a traffic cop. "It's been in the news," he said. "And I have my own sources of information—good sources, too. So please don't insult me, Richard."

"What's your fuckin' point," I asked, a tinge of exasperation creeping into my voice. I hate to be toyed with, and Fred was fast approaching the point of toying.

To his credit, he realized it. "From the start, Berlin wanted me to use you as"—he hunted for the right word—"*das Strohmann*—the schtraw man, the schalking horse."

Oh, that was good. "You track me, keep an eye on me, and then cut in front at the last minute, grab the ADMs, and Berlin gets to create a diplomatic incident that'll give it some leverage with Washington."

"*Ja*, that was more or less the idea," Fred said, his lips pursed. He wagged his head. "Now, I know you, Richard. We have operated together, and loyalty to an old comrade in arms is a very basic loyalty, and so I am opposed to doing that, and I told Berlin my decision three days ago, while you are still in Mainz."

I was happy to hear so, and I said it.

"But Berlin still needs results," he said. "Berlin must have something—political *Kapital*—to hold over the Americans, and right now, nuclear weapons that we were never told about are as good currency as anything. For me, I don't give a damn about the weapons. The Cold War was the Cold War—and we had to be ready to do what had to be done if the Soviets invaded. You and I both know that. So I will let Berlin and Washington fight the problem of hidden weapons out between the men in the pinstriped suits and the laced-up shoes and the uncomfortable starched shirts. But this other thing: the problem of Lothar Beck and Franz Ulrich and Prince Khaled. The potential for long-term damage is real, both for you and for me."

"Not from Khaled. He's dead. I killed him."

Fred nodded. "And good riddance. But his demise doesn't stop a whole litany of problems we both have to face these days. I worry about the neo-Nazis. They're making a resurgence, you know, recruiting."

"From the skinheads?"

"Some of the time. But also from other areas of the population. There have been neo-Nazis discovered of late in the police—not a good thing, Richard. Even in the Bundeswehr, internal investigations uncovered more than a few rotten apples. Very quietly, hundreds of soldiers have been discharged in the past year alone for neo-Nazi activity. And also in the Bundeswehr, a few members of"—he struggled for the right word—"ultranationalistic paramilitary organizations."

"Like our crazy militias?"

"*Ja.*" He drummed his fingers on the table. "*Und zooo,* I did some investigating. Very quiet investigating, you understand, and I discover that some of these organizations are being funded by people close to Lothar Beck. Now, we Germans have always had what you can call fringe groups. On the left we have the Greens, who want to disband NATO and give our military secrets to anyone who asks. On the right, we have people like Beck. But now, some of these crazies, they're beginning to exert real political power. Moreover, it is hard to deal with them because the ones in charge have much clout with certain segments of the government these days."

"What do they want? A Fourth Reich, Fred?"

"Not in the old sense," he said. "But there are those who would like to see a German hegemony over Europe in the twenty-first century. But the domination would be economic at first, not *politico-militar.* The political garbage would follow." He took a huge swallow of his beer. "And then, there are those who want to do it the opposite way. People like Lothar Beck, who wants political control first, followed by economic supremacy. I read the papers. And his PR people have been in overdrive lately, Richard. Beck is pushing political domination followed by economic subjugation."

"Fred, you have the capability to go and ream Beck and his

friends new assholes. You know it. So why not just go out and kick some ass?"

"Oh, I may have been given certain capabilities—on paper. And my best operators are as good as any in the world. But there's a real concern here about using the German military in any way that might be construed as political. We may be more than fifty years post-Hitler, Richard, but we're still suffering from the aftershocks of the Nazis."

He gave me an unhappy look. Fred was stuck between *der Fels*[46] *und der* hard *Platz,* and I told him so.

He nodded in melancholy agreement. "And to make things worse, finally, I have been given the responsibility of containing terrorism directed against foreigners—including Americans, because terror against foreigners is most often perpetrated by neo-Nazi or ultranationalists."

I knew what was coming next: all the problems Fred had just explained to me were about to come to a head.

"Und zoon, I sink. And I am convinced that it is a few people like Lothar Beck—ultranationalists who hate a system that encourages free expression and democracy—who are encouraging much of this mess."

I thought of the probes against U.S. facilities John Suter had told me about. Things were beginning to make sense. "So, why not take Beck and his pals down?"

"As I said, it is not that easy, Richard. Beck is an influential man. He has a huge public relations machine that wages *Blitzkrieg* in the news media. He does billions of marks worth of business with the Ministry of Defense. He has friends in Berlin who protect him—some we know about, others are in the shadows. He has informers in the police, the military, and the intelligence apparatus. And so it becomes hard to move against someone like that if you are someone like me."

I realized now why Fred had put his unit in isolation. He was

---

[46]Rock

keeping KSK uncontaminated from what was going on in German society. It was an OPSEC procedure, just as Jim Wink had thought.

Fred looked at me intently. "There is a security problem in Germany. And I have been tasked by those at the highest level of government to fix it. And those who are causing the problem, I believe, are some of the same people who are digging out your ADMs and selling them . . . or trying to." He cracked his knuckles. "*Und zooo*," he continued, "I make a proposal. I say we act *konzertierte*—together. Like the old days."

I thought about it. "Our governments have separate agendas, Fred."

"*Ja*, that is under*schtood*." He tapped a thick index finger on the photograph of Lothar Beck, Khaled, and Franz Ulrich. "But you and I, Richard; *we* are after many of the same targets. And you are an outsider. I may be restricted, limited, constrained, when I go up against Lothar Beck. You, however—"

He took my empty beer mug, filled it, and handed it back to me. Then he refilled his own. "You are looking for those who stole your devices and want to use them against you. I must hunt down those who would hijack Germany and take it from a democracy to a totalitarian system. I invite you to join with me, Richard."

As he spoke, something hit me like *der Blitz aus heiterem Himmel.*[47] Everything goes back to the *Kuz Emeq.*

Khaled was tied in to Franz Ulrich and Lothar Beck. How that knot had come about I had no idea. But when you thought about it, and I most certainly did right now, it made a lot of sense.

I'd always assumed that Khaled's target would be somewhere in CONUS. But I'd forgotten my own SpecWar Commandment: I'd *assumed*. But it was just as possible that Khaled planned to strike against America right here in Deutschland. Indeed, if he did that, the terror would serve a dual purpose. It would further

---

[47]That's "bolt out of the blue" in German.

Khaled's anti-American program. And it would help advance Lothar Beck's objective of German destabilization.

Then it hit me with the squash-power of an old-fashioned ton o' bricks. What we were being confronted with was a modern-day configuration of an old alliance. What we had here was a new kind of Axis. But instead of an alliance of totalitarian assholes, e.g., Hitler, Mussolini, and Tojo, this new Axis brought together transnational terrorists, who allied with one another out of convenience, not politics.

Because, now that I'd stopped to ponder the nasty possibilities, I realized that Khaled's goals weren't all that different from Lothar's. Each wanted to spread chaos and disorder. That made each of them a tango. Oh, they had different goals and separate agendas, just like the German government in Berlin and my own back in Washington. But that didn't mean they couldn't work together—just like Fred and I could—to pursue a common series of targets and bring destabilization—or worse—to Europe.

And there was something else I realized about the unholy trinity in the surveillance photo, too. There was one simple fucking truth about Khaled, Lothar, and Franz. That truth was that each deserved to die.

Well, I'd already made sure Khaled rode the magic carpet to Allah's side. Now it was time for me to help Franz Ulrich and Lothar Beck get to Valhalla.

But there were some things I needed to know before I was going to commit my men to a joint operation. I drank deeply and looked probingly into my old comrade's eyes. "Look, like you said, Fred, Berlin has its own political objectives in all of this. So does Washington."

Fred's face grew somber. "I understand, Richard, and, as you know—"

I broke in. "Oh, yes, I know. Berlin wanted you to use me as a fucking sacrificial lamb in this little exercise. But frankly, Fred, you've known me long enough to realize I don't give a rusty fuck about politics or politicians, and I certainly don't give a shit whether I ever get a star on my collar. All I care about is making sure the scumbags who tried to sell these things go down, and I mean go down permanently. But you gotta understand that we're talking about killing assholes who could make trouble for you, even after they've been wasted."

I watched as Fred drank in what I was saying and pondered the unhappy consequences. You see, he was a general now. He wears stars. If things went well for him at KSK, he essentially had a limitless future in the Bundeswehr.

Like I just said, I'm a hairy-assed SEAL captain, and I know I won't ever be promoted again. I exist only to break things, kill people, and make sure the merry marauders under my command remain WARRIORS in body and in soul. I don't give a shit about wearing stars. What *I* wear is scars.

But I wear those scars with more pride than any fucking admiral with four stars on his collar, scrambled eggs on his hat— and shit for his brains.

There was what you could call a LFP—a Long, Fucking Pause. Then Fred toasted me with his mug. "I understand," he said. "And, so be it, Richard."

His face was a mask of determination, boldness, and steely resolve. "To hell with politics. To hell with bureaucracies. To hell with apparatchiks. Let's drink to making WAR—to making WAR *together.*"

ABSCHNITT ZWEI

Chapter

10

According to the maps, it looked like just about an hour's run from Bonn to Düsseldorf on the autobahn. I drove up with Boomerang in forty-two minutes, in a clandestine-ops BMW Fred had loaned to us for the duration. It was another in the big, sleek 7000 series: black, with smoked windows and a hufucking-*mong*ous engine. (I flattened Boomerang against the passenger seat when I hit 209.5 kilometers an hour in the passing lane— only to have to pull over into the "traveling" lane and slow down to a mere 170 because some asshole in a Porsche Carerra wanted to pass *moi.*)

I was TBW, which you can probably guess stands for Tired But Wired. I'd spent sixty straight hours at KSK researching our targets. I'd had the opportunity to peruse Fred's intel files and news clips. I'd used his secure phone to get hold of my old friend Wink back in the States, and my new one, John Suter, down in Stuttgart.

Wink, who lives up in the Blue Ridge in an anonymous little town called Pine Grove, drove down to his office at Langley, quietly perused the counterterrorism files, and called me back from his secure telephone with the information I needed within eight hours. John Suter scanned the Ivans' fingerprints into his desktop and E-mailed 'em to me within minutes. Fred took the printouts and galumphed down the hallway like a kid with a birthday present.

While I waited for Wink to get back to me, Boomerang, sly child that he is, had used one terminal of the big Dell server belonging to KSK's intel squirrels to tap into the DOD computer at Nuremberg, giving us access to DIA's files and a smattering of NSA intercepts. Just for good measure, Boomerang siphoned off all the commo between Patch Barracks and CINCUSNAVEUR, so I'd be able to see how bad they actually wanted our hides tacked on the wall. Let me put it to you this way: hunting licenses had been issued by Eamon the Demon, and I was designated as trophy buck.

Sixteen hours after we'd arrived at KSK, I'd assembled all the pieces of the puzzle. Twenty-eight hours of strong coffee later, I had crafted a scenario for action, based on what I'd discovered from the begged, borrowed, and stolen intel factoids and info-bits.

Now, you may ask what makes me so fucking special that I can do in just over a day and a half what none of the vaunted G-2 staff in Stuttgart, or Nuremberg (or anywhere else for that matter), has been able to do in months.

The answer lies at the real quintessence of intelligence gathering: the concept that information is the raw material out of which political power can be produced. And because political power is something that budget-intensive organizations (which obviously include all the intelligence agencies) do not want to relinquish, forgo, or sacrifice, most of 'em treat their material as wholly proprietary.

Indeed, they're like only children who won't share their toys in kindergarten. The unhappy result is that most intel is stovepiped. It's kinda like all those smokestacks you used to see in the old industrial zones before the tree-huggers outlawed smokestacks. Each existed parallel to the others. Each vented its own hot air

(Now that's an apt image, since this is intel we're talking about here, huh).

Anyway, since DIA doesn't get to see CIA's stuff, and Naval Intelligence routinely tells Army Intel to get fucked, seldom does anything get cross-checked. Male tab "A" is never allowed to be inserted in female slot "B" because the slot and the tab belong to different, and competing, Intelligence organizations.

Moi, on the other hand, is well practiced at male/female slot insertion. And so, just as my old sea daddy, the late (and much lamented) Warrior CNO named Arleigh Secrest had once taught me, I took every shard of information I'd been able to assemble, laid it out, and went over it as if it was a piece of a three-dimensional puzzle, the scope, complexity, and design of which I didn't know.

Admiral Secrest used to say that if you do this little exercise and there's even a hint of preconception in your mind, you'll screw it all up. "Dick," he'd once growled at me in that wonderful gravelly voice of his, "you have to make your mind a blank, which for you doesn't happen to be much of a task at all."

And then, he said, you treat every piece of information as if it were new. You see where it fits, and where it doesn't fit; you layer it once, twice, thrice, and more if necessary. You look for patterns. You check for coincidence and happenstance, because you know there's no such thing in the Warrior's cosmos. And when you're done (and only you will know precisely when you are done because it will feel right), you will have been able to assemble a holographic image of the problem, and you will instinctively understand precisely how to solve it.

Okay, that's the procedure. Here's a bit of what I'd been able to put together.

• Fred's material indicated a Russkie involvement. That made sense to me, because we'd waxed a bunch of Ivans at the ADM site. But it wasn't clear what that Russkie involvement was. It could be as simple as imported muscle; it could be as complex as transnational terrorism. This inquiring mind wanted to know.

• From the Nuremberg computer I discovered that No Such Agency had been tracking a series of phone calls from Düsseldorf. One of the NIQs[48] was the same as the one the dead Ivan had written on his hand. The identities of the participants were annotated only as FN1,[49] FN2, FN3, and so on. But the subject of the conversations, which were larded through with code words and other gobbledygook, led me to assume that NSA had been assigned to help track stolen ADMs. I gave myself a mental note to pass the number to Fred and have him check it.

• Another info-shard, this one from the CIA, hinted that Lothar Beck was selling dual-use equipment to the Russkies, who were reselling it to such gentle and kind sovereign states as Iraq, Iran, and Libya. Dual-use stuff, you will remember, is what can be used to make fertilizer, but in a matter of hours it also can be switched over to make chemical and biological agents. As a student of history, I recalled that just prior to World War II, Nazi Germany did much the same thing: Hitler used the Third World as his weapons lab. It appeared that Lothar Beck was doing the same thing at the dawn of the new millennium.

• Fred had been able to link Lothar to half a dozen ultranationalist organizations inside Germany. The folks at Patch Barracks, e.g., John Suter, were looking at many of the same groups as KSK, because American installations were being probed.

• Wink told me that so far as the Agency was able to find, there was no Peter Grüner in the West German government. That puzzled me. I was certain that Heinz Hochheizer had been telling me the truth when he'd described his former agent, code-named Rottweiler. Still, the Stasi was a formidable opponent during the Cold War, and maybe Heinz had been better under duress than I'd given him credit for being. Maybe "Peter Grüner" was an alias. Whatever the case, I decided to abandon my search. It was a waste of time.

---

[48]Numbers in question
[49]Foreign national

• That was all in the minus column. On the plus side, Wink had been able to determine that Lothar's contracts with the Ministries of Defense and Interior in Berlin, not to mention agreements with Germany's newly privatized telephone companies, gave him potential access to fucking boxcars full of confidential information. "This guy Lothar, he's tight with the deputy assistant underminister of defense, some asshole named Markus Richter," Wink drawled in his North Philly accent. "Richter spends a lot of time eatin' an' drinkin' onna cuff at Beck's *Schloss* in the Mosel Valley."

I asked how come Richter had blipped on Wink's radar screen, since he appeared to be nothing more than yet another civil servant in search of a free meal.

"'Cause this particular asshole spent a lot of time recently in Moscow," Wink said. "An' I mean, hey, like he goes there on his own. I mean, no official stuff, y'know? Okay, nothing wrong with that. There are some people who like to go to Mogadishu for a vacation, too. But then, this guy Richter has a five-freaking-hour meeting with the Russkie foreign minister. Not just that. Guess where they had their little tête-à-tête? The bubble. The two of 'em spent those five hours in the friggin' bubble at the foreign ministry. Five hours. No way we could get a hint of what they were talkin' about. Dick, when I hear about something like that, it just sets my teeth on edge, y'know? I mean, it was bogus."

• Boomerang broke into IntelNet, the allegedly secure computer network shared by the Departments of Defense, Justice, and State, and typed in Markus Richter's name. The LEGAT[50] in Berlin had written a cable chronicling a series of kickbacks Richter probably took, and his possible involvement with the Russian Mafiya, and Richter's ties to the German ultranationalists, including one Lothar Beck.

Our ambassador in Berlin, yet another in the State Department's never-ending supply of pocket-change-jingling, heel-

---

[50]LEGal ATtaché: resident FBI agent

rocking, pinstripe-suited, can't-cunt bureaucrats, had the cable killed because he thought it might just possibly offend someone, someplace, somewhere. But the FBI agent's damning memo was still in the system. It didn't prove anything, but it gave me another avenue to search—and it tied Beck and BeckIndustrie to the Ivans.

Boomerang and I were the tip of the spear. As soon as I'd reconned BeckIndustrie, I'd send for the rest of my men, and we'd do the sonsofbitches some real damage. And so, Boomerang and I flew up Autobahn 61, then swung east at the Mönchen-Gladbach interchange. Just past M-G, I hit heavy traffic and had to slow down (to a mere 180) as we sped Düsseldorfward, cruising across the Rheinkniebrücke into the city. Off to my right stood the huge Rhine Tower, with its big round restaurant, observation deck, and digital clock tick-tick-ticking off the seconds.

I was so intent on the tower that I almost missed what I'd really come to see. At the last second, I swung my gaze to port. There it was, right on the waterfront: the huge steel and glass skyscraper, atop which revolved a ten-meter disk. One side was a huge clock. The other bore the logo BeckIndustrie, superimposed above the same pretentious coat of arms I'd seen on the door of the Mercedes limos at the pasture.

Even though we'd all done our map homework, Boomerang still missed the turnoff for Graf-Adolf Straße.[51] That meant we were carried along by the traffic flow south of where I wanted to be by just over a klik before I could start back. And so we sat in grid-locked traffic for half an hour as we worked our way north through a series of unfamiliar one-way streets, with Boomerang squinting at the tiny print on the map on his lap, pointing one way or the other, and intoning, "I'm fucked if I know where the fuck we be, Boss Dude."

---

[51]Remember that in Kraut, the "ß" sounds like a double "s." Hence *"Straße"* is pronounced "Strasse."

But being SEALs, and therefore eloquent in the art of naviga-
tion, it didn't take long for Boomerang to finally eyeball a huge
cream and red three-sectioned trolley car that bore the number
91, and the logo HAUPTBAHNHOF. "Follow in that sucker's wake,
Boss Dude," quoth he. "I can get us where we want to go from
the train station."

And follow in das sucker's vake I did, even though before I
could, it required what in SEAL terms is known as an ill-fucking-
legal U-turn followed by a nasty series of hit-or-shit situations
mit der pedestrians.

And lo, after a mere six minutes of bustling urban pilotage, we
schtood at the intersection of Bismarck Straße[51] and Konrad
Adenauer Platz, directly in front of the wide, modern main
railroad station which, in Kraut, is what they mean when they
bark, "*Hauptbahnhof.*" "Now, we face due west," Boomerang
intoned, his narrow nose still buried in the map.

I checked the sun and turned the car accordingly, steering
carefully around a traffic cop who vas giving mit der dirty looks.
And *violà!* There it was. "Graf-Adolf Straße's right in front of us,
my shit-for-brains naviguesser."

Boomerang peered over the top of the big map, squinted, then
flashed his big, nasty grin. "*Jawohl, Herr Schwanzkopf Boß Dude.*"

A mere three of east-west traffic minutes later, we found
ourselves directly across from der Holiday Inn's green-and-white
marquee. And after one last illegal U-turn, I pulled down the
tight circular driveway and into the subterranean garage.

They gave us a big double room on the sixth floor, looking out
across Düsseldorf's skyline. Off to the starboard lay the Königs-
Allee, the long shopping street with a canal running down the
middle known as the Kö. Dead ahead was the *Altstadt,* where the
beer never stops flowing. And lying to our port, dominating
the skyline, was the huge BeckIndustrie tower, its rotating clock
ticking off the hours, minutes, and seconds. Most Düsseldorfers
checked their watches against the BeckIndustrie clock. So far as I

---

[51]Remember that in Kraut, the "ß" sounds like the double "s." Hence "Straße"
is pronounced "Strasse."

was concerned, that clock would provide the countdown until Lothar and Franz met a timely demise.

I'd given serious thought as to how I was going to approach this problem, and decided to attack things head-on. There was no need to contact Heinz Hochheizer's agent Peter Grüber, aka Rottweiler, and work our way up the food chain. We already knew who was at the top of that chain: Lothar Beck. Besides, Franz Ulrich had already run a check on me. He knew I was prowling and growling somewhere in the neighborhood, and if he knew, Lothar knew. There was no use in trying to be stealthy; no tactical advantage to playing coy.

Indeed, the best way to execute a successful mission in a situation like this one is to attain the offensive. Here is the Rogue's First Law of Warfare: attack, attack, attack. This is something basic to Warriordom. The Warrior, after all, does not give up ground. The Warrior *takes* ground. The Warrior occupies your *fucking* space and drives *you* backward; the Warrior does not retreat. The Warrior forces *you* to retreat. And what if you have set up an ambush? The Warrior will sense it, and he will counterattack with such ferocity that your attempt to defeat him will fail.

Now, the tactics I have described above can be achieved in the boardroom just as effectively as they can be on the battlefield, so there was no reason NOT to use them here, against Lothar Beck, on his home turf.

Besides, I have discovered in the past that by confronting one's opponents (and I do mean CONFRONTING them, not just meeting with them), I put them at a disadvantage, knock them off their game plan—and I prevail. And so I am a practitioner of what might be called an old-fashioned, snout-to-snout, full-tilt, boogie-aggressive, rock-and-roll Roguish disorientation process. Or, to put it in the terms first defined by Roy Henry Boehm, godfather of all SEALs, I will totally fuck the fucking fuckers. First I fuck with their minds, then I fuck with their bodies. And I know that if I am consistent, and aggressive, and properly Warriorlike, I WILL NOT FAIL.

And so, I talked myself out of a quick tour of the *Altstadt* and its breweries. Instead, I picked up the palm-sized, untraceable, Motorola cell phone Fred had given us and punched in the number Baby Huey had taken off the dead Russkie's hand. Yes, I realize that I'd forgotten to mention it to Fred. But I figured WTF: here I was, and it was a local call. And so, I tap-tap-tapped the number onto the keypad, pressed the transmit button, and waited. The phone *bring–bringged* twice. And then a voice answered. "Ulrich—"

I slapped the Motorola shut. You know as well as I do that Franz had just signed his own death sentence. But everything happens in its own good time, and now the time wasn't right (after all, this book is just a little bit more than half over, and the bad guys always get killed off last), and so I hung up without saying a word, and then I marched Boomerang *eins–zwei, eins–zwei,* to the far end of the Kö where, at the same Schadow Arcade department store the late and unlamented Russkie *bandity* had done their shopping, I bought each of us a suit, two shirts, two ties, and all the other appropriate furnishings.

An aside: the ability not to have to wait for alterations is one of the better things about some European department stores. At the biggest of the chains, whether you are in Paris (Galeries Lafayette), London (Marks & Spencer), or Düsseldorf (Schenks), trousers come presized by short, medium, and long inseam, and if you're not too concerned about how the cuffs drape, you can walk in and ten minutes later emerge ready to do trendy beeziness.

Another aside: maneuvering Boomerang all the way down the just-under-half-mile-long Kö was not easy. The Kö is one of the most fashionable shopping streets in all of the world. From Hermés to Gucci, Fendi, Bally, and Joop, there are stores. The chocolates go from fifty to seventy-five dollars a pound. The women are much more expensive than that. And the women who shop there tend to wear very short skirts and have great legs and outstanding tits, so walking gets difficult when your companion keeps smacking into lampposts, telephone booths, and other sundry obstacles because he is disfuckingtracted by all the beautiful *fräuleins.*

Asides finished, I selected a couple of boss Boss suits for us. A slate gray double-breasted for me (a mere nineteen hundred bucks), and a sixteen-hundred-dollar fawn-colored single-breasted model for Boomerang's extralong frame. And while we tried them on, I made small-sprechen mit der salesman, a loquacious, amiable chap inappropriately named Fred. I mentioned I was here because ten of my friends had recently bought Boss suits just like the one I was wearing.

He said he remembered my "pals." His expression told me that he hadn't liked them very much.

"A little loud, aren't they?" I asked.

He retained his salesman's demeanor. "Oh, the Russians are not so bad," Fred said, rolling his eyes. "The Japanese are far worse. At least these gentlemen had some manners. They waited in line for the changing booths. The Japanese . . ." He threw his arms into the air. "Impossible."

I kept him talking. It didn't take long to discover that the Ivans had been shepherded by a Kraut, who'd paid for their clothes in cash. "A German with a scar?" I wild-guessed, my index finger tracing a jagged line across my cheek.

"*Ja, mit ein Narbe,*" Fred nodded, his finger mirroring mine on his own cheek.

Talked out, we double-timed back to the hotel, changed, and hit the street. This time we stayed away from the Kö, walking north until we reached Karl Platz, then veering off toward the Rhine, past Saint Maxim's church, took a hard left onto the Berger Allee and a hard right onto Thomas Straße.

The main entrance to BeckIndustrie lay directly ahead. One could drive in by going past a primer-colored security gatehouse occupied by three blue-blazered young men. I took a closer look at the narrow glass panes and knew from their color and thickness that we were talkin' class III-A bulletproof material here. Attached to the back side of the gatehouse was a red-and-white-striped pole on an electric arm, the same kind of barrier that they use at toll plazas, which won't even stop a bicyclist. Beyond it, however, I picked out a heavy, hydraulically operated solid steel, with eight feet of concrete footing, antiterrorist barrier, the type they are currently using on Capitol Hill back in Washington to prevent truck bombs from accessing the Capitol's East Front Plaza and blowing up the House of Representatives and the Senate.

BeckIndustrie itself was an architectural wonder. The thirty-plus floors of glass and steel sat atop a series of ten-foot-in-diameter, twenty-five-foot-high, pilings. The only access was by going up three narrow escalators leading to three separate entry doorways on the first floor. The right- and left-hand escalators were currently shut down by thick wire-mesh grates at the top end, so that access could be shut down in a matter of seconds.

Visitors were shuttled to the center escalator, where a large sign said EINFAHRT, which is not an invitation to break wind once, but actually means *entry*. Boomerang and I rode up, walked three meters to a thick smoked glass door, and pulled it open.

I'd expected to find the sort of big, two-story foyer one normally sees in office buildings. But this was almost like the kind of cramped portcullis you see in medieval castles. We were trapped inside a narrow passageway. Behind us, I noted that the doors had electronic locks—and they'd clicked. Ahead was a one-at-a-time full-length revolving door made of steel. The door could be made to work by running an entry card through an electronic reader. For the rest of us, there was a fish-eye camera lens secured behind thick glass and steel plate. Below it was a button that activated a buzzer, or a speaker. Above was a sign that read: ANMELDUNG, which is not a quaint way of saying horse, cow, or pig shit, but means *announcement* in German.

When asked, I announce. No shit of any kind. I pressed the button. "Hello."

An almost unintelligible voice, muffled by the muted metallic timbre of the small, weather-proof speaker, came back at me. *"Bitte?"*

Why waste time? "Dick Marcinko to see Lothar Beck and Franz Ulrich."

There was a click, and then silence. We waited one minute, then two, then three. Finally, I heard a soft electronic whine, and saw that that camera lens was moving. There was another wait. This one was less than two minutes. The disembodied voice mangled something that I took to be, "Please pass through the gate one at a time," and then I heard an electronic click.

I pushed, giving the revolving door a hefty shove. It didn't react to my pressure (considerable), which told me the whole apparatus was hydraulically controlled. I pushed again, and the door slowly moved forward a few inches. At the precise instant when I was trapped halfway, the hydraulic mechanism shut down, and it became impossible to move. After a two-second pause, there was another click, I pushed once again, the door moved, and I emerged into a low-ceilinged foyer about eight feet wide by twelve feet long, with a single steel door at the far end. Here, the walls were carpeted, and the floor was marble. A long sofa sat along one wall, a chrome and glass coffee table piled with magazines centered in front of it. Six chairs (two ranks of three), sat adjacent to the low table. The whole place was very . . . Spartan. Twelve seconds later, Boomerang's lean frame emerged. His eyes told me he'd seen the same thing I had, which is that the revolving door was built so as to be able to trap someone inside.

The steel door opened, and two young men in blue blazers, gray trousers, white shirts, maroon ties, and sensible black shoes emerged. They were wearing photo IDs on chains around their necks and carrying handheld metal detectors. The first of the security guards, whose blazer bore a metal name tag on its pocket, looked at me as if he knew me and said, *"Guten Tag,* Captain Marcinko."

I eyeballed his nameplate. *"Guten Tag,* Otto." I allowed Otto to run his detector over my body. It worked well enough, because it picked up the Heckler & Koch P7-M13 that sat in an inside-the-pants holster just behind my wallet pocket, as well as the Spyderco folder clipped to my right-hand trouser pocket. As he gave me the once-over, his compadre, whose nameplate bore the legend FRITZ, worked Boomerang stem to stern.

"You must give me the weapons, Captain," Otto said politely. "They are not allowed in the offices."

I snapped back at him in rapid German. "But of course. And you will give everything back to me when we leave. That is correct, is it not, Otto?"

"*Jawohl,*" he said, snapping to attention.

I handed over my pistol and knife. Boomerang surrendered his long, serrated Benchmark folder and the stainless little Sig Sauer P-230 he invariably carries as a backup weapon. Otto and Fritz had missed a total of five other weapons on our bodies, but I wasn't about to clue them in. Instead, we followed as Fritz ran his ID card through an electronic reader and we were passed through the door at the end of the foyer, and into BeckIndustrie's headquarters building itself.

It was like being transported into another world. We emerged into an expansive, three-story atrium, all faced in black, green-veined marble. There were three banks of elevators to our left, and another three to our right. Sunlight cascaded through the lightly tinted windows, reflecting off the marble walls and floor. It was all very impressive.

We took one of the starboard-side elevators, whooshing up to the twenty-eighth floor—the very top of the building, judging from the push buttons. There, the elevator went *bing*, the doors opened, and we emerged into a lushly carpeted receiving area. An attractive young woman in a short-skirted black wool Chanel suit, and the klunky, high-heeled, inch-and-a-half-thick soled shoes so fashionable in Europe today, was waiting as the elevator doors opened. She nodded in the general direction of Otto and Fritz, dismissing them with a haughty glance. "Follow me, please, Captain Marcinko," she said with the impersonal tone of an automaton. She turned on her well-turned four-inch heel without waiting for an answer and started down the wide corridor, her pantyhose making an interesting sound as she walked. Boomerang, who was drooling, and I, who was not, followed in her Chanel No. 5 wake.

First of all, fantasies are for the young. More to the point, I had Warrior work to do. I perused as we padded behind on thick, floral-patterned carpet, the kind of stuff that sells for a hundred bucks a square yard, my feet probing for pressure sensors in the thick wool. Hey, since Ms. Chanel was obviously too preoccupied to keep an eye on me, I'd use the time to do a little target assessing. For example, there had been two video cameras by the elevators, but I saw none as we started down the corridor.

I kept scanning as we walked. This was obviously the floor where all the top executives lived. The doors to the offices (or suites; I couldn't tell) were costly wood, not utilitarian metal. There wasn't a cubicle to be seen. Even the secretaries had expensive, Queen Anne desks, with inlaid wood and leather tops. Their chairs were leather, too. And except for one trio of scuff-shoed, baggy-pants, four-eyed dweebs in blue lab coats mit plastic penholders waiting while a nicely turned-out secretary scanned an credit type I.D. card and pulled open the only door on the floor marked BUTRITT VERBOTTEN,[52] all the men were dressed in the kinds of thirty-five-hundred-dollar slash four-grand Italian and English–cut suits whose jacket cuff buttons actually buttoned and unbuttoned; suits you don't buy off the rack and wear *sans* alterations.

I had to hand it to Lothar Beck—or perhaps more accurately to the people who worked for him. The security at BeckIndustrie was pretty good. For example, as we proceeded to wherever we were going I noted that each of the office (or suite) doors was equipped with an electronic card-reader. To get in, you slid an ID card into a reader. Once it had been scanned and you'd been

---

[52]No entry

cleared, the door unlocked, you pulled it open, and *voilà*, you're in.

They're using the same kind of thing at the White House, the State Department, and the Pentagon these days. But only on the perimeters. Here, every fucking door was wired, which made it possible for Lothar Beck to track every single employee as he/she/it moved around the building. I knew he could even get printouts that told him who was inside the HQ at any specific time, as well as when they'd come, and where they'd gone. Even the *Herren* and *Damen* bathroom doors had scanners. Oh, yeah, it was all very anal retentive. But then, this after all was Germany. And this place, in which Lothar worked? Think of it as LODAR: Land Of Der Anal Retentive.

That was all on the one hand. On the other hand, these scanner devices are not impenetrable. In fact, by the time we'd been quickmarched down the corridor, I'd already figured out how to bypass the fucking things. I especially wanted to get a peek behind the doorway with the "No Entry" sign, where the out-of-place dweebs had scurried.

And guess what? By the time we'd arrived in front of a huge set of wrought iron banded, double-thick wood doors, each of which was emblazoned with the omnipresent BeckIndustrie crest in red, black, and gilt, I'd worked out a doable scenario for getting *moi* and one of my boys back into this place after-hours for a quiet little sneak-and-peek.

But that would be later. This was now, and now we were being ushered into the holy of holies. The doors parted, Ms. Chanel departed, her thighs still making come-hither sounds, and we found ourselves in a huge, pentagon-shaped antechamber, with a vaulted ceiling supported by hand-carved stone ribs formed into the shapes of stars, or perhaps flower petals. Who cared: it was like going back in time about five hundred years.

I experienced an incredible, contrapuntal feeling when I juxtaposed the five-walled room in which we were standing against the austere, futuristic glass and steel building, and the contemporary design of the executive hallway. This room had been designed as the reception hall of a fucking castle. It was so authentic it was breathtaking.

Directly to my left, a pair of narrow, faux arched windows sat ten feet apart. The windows were framed by weathered beams and held ornate stained glass that pictured scenes from the Crusades. Between the windows was an inlaid wood-framed display table. Under its glass top, a dozen seventeenth- and eighteenth-century pistols were displayed atop green striated velvet. There were bulky matchlocks and elegant flintlocks, displayed muzzle to muzzle with Teutonic preciseness. In the middle of the display, two sets of ornately decorated eighteenth-century dueling flintlocks sat in opulent burl walnut boxes trimmed in gold.

I turned away from the weapons to drink in the rest of the room. Ornately carved and delicately painted wood rosettes were positioned at the centers of each of the ceiling vaults. Each wall of the pentagon was painted in a different and wonderful pattern. Mounted against the near right-hand wall, which was finished in a floral pattern, were two complete armor suits, mirror polished and bearing the broad-bladed swords common to the late fourteenth and early fifteenth century. The adjacent wall was painted with coats of arms, each set into a trompe l'oeil "frame" of gold and faux wood. The far left-hand wall was covered by a well-restored tapestry depicting the founding of Rome; the wall next to it repeated the window design, but with different stained glass images, and a display of long-barreled muskets and blunderbusses.

There were tables thick with gilt and scrollwork; curved, heavy wood chairs; pikes and halberds displayed in racks. There were crossbows. It was a true Warrior's haven, full of the instruments of death that mean so much of life to me.

Then, with an ominous creak, a thick, hidden doorway so cunningly cut into the coat of arms wall that I hadn't been able to pick it out, swung out toward us. Lothar Beck emerged, strode in, and broke the mood.

184

Chapter

11

LOTHAR WAS AN IMPOSING MAN—AT FIRST GLANCE. HE STOOD SIX feet at least, maybe six one. And, although I hadn't noted it in the clip file photos I'd perused with Fred, his body was dwarfed by a huge, out-of-proportion head with the kind of exaggerated features common to TV anchormen or movie stars. He had a wide, platycephalic forehead accentuated by thick dark hair combed straight back, massive, bushy, wild-haired black eyebrows in the Brezhnev style, and a broad nose that looked as if he'd been run into one or more walls at one point in his life. His lips were thick, like Mick Jagger's. He had the kind of faux-tan complexion rich folks get from their own private tanning beds.

"I hope you like my . . . foyer," he said in gently accented English. "It is an exact duplicate of my favorite antechamber at my country house. The weapons, there and here, are all real, and all operational." He grinned, and paused to wipe a tear of spittle from the left-side corner of his mouth. "There is no use in owning a nonfunctional weapon, Captain, don't you agree?"

I said nothing, and he continued his monologue. "I like to come here from time to time and meditate with my weapons; it is a way to interrupt the rigors of the day's stress and renew my spiritual side."

Those words struck me as odd, because Lothar Beck didn't seem to be the sort of man who'd have a spiritual side. He didn't look meditative, either, but rather sepulchral. He was dressed all in black. Black Bally boots, soft, black flannel trousers, a black-on-black jacquard silk short-point collared shirt buttoned all the way to his throat, and a black double-breasted cashmere jacket with narrow, peaked lapels. On his left wrist was a discreet solid gold Rolex Oyster Datejust. Cinched around his right was a gold chain fashioned of miniature links in the shape of those used in horse bridles. He wore tortoise-enamel framed, round-lensed glasses with rose-tinted lenses. The ensemble was cosmopolitan, urbane, sophisticated. It was absolutely *bec-fin*[53] perfect.

But *he* wasn't perfect—or even close. There was a distinct warped angularity to his frame, almost as if he had forgotten to take the hanger out of his jacket before he'd put it on. And then I realized that the lopsided motherfucker was as hunchbacked as Quasimodo, which was something none of the surveillance photos had indicated, and Fred (who says German generals don't have a sense of humor?) hadn't bothered to tell me.

I grabbed a second look at this Hunched Beck of Düsseldorf, because there was more: the sole of Lothar's left Bally boot was three times the thickness of the right Bally's sole. But that didn't cause him any problems. He lurched across the expanse of the room at flank speed, like some caricaturing, dinner-theater actor playing Richard the Third, his platform sole stridently smacking the off-beat on the uncovered stone flooring, tha-*wump*, tha-*wump*, tha-*wump*. His right arm was outstretched, as if to take my hand.

"*Kapitän* Marcinko," he trolled.

Olé. I fooled him with a *pase* that would have done credit to Manolete, then sidestepped, careful not to bump into Boomer-

---

[53]That's how they say up-to-the-minute fashionable in Paris.

ang, and let Lothar's speed and bulk carry him past me. He stopped, whirled like a dervish, and headed back in my direction: tha-*wump*, tha-*wump*, tha-*wump*.

This time I stopped him by stepping in front of him. He came to a Krameresque halt, and flailed his shoulder in my direction, his right hand still flapping, although I now realized it was flapping quite uselessly. He slapped the right hand down with his left, and gave me a TVE[54] that was much less appreciated than the one I'd received from First Sergeant M. Walsh. Then, satisfied about whatever the fuck he had to be satisfied about, he offered me his south paw.

I took his hand and gave it a healthy squeeze. There's a nasty technique to this: you grab the asshole's fingers on the joints just north of the metacarpus before he can get a firm grip on your hand, and by doing so you can cause excruciating pain if you squeeze h–a–r–d, which is exactly what I planned to do.

But the sumbitch was too fast for me. He gave me a rose-tinted grin, those thick, Jaggeresque lips parting to display perfectly capped & bonded teeth. He gripped my hand squarely, and then he squoze back, exerting almost as many pounds per square centimeter as I am capable of. He caused me enough pain to make me impressed.

Here is a truth, folks: people with disabilities, be they physical or mental, often work hard to overcome their limitations, by stretching in new directions. And Lothar Beck was obviously one of those types.

Well, good for him. And better for me. I am an EEO kind of Rogue, which means I treat everyone alike: i.e., JUST LIKE SHIT. And that's the way I was going to deal with Lothar. I didn't think of him as handicapped, crippled, or (as one might legally be forced to say in these politically correct days), spinally challenged. I'd deal with him just as if he was any other scumbag asshole cockbreath tango.

---

[54]Thorough Visual Exam, remember?

And so, I looked Lothar in the eye, grinned a Roguish grin, used the pain he was causing me as an energy multiplier, and then slowly, inexorably, began to apply my own gentle pressure on his sinistral appendage until he wrestled it back from my hand, tears of discomfort forming in the corners of his eyes.

My fun was interrupted by a vaguely familiar odor and a long-unheard voice, and a, "Long time no see, Dickie. When was it? That joint operation in the North Sea just before they removed you from command and threw you in jail, *ja?*"

I turned to see Franz Ulrich, his arms crossed, standing in the doorway, a smirk on his face. Now I remembered the smell, too: he wore a sweet, citrusy aftershave called 4711. A lot of it, too. The stuff was expensive. It was made in Köln, the city where (obviously) cologne originated.

Franz was backed up by two bulked-up hulks in badly tailored but expensive Italian suits. They weren't wearing an 4711. No— the only fragrance these guys were sporting was Touch of Garlic. Obvious *bandity.* Now I knew at least part of Lothar's Russkie connection: imported muscle.

Peculiar, isn't it, that someone like Lothar, who bitched so publicly about foreign workers, had hired his own foreign workers—these Mafiyosi *baklany*[55]—as his personal goons. See, assholes like Lothar don't believe the rules apply to them. And believe me, it's not just assholes like Lothar who have this sort of blind spot. Our congressmen and senators do, too. Too many of 'em believe that rules you and I have to live by, just don't apply to them.

But I don't have time to talk about that now. No—instead, I focused on Franz. Nothing had changed. He was still the same mean-looking motherfucker I'd known when he worked for Ricky Wegener at GSG-9. He wore his close-cropped steel gray hair in a kind of *I, Claudius* cut. His oblong, cruel face bore a

---

[55]That's Ivan slang for *punks.*

nasty, jagged zipper of a scar that ran down the right cheek and disappeared into the soft collar of his cashmere turtleneck. He liked to brag that it was a dueling scar from his days at university.

I knew better: Franz had never gone to university, and the scar was the souvenir of a back-street brawl over a ragged-looking hooker in some Third, Fourth, or Fifth-World country. He shifted his weight on booted feet. The soft, pleated black slacks and double-breasted jacket were absolute *doppelgängers*[56] for what his boss was wearing.

He pulled his shooting glasses off so he could give me the full-bore steel grays.

I took a good look. Guess what? Franz was obviously dilated to see me. I say that because if his pupils had been a camera lens, they would have been set at f-1.2. That kind of glassy, Victorian, Wilde-eyed look comes with drug use. Cocaine, to be precise. And even if he hadn't been coked up, I wasn't about to be impressed by his version of the killer stare. After all, I'd seen Franz operate. Oh, he could hop and pop and shoot and loot and snoop and poop; he could double-tap and fast-rope and do all that other operator shit. But he was careless, which had gotten some of his men killed. And he was impetuous, which meant he acted without thinking, a fatal flaw in SpecWar. He was arrogant, too. He was also needlessly cruel. Franz Ulrich took too much pleasure in inflicting pain.

My philosophy toward the enemy has always been like my old friend and comrade in arms Charlie Beckwith's: kill 'em all and let God sort it out. Franz Ulrich liked to kneecap 'em, or gut-shoot 'em and let 'em flop around for a while before he finished 'em off. It always seemed like a waste of ammunition to me.

"Long time no see, Dickie," Franz Ulrich said once again, his voice betraying impatience. "You vill tell me just how long has it been. The North Sea, *ja?"*

---

[56]Doubles

I told you he was arrogant. I didn't even bother turning in his direction. "I heard you the first time, asshole," I said over my shoulder.

I finished causing discomfort to Lothar's hand, then raised my hand and gave Franz the finger. "Last time I laid eyes on you wasn't more than four days ago, you worthless Kraut cockbreath. You know it, and I know it, so why bother to lie?"

The expression that spread over his nasty puss gave me everything I needed. That had always been another of Franz's problems: he was a lousy poker player.

He balled his fists and took three short steps in my direction. "Fuck you—"

I closed the distance between us before he could do any more. I took him by the lapels, slammed him up against me, and kneed him in the balls hard enough to drive them up into his throat. That ersatz killer's gaze vanished fast enough as his eyes crossed and the breath went out of him.

GBO (you can read that either as garlic body odor or goonish bandity one, either one works) clenched his fists and stepped in to protect his boss. I took his throat in my right hand, squeezed just enough to make his larynx hurt, and lifted straight up. I was smiling into his eyes as I brought his toes half an inch off the floor.

He finally brought his arms up in the classic counterplay to break my hold. But he'd telegraphed the move. So I simply released him, throwing him backward into the nicely painted wall.

His head went *bonk*, and he went down. Which was good, because Bandity Two finally realized that something was amiss. Except that Boomerang was on him like stink on shit. I never saw Boomerang's hands move. But the Ivan dropped like a sack of goatshit.

Franzie finally found his voice. He falsetto'd "You bastard" at me. Then he pushed off and came full tilt at me, fists clenched, head down, shoulders straight.

Which is exactly what I wanted him to do, because I knew that cocaine fucks with your timing, and from the look of him, his timing was completely FUBARed.

I sidestepped, waited, and chopped at his thick neck as he went past me. The blow dropped him to his knees. I wrenched his right arm up and behind in a painful come-along, which brought him back onto his tippy-toes. From inside my trouser waistband, I retrieved one of the two Mad Dog Micro Flyer composite blades I was carrying, both of which Otto and his metal detector had missed. I put the tip of the little knife far enough into Franz's neck to draw blood, and close enough to his carotid artery to cause him anxiety.

"Y'know, Franz," I said, making sure the asshole was in considerable discomfort, "I didn't like you very much when you worked for Ricky Wegener." I pricked him another eighth of an inch with the knife. "And guess what? I don't like you any better now than I did then."

I could tell from Lothar's expression that he realized this little encounter wasn't producing the kind of social intercourse he'd anticipated. Which is precisely the reaction I wanted from him. I wanted the son of a bitch off balance.

But then Lothar did something else totally unexpected. He smiled that big, toothy grin at me and started flapping the useless dexter again. "If that is how you feel, you simply must come with me, *Kapitän*," he said, as if nothing had just happened. "We will talk, you and I, and I can see now this is not the place."

He waved the pair of wounded *byki*[57] off; the Ivans withdrew in silence, casting worse-than-dirty looks at Boomerang and me as they did. Lothar gave Boomerang what passed for an aristocratic glance. "You, the tall one with the fast hands," he leered, his tongue running across his lower lip, *"Kommen Sie,* too."

Boomerang giggled. You and I know that when Boomerang giggles, he wants to kill something. But Lothar didn't know that,

---

[57]Russkie slang for *bodyguards*

RICHARD MARCINKO and JOHN WEISMAN

and from his expression, he'd put Boomerang's reaction down to nervousness. You could see it in the disdainful expression on his face. *B–A–D* mistake.

I brought Franz around and took the knife out of his neck. The sonofabitch actually tried to suckerpunch me. But like I said he's a bad poker player, and he gave the move away.

I stepped up, grappled him close, chopped his clavicle, then as he collapsed I kneed him in the balls again for good measure. I spun him around and released him in a rude bum's rush, sending him crashing across the room into the display case of antique pistols. Franz went face first into the glass, and if it hadn't been reinforced, burglar-proof stuff, he would have had a new scar or two to show off. He dribbled off the table frame and collapsed onto the floor.

"I don't deal with *byki* assholes like him," I said, indicating the ex-commando, who lay sprawled facedown and groaning. I plucked the little knife off the floor, slid it back into its sheath, and waited to see what Lothar had to say.

Except he didn't say anything. He just stood there, his hands on his hips, looking at the damage I'd just wrought. "You shall deal with me—and only me," Lothar finally said, a new and dangerous edge creeping into his tone. He galumphed over to Franz, bent over, took the creep's face in his hands, and slapped him rudely until Franz opened his eyes. Lothar held on to Franz's chin and machine-gunned a bunch of idiomatic German I didn't understand at him, speaking so fast that globs of spittle spewed off Franz's scarred cheek.

Oh, Franzie didn't like that at all. In fact, the look he gave his *Boß*[58] was not to be believed. But finally, he shook his head, and grunted something I took to be a reasonable facsimile of "*Jawohl*," pulled himself to his feet, and goose-stepped out the door we'd entered, his right hand pressed to his nicked and bloodied neck.

---

[58]It pronounces like *boss.*

Lothar's eyes followed Franz as he exited. Then he turned in my direction. "*Zooo*," Lothar said, looking into my eyes. "Now, we are alone. Follow, please."

I stepped aside to let Lothar lurch and lunge back the way he'd come. I followed, with Boomerang playing rear security. We walked down a short dark anonymous corridor that ended at a simple steel door.

Lothar pushed it open, and we emerged from the Middle Ages into the twenty-first century.

Lothar's office was all black and chrome. His desk, which commanded a view encompassing the river from the Rhein-brücke to the *Altstadt*, sat atop a skeletal textured steel platform. The ceiling was twenty feet high, and the window was a huge expanse of steel-reinforced glass. Facing the desk were four Mies van der Rohe chairs. A separate conversation pit was placed at the far end of the forty-by-forty-foot expanse.

"Do you like it?" Lothar pressed a button on the intercom that sat atop his desk and *rat-a-tat-tatted* German into it. "I bought the building because it has the best view in Düsseldorf. What do you think?"

It was moderately impressive and I told him so.

"*Ja*." He laughed, his big head moving up and down, his perfect horse's teeth gleaming. "'Moderately impressive.' Oh, that is good, *Kapitän*" He indicated that we should be seated.

I remained standing. This was combat. I don't fight sitting down. More to the point, I don't like to fight on my enemy's terms. I am an unconventional warrior. That means I don't take the field in neat ranks, and march to battle with pipers piping and drummers beating tattoos. I hit you where you don't expect to be hit. I am your worst nightmare. I come out of the dark and slit your throat.

But Lothar didn't know that. Or, if he did, he wasn't letting on. "Franz told me you were *ein Original*," he said. "I didn't realize how right he was."

I said nothing but waited Lothar out, allowing him the opportunity to hang himself with his own words.

My reasoning behind this course of action lies with Roy Henry Boehm, the godfather of all SEALs. As a young man, Roy was a devoted student of oriental philosophy. Tao, Shinto, Buddhism, Confucianism—he mastered them all. He scrutinized Islam. He read the Bhagavad Gita. And from all those studies, he extracted a series of precepts that became the philosophical nucleus of his Warriordom.

I remember one night a long time ago when Roy and I were sitting on adjoining bar stools, staring into space. Roy slapped his bottle back onto the bar, swiveled toward, me and growled, "Krishna says, 'A man can accomplish much by doing, but a man can also accomplish much by not doing.'" Then he turned away, retrieved his beer, took a long pull, and was silent for the next hour and a half.

Now, this kind of talk was confusing to me, especially as I was only a bare-balled tadpole in those days. I didn't want to listen to any oriental bullshit—even from Roy. I was impatient. I wanted to break things and kill people. I wanted endless supplies of hot pussy and cold beer. And so, Roy's words bounced off my young and empty head, broke into a million pieces, and were lost in the sawdust on the floor. And he, inscrutable bodhisattva that he was, didn't bother to clarify things.

Now, however, in my maturity, I realize what he was getting at. What Roy was saying is that timing is everything. Sometimes, you must act—now. And sometimes, you must wait. Impetuosity, he was telling me, is a bad quality in the Warrior. Decisiveness, i.e., knowing when to act, is one of the qualities that differentiate the true Warrior from the rest of mankind.

But Lothar didn't know that. Lothar never had the pleasure and honor to study at the gnarled flippers of Roy Henry Boehm. And so, he looked at me, and thinking I was tongue-tied, he continued talking.

"*Ein Original,*" he repeated. And then he launched into a monologue that I won't bother repeating here, except to say that it was quite unfuckingbelievable in its complexity and range.

He quoted Heine and Schiller, Frederick the Great and Bismarck, all to buttress an argument that went, more or less, as follows: It was Germany's destiny, Lothar argued, to become the dominant economic and political force in twenty-first-century Europe. But to do so, he insisted, the weak, spineless current coalition government would have to be changed; altered; moved to the right, just the way the Deutsche Volks Union,[59] which Lothar called a "patriotic front," but I know from my research to be a bunch of radical right-wingers, had already accomplished that goal in Saxony-Anhalt, a federal state in what used to be called East Germany.

It was his own destiny, Lothar said, to help Germany achieve these goals. He had made no secret of his ambitions, and so he felt no reticence in explaining them to me. And he would brook no interference—either from me, or from my government—in the fulfillment of this God-given objective. "I will do what I have to do," he said. "Whatever it takes." He paused. "You know, *Kapitän*," he said, "before what you call the Second World War, Hitler made a pact with the devil—the devil being Stalin—because that was what it took to achieve his goal."

He grinned malevolently. "Hitler didn't go far enough," he said. "That was his mistake."

He turned away from me for an instant, to peer out over the Düsseldorf skyline. When he turned back, the deranged, sociopathic expression on his face cannot be described, other than to say it was truly frightening, even to me.

"I will not make Hitler's mistake," Lothar Beck said. "I will go as far as I have to, to achieve my goals."

Lothar's lips rolled back from those perfectly capped teeth in the beatific smile of the truly loony. "Full schtopp, *Kapitän*," he said. "End of schtory."

As Roy told me, a man can accomplish much by not doing. But a man can also accomplish much by doing. And now it was time to do.

---

[59]German People's Party

I advanced on Lothar, moving around the desk and getting up close and personal to him. He backed away. That told me he didn't like to be squeezed. Some societies, Latinos for example, don't mind your getting real close to 'em. They love in-your-face *fuertes abrazos.*[60] Germans don't. Krauts like to maintain a sensible, Teutonic distance between you and them. So I put my schnozz in Lothar's puss, and my body up against his, and gave him my best War Face and said: "Tell you what, Lothar, maybe someday, if you're still alive, we can go someplace and have a couple of bottles of schnapps, and a steak or two, and talk things over before I kill you. Maybe if the food's good and we have enough to drink, I'll think you're less of a crazy, dangerous, pencil-dicked, pus-nutted, shit-eating, motherfucking cocksucker than I do right now. But it ain't likely."

Lothar backed away, muttering nonsense to himself as he scampered (tha-*whomp*, tha-*whomp*) up the textured steel stairs to put some precious distance (and his big, polished Bauhaus desk) between us. I saw as he reached his left hand under the shiny black surface of the desk as if to push something.

Boomerang's eyes caught the move, too. He turned and headed for the main office door, located at the far end of the big glass-walled room, dragging one of the Mies chairs as he went.

Lothar's face took on a more-than-slightly fretful expression.

"Not to worry," I said. "He's just going to make sure that we can talk without anybody interrupting."

I advanced up the stairway toward Lothar, who was now fumbling in one of his desk drawers.

Lothar was quick, but I was quicker. I caught the edge of the drawer and slammed it shut, catching his left hand in the process. He screamed in pain and spasmed, his useless starboard paw flailing wildly, flapping air in my vague direction. I slapped it down, then jerked his left hand out of the drawer, reached

---

[60]Big, strong hugs

inside, and extracted a shiny, blue pre–World War II Walther PPK.

"Nice piece." I dropped the mag, racked the slide back, and caught the extracted round in my hand. I took the rest of the bullets out of the magazine, then fieldstripped the pistol, put the spring in my pocket, rendering the weapon useless, and tossed it back in pieces at Lothar. They landed bouncie-bouncie on his desk, putting a couple of small dings in the perfect finish. Lothar's expression turned from shock to hatred. Yeah, I'd read him like a fucking primer. He was the kind of anal-retentive Kraut who couldn't stand his expensive furniture being marred.

I saw that Boomerang had wedged the chair under the door handle. The kid threw me an upturned thumb, and I returned the gesture.

Down at Boomerang's end of the office I heard pounding from the outside. Lothar's security people were trying to get in. Well, it would take 'em a few minutes. Meanwhile, I'd come here to shake this asshole from his hump to his toes. So it was time for what we few warrior's left in Naval Special Warfare call the Rogue's no-shitter.

"Okay, Lothar," I said, pushing him down into the leather and steel chair behind his now not-so-perfect desk. "You said your piece. I think you deserve to know what I've got in store for you. So you know what I'm gonna do? I'm gonna *aufdekken die Karten* for you, just like you did for me."

He glared up at me, his tongue running lizardlike over his thick lips.

"Here's *Karte eins.* You're a fucking terrorist," I said, staring down at his suntanned face.

He started to say something. I leaned down and smacked him, *whap-whap,* just like you used to see Erich Von Stroheim do to captured pilots when he played the monocled, nasty Nazi officer in all those World War II movies.

"*Karte eins.* You're a fucking terrorist," I repeated. "Now, here's *Karte zwei.* You're in bed with Khaled bin Abdullah."

Oh, the look he have me was ineffable. Pure hatred is an understatement.

Whap–whap. "*Karte drei,*" I said, "is that you're involved in selling nukes."

He started to rise in protest. I put him back in his big chair with another backhanded double swat.

"*Karte vier,*" I continued, "is that you're mixed up with the Ivans. Just like Ribbentrop, who Hitler sent to see Stalin before the Second World War, you've made a deal with the Russkies. Except that you made your deal with the Mafiya, not the government. Like you said, you didn't think Hitler went far enough. So you took it one step further."

I paused and stared down at his face. Oh, Lothar was good, He tried to control what was going on inside him, but he couldn't. So I continued my little monologue. *Whap–whap.* "And *Karte fünf?*" I paused rhetorically. "*Karte fünf* is that you're a dead man."

I paused just long enough for Lothar to start to say something. When I saw that he was about to speak, I cut him off with another double slap. "Those are my *Karten,*" I said. "And they look like a royal flush to me. Now, just in case you didn't know it, a royal flush is an unbeatable hand, Lothar. Which means, I'm gonna flush you . . . royally."

I gave Boomerang a high sign, he removed the chair from under the door handle, and a bunch of blue-blazered Keystone Krauts burst into the office, burbling in German and looking for their boss.

I smiled in Lothar's direction and cocked my right index finger at him the way General Crocker does at me.

"See you in hell, Lothar," I said. I dropped Lothar's ammunition into the palm of the closest Kraut security dweeb, whose expression told me he was obviously confused about the situation. "No problem, bub—we're about to leave," I said. "But I'd like our hardware back, first."

Chapter

12

CONFLICT ALWAYS MAKES ME HUNGRY AND THIRSTY. AND SO, THE preliminaries over, and little, with the exception of obtaining certain equipment, to be done until the *Glom*,[61] it was time for a world-class lunch. I led Boomerang past banks and municipal buildings, working our way north on a course roughly parallel to the Rhine, until we came to the crowded, narrow streets of the *Altstadt*. We stopped at the first *Bierstube* we came to and downed a couple of glasses of Schlösser Alt, brewed in the cellar and drawn from a ten-liter keg. Then we threaded our way through the knots of tourists, students, and drinkers until we stood before the smoky, thick plate glass front window of an Argentine steakhouse called El Lazo.

It had been perhaps two, maybe three years since I'd been here. But Señor Francisco, who owns the place, never forgets a French braid. "*Conjo*, Señor, Ricardo!" He stood in the narrow doorway, hands on hips, and laughed at the very sight of me.

---

[61]*Evening*

Then he ran into the cobblestoned street and gave me a tight *abrazo*.

I hugged the roly-poly little man back. "So, Herr *Franceesko*— is the best wine still Spanish and the best beef still Argentine?"

"Jawohl, mein Frigatenkapitän!" Francisco ran a manicured finger along the top of his little mustache, stood aside, and beckoned for us to come inside with a courtly little bow. "Everything is just as you remember it, except that the wine is more potent and the *bief* is better."

I pushed Boomerang through the cheesy beaded curtain and down a narrow entry corridor. The interior of the restaurant was as dim as ever. I took a quick look around and was delighted to see that indeed, nothing had changed in the couple of years since I'd last been in the place. Dusty pots of wilted plastic flowers still hung suspended over the booths. Worn faux pinto horsehide still covered the bar stools. On the whitewashed, rough-finished plaster walls, the same mélange of hand-hewn wood ox yokes, hand-wrought branding irons, and heavy, fringed leather saddlebags was still mounted haphazardly in a disorganized, *primitivo* paean to the Gaucho gestalt. The huge open-faced, wood-fired *parrilla*[62] where Francisco cooked thick *churrasco*, *lomito*,[63] T-bones, and garlic-enhanced Argentine *chorizo*[64] sat right in the restaurant's big, greasy-opaque plate-glass front window.

Was it fancy? Absofuckinglutely not. But ever since I was a beemish boy in Northern New Joyzey and I worked behind Old Man Gussi's lunch counter short-order-cooking and sizing up the pussy, I've made it my business to discover and hang out in joints like this one. Whether it's Casa Italia, Mama Mascalzone's family-style trattoria in Huntington Beach, California, where I

---

[62]That's Spanish for *grill*.
[63]These are Argentine steaks.
[64]*Sausages*

used to play with my beloved shooters from Red Cell, or Café Augustin, the French *boîte* owned by *mes amis* Henri and Collette LeClerc, they all provide me with a home away from home, and some of the best cooking this side of my own kitchen back at Rogue Manor. Not to mention the fact that the folks who own 'em don't mind if every once in a while the boys and I get a tad rambunctious and break a dish (or a customer) or two. After all, we always help clean up the mess—and we pay our bar tab every night.

I was delighted to see Boomerang's look of hungry anticipation. So far as I am concerned, the world is divided into two categories of people. There are those who, like me, appreciate eating in greasy spoons, old-fashioned diners where the waitresses sport tattoos, and trattorias where the food's served family style at long tables and in big bowls. And there are those who believe they're not eatin' unless they're *bluten*.[65] Boomerang, I am happy to report, is from the former category, not the latter.

And so, we piled into the rearmost booth, three yards from the closest customers, and polished off the two small glasses of Francisco's dry sherry that precede every meal at the Lazo. He followed the sherry with two *churrascos*—rump steaks, a kilo each, seared to black-and-blue perfection, served alongside piles of freshly made *frites*, and carafes of the restaurant's rich, red *Rioja riserva*, while Boomerang and I discussed our options for the near future.

So far as I was concerned, there was only one option: a foray into BeckIndustrie. Now, perhaps we'd find something of great value to us that would help crack this nasty chain of events right open. And maybe we'd come up dry. But either way, the op would serve the real purpose of forcing Lothar Beck and Franz Ulrich to act precipitously.

---

[65]Kraut for "paying through the nose."

We have been over this ground before, but it is significant stuff. Besides, like the old chiefs used to tell me, "You will see this material again, tadpole."

One of the most basic lessons of warfare, something that has been taught from the days of Sun Tzu, Tai Li'ang, General Chi, and all the other masters of Warriordom, is that by provoking your enemy to act before he is ready, you will carry the day. Sure, it's common sense. Sure it's simple. But believe me, simple has worked for thousands of years, and it works today.

Here is simple: we break into BeckIndustrie. We leave just enough of a telltale track so that Lothar knows he's been burgled.

And what does he do? He comes after *moi*. Who is set up in a Froggish ambush, waiting for *lui*. Result? Nasty, blood-and-guts confrontation, followed by Roguish denouement, followed by no more Lothar.

Now, I mentioned a while ago that I'd seen enough to know I could get into Lothar Beck's impregnable fortress of a headquarters, and once inside, break into the office where those dweebs were working. And I hear you asking me how I planned to do that.

My answer is that I'm not a "tell" kind of guy, I'm a "show" kind of guy. And so, you (along with the dweeb editor), will have to wait and see. I will tell you, however, that before the steaks were served, I was on the secure cellular to Fred, because he was going to have to provide me with one basic element of the night's work.

When he heard where I was calling from, he gave me a memorable demonstration of compound-complex German idioms all revolving around the *F*-word. I can report that even though he's a general these days, Fred still swears like a sergeant-major.

By the time we'd finished our flan, and downed two cups each of Francisco's perfect espresso, Fred had called back to say that he'd arranged for what I needed, and that I could have it all. *If*, that is, he could join in the evening's fun and games.

Guess what: since we couldn't play without his equipment, I was in no position to refuse his request. And to be frank, I was delighted to see that despite the fancy estate HQ, the stewards serving lunch, and all the antique china, he hadn't lost his taste for down-and-dirty operations. It told me that Fred still followed the two-word definition of leadership written in blood many years ago by Roy Boehm. Those two words are: *Follow me.*

2045. We assembled in my room and I drew up the evening's assignments. Actually, things were going to be pretty KISS-simple tonight. Since Fred wanted to play, he and I would make the entry and do the sneak-and-peek. The rest of the team—all my guys and an equal number of Fred's operators—would stake out the BeckIndustrie headquarters, to make sure we weren't going to be surprised. Of course, if we *were* surprised, we'd be dog meat, since all the available backup would be outside, right? But what's life without a challenge.

2100. I grabbed a twelve-minute combat nap followed by a two-minute cold shower. I got dressed, and packed what I was going to need in a small black, ballistic nylon duffel. Then I met Fred, dressed in soft Adidas CT boots, black jeans, and turtleneck, and sporting a black civvy beret, in the Holiday Inn's compact lobby, and we jumped into one of his big undercover Beemers. This one was a slate gray 7000 series job piloted by a six-foot, T-shirt-and-leather-clad skinhead driver named Wolf.

Wolf der Kraut kame komplete mit multiple earrings, a blue "cut on dotted line" tattoo around the base of his neck, a second tattoo—a triple strand of barbed wire—wound around his right bicep. The kid had the sort of aggressive, wiry build that reminded me of an NFL linebacker, and a set of big, even, white teeth that gave his face a kind of squared-off, Schwarzeneggerian look. Wolf obviously didn't bother saluting or doing anything else that might identify him as military. In fact, he called Fred, "*Boß*," and me "Sir," spelled *cur*, and, a big grin on his wide linebacker's face, he ushered us into the Beemer's leather backseat, made sure we were properly buckled in (it's a moving violation not to use your seat belt in Germany even if you're a clandestine shoot-and-looter), retrieved an HK P7M13 from the glove compartment and slid it under his thigh, checked his side mirrors, then squealed and wheeled into the knot of late rush-hour traffic, which in Düsseldorf can go as late as 2100, on Graf-Adolf Straße.

After four minutes of urban driving that told me Wolf was NASCAR[66] qualified, he turned onto Autobahn 46, which ran roughly east/west, just south of the city center. He high-speed merged (that's a fucking understatement), sped east for five or six kliks, then veered south (the sign said MONHEIM), onto another well-lit six-lane highway—this one labeled 58. After he'd completed the maneuver, he half-swiveled his head and looked at me, smiling. "I learned to drive like this in the United States," he said. "At BSR, in Vest Virginia. There, I trained mit your Delta Force."

"You see, Richard, I still believe in cross-training," Fred said.

"I'm glad you have the budget for it," I said. This fucking administration has cut the heart and lungs out of cross-training budgets. They're spending more fucking money on recycling than they are on making sure the men and women in uniform can do their jobs.

Fred grunted and fiddled with a fingernail, finally biting it down to where he wanted it. Off to our left, I could barely make out a huge, dark expanse of green in the darkness.

I poked my thumb to port. "What's that?"

"The *Stadtwald*," Fred said without looking. "The city forest of Düsseldorf. We're headed just south of the main park for the pickup."

As I nodded, Wolf suddenly kicked the speed past 235 kliks an hour, fast even for a German driver and fast enough to flatten Fred and me against the rear seat. Fred strained against his seat belt, leaned forward, and machine-gunned some Kraut at the

[66]NASty CAR.

back of the driver's head. The kid nodded, and we increased our speed another fifteen kilometers an hour.

"Problem?"

"Wolf says we're being followed. Two cars, minimum. Maybe three, maybe four. They picked us up back on Graf-Adolf Straße."

I swiveled and looked through the rear window. I saw a bunch of headlights. Nothing looked out of the ordinary. "Are you sure?"

Wolf's close-cropped head bobbed up and down. "*Ja*, Herr Dickie. They are moving well, weaving in and out, und changing the headlamps. But they are *mit uns*, all the way."

I slid across the seat so I could release the rear seatback and get to the stash of automatic weapons I knew lay in the trunk. "How do you want to handle 'em?"

Fred put a restraining hand on my chest. "Let them follow," he said. "We can deal with them later."

I would have taken 'em out ASAP. But it was Fred's car.

From the rear-view mirror, Wolf's eyes smiled at me. He'd read my expression. "Don't worry, Herr Dickie, we'll have fun with them—just like I learn at BSR." He pulled back into the passing lane and floored the accelerator. I turned and looked. Now I saw them—at least two of 'em, as two pair of halogen headlamps veered into the hammer lane behind us one after the other.

Wolf took us back to 235, stayed in the hammer lane, and flew south on the 58.

Fred had obviously thought about what I'd suggested, because he used the back of his hand to shoo me to my left. As I scuttled port, he pressed on the button release just behind the center of the backseat, and as the seatback sprang forward, he reached behind and into the trunk. He emerged with one, then another loaded HK MP5-PDW, followed by two pair of MP5 magazines in tandem clips. He handed me one of the weapons, and one of the double mags. "Just in case, Richard."

Fred latched the seatback, pointed the submachine gun's short muzzle to the floor, dropped the mag out of his PDW, checked the bolt to ensure that there was a round in the chamber, then slapped the mag home. I did the same.

Wolf jerked his thumb backward, at what looked like a quartet of rubber plugs set across the rear window. "You"—he fought for the word, then found it and used his free hand to give it the right body English—"*punch*, ja? The *Stöpsel mit* the barrel, Herr Dickie," he said, "and zen . . . you shoot."

The fucking car even had windshield gunports. The Krauts think of everything, don't they?

Fred barked something at Wolf, who nodded, and retrieved a set of night-vision glasses from the glove compartment. He handed them over his shoulder to the general, who turned and focused the NVGs on the pursuing vehicles, then called out a series of letters and numbers, which Wolf scribbled on a pad sitting on the console by his right knee.[67] "We'll track the license later," Fred said. "Meanwhile, I want to get to the rendezvous without furser incident." He machine-gunned another series of orders.

Wolf's *Kopf* went up and down in agreement. "*Jawohl, Boß.*" He slowed the Beemer by fifty kliks an hour and allowed our pursuers to gain on us. Then, as we came alongside a solid line of double-trailer trucks in the slow lane, Wolf slipped from the passing lane into the center one, edging behind a big Mercedes. Then he put pedal to metal and threaded a pucker factor 100 needle between a gasoline tanker and a tandem freight hauler, careened onto the wide asphalt shoulder, hit the accelerator again, and we sped onto a single-lane off ramp that wound in a

---

[67]The editor wants me to remind you that, being Krauts and therefore meticulous, Fred and Wolf have STS Model 2722 LP/NVGs (Low Profile Night Vision Goggles), which transition in milliseconds from low light to brightly lit environments. This state-of-the-art see-through capability (that's what it's called) allows the NVGs to scan past headlights and other bright light sources without blinding the wearer.

half-horseshoe from the unlighted *Autobahn* onto a wide suburban boulevard.

Fred checked our six. I did, too. It was clean—for the moment,
anyway. If Herr Murphy was around this evening, he was riding
with the competition.

There was a traffic light at the bottom of the off ramp, but Wolf
paid no attention to it. He slowed, checked *rechts*, checked *links*,
then hit the gas and drove toward an unlighted overpass,
heading east. As we accelerated, he killed the Beemer's lights.

As we emerged from the underpass, I could see the reflection
of headlights coming off the *Autobahn* half a klik behind us. Then
I lost 'em as Wolf veered sharply right, off onto a narrow,
residential street, turned right, then left onto a two-way street
and followed a single set of tram tracks for two blocks. He flicked
the car's lights on again, then drifted the big car left onto a well-
lit, four-lane thoroughfare. I caught a glimpse of street sign and
read, BAUMBERGER STR. If that means something to you, write me
in care of the publisher, because it didn't mean shit to me. I had
no idea where we were or where the fuck we were going.

Until, that is, we followed the tram tracks back under the
Autobahn. There, Wolf turned right, then immediately swerved
left, accelerated up the on ramp, and we were back on the 58
Autobahn—heading north this time.

The kid drove carefully, checking our six as he went. He pulled
over and stopped. Waited as traffic sped past. Drove another klik
or so and stopped again, repeating the exercise. Finally, Wolf
pronounced us clean. At that point he retrieved a cell phone from
somewhere under his seat, punched the send button, and
handed the phone—and the license plate number—to Fred.

Fred read the sequence off to someone, machine-gunned some
more Kraut, and hung up. "I'll have everything waiting when we
get back," he said confidently.

Wolf took the phone back as he steered one-handed, exiting
the *Autobahn* adjacent to the *Stadtwald*. We looked out at the mass
of dark evergreens bordering the forest. He followed the tree line

for about fifty seconds, until he came to a set of barriers manned by half a dozen police officers. He flashed his lights thrice, steered around them, and turned onto a gravel path that curved gently to our right.

We drove slowly along the path perhaps another half klik until the trees parted, and I saw what looked like a wide expanse of grassy field dead ahead.

"Für football," Fred said as the car's headlights picked up a series of low goal cages set into the grass.

Beyond the tubular cages, I could make out three choppers: two Pave Lows with all their running lights on idled noisily, their long air-refueling nozzles protruding from the right sides of their fuselage. Beyond them, a pair of MH-6 NOTAR (no tail rotor) stealth-fitted Little Birds sat, rocking in the big choppers' prop wash. We pulled onto the soft turf of the soccer field, drove past the Pave Lows, and pulled up behind the starboard-side Little Bird.

With the enthusiastic impatience of a child, Fred folded his beret, stuck it in the seat pocket, popped his seat belt release, jumped out of the car, and pounded on the black skin of the MH-6 with the meat of his hand as if he were pummeling his favorite stuffed toy. "Now begins the real fun, *ja?"* He shouted over the noise, his eyes smiling with anticipation.

Chapter

13

2222. FRED AND I PULLED ON DARK NOMEX COVERALLS. I EX-
changed my sneakers for a pair of Adidas SpecOps boots just like
his, retrieved the web gear I'd brought with me from the ballistic
nylon bag sitting between my feet in the Beemer, cinched it
around the coveralls, played with the straps until they sat just
right. Then I affixed the sheath for my big, Mad Dog Taiho3
serrated assault knife to my left shoulder strap, hanging it upside
down. I secured the rigid Kydex sheath with rubber straps and
black duct tape.

Fred looked at the thick, seven-inch long, quarter-inch-thick,
chisel-pointed weapon. "Isn't that *kleine* overkill, Richard?
Whose throat are you planning to slit tonight, eh?"

I shoved the blade home, then yanked it out twice to make
sure I could get to it if I needed to. "Nobody's—I hope. But every
time I fucking go out without this, I end up needing it."

The knife affixed, I took the other tools I'd be needing tonight,
fitted them in their pouches, Velcro'd everything shut, then did a
handstand to make sure it was all secure. Yes, friends, I've been
at the end of my rope (literally), and watched as Herr Murphy
slid down alongside me, plucked open my equipment pouches,

and dropped my tools into the void, leaving me with very little more than my big Marcinko dick to work with. And believe me, assault with a friendly weapon may be fun, but it's not very effective in wartime.

My gear all secured and double-checked out, I clambered over the coiled fast-rope and climbed aboard the Little Bird, slipped a headset and mike on, strapped myself into the rear right-hand seat, and pulled on my thick fast-roping gloves. The Pave Lows had already lifted off, their huge jet turbines deafening as they rose and disappeared, outboard lights flashing smaller and smaller, into the opaque sky.

Fred climbed aboard and looked at me all ready to go. He grinned, and slapped the release buckle on my shoulder straps. *"Nein,"* he said. *"Nicht* fast-rope."

He pulled me out onto the turf, handed me a stabo harness—a rig similar to SEAL SPIE gear, and a lightweight helmet with integral wireless communications package installed. I slipped the stabo straps around my waist and legs, brought it up, and cinched it tight under my arms. Fred took the end of the starboard side coiled length of black rope sitting on the chopper's deck and hooked it onto my stabo harness. He went around to the port side of the MH-6 and did the same for himself. Then he flicked a switch on the underside of his helmet visor, and motioned for me to do the same.

I found the switch. Immediately, his voice filled my brain. "Is okay to talk," Fred reverbed in my ears. He tapped the helmet and mike with his finger. *"Alles geschützt*—we're secure."

"Good." I patted my stabo harness. "Good thinking."

"Ja," Fred said. "The chopper will spend less time than if we fast-roped, and make the extraction easier, too."

If you believe that extracting, i.e., grabbing at the end of a one-inch rope from a moving chopper, affixing your stabo harness to the eye of the loop, and then lifting off without smashing into something hard or sharp is easy, I still have this bridge in

Brooklyn to sell you. But I knew that Fred was talking in relative terms. And in relative terms, he was right on the old pfennig.

Fred's knuckles rapped on the chopper skin impatiently. He was standing opposite me, looking through the open hatch of the chopper. "*Achtung, Achtung!* Are you ready, Richard?"

I tightened the strap on my ballistic goggles and gave him a double thumbs-up. "Let's do it."

"Max, Werner—*Los!*" Fred gave the pilots an upturned thumb, and the nose of the MH-6 tilted forward. It lifted off gently, taking the ropes with it, until we, too, rose off the grass, dangling at the end of our twenty-five meters of rope.

Just as my feet cleared the ground, the Little Bird banked sharply, and thrust into the darkness. The soccer field disappeared beneath my feet. The air grew cold as we rose to a thousand feet or so and swung in a wide arc to the south and east, the lights of downtown Düsseldorf disappearing in our wake.

Fred and I hung suspended, facing each other, twisting Nixon-like in the wind. Below, the lights on the *Autobahn* grew smaller. As we continued in the wide circle, I began to see the orangy, sodium lights of downtown Düsseldorf off in the distance.

Fred checked his wrist. He must have been wearing an altimeter, because his voice said, "Two thousand meters," in my ears. I wagged my head. He gestured earthward with a gloved hand. "Mnhm—Monheim," he said, somewhat incoherently, his voice affected by the wind and our speed.

I nodded. I let myself swing free, threw my arms wide, and let the wind take me where it would. There is very little that feels so wonderful as flying through the air, whether it's the adrenaline surge of a HALO insertion, or the slow descent from 35,000 feet on a HAHO glide.

I could make out the Pave Lows ahead of us, flying with all their lights full-tilt boogie.

What I'd suggested to Fred was an old-fashioned, KISS diversion insertion. I'd last practiced the technique in Central America when I ran SEAL Team Six, and we'd been assigned to take down an FMLN headquarters in a little town called Chinameca, in the rough-country shadow of the San Miguel volcano, just north and east of Usulután Province.

What's that you're saying? I can't hear you with all this ambient noise. Oh—you're saying that American forces, including SEALs, were forbidden by Congress from engaging the enemy in El Salvador. You're right. But we fucking did it anyway, and with the tacit approval of the White House, no less.

Remember, this took place during the Reagan administration, which was proactive, when it came to terrorists, and prodemocracy, when it came to Communist-run insurrections. Unlike the fellow who sits in the White House today, Ronald Reagan was a real commander in chief.

Anyway, Six was called in because the Salvadorans had security leaks, and snatching rebel comandantes had become a virtual impossibility for them. So, every once in a while, if the target was important enough, a gringo SpecOps unit would covertly slip in country and help 'em out. And this was one of those times.

We knew that the FMLN asshole, war-named Comandante Lobo, real name Francisco Zamora, was basing out of the Chinameca. The Salvadorans—even the elite commando brigade known as *Los Panteros*—had gone there half a dozen times, to no avail. The FMs would hear 'em coming, and Lobo would hightail it outta Dodge. Now it would be up to us. But I knew that if we staged a frontal assault, we'd give ourselves away— and he'd skip yet again. Let me interject here that this guy Lobo was responsible for the summary execution of two American Agency for International Development (AID) civilians, whose chopper had crash-landed in Usulután Province. And as if that weren't enough (it certainly put him on my death list), he had also seeded Usulután's rough countryside with between twenty thousand and fifty thousand land mines. Given the density of the population there, that meant he was responsible for blowing the feet off hundreds, if not thousands, of innocent kids as a way of inspiring terror and keeping folks in their villages, making it impossible to farm and eke out a living in the hardscrabble Salvadoran countryside.

Now, though kids may die in wartime, the Warrior does not target innocents as a way of doing his bloody work. If a twelve-year-old is holding an AK-47, or a grenade, or any other form of weapon, I will blow the little motherfucker away and think nothing of it. But I won't go planting land mines to blow kids' feet off just to terrorize their parents. Not in this life at least.

As you can probably imagine, I wanted Lobo's murdering ass in a body bag. The Salvadorans, however, wanted him alive, as a propaganda victory. To snag him, what we did was something the SEALs in Vietnam often did when they went in to make a snatch: they created a diversion.

I lifted out of Dam Neck, Virginia, with a squad of Six's plank-owners: Sergeant Ahas, Pooster the Rooster, Baby Rich, Carlosito, Gold Dust Larry, Gold Dust Frank, and Horseface. We RON'd[68] in San Salvador three days at a safe house, clandestinely gathering intel and poring over maps.

Our evenings were spent at the home of the MILGRP commander, an Army O-5 named Eduardo Rodriguez. Eduardo, a Bay of Pigs survivor, was one of the 2506 Brigade veterans who'd volunteered for the Army back when John F. Kennedy was still president. He had *cojónes* as big as bowling balls, which meant he managed to bring us in country unbeknownst to the ambassador, a pinstriped, pocket-change-jingling, heel-rocking, equivocating, C_2 fudge-cutter named Reginald something-or-other the Fourth. Anyway, our intel work completed, Colonel Rodriguez slipped us onto Ilopango Air Base, which sits at the eastern edge of the capital.

In those days, Ilopango was commanded by General Juan Bustillo, one of the toughest COs I've ever come across. This guy was ramrod straight. A Warrior. And he was lean and he was

---

[68]Remained OverNight.

mean when it came to dealing with the FMLN. He showed them no fucking mercy. He wasn't easy on his troops, either. He demanded results. Just the week before we'd arrived, Rodriguez told us, a company of Bustillo's paratroopers had hesitated before moving up a certain hill in San Vicente Province because the intel reports said it might have been seeded with land mines.

The general choppered to the scene, fired the company commander on the spot, and personally led his troopers up the fucking ridge. That is called LEADERSHIP.

Anyway, Bustillo gave us one of his two MH-6 NOTAR stealth choppers (we called them Hughes 500s in those days). Then Colonel Rodriguez personally flew us in, navigating a tough, terrain-hugging course that put us down at zero dark hundred close to the edge of the volcano, slightly southwest of the Salvadoran Army airfield at Quelepa.

We humped around the perimeter of the volcano, making our way through scrub brush and boulders, moving all night. We covered sixteen miles in nine hours. You say it doesn't sound like a lot of ground to cover? Fuck you—you've never had to hump through hostile countryside carrying fifty pounds of equipment and no maps of the minefields.

We made it to our ambush site, about half a mile due west of the village by 0650. Then we dug in, camouflaged our position, and waited until the critters settled back into their normal routines. Our site was situated along the one well-used escape path we'd found, using infrared photographs, courtesy of Christians In Action. Six hours after we'd settled in, I sent a series of secure radio signals. Colonel Rodriguez commandeered a regulation Salvadoran Army Huey at Ilopango. The Huey, you'll recall, is the loudest motherfucking chopper we had in El Salvador, and the Salvadoran Hueys were rougher than most, because they were used day-in, day-out.

Anyway, Colonel Eduardo flew in at full throttle. You could hear him coming for fucking miles. Then he made a series of touch-and-go landings in the scrubby countryside directly to the east of Chinameca. From the village—hell, from our ambush position, too—it sounded just like a fucking company of Salvadoran regulars were about to hit.

Lobo and his people heard all the noise, and of course, he ran west, which was precisely where I and my squad of shoot-and-looters was waiting. We bagged him up—literally—and then Pooster the Rooster popped purple smoke. That was the signal Colonel Rodriguez was waiting for. He came in and hot-zone landed, we tossed Lobo into the Huey, jumped aboard, scarpered the scene, and flew direct to the reinforced roof of the Estado Major, El Salvador's military intel staff HQ, where we touched down three-quarters of an hour later.

I was still hearing the outraged howls from Reggie the ambassador and tasting the cold beers we'd had at Lou Rodriguez's place that night when Fred's voice broke into my reveries.

"Richard—target dead ahead," Fred barked.

I looked up and focused. The Pave Lows were flying about half a mile apart. We were slightly behind 'em, and perhaps five hundred feet lower. We flew the contour of the river, veered off slightly over the harbor area, and descended slowly as we came over the *Rheinkniebrücke.*

As the Pave Lows veered west, our MH-6 dropped like a stone, descending precipitously. Just north of the bridge, it swung us wide as it turned east, then north, and skimmed the tall building roofs.

And then, the huge BeckIndustrie clock was dead ahead, and the chopper swung me left, then right, in a rough-and-tumble slalom as the air currents running past the skyscrapers affected the pilot's moves.

"Ready?" Fred's voice came strong in my ears.

"Ready," I shouted into the lip mike. My heart was racing now, as it always does before I make a blind jump.

It was not an easy move. Fred and the pilot had to coordinate, bringing us down gently over the roof, then making the drop at the precise instant the big, round clock that turned 360 degrees once a minute allowed the MH-6's rotors to clear the big, electric disk.

And then it was too late for anxiety, apprehension, misgivings, or concern: we were over the perimeter of BeckIndustrie's roof. The pilot flared. The Little Bird dropped, and I hit the deck hard enough to drive me to my knees. My ankle gave way and I went down in a heap, dragged across the rooftop.

But I still managed to hit the quick release. The rope flew away, I tucked, and rolled, then scrambled to my feet. Fuck me—eight feet away, Fred was being towed facedown by his stabo harness. His quick release hadn't disengaged. I launched myself at him as he pulled away from me, managed a shoestring tackle and flailed at the release turnbuckle on his chest.

The fucking thing wouldn't give. The line was getting tauter by the millisecond. Worse, we were being dragged across the roof, close enough to the brink to make me very, very nervous. I raised my eyes long enough to look ahead. Shit: another ten yards and we'd either snag on a huge, parabolic fucking antenna, which would break, or tangle us up and bring the chopper down on top of us, or we'd catch on an air vent with the same nasty result. Oh fuck oh shit oh doom on Dickie. This was not a good situation.

I snagged the Taiho, jerked it free, and slashed blindly at the rope just above Fred's head. The line separated and the chopper pulled away into the night just as the fucking clock came around.

I rolled onto my side and tried not to hyperventilate. I didn't succeed, so I just lay where I was until my pulse slowed to 160 or so. Then I pulled myself onto my feet. Fred was already checking himself over for dings. He watched silently as I slid the Taiho back into its sheath. I gave him a look that told him I knew what he was thinking.

2242. It was time to go play break & enter. First, I checked for cameras. They had 'em at each corner of the roof. But they were pointed out and down, just as they should be, in order to catch folks trying to climb the sides of the building. Companies don't as a rule protect their headquarters buildings from airborne assault.

We worked our way around the roofline until we came to the air shaft vents directly above Lothar Beck's office suite. Then I paced, working my way backward in my mind's eye, along the entry passage, and the huge medieval foyer, until we were more or less atop the corridor where I'd seen the dweebs in lab coats.

There were three air shafts, each about two feet by two feet, sitting more or less where I thought we should make entry. We checked 'em over to make sure they weren't booby-trapped. They appeared to be all right. I tried lifting the cover on the first one. It wouldn't budge. Either it was secured from the inside, or it was frozen shut. I tried the next. It, too, wouldn't move. Neither would the last of the trio. So much for easy. I extracted the Taiho, put the wedge blade under the edge of the vent, and ran the knife around the perimeter. I felt the cover give slightly. I exerted more pressure and pried as I worked the heavy blade around. The cover seal broke and the cover moved slightly. I pried it up an inch or so. Fred reached over and shone his minilight up so we could take a look and see if it was wired.

He ran the light around the underside lip of the vent cap. "*Nicht*," he said. "Go ahead, Richard."

"*Jawohl, mein general.*" I finished running the thick-wedge blade around the perimeter of the cap, then stowed the blade and pulled the cap off.

I took a minilight out of my web gear and shone it downward. This shaft wasn't gonna do us any good. It ran straight down, farther than I could see. Fred stuck his nose over the edge, peered, and shook his head. We replaced the cap and tried the next one over.

2253. *Zack* (which is how they say "Bingo" in Düsseldorf). This cap opened up onto one of BeckIndustrie's main electrical shafts. Fred uncoiled the knotted climbing rope he'd packed in his CQC vest, we rigged it off a plumbing vent, double-secured it to the base of the big, turning clock, and dropped over the side. Three wiggles, two shimmies, and one skinned knee later, I slithered through an air return, and lowered myself onto a convenient commode in one of the BeckIndustrie twenty-eighth-floor bathrooms.

I stepped off the seat cover and helped Fred down onto the

black-and-white tile floor. We made our way to the door. I turned
the lever handle and—nothing happened. I tried again. Nada.
The fucking thing was locked from the outside.

Of course it was. First of all, I'd forgotten that we hadn't been
alone on the Little Bird tonight. Herr Murphy had stowed away,
too. Second, *you* will recall, even though *I* suffer from CRS
Syndrome,[69] that each of the doors on the corridor had electronic
locks that had to be scanned from the outside. And outside was
where the hinges were, too. Obviously, these were smart locks.
Once you'd scanned your way inside, the door would let you out.
But if, like us, you'd dropped out of an air shaft, you were stuck
inside. Moreover, I couldn't pull the hinge pins from in here.

So much for "easy." I jerked my thumb at the air return. Fred
didn't look happy.

2307. I slit the silicon seal at the back of an air return, removed
it, stowed it in the air shaft, and then slithered down and into the
corridor I'd traveled earlier in the day. Fred followed. We
scanned the area. The lights were still on, but so far as I could
tell, no one was home. I'd checked earlier for TV cameras, and as
I recalled, there were none here. Even so, we moved cautiously,
wary of pressure plates in the wall-to-wall, and other nasty
devices that could bring the blazered security men scrambling.

I pointed out the doorway I wanted to breech. I gestured at the
hinges, then extracted a nail punch and a small rubber mallet
from my vest. This was going to be easy: punch out the hinges,
slide the door to one side, and we'd be inside, all without
disturbing the electronic lock.

I moved to the top hinge. Fred put a restraining hand on my
shoulder before I could tap it out.

He examined the hinge. He slid his minilight out and examined each one of the door hinges closely, then turned to me, a
somber expression on his face. "Electric," he whispered, pointing at the middle one.

---

[69]Can't Remember Shit

218

I followed his eyes. Sure enough, I made out the thin strands of wire that ran along the inside of the middle hinge.

Fred said, "You cut—*Alles kaput.*"

He was right. We were fucked.

I hunkered down, my back to the wall, and bemoaned my fate. Once again, I was being fucked by Herr Murphy, and there was nothing I could do about it.

It is at times like this, friends, when the spirit of Roy Boehm comes to me and gives Froggish inspiration. Roy and Mister Murphy engaged in mortal combat for thirty-some years, and Roy never gave in, not once.

And so, as I sat there, Roy's advice: "attack, attack, attack, you asshole," rang in my ears. I pulled myself to my feet.

It was so fucking obvious I don't know why I hadn't thought of it immediately. I went to the first secretary's desk I saw. Pried open the big center drawer in the Queen Anne desk and pillaged it. I came up empty, and so I shifted to the next one, and did the same thing. Fred looked at me quizzically.

Until I retrieved what I'd been looking for.

I waved the magnetic card at Fred. *"Das Schlüssel,"* I said, proudly remembering my German language training. I took the credit card-sized piece of plastic and ran it through the scanner.

Nothing happened. I tried again. Nothing happened again. It occurred to me at that moment that my well-laid plan was being fucked by Herr Murphy more than normal, even for me.

Fuck me? No: fuck *Murphy.* Because you know as well as I do that as I walked past the "No entry" door this very afternoon, a secretary was using a card to open its magnetic lock for those silly-looking dweebs in blue lab coats.

Okay: I simply had the wrong card. I proceeded to the next desk and pried away, leaving a nasty laceration in the dark wood in my eagerness. You might think I was careless. No, friends— that's the little telltale sign I was talking about leaving for Lothar that I'd been snooping around. I'd just started to rifle the drawer when a faint but nonetheless audible *bing* blipped on my radar screen.

Simultaneously, Franz's voice erupted inside my head. *"Richard, Richard—das security ist gelandet."*

I have said it before, and at the risk of being a redundant Rogue I will say it again. I am going to kill Mister Murphy when I finally meet the no-good cocksucker face-to-face.

I eased the drawer shut, hoping that the gouge I'd made on the drawer edge wouldn't show up in any cursory examination. I wanted it discovered, all right—but not yet; not *now*.

We had no place to go. The fucking desks had no privacy panels—they were Queen Anne, remember, and they looked more like library tables than office desks.

The men's room was thirty feet down the corridor, in the opposite direction from the way security was approaching. I pointed toward the bathroom, waved the card in my hand at Fred, and we scampered toward the doorway marked HERREN. I reached it first, ran the card through the reader, and pulled at the door.

Nothing happened. I scanned it again. Bupkis. Nada.

Fred grabbed the fucking thing and tried, too. He had as much luck as I'd had.

Okay, what about some EEO? I took the card and scanned the door that read DAMEN, then pulled. The fucking thing opened. We slipped inside, found two stalls in the darkness, climbed aboard the toilets, and waited, breathing shallowly in the darkness.

I felt stupid hunkering there, like some fucking kid playing a goddam game, wearing the fucking helmet and all the fucking gear, listening to me breathing and Fred breathing, and I told him so.

"Sei still!" he hissed back at me. "Be quiet."

2323. We waited. And waited. And waited. This was getting old fast. Moreover, it is uncomfortable hunkering atop a fucking toilet seat, wearing thirty or so pounds of assault gear. You are hot. You are stiff from maintaining the same position for a long time. I let my mind wander so as not to fixate on my discomfort. I also remembered that my current position was a lot more tolerable than, say, sitting in thirty-degree water with a leak in my diving suit, or lying in a shit-filled canal in some Fifth World country, with malarial mosquitoes the size of dragonflies sucking on me.

2340. I heard voices approaching. I'd slipped the helmet askew so I could listen to the corridor sounds. They sure had taken their fucking time. But that's the Krauts for you: methodical.

2343. I could hear the HERREN door being opened. There was a pause, some muffled Kraut that I couldn't make out, and then the door was pushed shut.

I held my breath as the door three yards from where I hunkered clicked audibly. A swath of light cut into the bathroom and then the bright overheads were turned on. I blinked at the sudden light and hoped that whoever had made entry hadn't heard my eyelids slamming. I heard the sound of shoes scuffing on tile, then as I looked, I saw a pair of polished black lace-ups, and gray trouser cuffs, as the security man walked past the stalls.

"*Alles in Ordnung?*" a nondescript voice asked matter-of-factly from the doorway.

"*Ja,*" came the answer from Herr Lace-Ups. You and I might quibble with what he said, because we know that *alles* was *nicht in Ordnung,* but this was one of those times when it's better to take "*Ja*" for an answer, and just S^2.

Which is exactly what I was doing when Herr Lace-Ups stopped just before he pulled out of my narrow frame of vision. That's when I glanced down at the deck and saw what he saw.

Let me put this in KISS terms: there were overhead spotlights above each commode. I am a large Rogue, and I cast an extensive, dense, Roguish shadow. Ergo, I'd cast a shadow that traveled beyond the stall wall; a silhouette that didn't match any of the others in the God-*Damen* pissoir. And remember: Krauts are methodical.

Herr Lace-ups turned back toward me, and I heard the intake of breath that precedes what Billy Shakespeare used to call "various alarums and excursions." I didn't wait. I threw myself forward to catch Herr Lace-Ups as he opened the stall—and nearly knocked myself cold as he threw the door open, my heels caught on the toilet seat, and the edge of the door caught me in the forehead.

Oh fuck oh shit oh doom on Dickie. I tell ya, I could have gotten a job as a talent spotter for Louis B. Mayer right then, because I saw more fucking stars than ever worked at MGM, believe me.

It didn't stop me, though. I flailed at him, grabbed a fistful of blue blazer, and tackled the sonofabitch as his eyes went wide when he saw *moi* coming at him. We crashed to the tile floor, making a lot of noise. Out of the corner of my eye I looked past the stars and saw Fred go toward the door and disappear into the corridor, heard a muffled thud outside, and knew that he'd stopped the second security man before the guy'd had any chance to do something aversely critical to our health and comfort.

I should learn to pay more attention to what I'm doing. As I was diverted, Herr Lace-Ups seized the initiative and tried to wriggle out of my arms so he could reach whatever he had on his belt and spray/slap/stun me with it.

We rolled across the tile as we grappled, hands finding hands, legs intertwined, seeking some sort of advantage. I was trying not to kill the asshole because there was no need to do so—and besides, killing him wasn't the objective here. First of all, these two weren't doing anything other than their jobs, and there was no reason for them to be caught in the crossfire between us and Lothar Beck. Second, killings would ruin the op. I wanted to provoke Lothar, not get him to call the police because a couple of his employees had been whacked during a second-rate burglary.

But it wasn't easy holding myself back. Rolling across a tile floor with thirty pounds of bulky, lumpy, hard-edged combat equipment is fucking uncomfortable. And it's noisy. And you never know what's gonna happen if you don't put an end to things as quickly and effectively as you can. And so, as I rolled atop him, I reached up and popped him one, snapping his head back hard onto the tile floor.

He went limp. I checked for pulse. He had one, and it was strong. But his shallow breathing and the soft spot on his skull told me I'd probably given him a hell of a concussion.

Well, TFB (look it up in the Glossary). I pulled myself to my feet and went after Fred.

I found *der general* in the corridor, taping the hands and feet of the second guard, who was also unconscious. "You okay?" I asked.

He looked up at me and finally nodded affirmatively. "But he saw my face, Richard. And yet I cannot kill him, you know that."

The fact that the guard had seen Fred's face was bad news. I didn't mind being spotted, because I wanted Lothar coming after me. But Fred added a whole new *Rünzel*[70] to the situation. Surprise: two targets are often easier to attack than one, especially when one of them is hampered by politics. And Fred was constrained by a whole passel of political limitations that I frankly didn't give a shit about. But what's done was done, and I'd adjust my op-plan to fit the circumstances.

Fred slowly pulled himself to his feet, then searched the inert security guard methodically until he came up with a master key-card. "*Und* now, we must *mach schnell*," he said, gritting his teeth as he worked the kinks out from the sudden burst of activity.

I caught myself doing the same thing, trying to limber up my scarred, dinged, and not-so-young-anymore body. You know how pain makes me feel I'm alive. Well, tonight, I was very much alive. Here's some SpecWar sooth for you: ops like these are for the young. And while Fred and I may be young in spirit and able to keep up with most any young pups when it comes to shooting & looting, the ol' Rogue body just doesn't respond as well as it did when we were pussy-chasing, screech-swilling, hell-raising lieutenants on the beach in St. Thomas.

---

[70]Wrinkle

223

Chapter

14

0003. I CRACKED THE BATHROOM DOOR, WENT BACK INSIDE, AND taped up the unconscious Herr Lace-Ups, took his pepper spray and radio, and all his passkey cards. Then I eased back into the corridor. Was the poor schmuck still out cold? You bet. But was I about to assume he'd stay that way until Elvis had left the building? What am I, crazy?

0004. We tried every single one of the passkey cards carried by Herr Lace-Ups and his colleague—and came up dry. The target door remained locked. Fuck me, and fuck Hans, because time was now becoming a factor. Sooner or later, someone was gonna miss those two security dweebs and come looking for 'em—and they'd know exactly which floor to come to, because as I've said so many times before, the Krauts are a methodical bunch of assholes.

0007. Time crunch or no, it was still back to S^1.[71] Have I ever told you how much I hate S^1? Actually, it wasn't quite square one. It was desk three—the one I'd pried open just before we

---
[71]Square one

were interrupted. It was the secretary sitting behind that desk—at least that's what I recalled—who'd opened the door for the blue-smocked trio. I retrieved the single passkey card from the center drawer, scampered to the locked door, and slid the card's magnetic strip through the reader. The audible click told me I'd struck paydirt.

I turned the knob, pulled the door open, pushed Fred inside, then quietly closed the door behind us.

0008. I plucked my flashlight out of its pocket and played the light around the room. It was utilitarian compared to the opulence of the surrounding offices. Five metal desks, each with a computer on it, a series of file cabinets—two with combination locks—and a large wallboard completed the furnishings.

We started with the file cabinets. I pried the first of them open, laid my knife on top where it would be easily accessible for working on the next one, and started with the top file drawer. There were spreadsheets and what looked like databases, all neatly arranged in numbered files.

"What are they?" I whispered to Fred.

He shifted from examining the wallboard to the drawer I'd opened. "Don't know. But it looks as if they're sorted by postal zones," he said. He held the minilight between his teeth and riffled through the deep drawer, his gloved fumbling with the thick files. "Zis iss some kind of political database, I think," he said.

I let him sort files because he'd know better than I what to look for. Meanwhile, I began turning on the desktops.

Now I know what you're going to say: that it is unlikely that anyone would leave important material on a computer without safeguarding it, either by using an encryption program, or at the very minimum, a password.

Gentle reader, welcome to the real world, where DGAS[72] is a way of life.

Whether it's White House memos, State Department cables, or

---

[72]Don't Give A Shit

the Pentagon's most secret mission profiles, materials tend to be stored on computers *sans* safeguards. People don't like to have to remember passwords. Indeed, they often write the passwords down and leave 'em in their desks. Or to make things easy for themselves (not to mention folks like me), they simply disable all the built-in security devices and make their computers user (and thief) friendly.

And so, despite my rusty German, it didn't take me long to find a document that caused Fred's eyes to go wide in shock. The desktop had an internal Zip drive. I popped the release and looked at the hundred-meg floppy. Two words were written on the label: OPTION DELTA. I slipped the disk into my pocket.

0015. We'd been in the room for what I considered a lifetime for this kind of op. Fred was flipping through files as quickly as he could. I'd found three more labeled disks, which were added to the one in my blouse pocket.

0016. I could see that time was really getting short: Fred checked his watch for the third time in thirty seconds and looked over at me. "We must go, Richard—the chopper starts its approach in three minutes."

"*Jawohl, mein general.*" Shit, that *was* really cutting things close. I stopped what I was doing and started flipping computer switches to off.

0020. Back on the roof. We hunkered in the glow of the huge revolving disk. I heard the big Pave Lows as they swept up the Rhine, their huge engines reverbing off the city's skyline. And then suddenly there was the Little Bird, flaring just off the northwest edge of the roof, the stabo lines dragging across the rough surface.

I sprinted toward the starboard line. I chased the line down, slipped the hook through my harness, wrapped my hands around the thick nylon, and let the rope take my weight.

Fred went for the port side. And came up holding his *Schnüffler*[73] in his hand. The fucking rope was sliced where I'd cut it to release him as we'd come in.

---

[73]That's a Kraut's dick.

226

I shouted, *"Halt-halt-halt!"* into the mike on my helmet, hoping to hell I hadn't wrecked the fucking thing during my ground exercises with Herr Lace-Ups in the *Damen*. I dropped to my feet, hit the release on my harness, and rolled under the chopper skids.

"Fred—here!" I grabbed him by the stabo harness and pulled him starboard. "Pilot—drop one meter, *now!*"

There is a God. I knew it because the fucking mike was working: the Little Bird eased down a yard. I took all the slack I could, slid the stabo line through Fred's chest straps, looped it once to secure him in position, then reattached myself to the end of the line.

It was right at that precise instant—when my hand brushed the empty sheath on my web gear—that I realized I'd left my beautiful fucking Taiho knife sitting atop the goddamn file cabinet. But this was no time to do anything about it. I slapped at the rope in frustration. *"Raus-raus-raus*—get the hell outta here!"

Easier said than done, friends. Let me pause long enough right here to explain one of the basic Roguish laws of physics: it is that every action has an equal and identical reaction.

You want to know what I'm trying to say.

Okay, I will be succinct. With the two of us hanging off opposite sides of the aircraft, the chopper was easily able to maintain its trim. Now, however, Fred and I, combined weight way over four hundred pounds including equipment, were suspended somewhat precariously below the right-hand skid of the small aircraft.

There is a precise, engineer's technical term to describe our situation according to the laws of aerodynamics. That term is: "Fucked."

Not that the pilot wouldn't be able to fly the MH-6 like that. The fucking MH-6 is one of the most stable choppers ever designed. I saw an earlier version of one (designated as the AH-6) hit by ground fire when I was in Panama during the 1989 invasion. I was out of the Navy then, waiting to report to the federal prison camp at Petersburg, Virginia, to serve out my one-year sentence. To make some shekels to pay the lawyer, I took a contract with an unnamed government agency to snatch Manny Noriega's bagman, an Israeli spook we code-named Ehud. At zero dark hundred on 20 December I hit Ehud's apartment, but the spook had already skipped, along with a pair of duffel bags that DIA (oops—now you know who hired me) estimated held more than two billion dollars in negotiable bonds. How did Ehud know I was coming after him? Later we discovered he'd been given advance warning by his former colleagues at Mossad, the Israeli intelligence organization.

Anyhow, when you lose your primary target, you should always have a secondary in your sights. Mine was a money-launderer named Calderon, who DIA's analysts wanted to interrogate. And so, through happenstance (which is a polite way of saying Murphy'd fucked me), I ended up half a block away from the Modela prison just as a squad of Delta Force shooters snatched an American prisoner named Muse before Noriega's goons could execute him.

As the Delta AH-6 lifted off the roof of Modela, the Panamanians shot the hell out of the sturdy little aircraft with everything from M-16s to a fucking RPG. But instead of dropping like a rock the way Blackhawks and Pave Lows tend to do, the Little Bird pilot was able to auto-gyro down. There were a lot of dings suffered, some of them serious. But everyone survived, including the rescued American hostage.

But that doesn't make an unbalanced craft any easier to fly, especially in the nasty crosscurrents and wind shears you get in urban airspace. Oh, yeah: I could feel the pilot struggle with the controls as I tucked my knees so I'd clear the edge of the roofline. Suffice it to say that the return flight was a lot less pleasurable than the outgoing leg.

0145. We touched down in the *Stadtwald* just long enough to transfer into one of Fred's unmarked Pave Lows. Then it was off again, for a twenty-eight-minute flight to KSK headquarters.

By the time my guys and Fred's backup team arrived, Fred and

I were already knee deep in the intel we'd snatched. The more I saw, the less I liked it. I could take a couple of thousand words here to explain it all to you verbatim. But since there's not a lot of time for that, lemme give you what I learned in a couple of quick bites.

• Bite One: Lothar's analysts believed that the time was as ripe as Limburger cheese for a waaay-right-of-center, ultranationalistic Germany to reestablish Kraut political and economic control over the European continent. Their analysis indicated that the Russkies were too weak and fragmented to pose any credible threat to Germany, and that the rest of Europe had historically followed the German lead in matters politicoeconomic.

• Bite Two: the one real threat to this new German hegemony was the United States. But, the analysis went, U.S. attention was currently focused elsewhere and would remain so for the next nine to twelve months. There were domestic diversions (an ongoing scandal in the White House and the presidential and congressional campaigns). And there were foreign policy distractions: continual crises in the Far East (China flexing its muscle, Japan's saggy-dick economy, and Pakistan and India playing dueling nukes all managed to complicate things). Then there's the Middle East (Israel and the Palestinians; Iran, Iraq; Syria; Jordan), and a series of new and potentially dangerous crises brewing in the Caspian Sea region (Iranian-sponsored anti-Western activity in the wide swath of oil-rich geography from Tbilisi to Turkmenistan).

But how, you ask (yes, I hear you shouting out there), would Lothar and his allies accomplish their takeover of Germany? It's a democracy these days, you say, and putsches are not easily accomplished.

You're right. Good question, too. Here's the answer. First of all, Germany is still reeling from its reunification. When Ronald Reagan went to Berlin and said, "Mister Gorbachev, tear down this wall," I don't think that people realized that there could be negative ramifications as well as positive ones. But there are. While West Germany prospered in the fifty years after the war, the East was looted by the Soviets and by the Commie bastards like Heinz Hochheizer who kept the people enslaved. And so, the absorption of the vast and out-of-date East German infrastructure has been difficult. Unemployment is still high. And then there are the hundreds of thousands of foreign workers currently living and working in Germany. Germany is a refuge for Turks, Greeks, Kurds, Romanians, Bulgarians, Croatians— you get the picture. And there is deep-seated resentment against these foreign workers. Enough resentment, in fact, so that more than a few foreigners have been killed here in Deutschland in the past few years.

Added to those problems is the current government, which does not rule by a clear majority but has been forced into a coalition with the left-wing Green party.[74] Now, if someone could employ these elements to foment civil unrest, it might just be possible to "flip" the German government—and take it over, using a right-of-center political party as cover. And I already knew, courtesy of my research, that Lothar had a wide range of contacts in politics, industry, and the government, not to mention all those ultranationalistic, foreign-worker-hating scumbag groups of skinheads and other assorted malcontents. If he could fuse all of that, he might indeed have a shot at achieving his nasty goal.

Indeed, that's just what we found when we scanned the Zip disk I'd pocketed. The one marked OPTION DELTA.

Option Delta outlined a covertly planned blitzkrieg; a putsch that would overthrow the government in one blow (let me quote directly here for you), "and change the course of German history by blood and by fire."

To accomplish the blood and fire number, Option Delta called for the theft of weapons and ordnance from German military

---

[74]The Greens, you will remember, are basically against NATO and for total disarmament and the disbanding of all armies. They are the same kind of politically and ecologically correct sanctimonious politicians as Albert Gore— and just as untrustworthy.

sites, and from U.S. installations as well. So much for those probes John Suter was investigating out of Stuttgart.

Here's the most troubling information. The plan called for the pilfering of as many POMCUS cashes as could be located—with emphasis on ADM locations.

Holy shit. They knew about our pocket nukes. It was bad enough that Lothar had stolen God knows how many weapons and supplies already. But had they grabbed any ADMs?

Of course they had. Remember my interrogation of Heinz Hochheizer, the ex-Stasi agent I'd captured with Khaled? Remember what he told me?

No? You need to take a fucking reading retention course is what you need. Okay. I will go to the videotape. Der *winzig*[75] Heinz said that he'd gotten the ADM he sold Khaled from a Georgian Mafiyosi named Gabliani; and that Gabliani'd gotten it from some German in Düsseldorf.

What did that tell me right now, as I stared down at the computer screen with Fred looking over my shoulder, helping me translate?

It gave me two choices, neither of them very pretty. Choice One was that Franz Ulrich, former GSG-9 shooter, had been skimming from his boss, Lothar Beck, to support a cocaine habit. And what had he been skimming? Well, at least one ADM, which he'd sold to Gabliani the Mafiyosi. And if he was able to do that, it told me that Lothar had at least one more—and maybe two or three. Choice Two was even worse: Lothar himself was selling U.S. ADMs to folks like Gabliani, because he knew that Gabliani would sell them to terrorists like Khaled.

That was an even nastier scenario. And as much as I wanted to believe that Franz was simply a venal, greedy little puke who was selling out his boss the way he'd betrayed Ricky Wegener and GSG-9, it made more sense (remember the surveillance photograph of Khaled, Lothar, and Franz at die Silbermieze),

---

[75]Tiny.

that Lothar was the brains behind this noxious little operation, and Franz was die braun.

It further occurred to me that, since we had the disk for Option Delta, there had to be at least three other options—Alpha, Beta, and Gamma—as well—which made for a Class A migraine for Fred. Since the Delta option was the most violent, the others were obviously covert or clandestine plots. And it would be up to him to ferret 'em out.

But that was going to be Fred's problem. Mine was to get as much of this info as I could to General Crocker, and as soon as I could. As I have said many times during the course of these books, I'm not a political animal. I'm a War-SEAL. It would be up to the Chairman to deal with the political fallout.

While I sit-repped the Chairman, my guys would take one of Fred's cellular phones and drop out of sight. I didn't want them being Fred's responsibility—after all, he had enough problems to face. And I didn't want them moving south, under John Suter's wing, because we were going fight our fight in this neighborhood, not near Stuttgart.

And so, with Boomerang in charge, my seven merry, murdering marauders would take the RV, the Mercedes, and the two bikes, quietly track Lothar Beck and Franz Ulrich's movements, and wait for my call. The sneak-and-peek would do them some tactical good (the more you train the better you get), and it would help keep them out of the *Bierstuben* while I was gone.

Gone? Oh, yeah. As you probably know, the Chairman has his own secure communications system. Indeed, all the service chiefs have dedicated, secure communications systems, known in the trade as CINCCOMs. That allows 'em to talk politics and gossip to one another without being overheard by NSA or any of the other alphabet-soup agencies that like to eavesdrop on private chitchat.

Now, I knew that the four-star in command of USAREUR (U.S. Army Europe) had a CINCCOM shack close to his office.

But there was no way this SEAL was gonna get to use it without jumping through the well-known hoops. No. I had to get to a CINCCOM that I could use clandestinely.

And that, friends, meant London. Where Eamon the Demon held court at CINCUSNAVEUR.

Yes, there were risks involved. Eamon doesn't particularly care for me (and that is a fucking understatement). And going to London meant abandoning—for the moment at least—my hunt for Lothar and Franz, and the ADMs that I had a pretty good idea they were holding. That was all on the debit side of the tally sheet. On the credit side was that I know London like the back of my hairy hand; and I can get into Eamon's CINCCOM shed *sans* making any waves.

Why, you want to know? Well, because Hans Weber, the old master chief who actually runs CINCUSNAVEUR day in, day out, is one of the old-fashioned, black-shoe fleet sailors who make up my informal safety net, a net that has kept me from a captain's mast or a court-martial more times than I care to remember.

I met Hans when I was a wet-behind-the-bare-balls ensign snipe (that's engineering for those of you not familiar with fleetspeak) aboard the USS *Joseph K. Taussig,* and he was a gangly twerp E-3 fireman. As I have said before and will repeat here, E-3 firemen and bare-balled ensign snipes are both just one step above smudges of soot.

Today, the hair on my balls is turning gray, and that other sooty smudge has become an E-9, as high as any enlisted man can go. Hans was assigned to London more than a half decade ago, and he has managed to stay on through three vastly different admirals, which means he's managed to get things done quietly and capably. He has a compact but luxurious office down the hall from the CINC's that may not have the admiral's square footage, or its four-star collection of English antiques on display, but Hans's corner office commands a better view of Grosvenor Square than the admiral's quarters does. Moreover, it is the actual office once occupied by General Dwight D. Eisenhower when he planned Operation Overlord, the D-Day invasion.

And so, a copy of the Option Delta disk in my pocket, a small duffel over my shoulder, and a hearty "Fuck you very much" to my guys, I jumped in the back of Wolf's Beemer and headed for Frankfurt, where I'd grab the first commercial flight I could find to London. The whole fucking exercise wouldn't take more than a day or so. Then I'd be back, and we could all go hunting together.

Chapter

15

I TRUDGED UP THE STAIRS AT THE GREEN PARK TUBE STATION HUNG out, wrung out, and strung out. Obviously, the travel gods had decided that my quality of life was altogether too good, and so they'd put me on the flight from hell. What was billed as an easy, British Airways puddle jump from Frankfurt to Heathrow turned into a six-hour chamber of horrors. We'd rolled back from the gate, then spent so much time on the taxiway system that I started to think we were going to drive to fucking Heathrow. Then the pilot (and I use that term very loosely) pulled over and parked, engines idling, for an hour and a half without bothering to tell us passengers WTF. Then he taxied back to the gate, where we were not allowed to disembark while the mechanics tinkered with something or other in the landing gear for another hour and fifteen minutes. Then he refueled. And then, because we'd lost our takeoff slot, we had to wait sixty-eight more minutes until we finally wheels-upped, slipping in behind a green Saudi 747. Have you added that up yet, friends? It comes to 233 minutes, just under four hours.

The flight, when we finally got to it, was another ninety minutes, followed by sixteen more minutes of taxiing, followed by a sixteen-minute pause because of a British Airways gate that the fucking British Airways ground crew somehow couldn't manage to attach to the plane's hatchway.

So what am I complaining about, you ask. All of the above is normal treatment when you're flying British Air, you say. You're right. And, so, you ask again, why do I call the flight such hell?

It was hell because in addition to all of the above, the bathroom leaked. Yes, leaked. All over the rear of the cabin. Have I mentioned the fact that I was sitting in the very last row of seats? Next to the leaky head. On the aisle? In a puddle? Wearing my nylon running shoes?

Yes, I know that SEALs can exist in almost any hostile environment. But frankly, given the fact that by the time we landed, my shoes and socks and thick-soled feet were all very wet and somewhat fragrant, this was one environment I would have opted not to be tested in.

I squished my way up Piccadilly, turned left on Albemarle Street, right on Stafford, wheeled into the Goat, one of my favorite pubs in London, and drowned my sorrows in Theakston's best bitter. The place was empty except for the bartender—a new one who didn't recognize me—the omnipresent television, tuned as always to CNN, and two Americans. How did I know they were fellow gringos? One: they were ample and audible evidence that Britain and the United States are indeed two peoples separated only by a common language. Two: the shorter and slighter built of the two was wearing a golf shirt that read GULF OF TONKIN YACHT CLUB above the pocket, and a drawing of an F-4 Phantom on the back. That made him a former Navy jock who'd been shot down over Vietnam and plucked from the gulf. Three: the other guy, who was a few years younger and a lot heftier, wore a shirt exalting the virtues of the F-111 tactical aircraft.

They edged to the upwind side of the bar when I walked in, and looked at me *v-e-r-y* strangely. I gave 'em a roguish "WTF" War Face until I remembered what my feet and shoes smelled like. Then I ordered a round for the house, explained that my aromatic appearance was courtesy of British Airways, and offered to go barefoot if it would help the situation.

After five glorious pints and a welcome bout of drain-the-lizard, they'd discovered that I was a SEAL, and I'd confirmed that Mr. Rick (the F-111 shirt), and Mr. Bob (the Gulf of Tonkin vet) were former fighter jocks who currently worked as pilots for FedEx. They were more than halfway through a three-day layover in England, waiting for a shipment they'd ferry to Frankfurt tomorrow at zero dark hundred. There, they'd offload and pick up some more cargo, which would go to Riyadh. Then they'd head back to Rhine Main and pick up a big load that was headed back to somewhere in CONUS. Then they would deadhead to FedEx headquarters in Memphis, take five days off, and start the long circuit one more time.

I hadn't realized FedEx's network was so extensive, and told 'em so.

"One reason for that," said Rick, "is because we do so much government work. We move lots of embassy goods for the State Department—household effects for Foreign Service officers, computers and other miscellaneous office equipment for the department. We're moving a whole bunch of DOD files to Rhine Main tomorrow night. And the Frankfurt-CONUS leg is all DOD, too. Some fucking hush-hush flight complete with blankethead armed guards."

No shit. And if it was so hush-hush, I asked, then why the hell was Rick talking about it to someone he'd only just met?

"Oh, what we do isn't *classified*," Rick said. "Just hush-hush. By which I mean, DOD uses us when they don't want to run a big old olive drab C-5 or C-141 StarLifter into a civilian airport back in the States."

He was right about that. When I ran SEAL Team Six, I'd started out using a hufuckingmongous C-5A for the team. But lemme tell you, when you fly a hufuckingmongous C-5A into Ankara, Milan, or Nice; Caracas, BA,[76] or Singapore, it attracts ATTEN-

---

[76]Buenos Aires, for the uninitiated amongst you

TION. Which is something you don't want when you're running a clandestine operation.

And so, I switched to civilian aircraft. Rented three old Braniff jets: one 747, one 727, and a DC-9. It meant it was harder to move my vehicles around, but at the same time, we attracted little or no attention when we flew into the sorts of one- and two-mule towns on the Second, Third, and Fourth World a unit like SEAL Team Six gets sent.

"See, we're so obviously civilian, that when we land in our big orange and purple plane, nobody gives us a second glance, whether we're in Cleveland, or Cairo. It's like 'Oh, FedEx. Big fuckin' deal.' So, State and DOD use us when they don't want to attract attention. Hell, I could tell you stories—" Then he caught himself and laughed. "But I won't."

Rick drained his Theakston, called for another round, laid a tenner on the bar and frowned when not a lot of change came back his way. "Hell, if you wanted to go someplace and not attract any attention, all you'd have to do was stow away with us. We come in, get the once-over from Customs, and that's it. Ever since the EC, nobody even checks our passports anymore."

"You guys fly out of Heathrow?"

"Nah," said Rick. "Up by Cambridge."

"Lakenheath? Mildenhall?" They were a pair of joint Anglo-American air bases I'd used a number of times. Both of 'em were just a few miles northeast of Cambridge. But with the Cold War over for more than a decade they'd been closed for a couple of years.

"Lakenheath," Rick said. "It was demobbed back in ninety-six. Too bad—great facility, too. I was assigned two tours there when I flew the F-111. It's actually kinda nice to be back. And we really like Cambridge." He looked ruefully down at the pitiful change remaining from his ten-pound note. "The beer's a hell of a lot cheaper than it is down here. And hotel rooms are about one-fifth the price."

"Speaking of which," Bob said, "we'd better drink up. There's a twelve-hour rule at FedEx—and we take it seriously." He drained his pint glass. "Besides, we have a train to catch if we're gonna get back for dinner." He hefted the Marks and Spencer shopping bag that sat athwart his feet. "We wouldn't have even bothered coming down to London, except my wife really likes the sweaters from Marks and Spencer, and it's her birthday in two weeks."

I waved in their direction as they pulled their jackets on and wandered out into the afternoon chill. "Happy landings, guys."

"And following seas to you, too," Bob called. "See ya 'round, maybe."

Maybe. But probably not. It was time to get to work. I picked up a trio of 10P pieces, sauntered to the phone, and dialed Hans's number.

One *bring–bring,* two *bring–brings.* Then: "Master Chief Weber," the voice growled matter-of-factly.

"Fuck you, you underweight cockbreath lower-than-whale-shit snipe."

A pause. Then: "Either the admiral has suddenly developed a puckish sense of humor, or it's Rotten Richard, you nasty man, and puck you very much indeed." There was glee in his voice. "Long time no hear, you no-load dickhead. You coming my way and need a place to stay? If you do, I have a garbage can out back you can bunk in."

As always, Hans treated me with the respect I deserve. "Already on-site, Hansie."

"Where?"

"Just arrived at our favorite watering hole."

"Gotcha." Hans had introduced me to this place some years back. It was just far enough from both the embassy and CINCUSNAVEUR to make it inconvenient for officials from either place to hang out. We were, therefore, unlikely to meet anyone we knew when we drank at the Goat. Hans said: "Give me half an hour."

I downed two more excellent pints of Theakston before Hans arrived. He'd gone a bit more gray around the edges of his flattop since I'd seen him last, but he was still the same big, ham-handed angular Kraut New Yorker who I'd forced through his GED when we were shipmates together in the *Taussig.*

He removed the ten-for-a-fiver cigar from between his teeth and set it into an ashtray, then grabbed me around the waist and waltzed me around the room, my feet three inches off the deck. The man is a lot older than I, and it's been years since he's done any formal PT other than lifting a pint of ale. But he is still one strong motherfucker.

We went off and hunkered down at a small table in the window well where we could talk undisturbed and not be overheard. I explained what I needed. Hans's face screwed up in a perplexed expression.

"What's the prob, Hansie?"

"Things have changed since you were here last, Dickie. The CINC's a real tightass. Worse, he's brought in a whole new layer of middle management that's fucking things up. There are eight one-star admirals in residence these days—eight! Plus twelve captains, sixteen commanders, thirty lieutenant commanders, and God-knows how many wet-behind-the-balls lieutenants, jgs, and ensigns. And none of 'em have anything to do but second-guess people like me, so no fucking work ever gets done."

My friends, let's pause here just long enough for me to give you some interesting statistics.

Item: the day General Douglas MacArthur initialed the Japanese surrender agreement on the deck of the battleship USS *Missouri* back in 1945, the Navy had one admiral for every 130 ships. Today, with no global war to fight and no Soviet bear prowling and growling, the Navy has one admiral for every *1.6* ships—*an 80 percent increase.*

Item: when Marines stormed Mount Suribachi on Iwo Jima back in 1945, Uncle Sam's Misguided Children had one general for every 5,802 Marines. Today, the Corps has one general for every 2,190 Marines—more than double the rate. I could go on, working my way through all the uniformed services, but I think you get the point.

Anyway, one unhappy result of this out-of-control flag-officer inflation is that today's military is run by bureaucrats, not warriors. Why? Because a majority of this new legion of flag-rank officers has nothing to do with breaking things and killing people, which is, as you know, the only reason to have a standing military.

Instead, the current bloated flag-rank corps is made up largely of C^2 apparatchiks: public-affairs specialists, procurement dweebs, financial management experts, lawyers, and other non-essential (and more to the point), non-Warrior types. Eamon the Demon is a prime example. His master's degree from George Washington University is in economics. His Ph.D. is in systems analysis. He hasn't been aboard a fucking ship in twenty years. And guess what? He surrounds himself with officers created in his own image, because Warriors make the man nervous. After all, Warriors might kill somebody.

The United States doesn't need eight one-star admirals at CINCUSNAVEUR. All it really needs is a Warrior CINC who is willing to lead from the front. But that wasn't the way things worked these days, and you could see from Hans's face that he didn't like it at all.

That was all on the debit side. On the credit side, having this bloated bureaucracy also meant that the port-side paw seldom knew what the starboard paw was up to. And having a crew of non-Warriors aboard the command also meant that virtually all of 'em waged an eight-hour shift, left the instant the clock hand came up on 1700, and tubed to Waterloo station, where they'd catch the commuter trains to Woking, Farnham, Dorking, or Aldershot, or any of the other hundred suburban bedroom communities surrounding London where our military personnel lived. Once they got home, they'd work on their gardens, or play with their stock portfolios.

And so, Hans figured, if we simply waited until everyone went home, he could slip me through the back door, up the stairs (no video cameras in the stairwells), and into the admiral's communications shack without attracting any undue attention. He'd stand guard outside while I got on the horn to General Crocker, and then walk me back down the stairs, out the emergency fire door, and onto North Audley Street with no one the wiser.

It seemed KISS enough to have a good chance of success. So, it was just a matter of waiting until things quieted down. I checked my watch. The big hand was on "10" and the little hand was almost on "4." That meant I had just over an hour's wait.

Hans retrieved his cigar and headed back to the office. He'd call the Goat when it was clear to move. I took a gulp of ale and ordered a plate of bangers and mash, watching from my secure corner position as the first element of the eventide regulars pushed into the place. I knew it wasn't going to be a long wait, but given my mental state (I wanted to go to war NOW), any sort of wait was unacceptable.

2020. "Is there a Mister Herman Snerd in the house?" I scraped the last of the gravy from my third plate of bangers and mash and looked up as the bartender, who was waving a telephone handset, scanned the crowd.

"That's me—" I pulled myself to my feet and threaded my way through the four-deep crowd to the bar, reached over, and took the handset. "Snerd here."

"Sorry, Dickie," Hans's voice said over the din, "tonight's the night everybody decided to work late. Can you hold off for another hour and a half?"

Mister Murphy must really like me. Why? Because he's always fuckin' hanging around. "Do I have a choice?"

"Not really."

"Okay, Hansie." I checked the big clock over the bar. "See you at twenty-two hundred again. Where?"

"Remember the alley just north of the main entrance?"

"Roger-roger."

"I'll be waiting there. But do me a favor: come up the block from Oxford Street, instead of walking from Grosvenor Square. The security folks just installed a new surveillance camera over the main door. Of course, it only picks up traffic coming from the square." He paused. "That's 'cause they've decided terrorists never walk against traffic," he said contemptuously.

"Will do." That was Hans—always thinking. And that was also the Navy's security specialists—always assholes. I handed the phone back to the bartender, went back to my table, finished off the last Theakston, grabbed my jacket, and pushed my way through the crowd to the bar so I could pay my tab. The bar was too smoke filled, too hot, and too crowded for my taste. I decided to amble through Green Park, walk along the Mall, up Regent Street, and from there along Oxford Street to North Audley. It was a long walk to CINCUSNAVEUR by that route, but after three plates of bangers and mash I could certainly use the exercise.

Except as I was handing over my fifty-pound note, something on the television screen caught my eye. It was a map of Germany, with a big arrow pointing just west of Bonn. I couldn't hear anything, but I watched as a new visual flashed onto the screen—pictures of a crash site in a thickly forested area, the footage taken from above. It was a big chopper that had gone down, too. You could see pieces of the huge rotor where it had sliced through the trees and shredded itself in the rocky soil. The big dark chopper body had smashed hard, landing on its side. The damn thing was still smoking: there was video of rescue workers who'd fought their way to the scene applying chemical from back tanks to the smoldering fuselage.

I caught the bartender's attention: "Yo—could you turn that up, please?"

He reached onto the back-bar, grabbed a remote, and pressed the volume button, but with no result. He tried again, then shrugged vaguely in my direction. "Sorry, mate."

That was when Fred's picture popped up on the screen. It was an old picture, a decade at least, taken back when he was a colonel and running his beloved paratroop brigade. His square face displayed a cocky half-smile. He wore his beret folded neatly through the epaulette strap on his shoulder; his blouse was open at the collar, showing off the top of his hairy chest; his sleeves, as always, were rolled up high to intensify his biceps.

I remembered more or less when it had been taken. I was running Red Cell in those days. I'd arranged a three-day boondoggle to West Germany during one of our European FXs,[77] and Fred and I had staged a joint exercise at a German military air base near Hamburg, with Fred's paratroopers playing the counterterrorist role while my guys played the tangos.

And while we made mincemeat of 'em, which Fred's troops didn't like at all (evidence of which manifested itself during a series of rough after-hours beer hall brawls), Fred wasn't offended in the least. He knew why I'd done what I'd done.

"Richard," he'd said, "they are feeling pretty low right now, and resentful of what you did. But for me, I am happy. It is good that they should learn from their mistakes. That is how I believe we make here real progress. You cannot, should not, always learn only from positive experience; from winning. Sometimes, it is much better for the training that we learn from negative experience. Because, even if it is a hard lesson for the men, they are taught by their mistakes, and afterward we don't repeat our errors again when we do this in the real world, against real terroristin."

Now, standing there in the fucking crowded bar, with the acrid smell of cigarette smoke mingling with old ale suddenly making me puke-sick, I wanted to know what the fuck had happened to Fred—and who had done it. In my Warrior's soul, I knew it hadn't been an accident. That would have been too much of a coincidence. And we all know that in his line of work—and mine—coincidences seldom if ever happen.

And just then, suddenly, in that bright, white flash of understanding that hits you like a fucking underhanded sucker punch, I realized who had done it. And in that horrible split second, I

---

[77]Field exercises

cursed my decision to come here. I'd broken one of the most basic rules of counterterrorism: <u>*go for the direct threat first.*</u>

I'd come to London when I should have been hunting in Germany. And Fred had died because I'd made the wrong judgment. I have lost less than half a dozen men over my career. And each man killed on my watch has caused me indescribable pain. But I have used that pain and grief as a way of focusing my anger and honing my wrath. Kill my shipmate, and I will kill you.

Now, I'd erred in judgement—and Fred was dead. Well, I wasn't about to make the same mistake twice.

I headed straight for the phone, dropped a 10P coin into the slot, and dialed Hansie's number. I had to get to North Audley Street right now, and I didn't give a damn how many grade-A ruby red government-inspected one-star can't-cunt sphincters knew I was on the premises. There were more important things to worry about.

ABSCHNITT DREI

Chapter

16

THE STARCHED LIEUTENANT COMMANDER MANNING THE CINC's
radio shack scrambled from behind his desk, his London *Times*
scattering as he struggled to his feet. I saw he'd been reading the
court calendar—real Warrior stuff. He leapt to his left, stood in
the doorway, and blocked my access. "I'm sorry . . . , sir," he
half-whined, not quite knowing how to address me, but guessing
from my beard and French Braid that he could spell it with a *c*
and a *u* with impunity, "but I can't let you in without a written
order from the CINC."

I wasn't in the mood to argue. I picked him up with one hand,
lifted him six inches off the floor, moved him to the side, set him
down without releasing my grip on his shirt, and opened the
door.

"Young Mister Pritchard," I said, reading the name tag above
his right breast pocket, "I have to talk to the fucking Chairman
on a secure fucking line. I have to do it now. And if you get in my
way I will fucking kill you."

He realized I was serious because he could see it in my face.
And then, I saw his eyes shift toward the telephone. He was
going to call in the goddam Marines. And so, instead of letting

249

him go, I coldcocked the poor bastard with two swift shots, caught him as he dropped, shrugged at Hansie, dragged the unconscious young officer by the underarms into the CINC's inner sanctum, and closed the door behind me.

I picked up the receiver of the big secure telephone, one of three secure instruments on the console, and punched the Chairman's private number into it. It rang twice, and then a neutral voice answered: "Nine-six-two-two."

That would be Master Sergeant McWilliams, the soft-spoken intel squirrel who ran the Chairman's comms shed. I told him who was calling and that it was critical that I speak to General Crocker ASAP.

"He's in a meeting, Captain."

"Interrupt him, Master Sergeant. This is Designation Gold stuff."[78]

There was no hesitation. "I'll get him for you, Captain. Please hold."

It took about three minutes. During which time, Lieutenant Commander Pritchard came to, rolled over, puked, then collapsed in a heap. That was good news—I didn't want to hit him again.

"Crocker." I could tell the general was in command mode from the tone of his voice, and pissed off to boot.

So I didn't waste time. I explained where I was, gave him a quick sit-rep about what Fred and I had discovered at BeckIndustrie headquarters in Düsseldorf. Then I told him about the chopper crash—and the fact that Fred was probably gone. I said I was about to head back to Germany and kill Lothar Beck.

I heard a sharp intake of breath. But the reason for it didn't have anything to do with Fred, or Lothar Beck. "So you *were* in Düsseldorf."

"Aye-aye, sir."

"Fuck. Crap. Goddammit, Dick—"

---

[78]In Joint Chiefs language, "Designation Gold" means ultraurgent.

The Chairman seldom uses that kind of language. Unlike me, he takes the "gentleman" part of officer & gentleman seriously. "What's the problem, General?"

"The Germans filed a démarche with the embassy eight hours ago.[79] They've declared you persona non grata. They've threatened to break off some very sensitive negotiations if we don't rein you in."

"The Germans?"

"Well, the Ministry of Defense asked, and the Foreign Ministry complied."

I knew that Lothar Beck was behind it. "General—"

"Yes, Dick?"

I could hear the impatience in his voice. "Did the démarche come from someone named Richter? Markus Richter? I think he's some kind of deputy underminister of defense."

There was a long pause on the line. Then his voice came back at me, but *sans* the prosecutorial edge. "That's who signed the original protest. Fill me in, Dick."

I laid out what I knew about Lothar Beck, and the network of unholy government officials he'd put together. I told him about NSA's intercepts of contacts between Beck and a variety of German ultranationalists—the same ultranationalists who were snooping and pooping in John Suter's backyard.

"I was never told," the Chairman growled. "Who the hell do they think they work for over there?" It was a good question, but not anything for me to answer.

Instead, I briefed him about the CIA's theory that BeckIndustrie was selling dual-use equipment to nations that supported terrorism. I encapsulated the FBI memo that our ambassador had killed. I told him what my old friend Wink had discovered about Markus Richter's long and secure visit to the Russian Foreign Ministry. Finally, I described the surveillance photograph of

---

[79]That's a formal diplomatic protest, filed by a nation's foreign ministry, to the foreign ministry of another country.

Lothar Beck, Franz Ulrich, and Prince Khaled. And I told him that Fred and I believed Lothar had at least one of our ADMs, and quite possibly more.

He was silent for some time after I finished my monologue. Then he said: "We may have to handle this quietly. But it has to be dealt with."

"I agree, General."

"I'm going to get on the horn to John Suter," the Chairman said. "Let him work things from Stuttgart."

That was good as far as it went, but so far as I was concerned, there were a lot of Kraut tango nets to wrap up, and that wasn't the job of the U.S. military. The Germans would have to clean their own house, and that's exactly what I told the Chairman.

"I still have a couple of friends in the German Army," he said. "I can solve that problem—have it done quietly and efficiently, too."

So the tango nets would be handled by the Krauts. That was good news. But it still left me in the cold. I had to get back to Deutschland, to deal with Lothar and Franz. They'd killed my shipmate—and they'd pay for it.

The Chairman thought about that. "I think I can stall things for a while. Especially if no one can find you." There was another lull. "Does anybody know where you are?"

"Just one person—and he can be trusted," I said, looking over at Hans. Then I looked down at the deck, where Lieutenant Commander Pritchard was just coming around again. Oops. That made two. Which is what I told the Chairman.

"You put that lieutenant commander on the phone right now," General Crocker said.

By 0200, Hansie and I had copied the Option Delta disk, I'd recapped my thoughts on paper, and we'd sealed everything up nice and shipshape. Now, all I had to do was slip back to Germany without making any waves. My plan was simple: take the first available Chunnel train to Paris, then catch an express to

Frankfurt. The nice thing about the EC is that once they check your passport, you can cross borders at your will. So persona grata or non grata, I'd be in Germany by midafternoon. Once I was there, I'd link up with my guys, and we'd be well on our way to putting Lothar Beck on the endangered species list. I wanted the humpbacked cockbreath sonofabitch extinct.

I called to make a reservation on the Chunnel express and was told that the trains weren't running. There was a transit strike in France.

And how long would that transit strike last?

We do not know, came the answer. Please make alternative travel arrangements.

While I was being FVM'd,[80] Hans was arranging to send my package of goodies straight to Quarters Six, the Chairman's residence at Fort Meyer, so it wouldn't have to go through the Pentagon's labyrinthine internal courier system, or the State Department's diplomatic pouch, both of which are notoriously nonsecure ways of sending sensitive material.[81]

How was he going to do that?

"FedEx," Hans explained. "Keep it simple stupid."

I marveled at his master chief's ingenuity and repeated his admonition while I looked at a map of Europe, and doodled with a pencil, trying to work out an alternative route to Frankfurt.

Sometimes, dear friends, I do have fartbeans for brains. When I do, it takes a chief to set me straight. "Keep it simple stupid," I said again.

"Huh?" Now Hansie was confused.

"Can you get your hands on a car, right now?"

"Sure—I've the keys to the CINC's Jaguar. It's parked over at

---

[80]Fucked very much.
[81]Oh, they're secure vis-à-vis foreign governments. But there are often internal snoops who like to peek at what's being sent from one bureau to another. Bottom line: why take chances?

the Marriott." The London Marriott and its twenty-four-hour garage sits directly behind CINCUSNAVEUR.

"Then drive me up past Cambridge. I've gotta get to Lakenheath before zero five hundred."

0455. It's just over sixty miles from London to Cambridge on the M11. About ten miles south of town, we swung onto the A11, an old road that runs by the old SpecWar airfield at Mildenhall. We pulled off at Eriswell, and Hansie drifted onto the old high street that ran through the small village of Hundley, to the main gate at the old air field.

Things sure had changed. The razor wire was still in place. But the hangars, which had held F-111s and B-1 bombers, and the weapons stowage depots, which contained nuclear-tipped Tomahawk missiles and tactical nuclear bombs, were all gone—razed. In their stead were a pair of huge hangars built for 747s, DC-10s, or AirBus 300s.

And sitting on the tarmac, bathed in the warm orange sodium light, were three FedEx DC-10s, their running lights on and APUs[82] attached to their noses. Farther away, a big brown 747 cargo jet told me that UPS also used this facility. Hans flashed his ID at the gate, the rent-a-cop slid the wire mesh open, we pulled inside and headed toward the low building marked OPERATIONS.

I jumped out of the car and jogged to the doorway, pulled it open, walked inside, and made my way to the ops desk. A chap in shirtsleeves put his cigarette down and looked up at me. "Can I help you?"

"I'm looking for two FedEx pilots—Rick and Bob."

He checked a computer screen in front of him. "That would be FedEx N214 Heavy. Out the door to your right, straight on, and it'll be the far-right-hand aircraft."

"Thanks—" I wheeled and jogged for the door.

0505. I caught Rick on his walk-around. No F-111 shirt this

---

[82]Auxiliary power unit.

morning. He was all business: blue uniform, white shirt, narrow black tie, lace-up shoes, and a real surprised expression on his face when he saw me jump out of Hansie's Jaguar.

"Yo, Rick—"

He looked me up and down and gave Hans a once-over, too, pausing as his eyes acknowledged the ribbons and stripes.

Rick said exactly what was on his mind. "I sure didn't expect to see you here."

I hadn't expected to run into him, either, and I told him so.

"So, what brings you up to Cambridge so early?" Rick asked. His face told me that he already knew the answer to that one.

So I didn't disappoint him. I gave him what's known in the trade as a Roguish no-shitter. Which is to say, I told him that I had to get back to my men; that the Krauts had made me persona non grata; and that there was some pretty important unfinished business I had to attend to in the next few days—business that entailed national security considerations. I didn't embellish, but I didn't play coy, either. After all, I was asking a man I hardly knew to put his job on the line for me.

"I gotta talk to Bob," Rick said. "He's the senior man on the flight deck."

"Bob's heard enough," a voice came from behind me. The other pilot stepped out from behind the DC-10's front landing gear. "So far as I'm concerned, we don't want to know anything."

Fuck me. Doom on Dickie.

Then he surprised me: "So, just climb aboard, hunker down somewhere aft, and don't get off until you hear from one of us. I don't want to have to explain this little infil to anybody."

I looked at the two FedEx pilots and shook my head. "I don't know what to say, except 'thanks.'"

"Hey, you ever come to Memphis, dinner's on you, bub," Rick said.

"Screw the dinner, I'm sticking him with the bar tab," Bob said, a big smile in his dark eyes. He indicated the plane's forward stair unit. "C'mon, go climb aboard and make yourself to home." He checked his watch and jerked his thumb in Bob's direction. "We're allegedly wheels up in seventeen minutes, and this asshole hasn't checked jackshit yet."

0715. You'd probably like it better if Herr Murphy wreaked all sorts of havoc with the flight back to Krautland and caused me no end of problems. I know the editor would. But since we're dealing in the real world here, folks, not Hollywood bullshit, lemme tell you that the trip was smooth, and nobody paid the slightest fucking bit of attention to me at Rhine Main. I waited until the plane was unloaded, Rick wandered aft and gave me an upturned thumb. I picked up my stuff and walked down the roll-away stairs, crossed the tarmac to the American air base, waved my military ID in the general direction of the German rent-a-cop at the gate, and walked out into the bright Teutonic sunlight free as the North Joyzey boyd. Now all I had to do was find a pay phone, chase my men down, and go hunting.

At which point I slapped my forehead hard enough to make myself wince, to-the-rear-marched and hup-two, hup-two'd to the low, red brick building that housed the Intelligence staff. I was delighted to see that First Sergeant M. Walsh was womaning the desk.

She looked up at me and smiled. "Captain Marcinko. Nice to see you again."

"Ditto that, First Sergeant," I said. "I need to borrow your phone for a while. May I?"

She hefted the receiver atop the divider. "Dial nine for an outside line, then the local area code."

Boomerang answered on the second ring. "Yo, Boss Dude."

"Howdja know it was me?"

"'Cause almost nobody else has the number. Hold on a sec." I heard rustling, and a muffled, "Belay, assholes, I'm talkin' to the skipper," and then he came back on-line. "Sorry, Boss Dude."

"Where are you?"

"We're not secure, Skipper, so I'd rather not say," he said abruptly.

I might have been taken aback by his tone. But I wasn't. After all, he was right. I tend to forget things like that when I'm in my War Mode. "Gotcha. How're the men?"

"We're okay. Waiting for you."

He was real preoccupied. "Great—then come and get me."

"I'll send someone."

Whatever. Geezus, he didn't sound like himself. "Boomerang—is there anything you want to tell me?"

"No." There was more silence as he cupped his hand over the phone. Then: "Where's the pickup?"

I'd given that some serious thought. I needed someplace close by, but I certainly didn't want anybody showing up at the front gate of Rhine Main. Too much opportunity for Mister Murphy. I caught First Sergeant M. Walsh looking at me, and realized whatever I did, I'd better do it fast. "Remember where we met that lieutenant colonel just after we arrived? Lieutenant Colonel Smith?"

I could almost hear the gears grinding away in his surfer's brain. Then: "Gotcha, Boss Dude."

"Good. Pick me up there. Half an hour."

"Negatory, Boss Dude. No can do."

Hey—fuck no can do, which is what I told Boomerang in RBL.[83] I was impatient. I had white heat burning inside me. I wanted revenge, and I wanted it NOW.

"Fuck you back, Boss Dude," he exploded. "I've got some fucking complicated tactical considerations to deal with right now. We'll come and get you in three and a half hours—eleven twenty-five."

I didn't like what I was hearing and decided that when I rendezvoused with the team, Boomerang was going to get a

---

[83]Roguishly blunt language

genuine Rogue Attitude Adjustment. "It's your fucking call, Boomerang. You're the one who's got to do the fucking traveling." Oh, I wasn't happy about this at all. "Who you going to send?"

"You'll know when you see him."

The phone went dead in my hand. *WTF?* This was not the man I knew and trusted.

It took me a few minutes to cool down, but when I finally did, I realized that three hours wasn't going to mean much in the long-term scheme of things. Besides, there are a lot of tactical rules to follow when you are operating in a hostile environment, and so far as I was concerned, that's exactly what I was doing.

And so, I used the same anonymous, *fürshtunken* diesel minibus I'd ridden on our first day in Germany, and chugged sluggishly through Florsheim, and Weilbach, and Biebach, and Erbenheim, and Wiesbaden, and crossed the Rhine at Schierstein, and finally said *auf Wiedersehen* to the driver on Rhein Straße, just south of the Hilton Hotel and north of the Rhinehalle concert hall.

From there, I caught a tram and rode to the Hauptbanhof, jumped off, and worked my way down Binger Straße to Münster Platz, crossed against the light and wandered down Schiller Straße. There, I paused to admire St. Emmeren's church, which was just down the hill.

Now, you know as well as I that I wasn't sight-seeing. What I was doing was performing what's known in the trade as an SDR, or Surveillance Detection Route. SDRs are long, meandering walks, during which you perform certain elements of tradecraft, secrets that I'm not about to give away right now, which allow you to tell whether or not you are being followed.

And so, for the next fifty-five minutes, I played tourist. I window-shopped. I browsed the book stores. I meandered through the Höfchen Markt with its cheek-by-jowl farmers' market stalls set up in the big *Dom* square. And then, confident that no one was sniffing my spoor, I backtracked around the cathedral, worked my way up Grebenstraße, and up to the small platz onto which the Alt Deutsche Weinstube faced.

The minisquare was bright with brilliant sunlight and bustling with people, but I didn't see anybody I recognized. I checked the "big watch, tiny pecker" tick-tock on my wrist. Eleven-hundred eighteen. I was seven minutes early. And so I retreated to the Irish pub just up the narrow street from the Weinstube, ordered a Murphy's stout, found a stool outside in the sun, and sipped away.

I wasn't even halfway through my pint when a long, familiar-looking slate gray Beemer 7000 with dark-smoked windows nosed into the square. The driver's window eased down. Wolf, der skinhead who had been Fred's driver, raised his Oakley shooting glasses and, squinting, scanned the square until he saw me.

"Kommen Sie hier, Herr Dickie," he mouthed, beckoning me toward the big car. Wolf disappeared behind the sunglasses as his window slid upward with a whir.

Alert to anything untoward, I set the Murphy's down and jogged to the Beemer. I heard the electronic locks release, quickly opened the rear door, slipped inside, and slammed the door.

Brigadegeneral Fred Kohler, his muscular arms crossed, looked over at me. *"Willkommen auf Deutschland, Richard,"* he said, a bemused expression on his Kraut face reacting to my highly visible double-take.

Chapter

17

"WTF, FRED?"

"It is *kompliziert*—" He struggled for the English. "Complicated, Richard."

"Fuck complicated. I thought you were dead, you Kraut asshole." I was so relieved I didn't know whether to hug the motherfucker or smack him into next week.

He shook his head as the big Beemer K-turned and threaded through traffic toward the river. "Yes—and so does Lothar Beck. The son of a bitch."

"But the Pave Low—" I was so fucking confused I was shaking.

"A nasty accident, believe me. I lost an eight-man crew, and six of my shooters." Fred's expression was cold as steel. "They got to somebody at KSK. There was Semtex put aboard. It was a bomb."

"Holy shit."

"*Und zooo*," Fred continued, "I thought it was best that they think they have killed me."

"They—"

"Beck. It is Beck."

"But how—"

"You perhaps have noticed how I have isolated the unit," Fred said.

I nodded my head in the affirmative.

"It is not the way I prefer to do business, but given the current mission, it is necessary. Recently," he continued, "it has been raised to me the possibility of internal infiltration."

"Moles."

"*Ja,* moles—or perhaps even worse. *Verrätern*—traitors. So, also, I have been changing my flight patterns for a little while now. A long flight is scheduled, *und* it is at the last minute changed to a short one. Or I switch choppers. Or I go by car. That is what happened here. We have a long-scheduled training exercise in Hanover. A *counterterroristin* scenario at a bank. On the pad, I change my mind. Instead of the Pave Low, I decide to use the NOTAR we flew, you and I, when we go to BeckIndustrie. But it is not fueled. *Und* so, the Pave Low goes ahead without me. But I am still on the manifest, *ja*? And over the *Nutscheiderwald*"—his hands flung violently upward—"explodes. Goes down. Boom-boom—*und alles kaput.*"

Fred shrugged, his palms upturned. "*Und zooo,* I construct this current . . . *Scharade, ja*?"

"What about Berlin?"

Fred's face took on an ugly expression. "I let Berlin think what it wants to think," he spat. "I do not know who my friends are anymore in Berlin."

"And the unit?"

It was as if a black cloud suddenly washed across his face. "My men, too. They think I am gone. Except for the three who are with me on the NOTAR. Wolf here, Max the pilot, and Werner, my copilot."

He looked at me like a man who'd just lost everything. Which, in fact, he had. "It was from *within my own unit,* Richard. *My own unit!*"

There was nothing I could say to him. The thought was inconceivable to me. My whole career has been built upon one unassailable foundation: my loyalty to my men, and their loyalty to me, is absolute. Complete. Pure. Unqualified. Unconditional. Categorical. The thought that one of them would ever betray me was foreign to everything I was, am, or will be.

Fred is cut from the same bolt as I. And so I cannot fathom the psychological depth to which he'd been suddenly dropped. I looked over at him. He had aged in the day and a half since I'd seen him. The lines on his face were deeper. His eyes had sunk into his skull. There appeared to be more gray in his hair.

He crossed his big arms and stared straight ahead. "I am at how do you say, vit's end, Richard. We set the NOTAR down and hide it. I send Wolf for the car—it takes him half a day but he comes back with it. And while I wait, I have my Max telephone your Boomerang. He is carrying the phone I gave him, so we know how to reach him, but I do not want to talk myself because no one can tell me that Beck and his people have not compromised my communications."

Good point. It also explained why Boomerang had been so close-mouthed on the phone.

Fred uncrossed, then recrossed his arms. "*Und zoo*, we finally rendezvous late last night—and we wait for your call."

"And now?"

He looked evenly at me. "*Und* now, I am with you *für die Daur des Krieges*—until this war is over. You said to me before you left to London, you were going to go hunting. *Zooo*, Wolf, and Max, and Werner and I—we are with you. When it is over, then I will think about picking up the pieces."

He turned away, his eyes straight ahead as Wolf eased the car through the heavy Mainz traffic, north onto the crowded two-lane highway that ran along the Rhine. Just northwest of the city, we sailed up onto the 61 Autobahn and cruised at two hundred–plus kliks per hour past Koblenz, turned south onto the 48 at the big Metternich Interchange, and then ran southwest, roughly paralleling the twists and turns of the Mosel River. Wolf exited at a sign that read KAISERSESCH.

From there, he took a hard right onto a wide, two-lane

highway followed immediately by a second hard right onto a wide two-lane highway, which after about two kilometers crossed back under the *Autobahn*, heading south. After about a klik and a half, Wolf steered right again, onto an unmarked narrow country blacktop lane that wove through hilly pasture-land and freshly ploughed fields.

We drove for perhaps a quarter hour in silence. I spent my time watching Fred as he sat in the rear right-hand corner of the Beemer, staring at nothing. I am accustomed to operating UNODIR. Fred is not. He is one of those *alles in Ordnung* kind of guys. And so I understood all too well that every molecule of his being was out of sorts because his entire existence had just been turned upside down.

I told him about my conversation with the Chairman. Fred nodded his head. "That is good," he said. "And perhaps you will check with him—I still have a secure phone—as to what he has been able to do."

"Done and done."

"Once we know," Fred said, his voice rock hard, "then we can finish things." He steadied himself as a hard left took us onto a narrow, gravel road barely wide enough for the big BMW. Wolf steered gingerly; the car'd been designed for urban speed, not rural maneuverability. On a ridge to my right, I saw a small enclave of houses and barns. I nudged Fred. "What's that?"

"The village of Pillig," he said. "We are close."

The topography was changing. It became hilly, rougher. The fields slowly gave way to rough, untilled countryside, above which we began to see the sorts of craggy escarpments similar to those ringing both sides of the Rhine and Mosel Valleys. After about six minutes, Wolf turned right onto an unpaved track, drove another hundred feet, and stopped.

Dead ahead, in a small clearing, our RV, its roof camouflaged with evergreen boughs, had been pulled up close to the trees. Behind it was the Mercedes. It, too, was covered with branches, so as to conceal it.

Gator Shepard, Max the pilot, and the Rodent were sitting

under the RV's retractable awning. They'd brought out the portable picnic table and were scrubbing, swabbing, and lubing our field-stripped MP5s in an efficient assembly line. At the far end of the table, Baby Huey and Nod were working on pistols. Duck Foot perched on the rear bumper of the Mercedes, loading magazines.

Boomerang emerged from the RV, a taciturn look on his narrow face and a small block of what looked like C-4 plastic in his left hand. He put the explosive down on the edge of the picnic table and came toward me, trying to read my body language. "Welcome home, Boss Dude," he said somewhat tentatively. "I guess I—" He stopped and flailed in my general direction, at a loss for words.

I gave him nothing. Instead, I did a pretty passable imitation of Everett Emerson Barrett's compound complex use of the *F*-word in polysyllabic combination. Then I bounded over to the wide-eyed cockbreath sonofabitch and hugged the hell out of him to let him know how I really felt about him.

He shrugged it off, giggled that silly laugh of his, and grinned at me. "If that's the way you feel, Skipper, let the real fun begin soon."

I clapped him around the shoulder. "I thought you'd never ask, asshole."

1500. Boomerang's sit-rep was succinct. At about the same time I'd been sitting on the tarmac at Rhine Main, Lothar Beck and three chase cars had come barreling out of the BeckIndustrie headquarters and headed straight for the castle. Nod and Rodent had followed 'em to the castle on the motorcycles. They'd remained on scene until Boomerang could move the rest of the guys into position, something that had been complicated by Fred's predicament. Indeed, they'd had to leave Nod and Rodent on their own overnight.

But now things seemed to be more or less shipshape. Beck was bottled up in his castle, which was crawling with armed guards. They'd maintained a constant surveillance on the place—and no one had gone in or out. Indeed, Half Pint and Werner, the copilot, were out on surveillance for the next hour and a half. Then they'd been relieved by Baby Huey and Wolf.

"Where's Franz?" I asked. Franz was nowhere to be seen, although Nod swore that the former GSG-9 shooter had been riding shotgun in Beck's armored limo.

I nodded. That put them both under the same roof. So, all we had to do, was go play some hide-and-seek with 'em, which we'd do tonight.

1515. I wanted to see the target firsthand. I packed one of our waterproof rucksacks with the necessities for an afternoon in the woods: field glasses, our pint-sized radiation detector, and a suppressed weapon. Duck Foot volunteered to play guide. We were, according to the map, just about two kliks from Schloss Barbarossa, Lothar's castle, which was located above a winding tributary of the Mosel River. That's not so far, you say—just over a mile. You're right. But what a mile it would be. It took Duck Foot and me just over an hour to cover the distance.

The castle grounds, some eighty acres, abutted what had to be several thousand acres of national forest, with the myriad hiking trails and touchy-feely nature walks so beloved of lederhosen-wearing Krauts. And lemme tell you: Germans don't make things easy for themselves. We're not talking Disneyland-style gently sloping paths, graded for amateur hikers. We trudged through thick evergreen forest, our feet crunching on the dried needles and the occasional branch. The terrain was tough: one ridge after another, each no more than three hundred feet high. But climbing one after another while moving along the rough terrain at a fast pace becomes tiring.

After about forty minutes, having worked up a good sweat, we left the series of nature trails, crossed onto the castle grounds, and made our final approach from the west, so the sun would be in the eyes of anybody looking out for intruders. We passed the camouflaged OP (yeah—it stands for Observation Point) manned by Half Pint and Werner, exchanging our greetings in hand-signs.[84] Nod took point. He slowed the pace as he left the trail he had obviously taken earlier and began a long, deliberate encirclement that would take us where we had to be.

After sixteen minutes, he eased over the crest of the ridge, and beckoned me to follow. I caught up with him—and stopped cold.

Below us was the Mosel tributary known as the Eltz. The river wasn't very wide, perhaps twenty meters in some places, twenty-five or thirty at others, maybe a little more. But I could tell it flowed fast and cold through the narrow, S-shaped gorge that had been worn deep and smooth over thousands of years.

The bottom of the S formed a peninsula of solid rock about a hundred meters long by perhaps seventy meters wide. Built atop that solid stone foundation stood Schloss Barbarossa. It was impressive. From the river, outer walls, which looked to be six feet thick at least, had been designed in the same irregular elliptical pattern as the S-shaped peninsula, giving the impression that the castle had been hewed from solid rock.

The walls, which metamorphosed into parapets and towers, rose at least sixty, perhaps even seventy feet above the rock foundation. At each end of the ellipse, the walls separated from the castle, creating a series of narrow courtyards. The castle itself, six stories high, with half a dozen separate towers (some with crenellated bartizans), surrounded a secure inner bailey that was accessible only by going through the main castle itself.

I pulled my binoculars out to take a closer look. What I saw wasn't encouraging. The castle's natural defensive qualities had been augmented by a fair amount of twentieth-century technology. Efficient halogen and sodium floodlights were mounted on the towers and parapets. The most accessible of the walls were

---

[84]No, I wasn't being paranoid. The human ear can pick up normal conversation up to a hundred meters away. Whispered conversations can carry as far as eighty meters. You can pick up the sound of a hammer cocking on a weapon five hundred meters distant. Indeed, noise discipline is probably the most important tactical lesson you can learn during field exercises. It can keep you alive. And it can make it possible for you to find and kill your enemy.

all topped by four strands of razor wire and topped by a single strand of electrified fencing. The riverbank was edged in a double roll of concertina wire. The grounds around the side facing away from the river were combed, a sign of sensors or land mines.

Formal entry to Schloss Barbarossa was via a single lane of well-maintained private blacktop, which, according to Duck Foot, stretched two kliks to the two-lane country road along which we'd seen Lothar and Franz traveling only a few days ago, when we'd been searching for ADMs in the cow pasture. The castle's narrow private road descended in a series of sharp S-curves from the ridge directly opposite where Duck Foot and I hunkered down. I swept the roadside and picked up telltale signs of electronic sensors. The blacktop terminated at an arched stone gate, which was blocked by a heavy, pneumatically raised, steel antiterrorist barrier. Behind the arch, where the macadam was replaced by smooth cobblestones, stood a gatehouse big enough for a two-man detail, where the steel barricade was no doubt controlled from. The glass looked to be thick and bulletproof. The gatehouse itself was constructed to look as if it was flimsy. I knew better. Past the gatehouse, the road followed parallel to the walls, up a steep incline, to the outer bailey.

It was cleverly designed. That outer courtyard was in fact a fatal funnel—a killing zone—because it lay between two natural defensive ridges: the thick outer fortifications, and a row of four-story-high inner walls that protected the wood-framed, stone-walled structures that made up the *Schloss* itself.

I scanned left to right, and back again, looking for signs of life. It didn't take long to discover 'em, either. I panned along one of the parapets, then stopped. A pair of hoods in black overalls lounged, smoking, against a waist-high wall. I zoomed the binocs. One had a suppressed submachine gun slung over his shoulder. The other wore a pistol in a belt holster. Both had field glasses suspended around their necks. But they were too busy talking and smoking to bother using 'em.

I scanned some more, and spotted another half-dozen armed men, all looking like cheap hoods standing outside some social club in Little Odessa. Obviously, there was something valuable on-site. I plucked the radiation detector from my rucksack and turned it on. Even at this distance, through the *Schloss*'s thick stone walls, I got a reading. That's your tax dollars at work, folks. Once in a while, the Pentagon manages to do better than six-hundred-dollar toilet seats and three-hundred-dollar hammers. I checked the readout again. Oh, yeah: Lothar had his ADMs here.

And the guards? Indeed, from the careless, un-Teutonic look of 'em, I was looking at a pair of Lothar's foreign workers. *Bandity.* Ivans. Herr Subgun flicked his cigarette into the gorge. I followed its parabolic descent with my glasses until it fell onto the rocks sixty feet below.

I raised my glasses and swept the castle from northwest to southeast, catching another half dozen of the black jumpsuited, binocular-rich Russkies as they lounged in their duty stations, smoking, talking to one another, and paying almost no attention whatsoever to their jobs, which no doubt included looking out for people like me.

This, friends, is a common problem in military units. Sentry duty is lonely, boring work, and as we all know, war is 99 percent waiting, and 1 percent chaos. The waiting is what most sentries do. Young officers do not realize that after about half an hour, one's defenses start to wane, and concentration drops. But today's lookouts are often on post for hours, trying to do nothing except watch, and look, and listen. Frankly, it is no fun. It is easy to daydream, to become distracted. And yet, if you do not remain alert, then people like me are going to take advantage of you, with the result that you and your men will end up riding a body bag home.

Still, the best way to deal with sentries—good or bad—is to bypass 'em altogether. And that is what I planned to do tonight. I sat down, cross-legged, and sketched out a rough diagram of the castle. From the positioning of the sentries, it was possible to gauge where we had to go. Undefended areas were less likely to contain valuables—either human or otherwise. I noticed that the southwesterly walls were the least protected, while the heaviest concentration of Ivans was spread across the castle's easternmost perimeter.

I shifted position and checked through the binoculars again, trying to make certain I hadn't overlooked anything that could come back and bite me in the ass later. I've staged enough missions with Mister Murphy sitting on my shoulder to know I don't like surprises. Like Everett Emerson Barrett used to tell us tadpoles in the Second-to-None Platoon of UDT-21: "If you blankety-blanking blanker-blankers plan for every motherbleeping contingency, and then when that blanker-blanker Murphy blankety-blanks you over, you won't be blanking hurt too bleeping bad, and you'll still make your bleeper-blanking objective."

So, maybe I was taking a little more time than I should, but I wanted to cut the margins for error before we inserted and Mister Murphy started fucking with us. I mean, you had to hand it to Lothar and Franz: Schloss Barbarossa was well defended, and highly fortified. But as is the case with every well-defended, highly fortified position, there is *always* a way in.

1800. I put a call through to the Chairman on Fred's secure telephone, and received good news. For once, Mister Murphy wasn't screwing with us. John Suter was on full alert. He'd scramble on my signal. And best of all, the Chairman had managed to get in touch with an old NATO colleague, a German general named Dieter Schulz, whom he'd known for twenty years and trusted the way I trusted Fred Kohler. Dieter had promised the Chairman that he had enough assets to wrap up the Kraut nets quietly.

When I mentioned Dieter Schulz's name to Fred, the first hint of a smile since I'd returned spread across his face. "*Ja*," he growled, "Dieter is a *gut* man. He will handle his end—just as we will handle ours."

1840. I finished sketching out my plan of attack. So far as I was concerned, the only way to go was to come through the back door, the way they'd least expect us. Let me, therefore, take you through this little op before we get started, because once I've committed my forces, there won't be a lot of time to explain things.

Schloss Barbarossa had been built on a peninsula that sat, more or less, on a northwest-southeast axis. The gate was on the northwest side, the tail of the peninsula faced southeast. The sensors and land mines were planted across the landlocked side of the castle, around the main gate and single-lane road. Then came the razor wire-topped walls. Multiple layers of razor-sharp concertina wire were also strung around the southeasterly side of the *Schloss*, because the walls there were low and scalable. The one point that was obviously impenetrable, and therefore lacking in ancillary defenses, were the sheer rock walls rising from the river gorge on the castle's southern tip. At that place, where the waters rushed past a series of minirapids, there was no protection other than the bulwarks provided by *Mutter Natur*: fast-moving water, unyielding stone, and a long, dangerous motherfucker of a climb.

Now you know how we're going to get in. But I wasn't done yet. Castles are big suckers. There are lots of antechambers, and chambers, and rooms, and galleries, and all kinds of miscellaneous architectural detail shit, including secret passages and hidden rooms and the like. Now, as I saw at BeckIndustrie headquarters, Lothar likes those special details. The antechamber he'd had put into his HQ had a hidden door that even I didn't spot.

Now, if I were Lothar, or Franz, and I was being attacked by *moi*, I wouldn't waste any fucking time at all: I'd get the hell out, through a secret passage or similar. But before I did, I'd set the ADM timers so when big bad Dickie came a-hunting, he'd get the shit nuked out of him.

That knowledge made the job tonight even more difficult. We'd have to get in and cancel the opposition without alerting Franz or Lothar. Only when we were in position to take 'em down could we let 'em know we'd come a-calling. And even then, I didn't want 'em thinking I was on the premises. I needed a major distraction.

That would be Boomerang and Nod's job. The pair of SEALs would get moving now. They'd infil from the ridge on the *Schloss*'s west side, and plant a series of charges directly across the approaches to the castle. They'd rig timers. But as we all know, Mister Murphy likes to play havoc with explosives. And so, Boomerang would back the timers up with a radio-controlled detonator.

At 0130—or on cue if we needed them beforehand—the explosions would "walk" right up to the gatehouse. They'd accomplish two goals: first, they'd make Lothar believe a frontal assault was coming his way—right toward the fatal funnel he'd devised. And thinking so, he'd take a few extra minutes before making his escape. Second, they'd destroy the only means of escape from the *Schloss*: the narrow, winding blacktop road.

More than two thousand years ago, the Chinese Warrior General Tai Li'ang wrote: "Give your enemy false confidence and he will defeat himself, even if he outnumbers you ten to one." That simple advice is as true today as it was back then.

Because tonight, we were outnumbered and outgunned. Tonight we would win by stealth, and craft, and pure Warrior spirit. Fred's face was a mask. He'd lost men to these Teutonic traitors—and I could see the fury burning within him. He wanted to go—*NOW!*

So did I. These men were dealing in weapons of mass destruction that could kill tens of thousands of innocent victims. "Any questions?" I slow-panned my own merry, murdering marauders, and was all of a sudden transfixed. Their confident expressions, their belligerent body language, their aggressive, can-do attitude, and the self-assured killers' looks in their eyes made me humble in their presence.

I took a few seconds to offer my silent prayers and gratitude to the God of War, who has allowed me to lead such men into battle and kill my enemies with great brutality and in large numbers not once, not twice, not even thrice, but scores upon scores of times.

Indeed, all of these Warriors—Fred's and mine—were filled with the sort of resolve, persistence, tenacity, and determination that told me they had the ABSOLUTE WILL TO WIN. To them, the word *impossible* did not exist.

And so, no matter what the odds, no matter what challenges they would face, I knew in my own Warrior's soul, that, tonight, WE WOULD NOT FAIL.

Chapter

18

1944. I split our force into two six-man units. The first squad, Duck Foot, Gator, and Baby Huey, would be mine. Fred took the second squad: Wolf, Max, Werner, Rodent, and Half Pint. My four would be augmented by Nod and Boomerang, when that pair of lethal SEALs finished planting the charges. The plan was KISS. We'd cross the ridges above the castle on the network of trails until we intersected the river. Then we'd infiltrate down the Eltz bank until we reached the deepest part of the gorge. There, we'd go into the water and let the current carry us downstream until we reached the *Schloss.*

We'd crawl onto the bank below the castle's escarpment, wriggle under the concertina wire, then send a climber up the rough stones to the port-most of three small, barred cellar windows that looked out on the gorge, some thirty, perhaps thirty-five feet above the rocks that formed the castle's foundation. A pair of ropes would be secured to the bars and lowered. Then we would all clamber up, because from the barred window it was only eight or nine feet more to a pair of crenellated doors that opened onto a narrow, awninged balcony. Half Pint would make short work of the door lock. From there, we'd enter the

Schloss proper, split into two efficient killing groups, and work from the outside in, neutralizing the opposition as we went.

If things went well, we'd maintain surprise until it was too late for Lothar's goons to respond with any efficiency. If they didn't, well, we could always improvise.

On ops such as this one, it's preferable to have all the latest SpecWar goodies: thermal imagers and miniaturized, waterproof communications; night-vision devices, computer satellite imagery—you have a good idea what I'm talking about. Well, we were going in with very basic equipment tonight. We had eight radios, two climbing ropes, eight suppressed and four unsuppressed submachine guns, twelve pistols, our combat knives, one night-vision monocular—and that was just about it.

But my old friend Avi Ben Gal has a saying that covers this situation. *"Haver shelli,"* he says, calling me his friend in Hebrew, "you Americans sometimes forget that in wartime, *great* is often the enemy of *good."*

What is he saying? He's saying that we Americans tend to always hold out for the most sophisticated equipment, when sometimes, basic is more than enough to win the day.

Would the technogoodies make our work easier? The answer is sure they would. Except if the batteries on the thermal imager went down, and the waterproof radios leaked, or any other of the myriad things Mister Murphy can do to screw with an op.

So, tonight, as I said above, would be Keep It Simple, Stupid. Or, to paraphrase the old brokerage firm TV commercial, we'd make our corpses the old-fashioned way: we'd earn 'em.

2020. The clock was ticking. Boomerang and Nod had slipped out of camp half an hour ago, and now it was our turn. We'd planned on a 2300 rendezvous a klik and a half west of the castle. We'd leave the base in one group and traverse the forest and ridges, then (since we are maritime creatures) we'd head for water. We would use the riverbank for cover and get as close as possible before slipping into the water. Everyone would be tied together in pairs—no stragglers allowed tonight. My squad would make the first infil, and secure the LZ. Duck Foot, my most experienced climber, would do the initial ascent. When he secured the ropes, the rest of us would pull ourselves up.

2026. Since things were going so well, Mister Murphy paid us a visit. Duck Foot, my stealthy, surefooted, catlike hunter, the selfsame SEAL who'd spent his childhood silently stalking deer, Canadian geese, wild turkeys, and other miscellaneous game all across Maryland's Eastern Shore, forgot to pay attention to what the fuck he was doing, tripped over a dead branch in the darkness, went tumbling ass over teakettle, and sprained the hell out of his right ankle.

It took seven minutes to tape him up (thank God we had two first-aid kits between the ten of us because the small rolls of inch-wide tape in the SpecWar-issued kit is not designed to tape sprains but cover wounds) and feed him a handful of aspirin.

I put Gator on point—and on notice. He'd be the lead climber tonight. Have I mentioned in the past that Gator does not like to climb things? Heights, you see, make him nervous. Then why, you ask, is he in a trade where jumping out of perfectly good aircraft, slithering up ice-encrusted oil-drilling rigs, climbing miscellaneous structures from the outside, and doing other elevation-intensive assignments are an incessant, constant, even immutable part of his life?

There are two answers. The glib, Roguish one is that Gator doesn't have to like what he does—he just has to do it. But there is a deeper psychological element at play here as well. To Gator, as is the case with most SEALs, life is a never-ending series of challenges that must be overcome. To him—and them—the word *impossible* does not exist. And so, if I order him to climb a sixty-foot tree in a forty-mile-an-hour wind, he will refer to me by rude imprecations. But then, he will grit his teeth, and he will inch his way up the fucking trunk no matter how much it hurts or how nervous it makes him, because there is no way he is *not* going to succeed. That's how he manages to jump out of planes at thirty-five-plus thousand feet (that's more than *seven miles* to the ground, friends—a long way down when you don't like heights), without my having to toss him out. That's how he muscles his way up caving ladders, climbing ropes, drainpipes, and other sundry things, to climb the sides of buildings, ships, and those nasty oil rigs when he has to. Gator understands that WAR is an acronym for We Are Ready—and he's always ready.

2109. Back on course. There were, of course, all those rough-track nature-lover's hiking trails to follow, but we didn't take any of 'em. Walking along an established trail is a bad thing to do when you're on patrol. It was too late for hikers, which meant that any contact would be hostile. So I followed the same procedure I've done for years: we'd parallel the trail, so as to leave no new tracks. It made our progress slow. But it ensured that we wouldn't be spotted. Wolf followed Gator. I trailed behind the tall skinhead, with Rodent and Duck Foot behind me. Baby Huey trailed behind on a parallel course, keeping an eye on our flank. Sixty paces behind BH, Fred and his trio of shooters played rear security. I didn't want any surprises tonight.

Now, lest you think this is a cakewalk, it is fucking hard to move through the woods at night *sans* lights, *sans* noise, and *sans* conversation, if you are carrying nothing. It is incrementally harder to do it when you are hefting weapons and ammo, ropes, and other sundry items. Moreover, we had no way of knowing whether or not Lothar put out one or two or three picket lines of Russkie *byki*[85] to make things difficult for intruders, and so we had to err, if we were going to err, on the side of total stealth.

This is the long way of telling you that my three-hour window was slamming down on my hairy knuckles much faster than I would have liked. It was three and a half kliks to the rendezvous point. After just over an hour and a half, we'd moved only 1.25 kliks. That is a mere 1,250 meters, folks.

2114. Six yards ahead of me, Wolf froze. His right hand went into a fist and his thumb pointed toward the ground. *Enemy seen or suspected.* I reacted to his move. I stopped abruptly. My fist

---

[85]Goons.

clenched and my arm went up in the silent signal for an emergency halt.

Now Wolf's hand unclenched. Palm down, parallel to the ground, he moved it right, right, right. *Deploy, deploy, deploy.* As I dropped off into deep cover I gave silent thanks for cross-training. The kid had learned American military field signals—and that knowledge was paying off handsomely right now.

I rolled onto my back so I could see behind me. Everyone had cleared the track. And, I hoped, we were all on the same side. It is considered impolite in SpecWar circles to fire into your own team.

I rolled onto my elbows and held my breath, listening for anything untoward. Nothing.

And then . . . the hair on the back of my neck stood straight up. And I knew, there was danger somewhere out there. Just how this fundamental, instinctive early-warning device works I do not know. But it works—and it has saved my life countless time in the past.

There. Perhaps fifty yards ahead, a sudden shaft of light. It disappeared, and then it was back, probing at the undergrowth. It grew closer, jerked away, then back. Now I heard low voices in a language I didn't understand.

This is something I cannot comprehend. No—not the fucking language, you assholes, the *talking.* Sound carries. At night, a stage whisper can carry almost as far as normal conversation. Full stop. End of story. So, why talk at all? The answer is because most people are careless, and as I've said many times before, they do not pay attention to their work.

Inexorably, the light grew closer. Now it was twenty-five yards out, and getting closer. I shut my right eye. Didn't want to lose night vision. Fifteen yards. They'd be coming up on Gator. I knew he was making himself invisible. Waiting them out. Now I could hear the messy scrunch of footsteps on the thick bed of pine needles that made up the trail. Whoever these people were, they had no tradecraft at all. They sounded like a bunch of fucking heffalumps. All the better: when they went past Gator, he could turn and fire, and we could catch 'em in a classic ambush crossfire with suppressed weapons. They'd be dead before they fucking heard anything.

Except . . . they stopped. WTF had they seen? Were we compromised? There are hundreds of options that run through your mind in the space of a millisecond, and none of 'em are pretty. I mean, I didn't know if these guys had spotted one of my men and were figuring out how to wax us all. I had no way of knowing if one of 'em was wearing an open radio, and was being monitored by a security office somewhere in the *Schloss*.

And then Wolf just fucking stood up. Pulled himself to his feet and went toward the light, snapping branches and kicking leaves and pine needles and making as much noise as a fucking herd of oxen. I saw right away he'd left his gear behind. Shrugged right out of the CQC vest. Left the MP5 and his pistol belt behind, too. Nothing but his black T-shirt and Bundeswehr-issue moleskin fatigues.

I crept forward to a position that let me cover him while still remaining hidden. I slid the suppressed MP5 forward, brought it up into a prone firing position, and searched for a target. I found none. The thick trees and underbrush made target acquisition impossible.

Then I heard Wolf. He was chattering away in loud Deutsch. I got about every sixth word. Then he switched to English, which made it possible for me to understand every third word. Yes, I am using literary irony. Even here. Even now. That's the kind of guy I am.

And the gist of what he was saying? The gist was that these weren't security guards. They were fucking *touristen*. Hikers who'd gotten lost on the fucking trail. And Wolf, that Skinhead Samaritan, was explaining how the fuck they could take themselves back to civilization.

What he left unsaid, of course, was that these two assholes had almost gotten themselves whacked. Because my rule of engagement when it comes to suspected enemy contact, is to kill 'em all first, and ask questions later.

2220. We left the *Stadtwald* and began our descent to the Eltz. Mister Murphy decided to put in his second appearance of the night, guiding us down a nasty slope filled with hollylike evergreens, whose spine-tipped leaves did our pedal extremities no good at all. We reached the gorge looking as if we'd rolled down a hill of fucking barbed wire.

I checked my notes and pondered the hand-drawn map I kept in my left breast pocket. We should be just over two kliks west of the *Schloss* now, some five hundred yards from the rendezvous point with Nod and Boomerang. And despite Duck Foot's twisted ankle and the ATE (look it up in the Glossary), we were still slightly ahead of schedule.

2255. We stayed ahead of the curve for almost two minutes. Then it became obvious that we were going to be late for our *Treff*[86] with my plastique-planting mavericks.

We spread out into a long skirmish line and moved down the gorge, obscuring our trail in the soft riverbank by staying in the river itself. Now, for those of you who haven't done this sort of thing lately, patrolling down a riverbank is not like walking along Riverside Drive or strolling Venice Beach. The bottom is uneven. You're ankle deep one step, knee deep the next, and testicle-shriveling waist deep the next. The mud sucks at your boots (if you haven't knotted 'em tight they'll pull off and disappear), and the stones—where there are stones—are greased-pig slippery. And as if that's not enough, you can fucking multiply everything by a value of ten because it is nighttime, and what little light there is plays tricks with you. But despite the problems of terrain, and the fact that we were behind schedule, I was breathing a little easier now that our movements were covered by the white sound of fast-moving water.

As you know, every piece of good news has an opposite side.

---

[86]Remember, that's Kraut for *rendezvous*.

In the present case, even though the sound of moving water masked our movements, it also would muffle the movements of the opposition. And so, Gator took excruciating care as he advanced, foot by foot, through the fast-moving water, sixty yards ahead of us. Which made our forward progress into something of an oxymoron.

2328. Boomerang, Nod, Gator, and Wolf were all ostentatiously stargazing on the rocky riverbank as I slipped and slid around a sharp bend and they came into sight. I thought about saying something creative, but frankly, nothing came to mind except "Fuck you very much, assholes."

"Oh, really highly, coolly inventive, Boss Dude," Boomerang said. "And when, pray, does the real fun begin?"

"Right now, cockbreath. From here on, we'll be making our approach in the water."

Chapter

19

2340. I BEGAN THIS HERE SAGA A COUPLE OF HUNDRED PAGES AGO explaining how fortunate it is that I love the cold and the wet. It is always amazing to me how things change very little over time. I was still cold, wet, tired, hungry, and suffering from terminal lack o' pussy, and my circumstances weren't going to change anytime in the immediate (or even relatively near-term) future.

Of course, if it's the big picture we're talking about here, cold and wet were going to be the least of my problems. The Eltz, which moved pretty fast for a small tributary of a slow-moving river (the Mosel), was flowing even faster now that the gorge had narrowed and big underwater rocks pushed the current in mysterious and potentially dangerous patterns.

We'd tied ourselves into pairs of swim buddies and begun the short but nasty swim down to the small, pitifully narrow scrap of riverbank that lay directly below the *Schloss*. Nasty? Oh, it was definitely doom-on-Dickie time. You already know that the water was so cock-shriveling cold that even the SAP/BJ[87] I told

---

[87]Remember that acronym? It stands for Special Assistant to the President for Blow Jobs.

you about earlier would have trouble dewithering me tonight. What I hadn't anticipated was the raw energy and kinetic power of the Eltz's subsurface eddies, swells, and whirlpools.

I'd roped myself to Wolf, who'd allowed that swimming wasn't his best sport. Well, not to worry: there's no water, friends, that I cannot traverse.

Of course, having said that (even to you), the War God immediately decided that I'd committed hubris. And as we all learned in English Lit 101, the noxious consequence of hubris is nemesis.

And so, having just inserted waist-high into the fast-moving water, my right boot tip caught itself between two rocks, at which precise instant I was hit by a subsurface whirlpool in the current. The water stood me up, then knocked me over, and twisted me 180 degrees to the starboard, with the result that my right knee was quickly hyperextended in a way that nature never intended it to be.

Oh, I must truly adore both God and pain, because God, ever beneficent, has provided me with multitudinous gifts of acute, intense, passionate suffering over the course of my professional life.

It was like being butt-fucked with a cattle prod. Belay that. It was worse. My knee was bent sideways, then backward, then sideways again. When it did, there was no more wet, or cold, only the pure, white heat of absolute, perfect, God-given agony. My whole body lit up. And then the fucking water slapped me around, turned me over, flipped me free of the toe-holding rock, and sent me sluicing downstream, headfirst, before I could reclaim any semblance of control.

My cheek was opened up as it hit something rough. My left shoulder cracked when I bounced off one hufuckingmongous underwater boulder as I threw myself in the opposite direction (or whatever direction it might have been), trying to correct my roll, pitch, and yaw problems. But they didn't want to be corrected. My rucksack wedged between two rocks, holding me underwater. I'd no sooner pushed myself free—no mean feat,

282

given the speed and force of the current—when the MP5's web strap came loose. The pistol grip slammed into my kidneys, knocking out what little wind remained in my lungs. I inhaled water—*fuuck*—muscled myself surfaceward long enough to grab as big a lungful of air as I could manage under the circumstances, then rolled back into the roiling water and lunged for the submachine gun (no way I was going to lose it here and now), and managed to grab the CQC strap just as the fucking thing disappeared beyond my grasp.

And then, and then, the rope around my waist drew taut and I was brought up short. I managed to surface again, sputtering, in a narrow cleft between two nasty-looking flat rocks. I pulled at the MP5 and freed it from wherever it had stuck itself, and brought the gun toward me until I held it close. Three yards away, Wolf, teeth audibly chattering above the water's noisy rush, reeled me in, lay me in an eddy, separated me from the weapon, and ran his hands around my throbbing knee. "Is *nicht kaput*," was his verdict. "Not broken."

"But is *nicht gut*, Dickie," he said, strangely disapproving, given the circumstances. *"Du bist der Kampfschwimmer. Ich—"* He mimed a race-car driver's hands on a steering wheel.

I puked up about a pint of water, flexed my knee in the way it was intended to bend, and considered telling Wolf that perhaps we should trade specialties tonight. But it was getting late, and there was work to be done. And so, I clapped him on the shoulder, gave him a hearty "fuck you," reaffixed the subgun, double-checked my web gear, made sure the rucksack hadn't sprung any leaks, and then rolled back into the water with a groan. As the former dweeb editor was so fond of misstating, "No pain . . . no pain."

2346. We floated under the orange blanket of sodium security light from the castle that bathed the river gorge. Slowly, slowly, I made landfall, turtled onto the steep, stone bank, unknotted the rope from my waist, shifted my MP5, eased a mag into position, slid the bolt forward, rolled over onto my back, crawled oh, so carefully under the rolled concertina razor wire that ran parallel to the river, and took up a defensive position in the shadow of a boulder. On my starboard side, Wolf mirrored my movements.

I felt half dead, and we hadn't even begun the serious part of the evening's entertainment yet. But you see, that's what makes SEALs different. Take Rangers. No disrespect meant, but they ride in a plane, jump out, and take their objective. Or take Delta Force—again, no disrespect meant here, either. Delta rides a plane to its preinsertion destination, then jumps aboard a chopper to the insertion site, then fast-ropes down, and takes the objective.

Now let's look at SEALs. We'll spend ten days crammed inside a fucking submarine, hot-bunking atop fucking torpedoes and getting a shower every third day, then have to lock out into the ocean, which is nasty and cold (with all the nasty goatfuck factors lockouts often entail). Then, having not killed ourselves during lockout, we'll load up our combat gear and swim two miles underwater to a precise dot on some chart. And now that we've thoroughly exhausted ourselves (as you will remember from the opening scenes of this book, swimming a long distance with combat gear is not an easy thing to do), we must then climb an ice-coated oil rig, or perform some similar body-numbing, debilitating, potentially lethal exercise. And then, after all of that Murphy-enriched foreplay, *then* we get to take our objective and wax the bad guys.

Yea, and even so, thus it was to be in our current situation. We were exhausted. We were wrung out. We were overstressed. And yet we weren't even halfway through getting to the point of waxing the bad guys yet.

Half Pint and Max the pilot arrived not thirty seconds behind Wolf and me. They unhooked and scrambled under the concertina wire toward a flanking position on the yard-wide riverbank. Fred and Werner rolled ashore. Then Duck Foot and Gator pulled themselves out of the water, followed by Baby Huey, Rodent, Boomerang, and Nod. As they used to say in all those World War II war movies: "All present and accounted for."

2349. We weren't alone: Mister Murphy had crawled ashore with us. Even though we'd made it through the perimeter lights unnoticed; even though we'd managed to crawl through the concertina wire without anything but a few scratches and a ripped BDU or two, we were still fuckee-fuckeed. Why? Twenty feet above the fast-moving river, the castle wall was climbable— it was as uneven as one of those training modules used by rock climbing professionals. But the first six or seven yards were sheer, smooth escarpment. Even Duck Foot couldn't climb it. And Gator was no Duck Foot.

I looked over at Boomerang, tapped my watch face, and shrugged, as if to ask how much time we had.

He shook his head dejectedly and signaled back: "One hundred and one minutes until boom-boom. Just as you commanded, Boss Dude."

Fuck the boom-boom. This was doom-doom. Doom-doom on Dickie time.

Roy Boehm, who was and is a serious student of Asian philosophy, used to tell me, "When you're confronted by what looks like the impossible, just let your mind wander, and a solution will come."

I hunkered down at the base of the castle's foundation and let my mind wander. Fred hunkered down next to me, his shoulder brushing mine. At which point, Baby Huey, who'd been uncharacteristically quiet all night, said, "Hey—don't move, Skipper."

I didn't move. BH stepped between us, then put one boot onto my right shoulder and the other on Fred's left shoulder, his arms steadying him as he spread-eagled on the *Schloss*'s foundation. "Now stand up," he said.

We did—carefully. BH waited, then jumped down, gingerly. He turned to me, his face full of excitement. "It's like my cheerleading squad in high school," he burbled. "We use a four-man base, three guys on top of them, two on top of them, and then Gator—he can reach the castle, I think," BH said.

Nod looked quizzically at Baby Huey. "You were a cheerleader in high school?"

"Hey, can you think of a better way to get to feel up good-looking chicks on a daily basis and get phys ed credit for it?" BH's face clouded over. "Why, you wanna make something of it?"

"Hell, no, kid. But it answers one question I always had about you."

Gator gave his shipmate a quasinasty look. "Oh, *yeah?*"

Nod ruffled Baby Huey's hair and grinned. "Yeah—it tells me why you're so fuckin' perky all the time." He stepped out of the way as BH took a good-natured swing at him. "C'mon—Terry's got a great idea."

2355. We built the pyramid. It was hard, because the rock bowed outward slightly, which meant we couldn't stand up against it at the base. If anybody took a tumble, they'd end up on the rocks—and I didn't need any broken bones tonight.

Gator waited until I gave him an upturned thumb. Then he began his long climb. He used my sore knee as his launching pad, then clambered up onto my shoulder. I helped hoist him up as far as I could, Fred's strong arm supporting him as he went. Then Rodent, Werner, and Max took the strain. Gator went over them, passed along to Half Pint and Nod by the second level of the pyramid.

"Fuck—"

I couldn't see shit from my position on the bottom. "What's up?"

"He cramped, Skipper," came Nod's stage-whisper from above. "He'll work it out."

He'd better. The fucking clock was ticking.

0001. Nod worked his way down the human pyramid, followed by Half Pint. "Gator's on his way," he reported.

0002. I watched, squinting into the lights, as Gator did the Spiderman bit, picking his way up the rough stones, pulling himself inch by inch. Let me tell you something: thirty feet is a long, long way to go, especially when you are working without a net, carrying a weapon, and a long coil of thick, soft climbing rope.

286

0013. Gator rolled over the narrow wood balcony and disappeared into the shadows. Ten seconds later, the climbing rope dropped soundlessly. Wolf attached two more, and double-yanked. Everything was pulled back up onto the balcony, and some fifty seconds later, a trio of climbing ropes descended back toward us.

Now came the fun part. Baby Huey and Nod played rear guard. Wolf, Rodent, and Half Pint were first men up. I watched as they muscled their way up the sheer scarp of the foundation, and then used the uneven castle stones to ease their journey. Fred, Boomerang, and I went next. Instinctively, I put my weight on the rope to test it. Then I took it in a climbing grip, and began the long ascent.

Out of the corner of my eye I watched as Boomerang's boots scampered out of sight. I hate youth. It's so . . . young. My knee throbbed painfully. I could feel the fucking thing pulsate with each pull upward. Next to me, I heard Fred's breath, as reassuringly heavy as my own. I looked over at him. His arms were straining. His face was beet red and distorted in a grimace. His discomfort brought me a smile. "Having fun yet, *Brigadegeneral*," I wheezed.

"Fuck you," came Fred's taut response. "I bet I get to the top before you do, *Kapitän*."

0024. "Welcome aboard, Boss Dude." Boomerang grabbed me by the belt and heaved me over the balcony rail. I collapsed onto the narrow decking, every muscle in my body way past the burnout stage. Even the fucking cuticles on my toenails hurt. Boomerang, however, paid me no attention at all. He was too busy hauling Fred's aching Kraut butt over the rail. Fred collapsed next to me, hyperventilating. *"Weiß der Himmel—I'm getting too old for this,"* he wheezed.

I pulled myself to my feet and smacked him on the upper arm hard enough to make him hurt through the pain he was already feeling. "C'mon, *mein Brigadegeneral*, we have another ten feet to go."

0026. That final step was the hairiest. I climbed onto the

balcony rail, balanced, and stretched as high as I could. Balanced precariously like that, I could just reach the bottom of the thick, hand-hewn window ledge above. I steadied myself, and jumped straight up, caught the window ledge, and, just as if I were doing one of my three dozen daily chin-ups on the outside bar at Rogue Manor, pul-*l-l*-ed myself slowly, but inexorably, up, up, up. Once my chin cleared the bottom of the crenellated window, things got a lot easier and I was able to muscle myself over the low sill and crawl on hands and knees into the room.

I caught my breath, then went back to the edge to help Fred. I reached down, caught him by the wrists, and pulled him up, into the room. He, like me, decided that walking on hands and knees was just fine for the time being.

0029. Boomerang stayed behind to ensure that Duck Foot, who was last man up the rope, had a relatively easy time getting from the balcony to the window above. Then, he climbed out onto the balcony rail and, like a fucking dancer, leapt straight up about three feet, caught the windowsill, and pulled himself directly into the room *sans* any of the messy heavy breathing that had affected Fred and me. Like I said, I hate youth.

0030. We were all aboard. We'd made our entrance into a rectangular room that was perhaps eight yards by six yards. The narrow crenellated windows allowed more than enough ambient light from the security lamps to allow us to reconnoiter. The ceiling was low, with hand-hewn beams painted in a rustic design of vines and grapes. The plaster-over-stone walls continued the theme, with trellises and arbors. Along the entire window wall, a pair of heavy drapes, currently drawn back, hung from fluted poles. The ceiling beams were supported by a series of octagonal-cut, dark wood joists. The floor was plain, unpainted, worn wood, broken up by threadbare oriental rugs. There was a fireplace faced with tile on the far wall. Its small mouth was covered by a heavy iron sheet held in place by a pair of ornate andirons. The room's single door lay just beyond the fireplace. It was not more than five feet high, arched, and hinged with black wrought iron straps.

One slight tactical problem was that we had no idea where we were, relative to the bad guys. Normally, in an op such as this, you have intel—either diagrams or blueprints, satellite or thermal imagery, to help you figure out where the tangos are. Not tonight. Tonight we'd be operating blind.

Well, not exactly blind. There were three levels of windows above where we'd made entrance, and so we had to be somewhere in the middle of the castle. Now, since folks tend to have their living quarters above ground level, it was most likely that the ADMs were stored in the nether regions, while Lothar would have a room with a view, and the Russkies would be relegated to the servants' quarters: either up in some tower chamber, or down in the basement.

0031. We had just under an hour to find out for ourselves— less, if we were discovered. I positioned myself by the outer door. Boomerang closed the windows and pulled the drapes shut, so we wouldn't be silhouetted, then moved into position behind me. He'd be my backup. I could sense the rest of my stack form up behind me. Baby Huey was third in the daisy chain. Then came Duck Foot, with Gator following, and Nod playing rear security. Fred led second stack: Wolf was his number two, Max followed, then came Rodent, and Half Pint. Werner played rear security.

Good thinking. Fred kept the Americans together and sandwiched 'em with Krauts. That would take care of any language problems.

0032. I waited. SOP is to let the last man in the stack signal that he's ready by squeezing the right shoulder of the man in front of him, an act that is then repeated on up the line as each man is ready to go. I counted seconds. Sixteen of them. Then Boomerang squeezed my shoulder, I nodded my head once up/down in the darkness to let him know I acknowledged, eased the heavy wrought iron latch up, and cracked the door open.

Our chamber was at the dead end of a moderately long darkened corridor. Stop. Look around. There was diffused light emanating from my left. Go toward the light. I moved toward the light and experienced . . . déjà vu. Then I realized the whole gestalt was vaguely reminiscent of an early 1980s computer game called Zork. Well, fuck Zork. This was real, not some lines written on a green phosphor screen.

I eased through the doorway, my left shoulder to the wall, my suppressed MP5 (the fire selector in three-shot burst mode) in low ready position, its Tritium night sights bright in the murky environment. Behind me, Boomerang's suppressed USP covered over my right shoulder. Behind him was Baby Huey, whose MP5 worked the starboard side of the corridor.

We moved with the sort of symbiotic choreography that comes with operating together for a long time. Each shooter's motions came in synergetic counterpoint to the man in front of him. It was like we were one, big, lethal stealthy creature.

I forced myself to breathe in/breathe out; made sure that my head and eyes kept moving. Scan and breathe. That's the way to keep alive when you're in situations like this. And so, I scanned, and I breathed. And then, as I drew up, close to the end of the corridor, the hair on the back of my neck stood up, and I stopped moving and breathing altogether. I didn't hear any footfalls. But I knew that someone was coming our way.

I'm gonna give you a SpecWar insight right now, my friends. If you wanna be a SpecWarrior, do not wear aftershave or cologne. Do not douse yourself in Old Spice, or Obsession; Canoe, or Brut. Because if you do, I will detect you coming a mile away, and I will wax your naïve but sweet-smelling ass.

Story: at one point in my long and checkered career, I was assigned to train an antidrug unit known as GOE, pronounced *goy,* in the make-believe State of São Paulo, in a fictional country I'll call Brazil. The GOE boys were good shooters, and they were fast learners. But they always insisted on wearing their aftershave on the job. I guess it's an integral part of the Brazilian culture, or something, because it was impossible to change their thinking on the subject. But wearing cologne is what got eight GOEs killed on a drug raid in the Amazon basin. The fucking *drogistas* smelled 'em coming, and cut the unit to shreds.

I do not allow my men to wear scent. Or to use anything but basic, Mark-1, Mod-Zero hard soap—and in the jungle, I don't even allow 'em to use that. Because if you don't blend in with your environment, you will stand out. And if you stand out, you will get dead. Full stop. End of story.

Back to real time. The heady, overpowering, sickly sweet bouquet of Habit Rouge applied by the pint came my way, wafting up the wide Rogue nostrils.

As my nose twitched in involuntary protest to the pungent aroma, I silent-signaled a halt. Quickly, my right hand told the stack that I'd handle the situation. Then I raised the MP5, got myself a flawless cheek weld and perfect sight picture, dropped my trigger finger from its "index" position onto the trigger, stepped around the corner . . .

And sneezed.

Have you ever sneezed a big, wet, heart-stopping sneeze when you're driving at sixty-five on the freeway in heavy traffic? One of those pluvial, windshield-streaking sneezes that sound like, "Ka-*BLISH*?"

I have. And whenever I do, my eyes squeeze shut, my heart stops, I generally stomp on the accelerator, lose momentary control of the fucking car, and I consider myself lucky that I manage not to smack the car in front of me.

Yeah, well, just consider the exact same genus of sneeze when you've got your fucking finger on the fucking trigger of a fucking MP5, and the safety's off.

Here's the good news: the subgun was suppressed—and all anyone heard was the clack-clack-clack of the hammer dropping, the clatter of jacketed hollowpoint bullets striking the ceiling, and the tinkle of nickel-plated casings as they ejected onto the stone floor. Here's the bad news: the three-shot burst went completely wild, sending stone fragments all the fuck over the place—to be precise, slashing my face. And here's more bad news: the Ivan who'd caused my allergic reaction was swinging the muzzle of his own suppressed subgun—it looked like a Bizon, but to be honest I wasn't into a whole lot of brand recognition at that precise instant—up, up, up and onto the immediate threat, which of course, was *moi*.

As is usual in these situations, the events seemed to play out at an almost languorous pace. His suppressor (I saw it clearly now and realized in the absurd way one sees meaningless details at times of stress that it was a screw-on model), was swinging around, moving toward me. I'd lost shoulder and cheek welds on the MP5 and was holding it one-handed, its fat muzzle vaguely ceilingward.

I lowered my arm, and reactively squeezed the trigger, stitching him across the neck and shoulder.

Oh, yeah—it was pure luck, believe me. But I'm one of those people who know how to take "yes" for an answer, and when I'm in extremis like this, I don't give a fuck about technique. I'm paid for results, not methods. All I want to do is make the cocksucker DEAD—as quickly as possible.

He went down with a gurgle, his gun clattering on the stone floor. Before I could finish him off, Boomerang stepped around the corner, shouldered me aside, put a double-tap—*phwat-phwat*—in the Ivan's head, and then gave me a smug, vaguely smart-assed look.

"*Gesundheit*, Boss Dude," he mouthed.

Right. Sure. "And fuck you very much, too."

Chapter

20

0049. WE FOUND A WAY TO REACH THE PARAPET WALK: A WIDE, circular staircase that led to the innermost battlements. Following its irregular perimeter would take us around the circumference of the castle. Keeping low so as not to cast a shadow in the sodium light, I peered out across the inner bailey, then down through a narrow balistraria to the crenellated, merloned walkway below. Now, I had some idea where we were. If the main gate was at twelve o'clock, we were currently at about two-thirty, which put us on the opposite side of the castle from where I'd seen the heaviest concentration of Ivans during my sneak & peek. I turned the radiation detector on and checked the readout. Then I split the force into working groups. First, it was better, tactically, to come at 'em from opposite sides. Second, I wanted to take down the ADMs myself. So Fred and his squad went starboard. My merry marauders and I took the port side of the castle.

The thing about castles is that each is unique. There is no standard. Thus, unless you're familiar with the layout of the castle beforehand, you can't anticipate a single fucking thing. We, of course, had no idea where the fuck anything was. And so, we moved with great caution, which of course meant that we made less progress than I would have liked—especially as the fucking clock was ticking, we had just over thirty minutes until the explosives went off, which is when SWH.[88]

Let me add that creeping on hands and knees is not a comfortable thing to do. It gets old (and painful) fast, especially when one (read *moi*) has a recently hyperextended knee. After about nine minutes of crabbing, creeping, waddling, and duck-walking, my right kneecap had swelled up to cantaloupe melon size, with all the appropriate accompanying pain. I looked heavenward with a beatific expression, because I knew God loves me more than he loves most of His children.

So much for the down side. The up side is that castles and *Schlosses* have more nooks and crannies than an English muffin, which makes the sneaking-and-peeking a lot easier. Schloss Barbarossa's inner parapet, for example, was not one of those movie-set deals that ran in a nice, gentle sweep. Its four-and-a-half-foot-high, crenellated, merloned wall was filled with myriad ninety-degree turns, abrupt twists, and other unexpected obstructions.

0101. We worked our way along the low wall, and crept around a narrow battlement. On the far side, I saw a blind turn, and then the hair on the back of my neck stood straight up again. I turned and signaled for a complete stop so my instincts and senses could take over. I went forward, inch by inch, Boomerang so close I could sense his body heat radiating. We made painstaking progress, prowling inch by inch along the battlement. My nostrils twitched palpably at the scent of cigarette smoke even before the Russkie voices came into play. Boomerang smelled it, too, because he tapped me on the shoulder and gave me an, *"If you fucking sneeze again I'll smack you upside the haid even if you are the Boss Dude"* look, which brought a quick, tension-breaking smile to my stressed-out face.

---

[88]Shit would happen.

I dropped to the deck, *e-a-s-e-d* to the corner, and cut the pie, centimeter by centimeter, to sneak a peek. Now, in all those Hollywood action movies, nobody ever goes snaking along the ground to take a look-see. Which is why Bruce, and Brad, and Arnold, and Sly, and the rest of the comic book cannon-fodder who try to pass themselves off as big-time action-adventure heroes wouldn't last ten fucking minutes in any of my units.

The last thing you want to do when you are operating in a covert manner is to draw attention to yourself. And sticking your head up in a way that changes the silhouette of a wall, or doorway, or fence line, or—yes—a parapet, is just about as stupid as playing Russian roulette with a loaded semiautomatic pistol.

And so, sucking the stone deck, big Slovak nose as close to the ground as I could get it, I eased my head slowly, slowly to my left, moving at an acute angle to the rough stone of the parapet wall until I was far enough out to be able to see around the oblique-angled corner.

There were one-two-three-four-five-six of 'em, perhaps eight, nine yards away, lounging and smoking, and passing a bottle of vodka back and forth. Three had slung their weapons over their shoulders. Three more subguns rested against the outer wall. They had radios—I could make out three, no four, handheld receivers on their belts. But so far as I could tell, not a single one was turned on.

Boomerang and I eased back, and I explained the situation with hand signals. The situation was fraught with nasty possibilities. There could be another group of Ivans around the next blind corner—and if they heard anything untoward, they could cause us a lot of trouble. Oh, sure, we could all pop up shooting. Maybe we'd take 'em out before they made a sound. But most likely not.

I see you, looking incredulous. You what? You say I've always claimed that my guys could double-tap anything, anytime, anywhere. You say I brag that my units use up more ammo on the range than the entire U.S. Marine Corps on an annual basis, and therefore, they should be able to do whatever the fuck they have to do. That's all true—and I still hold to it. But six *simultaneous* double-taps presents a number of tactical problems. And no, I don't have the time to go into them now. Just take my fucking word for it.

But tonight, I didn't have a lot of options. I wasn't about to toss a pebble or anything similar, because I didn't want the Ivans reaching for weapons or radios.

I silent-signaled my instructions and got five upturned thumbs. We'd go on three.

One. We hunkered, weapons out and ready, on the balls of our feet.

Two. I glanced to my right. Boomerang nodded, his USP ready to go. So did Baby Huey, who also was working with a USP now. Duck Foot's expression told me he was ready. Nod's chin went up/down, the USP steady in his big hands. Gator gave me a silent, *"Jawohl!"*

Three. Up. Get a sight picture on the portmost Russkie. Got it. Hold it. Breathe. Squeeze the trigger. Squeeze the trigger. *The motherfucker went down.* Next to me Boomerang fired—I heard quick *thwup-thwups* all down the line.

Time slowed. *The Russkies are frozen, watching us shooting at them, and unable to react.* It is a truth of battle: in those first milliseconds, if you shoot first, your opponent will freeze for an instant. No matter how well he's been trained; no matter how much he practices. It is human fucking nature. You hear a gunshot, and you fucking freeze. The professional simply freezes for much less time than the amateur. These assholes were bush league.

I charged forward, my feet moving side to side, never crossing, so as not to trip myself. My MP5 was still up. No telling whether we'd waxed 'em all, and I wasn't about to take chances.

Rounded the blind corner. All six Russkies were down. Scan. Breathe. Gun pointed toward the threat.

And then–

Peripheral vision. Movement. Swing the MP5 left and bring it down.

Two shots. Loud—ergo Russkie. Oh, fuck. Behind me, a cry of shock. Sight picture fuzzy. Squeeze trigger at the motion. Squeeze trigger again. And then it hit me. WTF: I'm not some goddam neurosurgeon.

I flicked the MP5's fire director to full auto and hosed all the Russkie bodies on the ground. No use taking any chances here.

I may have killed the sonsofbitches, but I was still fuckee-fuckeed. We'd lost surprise. And lost it long before I'd wanted to. No time to waste now. I looked back at Boomerang. "Blow the fucking charges," I said.

He reached for his radio transmitter. "Fire in the hole," he giggled.

You could feel the vibration as the charges went off, coming closer and closer to the castle. Now I heard shouts of alarm from beyond the doorway.

I wheeled to check on the casualty. It was Baby Huey. He'd been hit in the bicep. It was a clean wound, and from my quick examination no veins or arteries had been hit. But he was still going to be in shock soon, unless we handled things RIGHT NOW.

Duck Foot was over his shipmate, his hands fumbling in the fanny-pack first aid kit. He whipped out a thick wad of gauze pads, and a tube of antiseptic dressing, slapped those on the wound and wrapped Baby Huey's upper arm with the last of the surgical tape. The pressure would help. He started to prepare a Syrette of morphine, but Baby Huey knocked his hand away. "I'll be okay," the big kid growled.

Duck Foot stowed the morphine. "Your call, asshole."

BH rolled over, struggled to his knees, and finally pulled himself to his feet. "Too much work to do," he said, his face wet with perspiration, his teeth clenched against the pain. "No time for that shit."

So far as I was concerned, Baby Huey had just earned his fucking spurs. At that instant, I stopped thinking of him as the

FNG. He was one of us now: blooded in combat. And as I looked at this big, bruising, beamish boy struggling and persevering, a shudder of wonderment ran through my body. Oh, yes: it is watching Baby Huey's kind of commitment, my friends, that makes officers like me weak in the knees, and I took a couple of seconds to marvel at the birth of the latest Warrior to be forged in my image on the anvil of pain and dedication. But I didn't take long. My reverie was interrupted. Lights were coming on all over the fucking *Schloss.* We had to move.

0117. We hit three more pockets of Ivans before we came to the doorway I'd targeted during my recon, and ammo was beginning to run low. That's a problem on an op like this one. You have to maintain fire discipline, because you can only carry so many magazines. Tonight, I had six thirty-round MP5 mags, and eight fifteen-round USP mags stowed on my body, totaling three hundred rounds available. I'd used two USP mags and two MP5 mags so far. It didn't leave me a lot of breathing room.

I took a radiation reading. I was getting closer to my atomic grail—and the fucking door was bolted tight. Lemme tell you something about castle doors: they tend to be big and heavy. That's why they had all those medieval battering rams, I guess. We hadn't brought a battering ram—but we did have a couple of slivers of John Suter's C-4. Duck Foot took one small piece from Nod, gimped up to the door, and placed the charge around one of the wrought iron strap hinges, ran a pencil detonator and a long piece of quick-burning fuse, ignited it, and scampered back as best he could on his game ankle.

He hadn't even finished shouting the requisite "Fire in the hole . . ." when the fucking door blew. The hinge shattered, sending shrapnel back at us.

"Anybody hurt?"

Duck Foot answered for everybody. "Just fucking move, Skipper—"

I pushed the shattered door aside, charged through the smoking door frame . . . and found myself in a huge, pentagon-shaped antechamber, with a vaulted ceiling supported by hand-carved stone ribs formed into the shapes of stars, or perhaps flower petals.

I did a TVE. Fuck: it was a blind alley. The only entrance to this place was the one we'd just come through.

And then, a weird sensation washed over me. *I've been here before.*

MP5 still held at low ready, I took the time to look—really look—at where I was. There were narrow, faux-arched windows framed by weathered beams. Between the windows was a display case of seventeenth- and eighteenth-century pistols. The far wall was painted with coats of arms, each set into a trompe l'oeil "frame" of gold and faux painted wood. There were ornately carved tables; heavy wood chairs; pikes and halberds displayed in racks. There were crossbows.

I might have experienced a complete sense of déjà vu all over again as my eyes scanned this perfect Warrior's haven. Except it wasn't déjà vu. I'd been in this room before. Not *here*—but the *doppelgänger*[89] of this room: the faux-antique antechamber to Lothar Beck's office in Düsseldorf.

Which means, my friends, that there was a hidden doorway in this room. And that secret entry led somewhere important, just as it did at BeckIndustrie headquarters.

I strode to the wall covered with coats of arms, and probed. It took me less than ten seconds to find the door. I ran my fingers around the cleverly concealed portal.

It was time to make my entrance. I pried the hidden door open, checked to make sure there were no unfriendlies waiting, and beckoned my guys to follow me.

We moved quickly down a short, wide stone staircase into a huge, vaulted foyer. There were two sets of double doors: one port, one starboard. Radiation detector time. The signal grew stronger as I swiveled to my right. I gestured for Gator, Duck Foot, and Baby Huey to go left.

---

[89]Double

299

With Boomerang tight on my right shoulder, and Nod behind him, I retrieved a DefTec No. 25 flashbang from my thigh pouch, kicked in the right-hand doors, averted my gaze, and tossed the distraction device into the room.

The nice thing about the DefTec is that it is so fucking loud and so fucking bright. The flash just about imprinted on my eyeballs right through the goddam castle wall.

MP5 ready, I bulled my way through the smoke.

Boomerang's voice was loud in my half-deaf right ear: "Boss Dude—*threat, Red Four.*"

Yes, I know that in a three-man room clearance, the lead man usually moves to the left, but the most basic operational rule for all room clearance is: you take the most immediate threat first. I edged right, toward the Color Clock position Boomerang had shouted.

Scan. Breathe. Don't tunnel. I used as much of my peripheral vision as I could (it was pretty fucking dark in here) to make sure we weren't being outflanked. Shit: there was a wide archway off to my left, and a staircase off the rear, which told me this humongous chamber was only a small portion of the area we'd have to clear. "Take the green side and clear it," I shouted. "I'll cover this room. We'll meet up at the staircase."

Oh, yeah. Right. My favorite Chinese tactician, General Tai Li'ang, once wrote: "Never steal more chain than you can swim with."

Guess what? *Glub, glub.* The room was immense: fifteen yards long, perhaps ten yards wide, and filled to overflowing with heavy medieval furniture, suits of armor displayed on pedestals, eighteenth-century flintlock rifles and all their accessories displayed in glass cases, and there, amidst all the cacophony of museum-quality stuff, perhaps half a dozen computers, all tied together by cables and wires.

GNBN. The good news was that this had to be Lothar's ops center, so I was pretty close to the belly of the beast. BN was that, even in full daylight, the place was an ambusher's dream, and a room-clearer's nightmare. Now, in the dim light, the shadows made it nigh on impossible to pick anything out. Target acquisition was gonna be tough.

From off to my port side I heard firing. Nod and Boomerang had engaged, and I was on my own. As if on cue I saw vague movement through the smoke. I fired a three-shot burst, and heard a scream. Smoke cleared. Movement at eight o'clock. Fired two more three-shot bursts, then let a second barrage go, too. Did a shadow go down? Couldn't tell. Damn. Changed mags and advanced toward the threat. Moved cautiously between a pair of full suits of armor standing atop pedestals. One, two, dead Ivans stared up at me from the stone floor. A third was crawling away. I stitched two three-round bursts into his head.

A metal fragment cut my cheek, and I ducked instinctively as small arms fire from somewhere on my six pinged off the armor. Shit. Turned to the new threat but couldn't make anything out. Swept the room with my MP5. My fire was returned. Fuck—this was getting old, fast. I retrieved the last of my flashbangs, pulled the pin, hunkered as low as I could get, shut my eyes, tried not to think about the pain I was about to cause my eardrums, and soft-balled the fucking device into the center of the room, toward the general direction I'd been taking fire from.

Oh, damn, but those things are loud. I saw nothing but bright orange spots, which gradually gave way to bright green spots. I rubbed at my eyes and was finally able to focus long enough to make out stuff shattering and sparks erupting as one of the computer screens twenty or so feet away exploded.

The green spots turned to dark blue. My head wouldn't stop Big Ben-ing. And things were still too fucking fuzzy. But not so fuzzy that I didn't sense the automatic weapons fire coming my way from behind one of the big glass display cases of antique weapons.

When in doubt, shoot back. I rolled away, spray-and-praying toward the flintlocks, which is when the goddamn thing exploded, sending shards of glass all the fuck over the place, including into *moi*.

What had I done, you ask? From the intensity and brightness

of the explosion, I'd scored a direct hit on one of Lothar's antique black-powder flasks is what I'd done. Hadn't he once told me he kept all his weapons loaded? God, that's stupid. You never want to shoot anything into black powder. Black powder is fucking unstable.

Then the ringing in my ears and the bleeding of my face was interrupted by a solid *thwock,* followed by a new volley of shots in my direction. I watched as the big, thick refractory table in the center of the room was upended.

Even in my altered state, I realized, *The threat's gone behind the fucking table.* I brought the MP5 up and shot at the hufucking-mongous table. No reaction. Fired again, one, two, three three-shot bursts through the glossy, dark wood surface. I could see the splinters fly as I advanced on the cockbreath, whoever he was, making sure I was keeping his head down—if I hadn't killed the sonofabitch already.

That's when the MP5 ran dry. There are a lot of key elements to remember in situations like this one. One of the most key elements is to count your fucking rounds, so you don't do what I just did. Because if you forget to count rounds, you will end up with an empty fucking weapon, and the bad guy will wax your ass.

No time to reload—but I had to react. I released the MP5, letting it fall away on its combat sling. I threw myself off to the left and rolled onto the floor—slamming my damaged knee quite brutally in the process, I might add—my right hand frantically groping my tactical thigh holster for my USP.

Which is precisely when Franz Ulrich vaulted the table and charged at me. In his hand was a huge, lethal, and altogether much-too-familiar fucking knife.

Familiar? Oh, yes: almost twelve inches in length; flat-ground, geometric clip, fully serrated, chisel-tipped blade. It was the very same Mad Dog Taiho I'd left behind in Düsseldorf.

Chapter

21

HERE'S THE SITUATION *mit "einem Wort, kurz gesagt."*[90] *Eins:* Franz was coming at me hot and heavy. He had his War Face on, too, which made him even uglier than normal, especially as the cut I'd inflicted on his neck hadn't quite healed yet. *Zwei:* there was going to be no time to grab my pistol, which was stowed securely in my tactical holster.

Tactical holsters aren't built for quick-draw. Indeed, mine was a doubly secure, SAS model, built by the former SEALs at Blackhawk Industries in Virginia Beach. It was a spec-ops holster designed for both parachute and maritime ops. It had a restraining strap, as well as a flap that covered the entire butt of the pistol.

And guess who'd forgotten to unsecure the flap. That was all I had a chance to perceive—and tell you—before the big, Kraut bastard was on top of me. After all, it doesn't take more than a second to cover five yards at a dead run, and Franz was at a dead

---

[90]That's the Kraut way of saying, "In a nutshell." They are a loquacious bunch of assholes, aren't they?

run, my long lost but still very lethal Taiho knife held in a striking position.

Now, I have said this before and I will say it again: if you get caught in a knife fight without a weapon, the probability that you will get cut is just about 100 percent. But those odds are not necessarily detrimental. Consider two additional elements. The first is mind-set. Your attacker is overconfident because he has the weapon and you do not. The second is that the body itself will give you an additional boost. Your adrenaline will be off the fucking charts. Endorphins,[91] your body's natural painkillers, will be working overtime.

Combine those elements with one more factor: the Warrior Spirit, and the ABSOLUTE WILL TO WIN, honed through innumerable training sessions, and YOU WILL NOT FAIL. That is, of course, all contingent on whether or not Mister Murphy happens to be out of the room at the time.

Franz came straight at me, the knife's sawtooth serrated blade horizontal, held in what's known in the trade as a hammer grip. I sidestepped and managed a blow to his neck as he went past. But he was fast: that fucking knife whipped around and slashed at my hip. I reacted with an elbow to the back of his head.

Good news: I fucked with his marksmanship. The blade deflected away from my body and caught on my web gear. Bad news: the Taiho, especially the serrated blade version, is a very efficient knife when it comes to cutting multilayered, tactical nylon—things like seat belts, and web gear. So Franz's misdirected blow sliced clean through my pistol belt and my MP5 strap. The fucking subgun fell away, clattering to the floor. The pistol belt, weighed down by all the extraneous goodies hitched to it by Alice clips, hung useless, still attached to me by the pair of single elastic straps wound around my left and right thighs. It was like being restrained by an absurd garter belt. My tactical

---

[91]Endorphins (a fusion of the words *endogenous* and *morphine*) are natural peptides occurring in the brain and other body tissues. They resemble opiates, and they react with the brain's opiate receptors to raise the pain threshold.

holster and the combination MP5 mag and flashbang pouches were Velcro'd firmly to my thighs, keeping me from moving freely. While Franz pranced freely, I was restrained by this ungainly, perverse, ballistic nylon hobble.

Doom on Dickie, because Mister Murphy was indubitably along for tonight's ride. I backpedaled, and frantically tried to fix the damage. But the damage was unfixable—at least right now. And why was that? It was because Franz had found his balance, whirled, and was coming back at me.

But this time he didn't charge. His face contorted with rage, his eyes filled with hate, the scar on his cheek bright red, he moved like a bullfighter, his left arm balanced in front of him as if it had a muleta over it, his right holding the big, thick, tanto-bladed Taiho flat against his arm in a Ninja grip, so he wouldn't telegraph his deadly intentions.

He whirled, slashed at my right arm—and missed. I stepped under him, trapped his knife arm, turned so as to hyperextend it, then brought him across my body with a nasty hip throw. Lemme tell you, friends, that the simple act of throwing him, combined with the fact that he caught in my tactical holster strap, which put pressure on my already swelled knee, made the pain in that damaged joint crescendo to a previously uncharted level on the Rogue scale. But let me also tell you that my endorphins must have been pumping opiates by the quart—because pain didn't fucking matter right then. I just kept going. I dropped him flat, elbowed him in the face, raked at his eyes, and tried to detach his ear with my teeth.

He screamed and called me unprintable names in *Deutsche* while he tried to wriggle his trapped arm free, slamming and slapping and kicking and punching like some fucking dervish. The activity didn't do him much good. After all, I outweighed the S.O.B. by maybe twenty-five or thirty pounds.

But I'll give him this much: the asshole didn't drop the knife. Instead, he quit playing around and caught me with a finger to the eye that got my attention good. And, as I slapped my hand to my injured face, he executed a well-timed snap and roll, separated from me, flipped back onto the balls of his feet, and kicked out—snap!—catching me *whap* in the cheek with the sole of his boot.

The impact knocked me backward into a goddam suit of armor. I went sprawling, tangled up in the fucking armor. Here is something I never knew: they tie the goddam separate pieces onto a fucking wire frame. But the suit itself is not whole, just wired together. So when I collided with the goddamn thing it kind of exploded, all the pieces coming loose—but still joined by wire. It was like somebody threw a fucking fishing net over me.

Franz has never been one to lose an opportunity. He was on me, blade first, like stink on shit. He stabbed through the breastplate. The fucking chisel point of the Taiho cut cleanly through the polished steel.

I grabbed hold of the pauldrons and wrestled the torso to keep the point of the blade from coming directly toward my face.

He yanked the knife out and struck again—this time the fucking blade punctured the elbow protector. I bent the elbow up—and trapped the goddam blade in an improvised metal vise, then popped Franz a quick double-tap with the front of the chestplate, catching him in the nose with the rondel that sits right at the shoulder joint.

That rocked the *Schei&kerl*[92] back a foot or two. I heaved the armor off me, launched myself at Franz, and grabbed his knife arm at the wrist with both hands, and managed to turn it aside before he brought his left hand up, fingers extended, and tried to rake my eyes. I managed to turn away, and he missed my eyes— but from the way my cheek burned (endorphins or no endorphins, that *hurt*), the motherfucker must have had pieces of flesh under his fingernails.

I broke free and used my elbow to catch him in the face. There was a satisfying crunch of cartilage as I broke his nose, and I heard a stimulating grunt (it was stimulating to me, at least) from

---

[92]Cockbreath asshole.

him as my arm impacted one more time, and he realized he had to bring his free hand up while trying to protect himself and breathe at the same time.

Bad move, Franzie. You old Rogue readers all know that I press 450 pounds 155 reps, day in, day out, hung out or hung over, on the outdoor weight pile at Rogue Manor. So, lemme tell you newcomers something: I am one very strong motherfucker. That attribute gives me a lot of fucking leverage when I need it most—like right now.

I rolled atop him, my right hand still clamped around his knife wrist. I slammed the arm up and back, trying to loosen his grip on the weapon. But Franz wasn't giving up. He brought his arm back, whipped the blade around, and caught me a glancing blow on my upper bicep.

Oh, fuck, I hate to get cut. But getting cut wasn't about to stop the intensity of my struggling. In fact, it made me more implacably, virulently deadly, dangerously bloodthirsty.

Oh, yes, this motherfucker was about to pay.

But not yet.

Mister Murphy must have snuck up on us, because somehow, Franz managed to wriggle out from under me. In a fucking frenzy he clawed, elbowed, slashed, and kicked. It worked: it moved me back just far enough for Franz's steel-tapped heel to catch me under the chin in a kick to my Adam's apple that must have started with his eyelids.

Because I saw fucking stars. Belay that. I saw the whole Milky fucking Way. Things went all black and white. I couldn't grab a breath. My vision was fuzzy and faint.

And then he was back, up close and personal enough for me to tell you that he'd been eating something with garlic in it not too long ago. He shoulder-tackled me, knocking me back across the floor, tangling me up in the armor again, the big-bladed Taiho coming up, up, up, toward my chin. The sonofabitch wanted to take out my carotid artery.

Not now, Scheißkerl, not ever.

I flailed at him. He was fucking implacable, his face a mask of rage and hate. The knife came up. I grabbed it with my left hand, swung inside and rolled, using my hip to pivot the two of us— and toss him onto his back. But Franz has been through the same martial arts courses I have. So he knew precisely how to break my hold, deliver a fucking effective knee to my rib cage, and follow it with a roundhouse kick that swept me right off my feet.

I whirled and scrambled away, regained my balance and tackled him, driving him into the stone floor. We rolled around, each trying to gain the advantage—something that is much harder than it sounds when your opponent has a nasty knife and he keeps trying to slice off parts of your body with it.

My right arm caught on something cold as we rolled. Instinctively, I grabbed and held on. It was one of the suit's two vambraces—heavy, unjointed forearm protectors with ornate, pointed tops.

I ripped at it, and the fucking thing came free of the picture wire. I took the vambrace and jammed it, pointed edge up, from below, the spined tip cutting deeply into Franz's chin.

The blow slapped his head back, he bellowed like a fucking stuck *Schwein*. I jackhammered him again, working the sharp, pointed tip at the top of the vambrace into his throat. He gurgled in a way that told me eloquently that I'd hurt him serious. I didn't give a shit: I was having a good old time. And anyway, I didn't have to be told anything. Franz's actions spoke louder than his gurgles. The fucking knife dropped away from my throat.

Too bad Franzie. It was time for him to die.

Now I used my weight to pull him down, down, into a vortex of pain. I kicked the Taiho clear. Wouldn't need it, because I saw something better. My right hand dropped the vambrace then reached out for another weapon: the mace that had hung from the suit's gauntlet.

No, it wasn't fun holding Franz down. He was a strong motherfucker, and I had a hell of a time maintaining a grasp on him because my hands were wet with my own blood. Moreover,

Franz knew all the tricks of the trade. He worked out regularly, too. But all that didn't matter, because I didn't have to like it—I just had to do it. And Do It I did. He struggled, but I was having none of it.

I was thinking about Fred—and how he could have died. I thought about his dead shooters, and that this traitor to the uniform he'd once worn was responsible for killing Fred's shipmates. I thought about all the shooters who have died because assholes like Franz Ulrich betray their shipmates, and their nations. Oh, my friends, the list of traitors is far too long. Jonathan Pollard. Buckshot Brannigan. Aldrich Ames. Grant Griffith. Edwin Wilson. LC Strawhouse. John Walker. Werner Lantos. Ehud Golan. Bentley Brendel. And now, Franz Ulrich.

My fingers found the hilt of the mace—I pried it loose from the wire attaching it to the gauntlet; wound tightly around its sturdy wood shaft. Brought the head up, around, and swung the fucking thing just like it was a hammer and I was laying decking.

The first blow caught Franz on the cheek. It shattered his jaw. That one was for Fred's men.

He screamed in pain, which made me feel real good.

The sonofabitch tried to crawl away from me. He kicked out again, but he was hurt, and he had no power in his legs anymore.

I swung the mace in a big arc and caught him in the knee. As he reacted to that, I hit him again, smashing the other knee; shattering his patella and both condyles. He roared in agony. But he kept moving, dragging himself across the stone like the robot in the original *Terminator* movie, moving slowly, inexorably, toward the Taiho, six yards away.

I pulled myself off the floor and went after him. I used my height and my weight, swinging the fucking mace in a paroxysm of fucking vengeance. My goal was KISS: break every fucking bone in his fucking body—and then kill the cockbreath.

My first blow caught him in the shoulder, snapping his clavicle. He tried to roll away, but there was no escape. I brought the mace down in a two-handed blow and caught him in the sternum, cracking his fucking chest open.

I looked down at him. The motherfucker was drooling now, bloody spittle running down into the ripped, soiled black cashmere turtleneck. His eyes peered up at me, uncomprehending because the motherfucker was already in terminal shock.

Too bad. I wanted him to know what was happening. I reached down and grabbed him by his short, steel gray hair, and put my face down next to his so he could read my fucking lips.

"You're a fucking cockbreath," I told him. "You're a fucking traitor."

He tried to say something, but no words escaped. Just more spittle.

I gave him a Roguish smile. *"Auf wiedersehen,* Franz, you *Scheißkerl."*

I smacked his head back onto the floor. From the "I dropped a melon on the floor" sound of the impact, I probably gave him a bad concussion right then. But frankly, a bad concussion was about to be the least of his problems.

I stepped back, took the mace, held it like a golf club, checked my swing, and addressed the business end to the side of Franz's head. As the spiked round tip of the mace touched him, his eyes rolled in my direction. That's when he realized what was about to happen.

Oh, his eyes were *r-e-a-l* expressive. But the motherfucker couldn't move. He was dead in the water. Maybe I'd severed some spinal nerves. Maybe he was beyond motion. I didn't know, and I didn't give a rat's ass. My body hurt like hell. My right hand was wet with blood from the cuts on my arm. But the blood, and the pain, meant fuck-all right now.

There was work to be done. I gauged distance, power, stroke, and force, then drew the mace head back over my right shoulder, and—*fore!*—let fly.

I am no golfer, but believe me, my form was Tiger Woods, Arnold Palmer, Greg Norman Great White fucking Shark perfect, right then. I used more than enough backswing to give the mace an incredible degree of raw, kinetic drive. My shoulders, my arms, my wrists, all fused symbiotically to achieve a perfect, powerful, hole-in-one stroke.

Thwummmp. It was a hole in one, all right—a big hole in one big asshole. The mace head buried itself just above Franz Ulrich's ear, and right below the zygomatic arch. The force of the swing (and, yes, I remembered to follow through), sent a big, bloody divot of Franz's brain matter ten feet down the room.

Just to make sure he wouldn't bother me again, I changed position and hit him a second time, caving his fucking Kraut skull in from the top.

I left the mace buried in his head, retrieved my long-lost Taiho, and shoved it back in its Kydex sheath. I readjusted the rucksack. I repaired my belt with duct tape from my fanny pack, reloaded the MP5, unflipped the security flap on my USP, and then limped toward the staircase that I instinctively knew led to Lothar Beck.

Indeed, the night's mission wasn't over yet. Not by a long shot. The American ADMs were here—and I wanted 'em back.

Chapter

22

0125. I LINKED UP WITH BOOMERANG AND NOD. IT WAS BOTH joyful and irksome that neither of them looked much the worse for wear. Bone tired, sure. Grungy, too. But still ready to go. That was them. As for *moi*, Nod gave me a critical once-over and shook his head. "Hey," I told him, "there's nothing wrong with me that the juice from a liter of Bombay Sapphire couldn't cure."

Nod, his expression somewhere between disbelief and be-musement, slit my BDU blouse sleeve, applied antiseptic, wrapped the four-inch slit on my arm with gauze bandage, and taped it securely to staunch the bleeding. "It could use some staples," he said.

"I'll get the fucking thing stitched later," I told him.

Nod checked his handiwork with a critical eye and decided that it would do for the present. Then he repaired my slit sleeve with duct tape. "Right, Skipper. Anything you say."

I hate patronizing, don't you? But to be honest, I was too fucking tired, too fucking pinged, and too fucking dinged to do anything about it right then.

Besides, all those wonderful endorphins were fading by the second. My arm was throbbing, my knee hurt like hell, and there was another traitor to kill. I started to pick my gear up. "Let's just fucking go to fucking work, okay?"

"I really do like your ironic repetitive use of the *F*-word, Boss Dude," Boomerang said, his head going up and down like one of those goddam doggie toys you see in the rear windows of 1956 Chevys.

There is an ironclad rule about officers smacking enlisted men upside the head that I considered violating at that point. But any thoughts of mischief were interrupted by the sound of gunfire below. I wasn't here to play around. I was here to TCB. I turned the radiation detector on (I was gratified to see that my recent bout of balls-to-the-wall physical exercise hadn't damaged it), and peered down at the readout. Just as I'd guessed: the signal was getting stronger every step we went closer to the stairway. Oh, I knew I was headed in the right direction.

That, of course, was precisely when the fucking thing emitted a pair of plaintive bleeps and abruptly shut down on me. Was it the batteries that had died? Or was it the fact that the cocksucking, motherfucking device had been dropped, flopped, and whopped as a result of my recent activities. I didn't know, and there was no time to care. I was on my own now. But at least I had a vague idea of where I had to go.

0129. I took point, moving cautiously in the shadowy half-light. The stairway was right out of one of those 1930s Hollywood Errol Flynn costume epics: wide stone stairs, perfect for swordplay. Except I didn't have a sword. I'd do my dueling with an MP5, thank you very much. I kind of expected big candelabras or sconces, lighting my way.

The firing was much more sporadic now—at least what I heard of it. That meant that Fred and his group were taking care of business, and that my second three-man squad was also hard at work mopping up the malefactors.

I descended stealthily but steadily. No time to waste. I cut the pie, checked for threats, and finding none, moved on, inexorably downward.

It was a long stairwell, and the air grew noticeably cooler as we descended into darkness. At the bottom, we turned a sharp corner and were greeted by a thick, iron-reinforced door. Light emanated from underneath—and shouting, too. I approached cautiously and tried to raise the latch. It was immovable. I tested the door. It was obviously barred and bolted from the inside. Unlike modern doorways, most of which can be shot open with a submachine gun, you can't fucking shoot the bar off a damn medieval door because the wood is too thick, and the straps are too heavy. You need a ram, or a big fucking shotgun, or similar, to shatter the strap hinges and blow the fucking door open. Or you need explosives—ribbon charges, for example, or C-4.

Tell you what: the next time I hit a castle, I'm gonna make sure someone is carrying a fucking breaching shotgun, a lot of fucking T.K.O. shells,[93] half a dozen two-pound blocks of C-4, a satchel full of breaching charges and lots of fucking detonators. That way, doors like this one won't stop us. But that wasn't the case tonight. Tonight, we were locked out in the dark, holding our limp *szebs*[94] in our flippers, while who knows WTF Lothar was doing behind that fucking door.

"Whoa—" Nod was rummaging through his pockets. He withdrew a dark plastic vial and unscrewed the top of it. Inside was a chunk of C-4 about thrice the size of a sugar cube. "This is the last of John Suter's stuff," he stage-whispered, dumping the three-quarter-inch lump of plastic explosive into the palm of his hand.

Great. Now we could blow the door. My elation lasted for all of three seconds, which is how long it took me to factor in that all

---

[93]The T.K.O. (Tactical Knock-Out) is a frangible 12-gauge slug that is made of compressed zinc powder. It disintegrates locks and bolts when fired from a shotgun whose barrel has been equipped with a standoff attachment.

[94]If you can't figure out what this means by reading it in context, look the fucking word up in the Glossary.

the detonators were in Duck Foot's fanny pack, and who knew where the fuck Duck Foot was.

Boomerang obviously had his own ideas about what to do. He held his long, calloused palm under Nod's nose. "Gimmee," he hissed.

Nod relinquished the cube. Boomerang worked it, rolling the explosive into a round ball. Then he pressed the plastique, doughlike, up against the big door's middle strap-hinge. It stuck there like a wad of chewing gum. "I'll be back," he growled in an almost passable Schwarzenegger.

Boomerang sprinted up the stairwell. I dropped to the ground and tried to peer under the door, but there was no way to look past the uneven stone floor. But there were fucking people in there, and they were doing something, because we could hear 'em moving.

0132. Boomerang was back. He was carrying a fucking five-foot-long flintlock rifle with an ornately inlaid stock, and a six-foot-long pike. I looked at him. "WTF?"

"Dig it, Boss Dude." Boomerang took the rifle and sat it butt end on the floor. He retrieved a powder flask from his pocket and dumped what can only be called a shitload of granular black powder down the muzzle of the rifle, found a wad of cloth, and tamped the cloth home with the wood ramrod. Then he opened the pan cover, added a spritz of powder to the flash pan, and closed the cover again.

Boomerang picked the rifle up, retrieved the ball of C-4 from the strap hinge, and tamped it just into the crown of the flintlock's muzzle. Then he pulled back the cock. He wedged the butt of the weapon into a crack in the stone floor, and tapped the weapon with his foot to make sure it was set firmly. The muzzle, C-4 barely extending, was smack up against the thick, wrought iron strap hinge of the big door.

"Stand back." He pushed us back up into the stairwell, took the pike, and reached it around toward the trigger. "Fire in the hole, Boss Dude . . ."

Let me tell you something about black powder. It is much more volatile than smokeless powder, and much more explosive. The fucking flintlock was louder than a goddam DefTec No. 25. It was so loud I thought my eardrums had ruptured. All I could hear was ringing. When I was able to see through the smoke, I saw that the door frame had shattered, and the door itself was ripped off its hinges. Geezus, that stuff is effective. There was nothing left of the flintlock except for a few splinters of wood from the stock. The rest of it had been fucking vaporized. I think that if the C-4 hadn't blown the hinge, the fucking black powder would have done the job by itself.

Show Time. I went through the door first, scanning through the thick smoke and squinting at the bright lights. There were one-two-three black Mercedes diesel trucks lined up, twenty yards away, on the far side of this cavernous chamber, engines running. I tried to see whether anybody was behind the wheel, but couldn't tell.

Nod's voice cried out, "Threat, Green Ten—"

I turned left, acquired the target and fired a three-shot burst that brought him down. Over my right shoulder, I heard the abrupt chatter of Boomerang's MP5, then Nod's. I kept moving to my left, my back up against the wall, scanning and breathing as I searched for targets, making my way abreast of the trio of trucks. I wanted to know where the fucking exit was because I didn't want these guys going anywhere.

A throaty growl from my twelve o'clock. The truck closest to me gunned its engine, and from somewhere in the cab—I couldn't see a silhouette of his head—the driver popped the clutch. The fucking truck jumped forward, heading straight at me.

I fired a burst into the windshield, but the goddam thing kept coming. Fired another burst—longer than the first. But the truck didn't slow down. I tucked and rolled as the fucking thing careened into the wall, jumped onto the running board, yanked open the door, and sprayed the interior of the cab one-handed.

316

Maybe the driver was already dead, but I wasn't about to take any chances. I head-shot him, reached in, and shut the ignition off.

Jumped off, ran back, and checked the rear. I opened the latch, stood clear, and raised the gate.

No reaction. Stuck the business end of the MP5 around, and took a peek.

The fucking thing was empty.

I heard bursts of automatic weapons fire from the far side of the chamber—and rounds hitting the starboardmost truck. My boys were really earning their pay tonight.

I closed the cargo gate and latched it, changed MP5 mags—it was my last one—then made my way around the far side of the bashed-in cab. Sixty feet away, on the far side of the irregular-shaped chamber, was a roll-away, corrugated steel door, the kind that's operated by a continuous chain. A lopsided figure in black was feverishly pulling at the roll-chain.

I brought my MP5 up and fired a burst into the gear mechanism, freezing it.

Lothar Beck yanked on the chain and realized that it was useless. He turned toward me, his face a mask of hate and disgust.

Then he lurched to his left, scampered *tha-whomp, tha-whomp,* behind the truck closest to him, and disappeared from view.

Doom on Dickie. I'd forgotten how quickly Lothar the Hunch-Becked Kraut was able to move.

I raced to close the distance between us, firing as I moved, putting burst after burst into the truck cab. I didn't want the motherfucker starting the goddam engine if I could help it.

Stone chips kicked up ten yards in front of my size ten double-E's. I shifted focus and saw that Lothar had flung himself on the ground, finding shelter behind the big, thick wheels. He was firing a small, silver-colored pistol from a prone position. But he wasn't doing very well.

Hey, listen, it's harder than you may think to shoot someone with a handgun when you have a useless right arm and must shoot one-handed with your weak hand,[95] and when your adversary is coming at you the way I was going at him, which is to say, trying as hard as I could to shoot the deformed little *Scheißkerl* until he was *mausetot.*[96]

His odds improved, of course, when my MP5 ran dry. I transitioned to the USP and kept going. Lothar fired twice more—and then his little handgun ran out of ammo, too. That was when he realized that he was about to enter the lose-lose zone. He gathered himself up, and ran, his Bally boots going *tha-wump, tha-wump, tha-wump* on the rough stones. Where the fuck was he headed? I lost sight of him as he disappeared behind the truck. I sprinted after him, came round the corner between the truck and the big steel door—and saw nothing.

The motherfucker had *vanished.* Impossible. Then I saw the doorway. It was open. Pistol in hand, I went up to it. My USP in low ready, I cut the pie.

Nothing.

I edged forward, moving deliberately, but not rushing things. You don't want to go too fast. Move too fast and you make mistakes. But move too slowly and the motherfucker has time to get ready.

I widened the slice of my vision, and assured that Lothar wasn't waiting on the other side of the door frame with a pistol pointed at my head, I came full around, and made entry.

It was a small room, maybe ten by twelve, with fluorescent

---

[95]These days, many shooting schools have stopped using the term "weak hand," which was deemed politically incorrect because the word *weak* did not encourage the shooter's self-esteem. Instead, they use the term "support hand." Well, fuck all that touchy-feely shit. My belief is that if you practice with your weak hand long enough, it will no longer be weak. You will be strong on both sides, and you will be able to kill your enemy ambidextrously.

[96]Remember, that's the Kraut way of saying I wanted the motherfucker as dead as a doornail.

lights that gave everything a cold, greenish tinge. It was empty, too.

Fuck me. Backed out. Kept going. Down a short corridor. A second doorway—a modern steel door. This one was closed. I tested the doorknob. It twisted. I turned it clockwise, and eased the door open, pushing it slowly away from me. It swung back silently up against a wall. I could tell that no one was behind it. Cautiously, I cut the pie again, peering around the doorjamb.

Lothar was up against the far wall, working at a folding table. There were four ADMs on the table—three SADMs, and a Russkie suitcase nuke.

Lothar had one package opened. He was trying to assemble a SADM. The devices travel in six separate pieces: three base rings about eighteen inches in diameter, containing the U-235 fissionable material, a shaft some twenty-eight inches high that holds the demolition substance, a detonating rod, and a top collar for the demolition barrel, which holds all the arming clocks and timing devices. The three U-235 rings have to be linked together, and then attached to the barrel. Then the detonating rod is inserted. Finally, the timing collar is screwed into place. That's when the SADM can be armed and the timing fuse set. Putting 'em together takes about three and a half minutes. Arming takes another thirty-five seconds.

Those numbers, of course, work only if you are trained, and Lothar wasn't trained. So he was having himself a hell of a time trying to fit Tab "A" into Slot "B." He didn't even have the U-235 rings in proper sequence.

"Lothar—"

He turned toward me. *"Kapitän,"* he said, his thick lips pulled back from those perfect teeth. And then he whirled, and went back to his work.

"Lothar—I killed Khaled. He ain't part of the equation anymore."

There was no response. I kept my pistol at low ready and spoke to Lothar's hunched back. "We have your nets. They're all being scooped up right now."

His movements became even more frenetic, frenzied, maniacal.

"We have your organization—all of it. I took your Option Delta files, Lothar. Option Delta's dead. Finished. You're finished, too, Lothar. *Alles kaput.*"

That hump of Lothar's was humping, pumping, jumping as the crazed Kraut worked at the SADM.

"And guess what, Lothar—Fred Kohler is alive. He's giving Schloss Barbarossa a fucking enema right now. Killing your people. Killing the traitors. I wish he were here with me right now so I could let him kill you, you *Schweißpaket* faggot."

Oh, *that* finally brought him around. Lothar Beck whirled toward me, his face white with rage. He'd grabbed the twenty-eight-inch-high, three-and-a-half-inch-diameter shaft that held the detonating rod. He'd screwed the timing collar on. His fingers were squeezing the detonating device buttons—but of course, nothing was working. That's not how you set a fucking SADM off.

Then, holding it like a club, he charged, unintelligible Kraut and saliva spouting from his lips.

I wasn't about to take chances. One does not look properly Roguish if one is in tiny fragments of flesh and bone, and I wasn't about to find out precisely what kinds of shocks the SADM barrel could withstand. I came up with the USP, got what the great American pistolero Colonel Jeff Cooper calls a "flash sight picture,"[97] and shot Lothar twice in the face with a very controlled but fast pair of shots. He went down in an anticlimatic heap, atop the demolition barrel.

I know, I know: you wanted me to take my time with the Kraut

---

[97]That's when you don't spend a lot of time aligning the sights, but simply put your target in your front sight, thus narrowing the channel down which you are going to shoot. It is a concept used by hostage rescue teams, where there may be lots of friendlies in the immediate area, and point shooting could be fatal to the wrong people.

Kockbreath. Kill him inch by inch. Or let Fred kill him in the Euro-manner—centimeter by centimeter. Well, friends, that ain't the way life works. Sometimes, you just have to shoot the motherfucker dead and screw the high drama of the moment.

I went up to Lothar, and just to make sure that he wasn't going to give me any trouble, I kicked him in the head to see if he was faking. He wasn't faking. So, I rolled him over with my foot and put a shot right into his forehead from eighteen inches away, splattering bone and brain in a pattern that would have done Jackson Pollock proud, all over the concrete floor of the work-room.

That's overkill, you say? Well, *fuuck you!* As my young friend Orca, the SF[98] master sergeant from Delta, is fond of saying to his troops, "Always head-shoot every one of the motherfuckers. If you *know* they can't get up, then they won't surprise you when you've moved down the line."

0157. We linked up with Fred and his team, and began a methodical shutdown of Schloss Barbarossa. Fred and his guys started collecting intel. He was about to personally rip the heart and lungs out of what Lothar had been putting together. Well, that was his domestic concern—not mine.

Me, I had my own priorities. I got on the phone to John Suter, *interruptus*ing some pretty good coitus from the way he groaned and grunted and growled. I gave him our coordinates, and told him I had four packages waiting for him. He gave me about twenty seconds of passable Ev Barrett profanity, followed by a "Can do," followed by a long silence to see if, maybe, I was kidding.

I guess he decided I wasn't, because he finally drawled, "Oh, fuck. See you in ninety minutes or so."

Then, to get even, he said, "Oh, by the way, I have a message

---

[98]Special Forces.

for you from the Chairman. He says he and SECDEF have a small logistical problem he'd like you to deal with." And then, the line went dead.

0214. I watched as Fred and his guys started going through the piles of raw intel. I grasped Fred around the shoulder. "You gonna be okay?"

He waved his hand in a dismissive way. *"Ja, Richard, alles gut."* He paused. "It will take some time. But I will fix it. Root out the bad ones." A black look came over his face. "I will deal with them myself," he said. "Slowly. Quietly."

I knew what he was talking about. There are many inconspicuous ways in which traitors can be dealt with. Parachutes that don't open during jump exercises comes to mind as the most common example. Shoot house accidents work, too.

But handling those German traitors was going to be Fred's problem. Me, all I wanted to do was go home. I had this quartet of pocket nukes to hand off to John Suter. I had a dinged-up, stressed-out platoon to make whole again. I had the kind of deep, endorphin-repellent pain that lets me know that God loves me more than He loves most others.

And, of course, there was the Chairman's message yet to come. John Suter'd said there was a "small logistical problem" that needed some work.

Oh, the Doom-on-Dickie potential was gonna be very, very high. I've heard this song before. And so have you—earlier in this very same book. For those of you who have bad recall, I'll recap the gist for you. When officers start talking about small logistical problems, I am always transported back to my days as an enlisted man. I learned early on that when someone who wears gold braid on his sleeve starts talking about "a small logistical problem," it means that *I'm* about to draw a nasty dose of swabbing latrines, or pumping out bilges, either literally, or figuratively.

But swabbing and pumping, or jumping and humping (or hopping & popping, and shooting & looting), whether indeed literal or figurative, would all have to wait. For now, we had just over an hour before John Suter arrived, in which to do some real SpecWarrior work.

That's right: we had to discover where Lothar kept the fucking beer.

Glossary

A²: aforementioned asshole.

A³: Anytime, Anyplace, Anywhere.

ADM: Atomic Demolition Munition. Pocket nuke.

Admiral's Gestapo: what the secretary of defense's office calls the Naval Investigative Services Command. See: SHIT-FOR-BRAINS.

AK-47: 7.63 X 39 Kalashnikov automatic rifle. The most common assault weapon in the world.

ATE: Accidental Tourist Episode.

AVCNO: Assistant Vice Chief of Naval Operations

Bandity: (Russian) Police slang for hoodlums.

BAW: Big Asshole Windbag.

BDUs: Battle Dress Uniforms. Now *that's* an oxymoron, if I ever heard one.

BFH: Big Fucking Help.

BIQ: Bitch-in-Question.

BOHICA: Bend over—here it comes again!

Boomer: nuclear-powered missile submarine.

BTDT: Been There, Done That.

BUPERS: Naval BUreau of PERSonnel.

BUWEPS: Naval BUreau of WEaPonS.

C-130: Lockheed's ubiquitous Hercules.

C-141: Lockheed's ubiquitous StarLifter aircraft, soon to be moth-balled.

C-4: plastic explosive. You can mold it like clay. You can even use it to light your fires. Just don't stamp on it.

C²CO: Can't Cunt Commanding Officer. Too many of these in Navy SpecWar today. They won't support their men or take chances because they're afraid it'll ruin their chances for promotion.

CALOW: Coastal And Limited-Objective Warfare. Very fashionable acronym at the Pentagon in these days of increased low-intensity conflict.

cannon fodder: See FNG.

Christians in Action: SpecWar slang for the Central Intelligence Agency.

CINC: Commander IN Chief.

CINCLANT: Commander IN Chief, AtLANTic.

CINCLANTFLT: Commander IN Chief, AtLANTic FLeeT.

CINCUSNAVEUR: Commander IN Chief, U.S. NAVal forces, EU-Rope

clusterfuck: see FUBAR.

CNO: Chief of Naval Operations.

cockbreath: SEAL term of endearment used for those who only pay lip service.

CONUS: CONtinental United States.

CQC: Close-Quarters Combat—i.e., killing that's up close and personal.

CRT: Cathode Ray Tube. Computer screen.

CT: CounterTerrorism.

DADT: Don't Ask, Don't Tell.

DEA: Drug Enforcement Agency.

DEFCON: DEFense CONdition.

DEVGRP: Naval Special Warfare DEVelopment GRouP. Current U.S. Navy designation for SEAL Team Six.

detasheet: olive-drab, 10-by-20-inch flexible PETN-based plastic explosive used as a cutting or breaching charge.

DIA: Defense Intelligence Agency. Spook heaven based in Arlington, Virginia.

diplo-dink: no-load fudge-cutting, cookie-pushing diplomat.

DIPSEC: DIPlomatic SECurity

dipshit: can't cunt pencil-dicked asshole.

***Do-ma-nhieu* (Vietnamese):** Go fuck yourself. See DOOM ON YOU.

Doom on you: American version of Vietnamese for go fuck yourself.

dweeb: no-load shit-for-brains geeky asshole, usually shackled to a computer.

EC-130: Electronic warfare-outfitted C-130.

EEI: Essential Element of Information. The info-nuggets on which a mission is planned and executed.

EEO: Equal Employment Opportunity. (Marcinko always treats 'em all alike—just like shit.)

ELINT: ELectronic INTelligence.

EOD: Explosive Ordnance Disposal.

F³: Full Fucking Faulkner—lots of sound and fury.

FIS: Flight Information Service.

flashbang: disorientation device used by hostage rescue teams.

FLFC: fucking loud and fucking clear.

FLIR: Forward Looking Infra Red.

FMs: Fucking Monkeys.

FNG: Fucking New Guy. See CANNON FODDER.

Four-striper: Captain. All too often, a C²CO.

frags: fragmentation grenades.

FUC: Fucking Ugly Corsican.

FUBAR: Fucked Up Beyond All Repair.

Glock: Reliable 9-mm pistols made by Glock in Austria. They're great for SEALs because they don't require as much care as Sig Sauers.

GNBN: Good News/Bad News.

Goatfuck: What the Navy likes to do to the Rogue Warrior. See FUBAR.

GSG-9: Grenzchutzgruppe-9. Top German CT unit.

HAHO: High-Altitude High-Opening parachute jump.

HALO: High-Altitude, Low-Opening parachute jump.

HICs: Head-In-Cement syndrome. Condition common to high-ranking officers. Symptoms include pigheadedness and inability to change opinions when presented with new information.

HK: ultrareliable pistol, assault rifle, or submachine gun made by Heckler & Koch, a German firm. SEALs use H&K MP5-Ks submachine guns in various configurations, as well as H&K 33 assault rifles, and P7M8 and M13 9-mm, and USP 9-mm, 40- or 45-caliber pistols.

HUMINT: HUMan INTelligence.

humongous: Marcinko dick.

Hydra-Shok: extremely lethal hollowpoint ammunition manufactured by Federal Cartridge Company.

IBS: Inflatable Boat, Small—the basic unit of SEAL transportation.
IED: Improvised Explosive Device.

Japs: bad guys.
jarheads: Marines. The Corps. Formally, USMC (Uncle Sam's Misguided Children).
JSOC: Joint Special Operations Command.

KATN: Kick Ass and Take Names. Roguish avocation.
KH: KeyHole. Designation for NRO's spy-in-the-sky satellites, as in KH-12s.
KISS: Keep It Simple, Stupid. The basic premise for all special operations.

LANTFLT: AtLANTic FLeeT.
LODAR: Land Of Der Anal Retentive.
LTWS: Lower Than Whale Shit.

M³: Massively motivated motherfuckers.
M-16: Basic U.S. .223-caliber weapon, used by the armed forces.
MagSafe: lethal frangible ammunition that does not penetrate the human body. Favored by some SWAT units for CQC.
MILCRAFT: Pentagonese for MILitary airCRAFT.
Mk-1 Mod-0: basic unit.
MOTI: Russian Ministry of the Interior.

NAVSPECWARGRU: NAVal SPECial WARfare GRoUp.
Navyspeak: redundant, bureaucratic naval nomenclature, either in written nonoral, or nonwritten oral modes, indecipherable by nonmilitary (conventional) or military (unconventional) individuals during normal interfacing configuration conformations.
NILO: Naval Intelligence Liaison Officer.
NIS: Naval Investigative Service Command, also known as the Admirals' Gestapo. See: SHIT-FOR-BRAINS.
NMN: No Middle Name.
NRO: National Reconnaissance Office. Established 25 August 1960

to administer and coordinate satellite development and operations for U.S. intelligence community. Very spooky place.

NSA: National Security Agency, known within the SpecWar community as No Such Agency.

NSD: National Security Directive.

NYL: Nubile Young Lovely.

OBE: Overtaken By Events—usually because of the bureaucracy.

OOD: Officer Of the Deck (he who drives the big gray monster).

OP-06-04: CNO's SpecWar briefing officer.

OP-06: Deputy CNO for Operations, Plans, and Policy.

OP-06B: Assistant Deputy CNO for Operations, Plans, and Policy.

OP-06D: cover organization for Red Cell/NSCT.

OPSEC: OPerational SECurity

PDMP: Pretty Dangerous Motherfucking People.

PIQ: Pussy In Question.

POTUS: President of the United States.

RDL: Real Dirty Look.

RPG: Rocket-Propelled Grenade.

R²D²: ritualistic, rehearsed, disciplined drills.

S¹: Square one.

S²: Sit the fuck down and shut the fuck up.

SADM: Special Atomic Demolition Device. Man-portable nuke.

SAS: Special Air Service. Britain's top CT unit.

SATCOM: SATellite COMmunications.

SCIF: Sensitive Compartmented Information Facility. A bug-proof room.

SEAL: U.S. Navy SEa-Air-Land SpecWarrior. A hop-and-popping shoot-and-looting hairy-assed Frogman who gives a shit. The acronym *really* stands for Sleep, Eat, and Live it up.

Semtex: Czecho C-4 plastique explosive. Can be used to cancel Czechs.

SERE: Survival, Evasion, Resistance, and Escape school.

SES: Shit-eating smile.

Shit-for-Brains: any no-load, pus-nutted, pencil-dicked asshole.

SIGINT: SIGnals INTelligence.

SLUDJ: Top secret NIS witch-hunters. Acronym stands for Sensitive Legal (Upper Deck) Jurisdiction.

SMG: submachine gun

SNAFU: Situation Normal—All Fucked Up.

SNAILS: Slow, Nerdy Assholes In Ludicrous Shoes.

SOCOM: United States Special Operations COMmand, located at MacDill AFB, Tampa, Florida.

SOF: Special Operations Force.

S&P: Spit-and-polish.

SpecWarrior: One who gives a fuck.

SSN: Nuclear attack sub, commonly known as sewer pipe.

STABs: SEAL Tactical Assault Boats.

STR: Smack the Rogue.

SUC: Smart, Unpredictable, and Cunning.

SWAT: Special Weapons and Tactics police teams. All too often they do not train enough, and become SQUAT teams.

szeb **(Arabic):** dick.

TAD: Temporary Additional Duty. (SEALs refer to it as Traveling Around Drunk.)

TARFU: Things Are Really Fucked Up.

TBW: Tired but wired.

TECHINT: TECHnical INTelligence.

TFB: Too fucking bad.

THREATCON: THREAT CONdition.

Tigerstripes: The only stripes that SEALs will wear.

TIQ: Tango-In-Question

TTS: Tap 'em, Tie 'em, and Stash 'em.

TVE: Thorough visual exam.

U$_2$: Ugly and unfamiliar.

UNODIR: UNless Otherwise DIRected. That's how the Rogue operates when he's surrounded by can't cunts.

VDL: Versatile, Dangerous, and Lethal.

VSV: Very Slender Vessel. A balls-to-the-wall fast cigarette boat, currently in operational use by DEVGRP.

Wanna-bes: The sorts of folks you meet at *Soldier of Fortune* conventions.

Weenies: pussy-ass can't cunts and no-loads.

WHUTA: Wild Hair Up The Ass.

WTF: What The Fuck.

Zulu: Greenwich Mean Time (GMT) designator used in formal military communications.

Zulu-5-Oscar: escape and evasion exercises in which Frogmen try to plant dummy limpet mines on Navy vessels, while the vessels' crews try to catch them in *bombus interruptus.*

Index

All entires preceded by an asterisk (*) are pseudonyms.

#1 *New York Times* bestselling author

RICHARD MARCINKO

Richard Marcinko first exploded out of the clandestine world of special forces warfare with his #1 *New York Times* bestselling autobiography *Rogue Warrior*. After coauthoring five successive Rogue Warrior novels, Marcinko now calls upon the warriors who fought by his side to tell their own stories.

ROGUE WARRIOR®
THE REAL TEAM

THE REAL TEAM introduces the real operators from the *Rogue Warrior* series, up close and down and dirty! See who the Rogue recruited, why they stayed and how he keeps them ready to kill!

Coming in Hardcover June 1999
from Pocket Books

POCKET BOOKS